SANDS

KEVIN L. NIELSEN

SANDS

FHP

Future House Publishing
Copyright © 2015 by Kevin L. Nielsen

Cover design by Garrett Hamon
Cover design © 2015 by Future House Publishing
Developmental editing by Helena Steinacker and Mandi Diaz
Substantive editing by Emma Hoggan
Copy editing by Heather Klippert
Interior design by Emma Hoggan

ISBN-10: 0-9891253-7-8
ISBN-13: 978-0-9891253-7-6

Acknowledgements

This book is primarily for Kaitlynn, who upholds the flame.

However, I would be remiss if I did not name the others who were also important to the process. My writing group, Team Unleashed, has provided invaluable assistance. The people at Future House have been wonderful to work with and I thank each of them in turn—they know who they are. My parents also deserve their moment, for supporting me when I needed support and giving me tough love.

And finally, the two who originally inspired me to write: Kevin Bailey and Ms. Wolfe. Thanks for the motivation to start. May death's shadow pass over you all. Always.

Part 1

Sidena

CHAPTER 1
Payment

"I know the voice of the girl child screaming. Am I the cause of those screams? The enemy has come."
> *-From the Journals of Elyana*

The crowd pressed close as the outcast juggler tossed flaming brands into the air. Near the middle of the crowd, three children scuffled. Two boys pushed a little girl out of the way and scrambled to get a better look. The little girl fell with a muffled shout, landing hard enough to scatter sand across the stone floor.

Lhaurel watched the children out of the corner of her eye, waiting for the parents to step in. None came. She moved to the girl's side, gently helping her to her feet. One of the boys, perhaps no older than seven or eight years, made a face at her, but Lhaurel glared at him until he sniffed and turned back to the show. Lhaurel turned back to the girl and dusted her off. There was a small cut on one of her cheeks that bled down in a thin, red line.

"Hey," Lhaurel said softly, licking her thumb and wiping away the blood. "It's alright. Do you want to see the juggler?"

The little girl swallowed and bowed her head, shuffling her feet and sniffing as her nose ran.

Lhaurel sighed. Most of the children in the clan had been told to stay away from her—the clan's bad influence—at one point in their lives. It appeared they were starting even younger now.

"Come here." Lhaurel swept the girl into her arms and then up onto her shoulders.

The girl whooped, drawing angry glares from more than one of the watchers, but none of them said anything. Little hands fastened in Lhaurel's bushy hair, and a little chin dropped onto the top of her head. Lhaurel smiled and turned her attention back to the performance. And for a moment, at least, the stresses and weight of the next day faded away.

The juggler gave way to a pair of acrobats, who contorted themselves into strange positions and performed stunning jumps and leaps that left the crowd gasping. The little girl laughed and clapped her hands. Lhaurel laughed along with her.

Castoffs from the seven clans of the Rahuli people, the outcasts, were typically shunned and ignored, left to wander the Sharani desert alone unless they found another of their kind. Except, of course, when there was cause for celebration. Then they were commissioned to perform.

Even under invitation, though, they were kept at arm's length. Unwary people were sure to lose any valuables they had on hand if they let an outcast any closer.

The little girl—Lhaurel thought her name might be Kesli—tugged on Lhaurel's hair. "Look. They've got red hair like you." The girl pointed one pudgy hand at the acrobats, who bowed to the clapping audience and stepped away from the stage.

Lhaurel tugged on the girl's foot, and she giggled, dropping her hand.

In truth, Kesli was half right. Lhaurel's hair did have a certain reddish cast to it, especially in the sunlight, but it was a deeper shade of brown beneath. The acrobats had hair the color of fresh blood, bright and vibrant even in the dim light of the cavern in which they performed.

Not many people paused to consider the difference, though. More than one family had passed Lhaurel along based on the color of her hair. That and her height, another similarity she and many outcasts shared.

Kevin L. Nielsen

The acrobats vanished into the small group of waiting performers behind the stage, and an older woman stepped forward amidst the claps and shouts from the crowd. This woman's hair was streaked through with white, only a few strands of brown remaining. She had been acting as the main narrator, introducing the next performance and interacting on behalf of the group as a whole. It was almost as if she were their leader, a preposterous idea. Even the Matron of the Warren had to bow before her own Warlord. Yet Lhaurel admired the outcasts for it.

In the back of Lhaurel's mind, seeing this outcast woman leading the tribe only made her that much more nervous about what lay before her.

"Wasn't that something?" the woman said, her voice a scratchy, grating sound like the wind against sandstone rocks during a storm. "We will now be graced with the story of a great warrior, a man of great stature and strength. Gavin, master of lore and legend, will tell the tale of Eldriean."

She raised her hands wide, and a young man stepped forward, garbed in simple, dusty robes. He adopted an easy, practiced pose just slightly off from true. His red-brown hair fell casually in his eyes, but he stood stiffly like he was afraid of something. *Or* he was simply nervous. If she were the one on the stage, she'd be stiff as well. And trembling on the inside.

The crowd applauded. Several of the younger children pushed forward through the crowd in an effort to get closer to the storyteller. Stories were rare, and this one was a favorite.

Lhaurel leaned forward slightly, though not enough to unseat Kesli. In her seventeen years, she'd only heard the story one other time, and it had been so long ago she'd forgotten much of it.

The man, Gavin, kept his eyes forward, focused beyond the crowd at a distant point on the wall behind. When he spoke, there was no quaver in his voice. It resonated and echoed off the cavern walls as if a chorus of men were speaking.

"The Salvation War, War of Recovery, The Deliverance. It went by many names. In the last years of the long, bitter struggle, Eldriean became leader of the Rhiofriar, greatest of the three clans."

A focused hush fell over the listeners. Even the small children fell silent.

"It was a happy time for the Rhiofriar, for the Enemy had abated its furious onslaught. The clans could take a few months, mere moments against the span of years of death that came before, to breathe once more. To have a few moments of peace.

"But the blood of past deaths rang heavy in Eldriean's ears, a clarion call to arms. He rode forth to the Lord's Council on the back of the Winds, his mighty Weapon at his side, won from an Enemy slain in battle. With a voice of thunder, he claimed leadership of all the clans, not just his own. He demanded their fealty and their strength. He drew forth his Weapon and brandished it in the face of those who opposed him. One, Serthim, stood against him longest, but all fell away, bowing to his might. They surrendered to his glory."

The man paused, letting the silence grow heavy with weight. Emotion roiled in the cavern, curiosity mixed with confusion. Who was this Eldriean? And the Rhiofriar? No such clan existed.

"The hordes came in waves," Gavin continued, "from the earth and from the air, leaving destruction and death in their wake."

"The genesauri!" Kesli whispered. Lhaurel felt her shudder in fear. A matching one worked its way into the pit of Lhaurel's own stomach.

"Yet Eldriean brought the clans together in unity in the one place where life still clung. The clans met the enemy there upon the cliff that surrounded this place of lush fertility. There they ringed the walls with bodies and with flesh, armed with lances and swords and spears and magic and will. There they faced the final charge. There the Weapon that so much sacrifice had earned was unleashed in full at long last, unleashed in all its might and glory and horror. There they found victory and defeat. There they found their salvation. And their destruction. There upon the cliffs."

Gavin waited, his eyes growing unfocused. His hands shook at his sides, and he clenched his fists into balls. Behind him, the older woman made a small grunt.

"Eldriean fell there, upon the cliffs," Gavin continued, his voice so soft that Lhaurel had to strain to hear. "Betrayed by Serthim, who had never truly bowed. His mighty Weapon, which had rallied the clans and unified them under one rightful King, pierced Serthim there, slamming the traitor into the rocks even as he fell, sealing the fate of the Rahuli.

"Leaderless, left to fight the enemy on their own, they became lost and broken. Three tribes became seven—and the outcasts. But it is said Eldriean's Weapon lies there still atop the cliffs of the Oasis, there for the time of great need when the clans shall once again need a King."

For a moment after Gavin stopped speaking, the silence seemed a living thing, an entity unto itself.

The man stood upon the stage, head bowed and fists clenched, as if telling the tale somehow left him afraid. Or maybe angry. Lhaurel couldn't decide which.

A bark of laughter shattered the ethereal blanket that had covered them all.

Jenthro, Warlord of the Sidena, stepped forward. "And every year in the Oasis, at least one of you fools dies trying to scale those rocks and find it. Now *that* is a performance I like watching," he said, raising one hand and spreading it before him.

Behind him, several people laughed. Atop Lhaurel's shoulders, Kesli giggled as well, though Lhaurel wasn't sure the girl knew what she was laughing about.

Lhaurel herself maintained her silence. The man was an outcast, but he was still a person.

"Wasn't it just last year there were two of them who tried?" Taren asked. He was an older warrior, the effective second in command behind Jenthro. "I think I remember watching that one. A husband and wife, I recall. One of them tried to fly when they fell, flapping his arms like a bird until he hit the sand." He mimicked flailing arms, and the Sidena laughed again.

The man on stage, the youth, really, shook with suppressed anger. Lhaurel was sure his nails were digging into the flesh of his palms. The outcasts who had already performed were stony faced or else turned away, backs stiff.

Only the older woman seemed unfazed. She stepped back up to the stage and smiled sweetly down into the jeering faces. With one hand she pushed the young man back in the direction of the others. He retreated with reluctant steps, leaving her alone on the stage.

"Mighty Sidena," she said with a bow that a woman her age shouldn't have been able to accomplish with such alacrity and grace. "We will take our leave now. If you would kindly provide us our payment, we will leave you to your festivities."

Lhaurel winced at the reminder. As much as she enjoyed the performers, she would rather they not be here at all.

No, I won't think about it. Not now.

Jenthro laughed and gestured with one hand. "Three goats, I believe."

A disturbance arose at the back of the crowd, followed by renewed laughter. A younger warrior came forward, pulling the leads on the three goats. Lhaurel felt a moment of pity when she saw the creatures.

Scrawny and obviously sick, the goats were in such bad health they were likely only a few moments away from being culled from the herd. Lhaurel could count the ribs on all three of them. One even had a large, festering sore on one flank that was causing the animal to limp.

Lhaurel felt a moment of simultaneous anger and pity warm her chest. The goat and sheep herds were a large part of what sustained the Sidena. They were cared for, fed, and looked after with more care than some of the children. These animals had been purposefully underfed and neglected to mock and demean the outcasts.

It was vain, foolish posturing. The act was one she should have expected. One more strike against a clan she would never call her own.

"Three goats," Jenthro said with a bow much less graceful than the lady's had been, "as promised."

The woman accepted them with another bow, not even raising an eyebrow at the condition they were in. She was an outcast. They were used to such treatment. At least they got paid at all. Other clans may have chased them out at the point of a sword.

Lhaurel admired the grace the woman showed in the face of such hostility, a grace Lhaurel wished she herself were able to imitate. She'd thought about joining them before but had always given up on the idea. Life in the protection of a large clan was better than life as a clanless nomad.

Yet, as the small group of outcasts gathered up their possessions and left the warren, pulling wide-wheeled handcarts and escorted by a half-dozen Sidena warriors, Lhaurel couldn't help but wonder if her life was really any better off than theirs.

CHAPTER 2
Blood and Leather

"Our lush, arboreal verdence lays desolate, crumbling from life to dust. Life is dissolution."
-From the Journals of Elyana

Lhaurel paused at the intersection of two passages, trying to decide if she should go back and accept her pending marriage or chance the desert sands on her own. If she was honest with herself, she knew there wasn't really much of a choice. She'd never survive the sands alone, not with the Migration coming in just a fortnight's time, but that didn't stop her from trying to avoid the bonding ceremony anyway. To give up was to condone the act, which she didn't.

Part of her toyed with the idea of running away and joining the outcasts like the group from the night before. But—

She took a deep, steadying breath as the sound of voices echoed down from the passage ahead of her, and she began walking at her normal pace, careful not to appear as if she had been running. The stitch in her side throbbed, reminding her of her lie.

A crowd of women appeared in the passageway.

Lhaurel mentally sighed, succumbing to the inevitable. *They would have found me eventually anyway.*

"Lhaurel," the woman at the front of the group said in an exasperated voice, "there you are! We've been looking everywhere for you! Didn't I tell you to meet me by the greatroom?"

Lhaurel inclined her head in respect, which also hid the grimace that crossed her face.

Marvi was a large woman, as equally intimidating by her size as by the blue *shufari* at her waist that marked her as the Warlord's wife. The Matron of the Warren, Marvi could tan the hide off of anyone with either her hand or her tongue as easily as a sandstorm stripped the flesh from a body.

"Your pardon, Matron," Lhaurel said as women with yellow *shufari* began to usher her down the hall with impatient clucks or gentle prods, "I needed to be alone for a moment to—to get ready. I didn't mean to cause you stress." Only years of practice kept back the bitterness from her voice.

Marvi snorted and rolled her eyes, brushing back her long black hair with an irritated flick.

"As well you shouldn't. If today weren't your wedding day, I would send you out with the children to tend the sheep and hunt for mushrooms. And Saralhn's no better. She was supposed to be keeping track of you. I put her to task working the salts." She sniffed. "Your head is as full of sand as a genesauri's nest. Why, just this morning I was telling the Warlord—may he ever find water and shade—that you'll need a strong hand to calm your vagrant spirit. He just nodded in that flippant way of his. As if I hadn't carried his children for the last twenty years or made sure the warren had food to eat and water to drink. Despite him, sometimes."

Even Lhaurel flinched at the words. Marvi was the only one who could get away with speaking so ill of the Warlord, and even for her it was dangerous. If her husband hadn't been so indulgent, he could have ordered her death just for referring to his nod as "flippant." Lhaurel grated at the irony of Marvi being the one to always punish her for acting unwomanly. Lhaurel had often found it to be true: those who most vehemently supported an ideal were often the ones to most egregiously and consistently violate it. As it was, what Marvi said was true, at least insofar as taking care of the warren despite the Warlord was concerned. She never let his temper get in the way of getting things done.

SANDS

Lhaurel did feel guilty about getting Saralhn into trouble again, though. She hadn't known Saralhn had been appointed to watch over her. Likely Saralhn had known Lhaurel needed the mental and emotional break and had let her go, knowing full well she'd get in trouble for it. That was so like Saralhn. Lhaurel made a mental note to thank her for it later. *After* she apologized.

"You're as wayward as a Roterralar, child," Marvi continued, ushering the procession through a series of passages normally reserved for women who wore a purple *shufari*. "Maybe one of the older, widowed warriors would suit you best. Sands knows I've had my hands full trying to find someone willing to take you after everything you've done." Lhaurel didn't have to see Marvi's face to know the Matron was rolling her eyes toward the heavens. "Taren would have you broken and gentled within the week." Her voice grew soft at the end, almost a whisper, and she grimaced.

Lhaurel couldn't suppress a scowl of her own. If she had to get married at all, couldn't it at least be to someone who wasn't old enough to be her grandfather? Part of her gave a mental shrug. What difference did it really make? The choice wasn't hers either way.

The young women around her broke out in whispers, each suggesting a potential match among the eligible bachelors of the clans. Taren was, surprisingly, one of the least objectionable choices.

"Enough of that now," Marvi said, noticing Lhaurel's scowl. "You will learn your place. Just as your sisters have."

Lhaurel had always hated how all the women of a certain age were referred to as sisters, even when there was little, if any, relationship between them. She had no true sisters, and the women in her own age group found her odd, almost as odd as she found them. Most of them were around her, wearing the yellow *shufari* that marked them as bound to a man, wedded within the last year. After that, they would wear the brown until their husbands attained a high enough status for their wives to wear the purple. Or, like Marvi, their husbands became the Warlord. Then they would wear the blue.

Lhaurel was as different from them as it was possible to be. She stood a full head taller than most of the Sidena woman, tall and thin and straight like a pole, all angles and bone without much of a figure to speak of. Where they were olive skinned with dark hair and dark, ovular eyes, Lhaurel was fair of skin, was covered in freckles, and sported an unruly mane of bushy hair the color of new-formed rust.

Sisters indeed. Well, she counted Saralhn as a sister, so they weren't all bad.

The procession led her to the bathing chambers, where steam wafted up from the salted hot spring vents. The water was unsuitable for drinking, but it served perfectly for bathing or washing out clothes as long as you didn't mind the fine grit of salt that was left behind. Honestly, it wasn't much different than having your clothes or body covered in sand. Either way you remained itchy.

The salt springs were the pride of the Sidena, and the salt harvested from them was a staple of trade for the clan when they were in the Oasis. The shallower pools, farther down in the caves, were a stable source of drinking water once the processing was completed. Lhaurel didn't understand it completely, but it involved capturing the steam. Somehow that produced non-salty drinking water. Or something like that.

Lhaurel stripped and stepped into the hot water while listening to Marvi prattle on. She smiled when the dirt, sweat, and sand were washed away, leaving her skin feeling clean and smooth. As she slipped beneath the water to rinse her hair, though, Lhaurel couldn't help but suppress a nervous little shiver that crept up her spine. She was getting married today. A small part of her was excited and nervous all at once. Another part of her, the larger part, felt an overwhelming sense of defeat. She'd have to give up so much. Her independence, the freedom to clandestinely do things women were not supposed to do, was at an end.

"You know, you really shouldn't provoke the Matron like that, Lhaurel." A soft voice said when Lhaurel broke the surface of the water.

Lhaurel opened her eyes. Marvi and most of the other women had departed while she had been under the water, leaving only one behind. Saralhn, the closest thing she had to a friend. As was custom, Saralhn, the most recently wed among the women, would prepare Lhaurel for her own union.

The short woman frowned at her, arms folded beneath her breasts.

"Running off like that on the morning of your wedding." Saralhn held out a towel so that Lhaurel could dry herself off. "Why do you always do that?"

"You know why, Saralhn," Lhaurel said, taking the towel.

Saralhn only sighed and shook her head.

Lhaurel ran the rough towel through her hair, making it stick out at odd angles over her head. "Thanks for letting me go anyway. I didn't mean to get you into trouble."

Saralhn smiled and helped dry Lhaurel off with another towel she took from a nearby stack.

"I don't see that you have anything to complain about," Saralhn said after a moment, a small note of envy creeping into her voice. "If you really do end up with Taren, you'll jump straight to the purple after your year with the yellow."

"We'll just have our children call him grandfather instead of father," Lhaurel said, making a face. "It'll be wonderful."

"Oh, Lhaurel, why do you have to fight so much? This is our life. It is a good life. Being married, being a woman, they have their own rewards. Besides, no matter how much you fight it, there's no way out."

Lhaurel maintained her silence as she finished drying herself. Saralhn was right, of course. There wasn't any way out, and that's what Lhaurel hated more than anything. Her only purpose, according to the clan, was to serve her husband and the clan by producing more children and tending to womanly tasks. All the other women in the clan accepted this and seemed to find some measure of happiness in fulfilling that purpose. Lhaurel sometimes wondered if there was something wrong with her since her thoughts dwelt on things generally denied to women. Mostly she wondered what was wrong with them.

Saralhn turned and retrieved a small box from a nook in the wall. Actually, it wasn't a box at all. It was something wrapped in a piece of white cloth.

Lhaurel looked a question at Saralhn, who gave her a small smile as she handed Lhaurel the bundle. "It's not much, but it was the best I could do."

Lhaurel slowly removed the cloth, revealing a thin white comb made of bone, teeth set wide apart. With Lhaurel's thick hair, the wide teeth would be a welcome relief.

"Oh, Saralhn," Lhaurel said, voice catching. "Thank you."

Saralhn held up a hand to silence her, a faint smile on her lips. "I understand, Lhaurel. Let's just pretend, for now, that I've convinced you to be happy and that you actually are, okay?"

Lhaurel smiled through the tears in her eyes.

No further words were exchanged between them. Not as Saralhn combed and braided Lhaurel's hair. Not when Saralhn garbed her in the robes of a bride. And not when the gaggle of young, married women returned and hurried her away. None were needed.

* * *

Lhaurel waited impatiently in the exact center of the greatroom, thick leather ties hanging from her left wrist—the bonding ties. Her hair was arranged in a beautiful net of braids and beads that spread down her back like dunes. She fingered her blue dress for perhaps the hundredth time, feeling the fine material and wishing she could scratch without appearing nervous. She would have preferred the dress be green, but blue was the traditional color of a bride.

All around her, the clan stood in neat rows, warriors in front, women and children behind. She stood alone, open and exposed.

The reality of it all hit her with the force of a storm wall. She'd put on a brave face for Saralhn earlier, but she had been right. There was no way out of this. Standing here in front of everyone, waiting for her first glimpse of the warrior to whom she would be bound—this was the beginning of the end.

She was devoid of *shufari*. It was the only time in a woman's life that her status was not openly displayed about her waist. In that moment she was nothing, a woman devoid of identity and life until her new husband arrived. When he did, she ceased being an individual and started being a possession. It was her last silent moment of freedom.

Lhaurel sniffed and swallowed hard, though her mouth was suddenly dry. She ground her teeth together, refusing to cry. Crying was a waste of pure, precious water. Instead she stood erect and raised her chin, putting on a smile. She saw Saralhn standing behind her husband, but the woman's eyes were dutifully looking elsewhere. Toward where the bridegroom would enter.

Lhaurel glanced around the room at the assembled clansmen, unable to look where they were looking. Maryn stood next to her husband, Cobb, the older couple looking stern and resolute, as always. Portly Jerria, with her gaggle of children around her, snatched one of them as they ran by and put the offending child back in line where she belonged. Lhaurel had spent nearly five full fortnights with that family before Jerria had asked Marvi to pass her along to another one.

A small group of children, all younger than eight years old, stepped forward as an older woman produced a set of thin reed pipes and began to play. The melody was a familiar one, played at every bonding ceremony. The notes of the song echoed in the large room, the effect being a broken duet. A call and then a distant echo. The children began to sing, though Lhaurel couldn't distinguish the words. A wash of jumbled emotions spread through her, so mixed up Lhaurel couldn't begin to pick out any one in particular.

From behind and to the left of the assembled crowd, hand drums began to pound. The sounds rang out in the sandstone chamber, echoing off the walls and amplifying the notes of Lhaurel's pounding heart. Beads of sweat formed on Lhaurel's brow as the crowd directly across from her parted and the Warlord led his procession, eight warriors forming a tight ring around her chosen husband.

Lhaurel tried to catch a glimpse of the hidden man, but the warriors around him stood too close together for her to make out anything but the standard brown of cloth and leather. A hard look from the Warlord, who had noticed her rebellious act, dropped her back on her heels. But she refused to lower her gaze.

The Warlord cut an imposing figure, full of hard lines and with a face as impassive as stone. His graying hair was pulled back into a topknot by a simple cord adorned with a metal pin shaped like a sword. He walked with the grace of a warrior but the poise and air of one who had lived with authority as a mantle since youth.

Growing up, Lhaurel had often thought the man arrogant. Looking at him now, she revised her earlier opinion. It wasn't arrogance. It was condescension. She almost took a small step backward as his gaze fell upon her once again. She realized that she was chewing on her bottom lip and stopped herself.

The crowd around them watched the ceremony impassively as the procession passed through a hallway of crossed swords and then parted, revealing the warrior hidden at their center.

Lhaurel couldn't push back the rush of despair that washed over her. It was Taren.

He smiled at her with a crooked grin, though there was no levity or humor in the look. His perfect brown robes and thick leather groom's vest were at odds with his bald pate and scarred hands. A long leather cord trailed down from his right hand. The sealing dagger hung at his waist.

Lhaurel's breath caught in her throat, and she fought a wave of panic. Her eyes sought out Saralhn, who gave her a small nod of encouragement. She could do this.

With a start, Lhaurel realized that the Warlord had come to face her and that the procession had arrayed itself around her, forming a half circle. The warriors' faces reflected a range of emotions, from pride to solemnity. Lhaurel's pulse quickened, and color burned on her cheeks. She felt hot and cold at the same time. The cloying smell of sweat and drink hung heavy on the air. Lhaurel clutched at her dress with both hands to keep them from shaking.

The Warlord began to speak. "Two hearts, two hands, two lives entwined." He grabbed Lhaurel's left arm and held it up alongside Taren's right. The leather thongs hung in the air between them, rocking back and forth like pendulums. "Two becomes one through the bonds of time. Two to become one, flesh of their flesh, heart of their hearts, blood of their blood." The Warlord pulled the sealing dagger from Taren's waist and slashed it across her left wrist in one swift stroke.

Lhaurel gasped. The pain was hot, incredibly hot, though the wound was shallow. Deep red blood poured from the wound, ran down her arm, and dripped from her elbow onto the sand. She almost expected it to hiss and steam. Instead it pooled and formed a dirty puddle.

The Warlord grabbed Taren's right arm and flipped it forward so the palm faced him. Four distinct scars stretched across his wrist, the one closest to his palm faded with age. Four scars meant four wives that had gone to the grave performing their greatest duty, bringing more sons into the world that could protect the warren from the genesauri and the other clans. At that moment, Lhaurel saw the scars as tributes to four women only remembered through the number of their sons still living.

Among the warriors, the scars were worn as badges of honor. Lifeblood pumped through the wrists. A cut too deep could lead to the loss of a hand or even their lives. Jenthro had years of practice, and no one, man or woman, had died from the sealing cuts for years.

Helplessness spiced with fear sank into the pit of Lhaurel's stomach. Blood pumped from her wrist and dripped into the sand. The last four women married to this man had died.

"His blood in her veins," The Warlord continued, slashing Taren across the wrist beneath the fourth scar, "pumping to her heart. Her blood in his, sealing the union. Flesh to flesh, heart to heart, blood to blood." He pulled Lhaurel's wrist up and pressed her cut against Taren's, wrapping the leather thongs around them both. She felt the older man's blood mingle with hers, hot and sticky, pumping through the slit in her wrist and down into her arm. She could smell the salty tang of it in the air. Less blood came from his cut than hers.

"And thus are they sealed."

It was done. The music ended.

A murmur arose from the surrounding watchers. Hands were raised into the sky, palms forward, exposing scars of varying degrees of freshness in a token salute. Tradition named it a gesture of honor and respect.

Lhaurel bit her bottom lip against the pain as Taren raised their bound hands high, nearly pulling Lhaurel from her feet. Even with her abnormal height, he towered over her.

"Hail the union!" Taren shouted into the chamber. His voice echoed and reverberated over and over until it was joined by other warriors' voices, shouting exultation to the heavens.

Lhaurel looked down toward the ground and swallowed hard against the bile welling at the back of her throat. Blood dripped over taut leather.

The echoes rose to a frenzied, cacophonous pitch. Then the sounds fell away, dying in a ragged succession that left the last note a broken, hollow thing. Lhaurel looked up and blinked, noticing that the assembled watchers had turned from her and Taren and were looking toward the northern side of the room. She turned in the direction they were looking.

A red-robed figure walked forward with the gait of a much older man, as if his presence there weren't unusual at all. He was one of a group of strange men who wandered the sands without a home and called themselves Roterralar, or wanderers. They weren't outcasts but something far more odd, always garbed in red robes and steeped in rumor and suspicion. The crowd parted with tones of fear and amazement, affording Lhaurel a complete view.

The Roterralar walked forward with a determined expression, his eyes hard, though there was a smile on his lips. He seemed to be favoring his right side slightly, taking a dragging limp forward with that leg while walking normally with the left. And behind him he dragged the body of a sailfin.

The eight-foot-long behemoth was clearly dead, but even still, Lhaurel struggled to hold back a gasp of fear. It came out as a mixed gasp of fear and amazement, echoed throughout the room by a half-hundred throats. Even though the sailfins were the smallest and most plentiful of the genesauri monsters, few there had seen one up so close. Fewer still could look at this one without a wave of fear and confusion.

Jerria's face hardened, and one of her smaller children started to cry. The woman had lost her first husband to a sailfin pack during the previous Migration.

Lhaurel fought back her own wave of pain and memories, though her thoughts had grown clouded with the blood loss and pain.

"What are you about, man?" Jenthro shouted, cutting over the small hum of amazement that had overcome the onlookers.

The man took another few shuffle-steps forward, dragging the corpse behind him, careful to avoid the poisonous purple spines of the sail on its back.

SANDS

"Well, aren't we all excited on this happy day?" the Roterralar said, meeting Lhaurel's eye and inclining his head slightly.

Lhaurel looked away, hoping that no one had noticed her breech of protocol.

Jenthro gestured and a number of warriors surrounded the man. They were careful to avoid the sailfin corpse. Even dead, the small genesauri was not something anyone wanted to be close to.

"What are you about?" Jenthro repeated, his tone hard.

"Well, I thought you should know the Migration has started."

He said it so unconcernedly. Lhaurel blinked, looking for humor in his expression. Who would joke about something like that?

"The Migration is over a fortnight away," Taren spat. "everyone knows that."

"But where'd the sailfin come from, then?" Lhaurel said quietly.

Taren yanked on their bound arms to silence her, nearly knocking her from her feet.

Lhaurel stumbled but caught herself as Marvi voiced the concern Lhaurel had already expressed. No one stopped her. She was the Matron and above all but the Warlord. Lhaurel swallowed her anger, fighting the onset of a strange dizziness.

"I killed it, obviously. Where else do you get a sailfin corpse? It's not as if I could trade for one down in the Oasis, could I?" The man's tone made more than one of the assembled warriors finger their swords.

Taren snorted. "You expect us to believe that pile of goat leavings? Few can boast of killing a genesauri."

The red-robed man smiled, an expression that didn't come close to reaching his eyes, and stood resolute, so different from the impression he had given during his entrance. His young face was plain, his hair the standard shade of brown, but his calm while being completely surrounded and heavily outnumbered belied his youth. Lhaurel doubted he was much older than her own seventeen years, but he acted as if he were the most senior warrior present.

"We can argue about that until we all turn back to sand and dust, but it doesn't really change anything. Open your ears. Can't you hear them coming? The faster ones will be here in just a few minutes."

Silence killed the soft hum of voices with the effectiveness of a plague. Even the smallest child in the group lay still, listening for the terrifying keening of the wind passing along a sailfin's spine. Lhaurel glanced at the people around her, seeing the same fear in their expressions that she felt within herself. Saralhn, standing by her husband, was as pale as bleached bones.

"I don't hear anything!" Taren snapped after a moment. Lhaurel tried to ignore the irritated tugs on her wrist as Taren gestured for the warriors to grab the Roterralar man.

"I hear it!" Someone in the crowd shouted.

"Me too!"

Other shouts joined in, but Marvi hushed them with a forceful command. The warriors who had been stepping forward to grab the man hesitated, listening again.

Lhaurel heard it then, a soft sound carried on the back of the winds outside the warren. The keening notes of a sailfin pack. Terror washed over her.

"Everyone to their tasks!" Marvi shouted, her thunderous voice echoing throughout the chamber and making everyone jump. "Cobb, take three warriors and secure the water urns."

Everyone hesitated, frozen in the moment of fearful, stunned recognition. Lhaurel blinked, her mind refusing to comprehend what was going on. Her world had come crashing to an end wrapped in blood and leather, and now the genesauri were coming? Sands take her, the *genesauri* were coming.

"Move!" Taren yelled, pulling Lhaurel forward by the tethers on their wrists.

The crowds burst into motion, scurrying into the warren like ants into their hole. Lhaurel watched in detached amazement as mothers grabbed their children, herding them toward rooms to gather their possessions while their husbands assembled with the other warriors. She noticed Saralhn turn to leave only to be yanked back by her husband, who shouted something unintelligible at her before shoving her back toward one of the cavern exits.

Lhaurel watched it all with strange curiosity while being pulled along by her left wrist. She wondered if loss of blood was affecting her thinking.

"Get me out of this thing," Taren demanded, dragging Lhaurel over to Jenthro. He reached for the sealing dagger in Jenthro's hand, still wet with blood.

Jenthro backed away, holding the dagger out of Taren's reach. Lhaurel stumbled forward, righting herself with difficulty as Taren tried to snatch the dagger anyway.

"Tradition dictates an entire night need pass to seal the bond," Jenthro said with a grin that bore no humor. "Figure it out yourself."

Lhaurel blinked. Was the Warlord seriously suggesting they run all the way to the Oasis bound like this?

"Please," Lhaurel stammered, part of her terror cutting through the mental slowness caused by loss of blood. "Please, take it off."

"Oh, enough!" Marvi snapped, walking forward with a drawn dagger. "We need him."

Without turning to face her, Jenthro backhanded her across the face. Taren growled in frustration but stopped reaching for the dagger. Marvi spat blood into the sand.

Lhaurel felt a fleeting moment of pity for the woman. Marvi outranked everyone there and could even speak for the Tribe in meetings in the Oasis, but not even she could hold a weapon. Lhaurel wondered what they'd do to her if they ever found out she practiced the sword forms in secret on her own. Still, she was grateful Marvi's actions had overshadowed her own pleas, but both were unimportant with the genesauri coming.

The Roterralar watched them from next to the sailfin corpse, running a stone over the edge of his blade. The steady rasp was an eerie accompaniment to the swelling screams of the approaching sailfin pack.

Lhaurel struggled to focus, shoving aside the growing dizziness and mental slowness just as warriors began to return to the greatroom.

Old Cobb limped forward, leading a small group of warriors who bore the water urns affixed to wooden poles between them. Women returned with their children, bearing heavy packs of all their possessions. Even the smallest child carried something, be it a favored toy or a sack of meal. Lhaurel caught a glimpse of Saralhn at the back of the group, carrying a pack that was far too large for her small frame.

Taren tugged at their bound wrists with a frustrated growl. Red blood dripped into the sand.

"Alright, everyone!" Jenthro shouted. He drew his sword and accepted a light pack from one of his sons. "Make for the stoneways! If the Migration has started early, maybe the rains in the Oasis have passed as well."

From the back of the room, someone screamed.

Sailfins burst up through the many caverns that opened into the greatroom. Their massive dorsal fins shone sickly grey, each of the supporting spines a deep, rich red tipped in yellow. A prick from one of those spines was death. Hovering a few feet off the ground, the monsters crashed into the assembled group like sandtigers among sheep.

A woman screamed and disappeared amidst a storm of flashing, twisting teeth and flesh. Long, serpentine sailfin bodies twisted around victims, massive maws taking limbs or torsos in a single bite.

Chaos took the group. Taren leapt to his feet, cursing, and yanked Lhaurel up behind him. He shouted out unintelligible orders as he yanked the dagger from Jenthro's stunned grip. With barely a pause, he slipped the dagger between their bound wrists and cut the bonds free, cutting into Lhaurel's already-wounded wrist in the process. Grabbing a sword from a passing soldier, Taren dashed into the fray, not looking back at Lhaurel.

Lhaurel struggled to her feet. Her limbs shook and trembled. Blood pooled everywhere, staining the rust-colored sand a deeper, more vibrant shade of red.

A sailfin flew by her, skimming across the ground and then back up into the air with a strange crackling noise, grabbing an old man by a shoulder and taking him to the ground beneath its massive weight. Lhaurel couldn't help but scream, her mind and memories shouting at her to run.

Lhaurel stumbled toward one of the exits, trying to ignore the chaos and carnage around her. A single thought kept her moving, pushing past the dead and dying around her. *The stoneways. We've got to make it to the stoneways. Run!*

Someone crashed into her, knocking her to the ground. She fell hard, cutting her hands on the rocks and sand. The wound on her wrist added to the red on the sand.

Must get up. Stoneways. Make it to the stoneways.

She froze halfway to her feet. Saralhn stood directly in front of her, struggling with her massive pack. From the side, a sailfin turned and, spotting the struggling woman, flashed toward her, mouth agape. Lhaurel shouted a warning, but the sound was lost in the chaos and confusion. She looked around, hoping to spot anyone who could help. A nearby warrior dashed by, glanced at the scene, and ignored it, fleeing down the cavern with a stream of others. To face the genesauri was death. To flee—run—that was the only chance at life.

Lhaurel glanced to her left, toward the narrow passage only a few paces away. She could make it if she ran quickly enough. The narrow passage would slow the sailfins' pursuit, giving her a chance. From there she could make it to the safety of the stoneways as fast as her legs could carry her.

The sailfin drew closer, a faint keen sounding from its vibrating fin.

Lhaurel got to her feet, a surge of adrenaline shooting through her, rushing through her veins like early morning frost, pushing her up despite the fear. She looked up at Saralhn and then back at the narrow tunnel to her left. Lhaurel was not a warrior, despite her clandestine training. She didn't even have a sword. But she wasn't going to let Saralhn die undefended. She wouldn't abandon her.

Lhaurel raced across the ground, spraying up sand. To the side, the water urns burst, spilling their contents across the sand and mingling with the blood. Saralhn looked up, finally dropping the pack so she could stand. Her eyes went wide with fear, terror freezing her where she stood as her gaze fell on the sailfin bearing down on her.

Lhaurel wasn't going to make it. She was going to watch Saralhn die, and there was nothing she could do—

Suddenly the Roterralar was beside her, his red robes the exact color of blood. He matched her pace, a sword in each hand.

"Here!" he shouted, tossing her one of the swords.

Lhaurel snatched it out of the air without thinking. Tradition and rules be damned to the seven hells. The man spun to the side, tackling

Saralhn out of the way just as the sailfin would have struck. Lhaurel kept running forward, sword tip leading the way.

The blade dug into sailfin flesh, the momentum of its forward progression tearing the sword from Lhaurel's grip. Lhaurel crashed into the rest of the creature's long, muscular body, spinning and dropping to the rocks and sand. She got to her feet almost instantly, adrenaline still pulsing through her, terror giving her a mental acuity she never would have had otherwise.

She found her sword still sticking from the sailfin's body. She ripped it free as the creature twitched, writhing on the ground and threatening to stab her with one of its poisonous dorsal spines. She brought the sword down on the sailfin's back, cutting deeply into the flesh until it struck something hard. Again and again she struck, terror, adrenaline, and fear driving her, cutting into the beast long after it had stopped twitching.

Heaving lungs forced her to stop. She paused, sword held in front of her with a shaking, trembling hand. There was red on the hilt, lots of red. She didn't know if it was hers or the sailfin's. She looked down at the broken, mutilated corpse in front of her and immediately felt sick.

She looked away, and her gaze fell on Saralhn and the Roterralar man, standing on the other side of the sailfin corpse. His expression was unreadable. Saralhn's was a look of horror.

Something cracked against the back of Lhaurel's head. Pain exploded through her consciousness, and she fell, sword dropping from her hand. She blinked once and then faded into darkness.

CHAPTER 3
Desperation

"There was a time when these people would not have let one of their children come within a thousand spans of me. Now they provide me with one, Briane. One whose presence is a constant reminder of their desperation."

-From the Journal of Elyana

"Well, you've gotten yourself into a fine old mess."

The voice resounded as if from a long distance away, though upon reaching her ears, it echoed in them like a beating drum. Her thoughts bounced around her head and left her swimming in confusion. Eyes fused shut, sight and senses gone, Lhaurel struggled to form a coherent thought.

Where was she?

Lhaurel tried to think but couldn't focus. The salty tang of blood and sweat hung heavy in the air. She tasted blood on her lips. All she could feel was pain, pain everywhere.

Boots crunched against sand and sounded against the rock as someone approached. She tried to move but was restrained. Someone pressed a waterskin to her lips, and she drank gratefully, regaining some clarity of thought despite the pounding, throbbing pain in her temples. She took another drink, and the pounding faded slightly. Whoever was there turned and walked away a few steps.

She noticed, for the first time, the orange glow behind her eyelids. Realization hit her with the force of a storm. She'd been strung up on the rocks—bait for the coming genesauri horde. Those sun-blasted, fever-stricken Sidena had finally done what they'd threatened to do all these many years. Lhaurel had finally pushed their tolerance too far. She tried to fight down the terror, though she didn't have the strength left to fight her bonds. Her head throbbed every time she tried to move.

The footsteps grew closer. Maybe they were here to watch.

Sunlight blared down on her, burning her pale flesh and searing her eyes, and she blinked them open. Two involuntary tears leaked down her cheeks and mingled with the dust and sand that clung to her face. There was blood there as well, both old and fresh, but the tears did little to wash it away.

A shadowed silhouette blocked out the sun.

"Who's there?" she asked. Her voice came out as a rasp.

A man smiled down at her, and even through the pain she noticed he had a wonderful smile. His face was plain, and he was far from the most handsome man she'd ever seen, but his smile was surprisingly endearing. *Foolish girl,* she thought, *you're about to die and you're concerned about his smile. Think! Figure out how to get out of this!*

"I'm trying to decide whether I should just leave you here." The Roterralar dropped to his knees on the stone next to her, leaning down so their faces were only a foot or two apart. How had she not recognized him before? He smelled of rust, earth, and sweat, though his breath carried a cloying freshness to it, as if he had been chewing herbs. "In fact, that is what Taren and the others would want me to do. I mean, you're the one they caught with a weapon. They'd want me to let you get eaten, flesh stripped from your bones bit by bit. I've seen the sailfins do it before. They peel the skin off you first."

His voice was jovial, as if he were telling a friend a favorite tale or even a joke, but his eyes were hard grey stones, locked onto hers, reflecting none of the levity with which he spoke. It left her suddenly cold despite the sun beating down upon her.

Lhaurel swallowed and almost choked on phlegm. It hurt to cough.

"Or I could save you," he continued in the same light, conversational tone, "Give you the chance to make amends for my intervention on your behalf. The choice is yours. You can stay here and be diced into fodder not fit for swine, *or* you can let me save you."

Lhaurel didn't respond. She had no reason to trust him. No reason to even speak to him at all.

"You've got about two minutes before the genesauri get here."

Lhaurel lay there, torn in the agony of indecision. The stories spoke of the Roterralar as wanderers, nomads that somehow managed to survive the Migration out on the sands on their own. For sands sake, that's what their names *meant*. Mothers whispered to their children of strange deaths and accidents attributed to these men. A calf born with two heads was the work of a vagrant Roterralar. A child sick with fever after one passed through the camp was attributed to the evil glare a Roterralar had given the child when he'd run across his path. At least, the mother would warn, the Roterralar hadn't eaten him. They were said to do that. It was also said that the Roterralar could make themselves appear a hundred feet tall and disappear into the sands, or else ride on the backs of the genesauri. And they would kill you as soon as look at you.

The sun beat down, burning her eyes and scorching her flesh. Blood throbbed and pumped from her wrists and ankles where the leather cut into her flesh. The silence was deafening—the silence that heralded the last few moments before the sailfin pack burst up out of the sand and descended upon their prey. The genesauri were coming, sands take them. Her fear of them outweighed any distrust. The indecision passed in a sudden moment of release.

"Fine," she said finally.

"First, you must swear a blood oath to the Roterralar."

Lhaurel blinked, though the effect was lost through her squinting.

"You have about one minute left."

Her clan had left her behind to die to aide in their own escape. Honestly, she couldn't blame them. She'd violated their laws and traditions. "Fine, I swear by the blood within my veins that my loyalty is now and forever to the Roterralar."

"You don't really mean that, but I'll hold you to your oath."

The man rose to his feet, appearing for a moment as if he were encompassed by a shroud of red-grey mist from the sun's brilliant radiance behind him. He pulled out a dagger, knelt, and cut Lhaurel free. Rising and putting fingers to his lips, he let out a shrill whistle that tore at Lhaurel's eardrums. An echoing response came almost immediately, but from above them.

Blood flew back into her limbs with a rush, leaving them prickling as if she had stepped on the spine-covered shell of a rashelta. The smell of sweat and blood grew stronger when the bonds fell away. She arose on shaky limbs, taking the hand that the Roterralar proffered when the pain threatened to drop her back to the ground. Her head ached, and she couldn't seem to keep her balance. The man's grip was like iron, keeping her on her feet

"Did Saralhn make it?" Lhaurel asked, steadying herself and letting go of his hand.

"Who?"

"The girl we saved."

"I don't know."

It would have been worth it if she'd saved Saralhn.

Something large passed in front of the sun. A creature of talons and feathers plummeted toward the earth, a streak of mottled brown and grey and yellow.

Lhaurel shrieked in a combination of surprise and awe as the creature spread its wings and reared in the air.

Clouds of dust sprang up beneath the creature's powerful wings. With an ear-shattering cry, the creature extended massive, taloned feet and alighted on the ground, standing with its head easily a span above Lhaurel's.

The man walked up to it and gently stroked the mottled plumage.

The creature's wings raked back in a sickle shape on either side of its long body. Black orbs, deep, dark pools of intelligence, studied her over the top of a hooked yellow beak.

The majesty took Lhaurel's breath away and, for a moment, at least, made her pains somewhat lessened.

"This is Skree-lar," he said, holding out a hand.

For the first time, Lhaurel noticed the leather harness buckled around the bird's torso.

"And it really is time we left here."

As if to accentuate his words, the high-pitched wail of a sailfin pack ripped through the air.

The man didn't wait for Lhaurel to respond. He seized her by the arm and dragged her over to the bird. She had completely underestimated the danger of this unknown man. His grip was strong, but she resisted despite the pain, and he stopped pulling immediately.

She glanced to one side, contemplating making a run for it.

He followed her gaze. "Don't be an idiot," he said, glancing out over the rolling dunes with narrowed eyes. "You can come with me and take a chance at living or stay here and welcome certain death. And it seems a pity, really, for you to have chosen to come with me already just to hesitate when confronted with something *out of the ordinary*."

He vaulted up onto Skree-lar's back, the bird having hunkered down into the sand so he could do so. His hands moved in a blur as he took leather leads from the harness and attached them to rings hidden in his robes. That done, he again reached down and offered her a hand.

Lhaurel hesitated. She could run and try to make it on her own. If she made it into the warren the Sidena called home, she could lose the sailfins and then try and make it to the Oasis on her own once that pack had passed. She dismissed that plan almost immediately. She wasn't about to brave the sands on her own with the genesauri loose. It was the same reason she hadn't left to join the outcasts, the same reason she'd never simply run away. She feared the sands and the demons they contained. She hesitated a moment longer.

A moment too long. The man lost his patience and seized her arm, pulling her up behind him as if she were no heavier than a small child. Just as she landed, the sand ruptured and spewed out a geyser of sand, and a sailfin burst into the air.

"Hold on!" the man shouted, and he gave a sharp, whistling trill.

The bird spread its wings and launched into the air.

Lhaurel awkwardly seized the man around the waist, feeling hard muscles beneath the cloth of his robes. She found herself blushing furiously and berated herself silently at the foolishness of it all. What was she? A girl or a woman?

All further thought was blown from her mind as the bird drove its wings downward in a single, powerful stroke that pushed it higher into the air.

The sailfin gave chase, sinuous serpentine body twisting into the sky as if it were swimming through the air. A row of black dots extending backward from the corner of the jaw seemed to crackle and spark the higher it rose into the air. Twice as long and almost as thick as the bird she rode, the sailfin's scream grew to a frenzied, cacophonous pitch.

Lhaurel wanted to scream, wanted to will the bird to fly faster, fly higher, but the sailfin matched the bird's beating wings surge for surge. Another sailfin burst out of the sand, flying upward. Two more followed, then half a dozen more a few seconds later.

The man swore under his breath and urged the bird onward with his hands and another pattern of whistle bursts.

The original sailfin was gaining on them. It was only a few inches away from the bird's gleaming talons, jaws agape as if it would attempt to swallow them all in one bite. Lhaurel looked down into the creature's gullet, seeing rotting flesh and yellow-stained teeth as long as her hand.

Skree-lar flapped harder, its wing beats strong and shallow, yet stiff and uncomfortable.

Fear tightened Lhaurel's grip at the man's waist.

Suddenly, the sailfin seemed to fall away.

An awful sound filled the air like bone scraping against rock. It took her a moment to realize that the sound was the man laughing, distorted by the wind. If her hands hadn't been locked around his waist, feeling the rise and fall of every wheeze, she wouldn't have believed it.

"How can you laugh at a time like this?" she asked, swallowing a mouthful of dust and sand that left her in a fit of coughs. Her pains returned as the adrenaline and fear faded.

By way of response, the man gestured down. The sailfins hovered nearly four spans below them, stationary in the sky except for the strange undulations that made up their normal movements. With each beat of Skree-lar's wings, Lhaurel was taken higher. The genesauri remained where they were. One of them seemed to swim upward toward them but only wriggled in place. It hissed, a high-pitched, grating sound, and then the pack turned and dove back into the sand. Scores of dorsal fins rose up out of the sand as the others descended into it, the rest of the pack welcoming back its companions.

"Why aren't they following us?" Lhaurel shouted, keeping her mouth close to his shoulder to avoid the dust and wind.

"Look!" he shouted, gesturing.

Lhaurel glanced where he pointed and then turned her whole head to take in the sight. A handful of the massive birds of prey, riders on their backs bearing long, metal spears, sped along the desert floor. High above them, more of the rider-bearing creatures circled in complicated aerial patterns. Light glinted off the ends of spears clutched in the riders' hands. With shrieks that rent the air, the birds and their riders descended upon the sailfin pack.

Who were these strangers? She'd never seen so many Roterralar before—in fact, she'd never seen nor heard of more than one being in the same place at any given time, nor had she ever heard anything, even legends, about these mysterious bird-warriors.

"That's why. Now shut up and hold on!"

Lhaurel started to reply angrily, but then a sudden thought struck the barb from her lips. She was flying on the back of a giant bird!

She looked down again, taking in the dunes, the violent struggle of life and death going on beneath her, the dizzying height. Over a hundred spans in the air, her only support was the man to whom she clung and Skree-lar's broad back. It was a moment of fearful wonder that she couldn't fully fathom. Her grip tightened even further around the man's waist.

They climbed high into the air, wheeling to the northeast and keeping the sun to their right. The sight and sounds of battle passed from her view. The man guided the bird with a few tugs on the harness and the occasional odd pattern of whistles.

Lhaurel was fascinated by the ride, though it was far from comfortable. The stiff wing beats brushed up against her already sun-baked thighs, and her skin was being torn at by the rushing wind and sand. Yet all discomfort vanished each time that she glanced down toward the ground. Sand stretched as far as the eye could see, rolling and cresting in endless waves. Even during the periods of safety when the genesauri hibernated beneath the sand, the desert was a constantly changing labyrinth of dunes, sand, and death for several thousand spans around the Oasis. Some of the dune fields moved over fifty spans in the course of the months that the genesauri slept, making them impossible to map.

The ground was firmer, less sandy, from the cave-filled plateaus the Rahuli people called warrens outward to the Forbiddence, the massive, grey-brown stone mountains that rose as sheer cliffs in a perfect circle around the Sharani desert. Full of scraggy bushes and hard, cracked earth baked hard over eons of constant heat, the plains there were generally safe from the genesauri, but there was little food to be found. And absolutely no water.

It was an intimidating yet awe-inspiring sight. She glanced southward, back toward the shallow cliffs where her clan held refuge during the Dormancy. She wondered again if Saralhn had made it to the stoneways safely. Skree-lar banked to the left, compensating for a sudden gust of wind that took him off course.

The thrill that ran through her had nothing to do with fear. *This* was freedom. To pass through the skies, move through the limitless currents of space—it defied reason and time. It was exhilarating. Pure, unadulterated joy.

The man let out a series of whistles and clicks, and Skree-lar banked to the left even more. Far on the horizon, massive cliffs reared up against the sky. Lhaurel peered toward them, ignoring the searing sun on her flesh and the fine grit of sand that cut into it and irritated her many cuts and bruises. The cliffs seemed to pierce the sky, thrusting upwards, striving to meet the clouds, almost as tall as the Forbiddence. The sides of the cliff were straight. Sheer. Impenetrable.

Within moments, they were circling the massive plateau, dropping incrementally closer and closer toward the top of the stone.

"Brace yourself," the man shouted against the wind.

Lhaurel laughed in exhilaration, her overwhelming emotions lending a note of hysteria to her actions.

Skree-lar screamed a note of answering joy as it flared its wings a few spans from the stony surface, pinion feathers bending backward with each stroke of its wings, tail curling inward, slowing it further. Talons stretched outward, grasped onto stone. They slammed forward with the force of the landing.

Unprepared, Lhaurel almost knocked the red-robed man from Skree-lar's back, but the man had braced himself as he had admonished her to do. Instead of knocking him free, her grip around him suddenly loosed, and she tumbled free of the bird's broad back, rolling down one wing and sprawling in the rock, afire with pain. She picked herself back up again with a curse, checking the new cuts and bruises that now graced her sun-scorched flesh and crisscrossed other, less recent injuries. The euphoria of flight faded in a wave of dull, aching pain. The cut on her left wrist dripped a steady stream of blood onto the deep, red rock. It mingled with the dust there, making a slurry of reddish paste.

The man looked down at her for a moment, an odd expression on his face, and then his mouth split into a grin, and he started laughing. It was a deep, throaty laugh, full of mirth, though dusted with something aloof and condescending, simultaneously different and similar to his earlier wheeze.

"What are you laughing at?" she demanded, her annoyance burning away the pain and soreness that had been threatening to take her to her knees up until that moment.

She had definitely passed her breaking point, being so confrontational. Cruel experience had taught her to hide her emotions as best she could. An emotional explosion like this back with the Sidena would have earned her a whipping. She was loath to live through one of those again.

The man stopped laughing but grinned at her, hopping down from Skree-lar's back.

The bird screeched and shambled off across the stone a short distance. It was far less graceful on the ground than it was in the air.

The Roterralar walked up to her, stopping only a few feet away. He was barely as tall as she, but his suddenly iron visage made him seem all the more imposing. "I am the man who saved you. I have every right to laugh when I please. There is so little humor left in our world,

Lhaurel, that I take the opportunity when I can."

Lhaurel took a half step back from the intensity of his words and the sudden light that flashed in his grey eyes.

He matched her step, keeping his gaze locked onto hers. "You didn't have to catch the sword. I could have saved the girl on my own, but you had to go and take the sword yourself. Ask yourself why. A decision like that doesn't just happen. You *already* chafed at their rules and traditions. You have to live with the results of you own actions."

Her temper flared at being called a fool. If he could have done it on his own, then why had he offered her the sword? Why hadn't he simply done what he, as a man, was supposed to do and protect the women and children of the clan? It was obvious. He'd done it to see what she would do. It angered her even more knowing that he was right. She felt, ironically enough, as foolish as a Roterralar suffering from the sun fevers. She'd *wanted* to fit in, but the things she wanted—desires originally inspired by the outcasts, of all people— were incompatible with the lives the Sidena lived. And as much as she wanted to be a part of something, to not feel alone anymore, she didn't want to be a part of that.

"Did she live, at least?" Lhaurel asked. She knew she'd already asked the Roterralar, but she had to know.

The man shrugged. "I saw her get out of the warren, but I didn't follow them to the Oasis. I had other things to attend to." Lhaurel felt a moment of pride and satisfaction rush through her. At least her actions had meant *something*.

"What is your name, anyway?" she asked, only then realizing she didn't know it. She simply thought of him as "the man," or "the Roterralar," as she'd always called the red-robed fanatics that wandered into the warrens.

The man smiled again, spreading his hands wide.

"I am of the sands and stones. I am he of the aevians, a warrior of the sands and metal that make up our world, a man of the Rahuli people."

Lhaurel glared at him. Pain damped what little patience she had left.

His smile widened. "They call me Kaiden. And I am sorry for

this."

He nodded, and before Lhaurel could move, rough hands grabbed her from behind. Something was placed over her mouth and nose, a cloth of some sort that smelled of the small purple flowers that grew in the Oasis. She struggled, but the grip around her shoulders and neck was simply too strong. Her muscles grew weak, and her eyelids grew heavy. She blinked rapidly and tried to scream, but all that came out was a ragged moan.

Behind Kaiden, Skree-lar clicked his beak and made a soft chirping noise. For some reason, that made her want to smile.

* * *

For a moment, Khari ConDeleza, Matron of the Roterralar, felt a flash of annoyance and disappointment as the girl slipped slowly toward unconsciousness. Despite the girl's wounds and obvious weakness, Khari had hoped to see at least a little vigor from the girl. She'd given the men careful instructions so that the girl would have ample opportunity to fight back and resist. But—

The girl suddenly dropped, pulling the sword from Rhellion's belt as she fell.

That's the spirit.

The girl was slow to react, slow to move, and a normal enemy would never have been able to take Rhellion's sword from him, but Khari had instructed him to let it happen beforehand. That was, if the girl had enough gumption to actually try something.

"Stay back," the girl said, eyes darting to the three men who had drawn swords and advanced on her.

Kaiden stood back to one side as he'd been instructed to do.

The girl took a step back, legs shaking visibly, though the sword point didn't waiver.

Khari watched from one side, curious to see what the girl would do. There was no way off the top of the plateau except for on the back of an aevian.

As instructed, Rhellion moved forward, a sword given him by one of the other men held low. "Calm yourself, girl," he said. "There's no need to fight."

The girl stepped back again.

Rhellion's face hardened, and he raised his sword. "Put that down, girl. You wouldn't want to hurt yourself."

Rhellion thrust, and the girl batted it aside.

Khari raised an eyebrow. The girl knew the basic sword forms. Rhellion swung back, and the girl batted it aside again, twisting the blade so the blow was deflected and allowing the girl a chance to reset. True, it was slow, but the move was executed perfectly. Khari stood upright and drew her own sword, striding forward.

"Your form is sloppy," Khari said curtly.

Rhellion backed away and allowed Khari to stand facing the girl. For a moment, the sword dropped, and the girl's face scrunched in confusion. Then Khari raised her sword and pointed it at the girl.

The girl raised her own blade.

Khari, obligingly, went on the attack, though slowly and deliberately. The girl responded with perfect form, her face intent with concentration and a little fear, though her movements were stiff. She really *did* know the basic forms. How had she managed that? Khari pushed her harder, and the girl's defenses broke, unable to match Khari's speed. Khari batted the girl's sword aside and dropped her own sword onto the girl's shoulder, the razor-sharp edge against her neck. The girl's eyes showed white with fear and confusion. Khari felt a twinge of regret at what she was going to have to do next, though it would be for the girl's own good. She hated having to break the new recruits. There were few of them, only three in the last decade, so she was not in very good practice, and a breaking was an extremely discriminating process.

"You will learn that nothing is the same here as it was in your little clan," Khari said in a flat voice made all the more powerful for its lack of emotion. "Forget everything you have ever learned, and you might survive life here. Forget your pride. Forget that you can even think for yourself. Your life begins and ends at my whim now."

The girl gulped, trembling either from fear or the effect of adrenaline wearing away.

CHAPTER 4

Cracks

"The true enemy of any ideal is a lack of persistence. And persistence is the true ideal of a fearsome enemy. The creatures are hardy, if not yet salvation. Change is the autumn leaf on its journey to the ground. It is not the first leaf that heralds autumn's hold, but the last, and all the ground is brown, and red, and gold."

-From the Journals of Elyana

Makin Qays, Warlord of the Roterralar, eighth clan of the Sharani, stepped back from the hidden opening high above the eyrie floor. Wrinkles born of the weight of leadership furrowed his brow. Age belied his once fine stature and slowed his step at times, but he still held himself with a proud and noble bearing. He had led the Roterralar against the genesauri for three generations now, over forty years. And during all forty years the genesauri pattern had never changed. Until now.

Though the sailfins were the smallest of the three genesauri, their vast numbers made them as deadly as the larger two. Thankfully, there were generally several fortnights between when the sailfin packs showed up and when the larger genesauri, the marsaisi and karundin, awoke from their hibernation.

Wind made the thin cloth that hid the opening flutter and shift slightly, but Makin Qays took no notice. The covering lay in a shadowed corner of the eyrie, high along wall. Even knowing it was there, he often had difficulty finding it from the eyrie floor. He sighed, pulling himself from his troubled thoughts, and walked back to the edge.

The woman that Kaiden had brought to the warren was still standing by the doorway, her gaze moving from one side of the eyrie to another in an aimless pattern. Confusion was a common sentiment among those they welcomed. This one was taking it better than most, he noted with interest. Perhaps she might even be ready to fight in this Migration. Sands knows they needed her.

Khari, his wife and the matron of the eyrie, entered the room and joined the table of silent observers. She must have had to jog the whole way to make it up here this quickly, but that was her way. Silently, he applauded her performance with the woman below. She hated having to break the young men and women down, tearing them apart one piece at a time. But it was requisite that something be broken before it could be fixed.

Breaking was a delicate process. It wasn't simply a question of taking a hammer to a crockery pot and bludgeoning it until all that was left was a few tiny pieces and a smattering of dust. No, with people, the breaking had to take place in a way where the pieces could be put back together. Trauma wasn't necessarily the best course. Each person was different.

"So," Makin Qays said, turning to the table of silent observers, "what news?"

Tieran, one of the cast leaders, grinned. "The new girl is a pretty one. It'll do my old bones some good to have her around."

Khari shot him a flat look.

Tieran's twin, a woman named Sarial who was nothing at all like her brother, snorted. "You're not old, and you say that about every woman," she said.

"Well, it's true each time."

Makin Qays silenced them with a word. "Any *relevant* news."

"She's got a stubborn streak in her," Khari said. "About a dozen spans wide, but she is decent with a blade. I just have to break her first."

"I have a feeling we'll need her before this Migration is through," Makin Qays said thoughtfully.

"I'll do what I can," Khari said.

"She won't break." Kaiden's voice was strangely resolute.

Khari blew out a long breath. "Let's hope you're wrong, Kaiden. For all our sakes. We'll give her a couple of days, and then I think we'll let her know that her friend didn't survive."

* * *

A single long cut along the sailfin's belly, then peel back the skin. It came off the flesh easily, only needing a few easy slices to loosen it from the muscle and sinew beneath. Once the skin was peeled all the way up to where the large dorsal began, Lhaurel had to roll the creature over and skin the other side. Long cuts sliced both the skin and the dorsal free, though she was careful not to let the tips of the dorsal spines pierce her flesh.

Now the real work began. Milky white cords of sinew and gummy flesh coiled around the long, tubular body, which had to come free. The coils were tough and hard to cut, but she persisted, even with just a single knife whose blade was shorter than the length of her hand. Her first sailfin had taken her nearly half a day to skin and slice up into chunks for the aevians to eat. Part of it had stemmed from the fear that coursed through her at the sight of the creature despite knowing it was dead. Now, two weeks later, she could get through four or five sailfin corpses in that same time. And she was no longer afraid. Fear faded in the face of familiarity.

What she hadn't gotten used to was the smell.

A foul odor came from the fat and the membranous white strands that she had to peel away layer by layer. The skeleton was also unique in that it was a mottled mixture of white bone and a dark grey, metal-like substance. It smelled of rust and age mingled with rotted meat.

She cut out a thick steak and set it aside, lost in her work and her own thoughts. The past two weeks had been both the most exhilarating and the most frustrating of her life. Being with the aevians all day long, every day, seeing to their needs and even sleeping curled up in the sands near them—that was wonderful. She loved the majestic birds, their nobility and playfulness. She felt a special attachment to and a love for them that she had never before experienced.

And she couldn't leave. There was no feasible escape. Even if she did manage to climb down the thousand spans to the desert sands below, she had no idea where to go, nor any reasonable hope of surviving the journey. The sailfins, though smallest of the genesauri monsters, were the most numerous. Their packs ravaged the desert and destroyed anything living upon the sands. And the bigger ones— Lhaurel shuddered at the thought.

Taking a deep breath, Lhaurel got to her feet and let out a shrill, piercing whistle, a skill that she had only recently mastered. Immediately, the aevians descended. Several skittered toward her low along the ground, rust-colored wings flapping and black eyes fixed on the meat she had prepared. Others dove from their places high along the cliff walls, sickle-shaped wings folding inward as they cut through the air, racing each other like children at play.

The sight of the approaching flock would have terrified most people, but it made Lhaurel smile. She closed her eyes and listened to the beat of wings, the cries of pleasure, and the shrieks of friendly competition. The sounds were the sounds of friends and companions—the sounds of the one thing she trusted in this place. They bore down on her, talons extended, hooked beaks clicking in hungered anticipation.

A thrill ran through her.

The aevians parted around her, diving for the butchered meat and avoiding her as if she were an immovable pillar in their way and not a mere woman half the size of the smallest aevian.

She breathed in and then let it out slowly, her frustration and anger burned away in the rush of adrenaline.

"I already knew you were stupid," a cold voice said, raised slightly to compensate for the noise thrown up by the feasting birds, "but *that* was sheer idiocy."

Lhaurel opened her eyes to find Kaiden before her.

His flinty eyes penetrated her. She refused to blush and then grew angry as she felt heat blossom on her cheeks. *Foolish woman*, she snapped at herself, *don't let him see that he's getting to you. Didn't all those years with Marvi and Jenthro teach you anything at all?*

"And I just realized the extent of your arrogance," she retorted. "Well, it's either that or you have a strange understanding of the meaning of an apology. Would *you* think someone was truly sorry if they left you a prisoner in strangers' hands?"

He shrugged, an expression heightened by his bare shoulders, exposed beneath his thin leather vest. An array of colorful bracelets adorned his arms above each wrist in differing patterns. Upon closer scrutiny, Lhaurel realized that they weren't bracelets at all but tattoos. Bands of color wrapped up his forearms, ending just short of his elbows. Most of them were a deep, dark brown that stood out from his lightly tanned skin and the other bands of color around them.

"You can think what you wish. My apology was sincere and so has merit. It is not my fault if it falls on deaf ears," he said.

"Arrogance it is, then."

He shrugged again and stepped around a group of aevians fighting over a particularly juicy chunk of sailfin. "From what I've seen, you seem to like it here. Well, the aevians at least."

They'd been watching her? Worse, *Kaiden* had been watching her. She felt more exposed than when he'd seen her in her smallclothes. He'd watched her work, watched her toil, and sweat, and rant, and pee. How many more of them had watched her?

"Lhaurel," Kaiden said, then hesitated.

Lhaurel looked over at him, chewing on her bottom lip to keep herself from saying anything else rash.

Kaiden's expression firmed. "The girl, Saralhn—she didn't make it to the Oasis."

Lhaurel felt as if she'd had a bucket of freezing water poured down her back. Her vision swam. Dread spread through her, clutched at her heart. Her lungs seized up, and she gasped for breath, afraid and angry at the same time. She felt suddenly dizzy.

Kaiden swore as she fell to her knees.

Immediately she could breathe again. The feeling of icy dread washed out of her, bursting free like water held back by a dam in the Oasis.

Kaiden knelt down beside her, resting an arm on her shoulder.

"Are you ok?" His voice seemed both annoyed and concerned, an odd combination.

She started to get to her feet, placing a hand on Kaiden's knee to give her support, but her hand touched a patch of wetness. Jerking her hand back, she felt bile rise up in her throat, and she almost heaved.

"It's not what you think," Kaiden said, his voice suddenly cold again. "My water pouch burst. Hence the cursing." As if to prove it, he reached into the pocket of his leggings and removed a deflated waterskin, a large hole in one end. He tossed it aside, making several aevians hiss and skitter out of the way. He held out his hand.

Lhaurel ignored it and got to her feet, pushing herself up with hands on her own knees. "Are you sure she didn't make it?"

Kaiden hesitated, then nodded.

Anger, pain, and despair welled up within Lhaurel. Saralhn had been the only true friend she'd ever had. It wasn't enough that she'd been forced to endure the strange ways the Roterralar had been treating her. What she'd gone through with the Sidena wasn't enough. Now Saralhn was dead.

Frustration, anger, and pain pushed past the inhibitions with which she had been indoctrinated. "You had no right to watch me without my knowledge, Kaiden," she said vehemently. "No right at all."

Kaiden's eyes steeled, becoming hard pools of grey reflectivity. "You don't even understand what you're talking about." He jabbed an accusing finger at her. "We have every right to protect ourselves. You have no attachments to life, no understanding of what it means to be part of a clan or even of a family. It is you who have no rights here. No right to claim understanding. No right to even demand answers to your questions. I saved your life from the genesauri. I could just as easily return it to them."

Lhaurel's shiver didn't come from the threat. Rather, it was the monotone way in which he said it. No anger or fear colored the words. It was a simple statement. Fact. It quenched the anger and the frustration, leaving behind only the pain.

"I didn't choose my life," she said, looking down. "I never had a family to be a part of. I don't even know who my parents were. Not really. I didn't choose this."

"You chose to take that sword. You chose to train."

She raised her chin, pride firming her resolve, but Kaiden's expression stopped her. He wasn't even looking at her, the arrogant little—Kaiden nodded at something over Lhaurel's shoulder, his face angled high along the wall.

Then he noticed her. "What?"

"What were you just looking at?"

Kaiden arched an eyebrow at her. "I wasn't looking at anything."

Lhaurel gave him a look that clearly told him she didn't believe a word. She'd already exploded once. One more outburst, albeit smaller than the last, wasn't going to make any real difference.

"Suit yourself," he said. "I really must be going now. Enjoy your solitude."

Lhaurel glared daggers into his back as he left, though once the door closed, she turned and glanced in the direction Kaiden had been looking. The corner of her lip tugged into a half smirk. He'd finally slipped.

* * *

A few hours later, after coming to terms with Saralhn's death as best she could, Lhaurel stood in the same spot where Kaiden had been standing when she had caught him peering up at the wall with far too much attention. She scanned the sandstone walls, studying the area for anything that would appear like an opening or place where one could perform observations. She must have stood for a good ten minutes, studying the stone.

Nothing.

The Lhaurel that had first arrived would have given up then, but Lhaurel's stubbornness had grown. As she started her second scan, a slight breeze wafted up from the chamber's opening, swirling in a complex pattern of eddies and whorls. High above her head and slightly to the left, thirty spans up, the rock *shifted*.

She almost smiled but stopped herself before the expression could betray her discovery. Someone was surely watching her even now, wondering what it was that she was doing. So she continued to study the rock, allowing her expression to show feigned frustration and disappointment. After a few long minutes she hung her head in resignation, allowing her auburn hair to fall in front of her face. Behind the red curtain, though, she smiled.

She put down her metal bucket and spade, leaning them against the wall of the cavern. Next, she divested herself of the nondescript brown robe she wore, leaving her only in her smallclothes. The robe would get in the way as she climbed. There were no steps carved into the stone—no easy paths of ingress or egress. Yet the entire cliff was made of the same rough sandstone, laden with streaks of dark grey metal. That meant it was rough and full of crags. She reached up, seized an outcropping of stone, and started to climb.

She continued to climb, ignoring the ache in her shoulders, the burning angry pain stretching up her arms and down her back, which screamed at the strain. Sweat dripped down her brow and pasted her hair to the side of her head. Her hand burned where she had been cut, and it continued to bleed, leaving a trail along the rock that marked where she had been. The occasional aevian would pop its regal head out of an outcropping or nest to peer quizzically at her as she passed, but she ignored them. Everything ceased to exist except the strange outcropping where she had seen the stone move.

Halfway to the outcropping, her muscles forced her to stop and take a momentary respite on a large promontory of stone that jutted out from the regular semi-flat sandstone wall. Lhaurel pulled herself atop the lip and collapsed onto the gritty surface. She blinked away the stinging sweat, though more dripped into her eyes, making the gesture a futile one. Her vision was slightly blurry around the edges, as though she had just woken up and had yet to become fully alert. One of her hands, the one with the cut, trembled uncontrollably, like the wings of a grasshopper in flight. She closed her eyes and breathed as deeply as her oxygen-deprived lungs allowed. Was she really so soft that a simple climb like this would leave her *this* winded?

Near her, Gwyanth, Khari's aevian and the only one of the creature whose name she had learned, and her son hopped from crag to crag, the younger aevian flapping his wings far less gracefully than his mother.

Lhaurel smiled. The young aevian, called a fledgling, apparently, was one of her favorites. He had a funny little chirp he seemed to reserve just for her.

A sudden thought struck her, one that left her sickened and enraged at the same time.

They'd never told her not to try to escape. No one had ever threatened her about trying to run away. In fact, they had done everything in their power to frustrate and enrage her. They had *wanted* her to try and escape.

Why else would they have forced her to do such menial tasks day in and day out. She'd forgone sleep for almost a fortnight caring for the aevians and Gwyanth's fledgling son. No one told her that Gwyanth would have done that herself if Lhaurel hadn't been there. There had been other fledglings born while she'd been working with Gwyanth's son, but none of them had been cared for by another person. Why had she?

The most powerful prisons were those whose bars were constructed by the one imprisoned within them. They had made her *want* to care for the creatures. They had used her own kindness and determination against her. She felt like a milk-besotted babe to have been so easily manipulated.

"I'm such a fool," she said aloud, clenching her fists and kicking some loose sand over the side of the ledge. Why hadn't she realized what they were doing to her? They'd expected her to attempt something. They'd expected her to figure them out at some point.

She looked up in a sudden burst of anger, her eyes flashing and fixating on the spot where she had seen the rock move. She could see it even though she was directly beneath it. Her ledge afforded her a slightly angled view of the spot.

"I know you're up there," she shouted, her voice carrying and reverberating off the close walls. "I'm done playing your games. I'm done waiting for you to explain. Show yourselves! Kaiden! Khari! I've had enough!"

Her voice echoed across the chamber, rolling and reverberating like a wave of rolling sand. The rock she was staring at shifted, and a head poked out over the edge and peered down at her—a head topped with dusty brown hair, a plain face, and grey eyes. And a frown.

"Well, you're not nearly as stupid as you've made Khari believe," Kaiden said, "but not nearly as smart or as stubborn as you're going to need to be."

Part 2

Roterralar

CHAPTER 5

The Smell of Change

"Having lived the solitary life, alone with my craft and with the creatures that I love, having another's presence within my walls is uncomfortable. The girl is always there—always in the way. And her ceaseless chatter gnaws at my mind and steals away what hope I have left. She is a leech, sapping away my strength."

-From the Journals of Elyana

Sheltered in a large stone bowl that mirrored the epic grandeur of the Forbiddence, the Oasis walls stuck up over the sands for dozens of span. The ground within the bowl the Oasis formed was covered in a thick, green grass that cushioned the foot when one walked. For Marvi, who was used to walking on the sandy covered floors of the warren, where each step was really the culmination of two motions—one forward and one slipping back marginally—the springy grass of the Oasis was unnerving.

The Oasis was a blessing, a shelter from the genesauri during the Migration and a sure source of water during the three months when the rains didn't make the Oasis uninhabitable. If it weren't for the nine months of rain each year, they could have stayed in the Oasis all year long and never worried about the genesauri again. But the flooding made living there during the Dormancy impossible.

Thankfully, the genesauri slept for that period, which made the Sharani Desert relatively safe.

Marvi doubted that the water oaths would hold up with all the Rahuli clans confined together for as long as they were. In truth, the peace barely held together each year. Fights often broke out between the clans who were sworn blood enemies. Tempers ran high, and fear and warmongering were facts of life. It was only common need that allowed them some respite from the chaos that awaited them on the sands. Fear was the great unifier of all men. Well, that and lust.

Marvi grimaced as she walked along the grass, holding up the hem of her robe so it wouldn't catch on the grass or get soaked by the thick beads of dew beading along the green strands. There was a muskiness to the air, an odor of dirt and plants and the close proximity of thousands of people and whatever animals they had managed to save that Marvi simply hated. It was a foreign smell found only here in the Oasis, the thick, ugly smell of wet.

Despite her efforts, her robes caught on the rough bark of a tall palm and tore with a loud ripping noise. She swore and dropped the robe altogether. Let it get wet. Where she was going, it didn't matter if she had on the finest robes or if she wore loops of gold in her ears. Eyes narrowed in determination, she strode through the grass and entered the camp of the Frierd clan. Though there was a water oath in place, it didn't stop the politics or the jockeying for power or influence of trade among the various clans. And it also didn't stop the jostling for the best encampments within the Oasis. The Frierd had been encroaching upon the Sidena borders, using the well maintained by the Sidena to water their sheep. It was a grievous insult. Were one to drink from the water sullied by the sheep of another clan, they themselves would be counted no more worthy than cattle to be driven and branded by another's mark. It was an emasculating maneuver perpetrated by Frierd's Warlord, Alarian, in response to some imagined slight. Marvi's husband, Jenthro, had rushed to defend their honor, thinking with his sword more than his brain.

Foolish man, she thought, tossing her head with an exasperated flick, *he's going to get himself killed one of these days, and I'll be damned to the seven hells before I step in to protect him.*

She reluctantly dismissed the thought. She knew her present duty to the Sidena, if not her husband. Do what he would, Marvi would step in to make up for all of Jenthro's lapses. And, sometimes, protect him from himself, as she was doing now. If she'd left it in his hands, they would have been in battle now, not just against the Frierd clan, but also likely against the Mornal and Olarin clans. The Frierd, Mornal, and Olarin had fierce trade alliances, such that many of their families were intermarried one with another. The bonds of blood ran deep, more deeply than Jenthro realized or even cared to acknowledge. That was a failing of men. They never understood the power of blood except to shed it. *Idiots!*

As the Matron of the Sidena, she had the power to speak for the clan, though that power was seldom, if ever, used. The Frierd would not stand in her way, though. She adjusted her robe against the stifling humidity, held her head high, and strode through the center of the Frierd camp as if she were their matron.

The Frierd camp was arrayed like most of the others, a half circle of tents nestled up against the protective cliffs and encircling the shallow market where others came to trade or else survey the wares they had brought to the Oasis. Or that was what it normally looked like. This year the market was just a barren stretch of grass, slightly flattened by countless trampling feet. Like the Sidena, there hadn't been time for the Frierd to bring much other than their own selves to the Oasis with them. *Damn the genesauri!*

The Frierd people themselves were arrayed in small groups around a central fire pit. Many were chatting among themselves or else attending to one of the score of little tasks that occupied both men and women when they camped. They looked mostly the same as the Sidena except that the men sported detailed tattoos around their eyes and down the sides of their cheeks. Also, they were devoid of topknot, instead leaving their hair long like a woman's, though the women in the clan tied their hair back in thick braids that hung down their backs. Some of the wealthier women of a higher rank, as evidenced by the color of their *shufari*, even had small stones or colorful bits of yarn interwoven with the strands of their hair. It was an opulent display of their wealth, and they did it because they knew that Marvi was coming.

The fire pit sat in the center of the clustered groups. Stones had been placed around the pit to reflect the heat properly. It was such a strange thing—an open fire. Fires were such a rarity out on the sands due to a lack of fuel that Marvi still marveled at how common they were in the Oasis.

The Frierd parted around her, leaving a clear path to where Alarian waited, arms folded across his chest. Even with her torn robes and water-soaked hem, she bore herself with a regality and authority that outshone the stones in the women's hair, sent even the proudest warrior to reexamine his masculinity, and cast a shadow over the entire message they were trying to present. By simply refusing to be intimidated, Marvi had changed the way this meeting would unfold, and she hadn't said a single word. It helped that even in her old age, if a trifle rounder than it had been in her youth, she still wielded a stately beauty.

As she approached, Marvi took a quick minute to study the man. He was a newer Warlord, and she had not had much time to get to know anything about him. Her informants knew little. He was a younger man, perhaps not yet past his fortieth year. His skin was weathered and bore the leathery toughness of one who has spent his entire life toiling in the blistering heat. He wore a simple vest and loose pants, exposing hard muscles and an array of scars that crossed his chest. Marvi thought they looked like the marks a sandtiger's claws might make. Only the bravest or most foolhardy warriors still hunted sandtigers.

His face was as weathered and hard as the rest of him, square nose, firm jaw, and thin lips, all set beneath dark blue eyes that shone with a shrewdness born of survival in a place where even the smallest of children played with death as they would a favored toy. Spikey tattoos lined his eyes.

Marvi was surprised to find that she liked him. He was even somewhat handsome when compared to her own homely husband. *Maybe he could be of use after all.* Marvi adjusted her plan in an instant, shifting her intent like the wind shifted the dunes.

"Greetings, Honored Warlord," she said with a slight inclination of her head, a gesture that just barely covered the tenants of propriety. "May death's shadow pass you by."

Alarian returned the nod, the slight movement far more appropriate coming from him than it had from her.

She waited for him to say something, conscious of the fact that the rest of the Frierd clan had closed in behind her. She almost smiled, but that would have destroyed the effect she was trying to create.

He said nothing.

Fine.

"A troubling matter has been brought to my attention, noble Warlord," she said. "One that concerns your cattle and our well."

"Why would Frierd cattle be anywhere near a well maintained by the Sidena?" Alarian asked. His voice was deep and rich despite the yellowed teeth. She could look beyond that.

"Why indeed. Perhaps they were so parched from the excessive heat and dryness here that they were driven to drink wherever they could find a place to quench their thirst." She was giving him a chance to get out of the situation before it became more than it was. Before it came to a test of honor. She knew it would be futile, but she had to offer him the chance.

"Or perhaps someone tried to lure them away from their rightful masters? Meat is scarce. The Migration took us all by surprise, and there is barely enough to go around. It would be understandable, if not forgivable, for a weaker, less honorable clan to attempt such a thing." He was trying to provoke her, get her to react in anger and issue a challenge that would lead to a direct confrontation between their two clans.

She couldn't risk that. The Sidena's flight from the genesauri had already diminished their ranks enough—they couldn't afford to lose any more, especially not with the clans all packed together here in the Oasis. It would be a massacre.

"Perhaps, but who would anger the clans by breaking the water oaths in such a way? Any form of provocation would be considered an act of war and would enact the full retribution of all the clans. That is not something anyone would want to face."

Alarian shrugged, though she caught a glimpse of something in the set of his jaw, the glint of his eye. Agreement.

No one wanted to violate the water oaths. None of them could afford the losses after the deaths meted upon them all by the genesauri. Outside the Oasis, out on the sands during a Dormancy, the clans could and *would* fight each other over the slightest perceived insult or merely to jostle for power and influence. Pride was the motivator of every fight. Inside the Oasis, mutual fear and need outshone the pride but didn't kill it.

"Perhaps not," he agreed with a slight nod. "Perhaps the cattle were merely so thirsty they were forced to find whatever drink they could. A pity it fell upon your well."

Marvi spread her hands wide in a gesture that took in the entire camp. "What happens to one affects us all."

The assembled Frierd watchers nodded and murmured their assent.

Marvi grinned inwardly. Now was her time to strike. "One would not be so loathe to share water with cattle if a portion of them were one's own."

"If only one were fortunate enough to have brought one's own," Alarian said slowly, his eyes narrowing as he tried to puzzle out where she was going with her reasoning. "One would not mind sharing with them. The animals grant us life and are worthy of sharing some comforts with man."

"From such sharing are other things gained," Marvi agreed. "The water gives life to both cattle and man, and the cattle can then sustain the man even when the water no longer remains. To share water with the cattle is to lay up storage for the future against unknown need."

Behind her, some of the warriors began muttering under their breath, realizing what it was that she was proposing. A trade between the two clans. The Sidena would allow the Frierd cattle access to their water for a portion of the herd. Alarian's eyes narrowed, his eyebrows coming together in small ridges over his nose.

"But the costs of such sharing can sometimes be toxic," he said, his voice hard. "Cattle spread disease, and once cattle get used to watering with men, they come to expect it and so strut around as if they were men. And men as if they were beasts."

Laughter erupted at this, deep laughs, from the men in the group behind her. Several small children took up the laughter, responding to the adult's mirth more than from any understanding of the discussion.

Marvi smiled and nodded slightly, acknowledging the skill of the veiled insult. "When hunger strikes, as it is wont to do, is it not easier to slay a beast that is close to you rather than far afield?"

Alarian smiled at this, a smile that spread from his lips to his eyes, a hot smile, one of conquest and lust.

She had known this would appeal to him. She had steered him toward it from the moment he had tried to provoke her. He was a bully at heart, a shrewd bully, but a bully, nonetheless. And to the core, bullies were the epitome of laziness. Having victims close at hand was something that appealed to the malicious nature within him.

"You are very wise, Marvi, Matron of the Sidena," he said at length, holding out his right hand, wrist up, exposing the multitude of scars there. She reached out with her left, conscious of the single scar on her own wrist.

"And your counsel is always sought, Warlord. May death's shadow pass over you, always. I will send a scribe to dictate the full terms."

He nodded and turned away, dismissing her in the same motion. Normally, Marvi would have rankled at the indifference Alarian was showing her with the gesture, but she ignored it this time. She'd been lucky—no, she'd used her talents and gotten what she wanted, but she wasn't about to push it any further. The spider didn't catch many flies by waiting in the middle of the web, hovering over its kill. No, it wrapped the fly in silken strands and then retreated, awaiting the next victim. And she was only a Matron, not a Warlord—her gender made her beneath him in social standing, if not in skill. Luckily, the latter was far more important.

Marvi turned and exited the way she had entered, torn robes dragging along the grass. She waited until she had passed the borders of the camp to smile and chuckle silently to herself. Alarian thought he'd won a great victory today, a position of power where he could lord himself over a lesser clan. He would soon discover it was the other way around.

* * *

Jenthro met her halfway back to the territory controlled by the Sidena. He sat, legs crossed and eyes closed, and his hard-edged face formed an impassive mask as she approached.

Marvi couldn't begin to understand how he could be comfortable sitting on such strange softness. Grass should be yellow, long, and tough, not green and springy.

"You haven't the right to do what you did," Jenthro said without opening his eyes. His arms lay outstretched, palms facing upward toward the sun, forearms exposed. Only a single scar graced his right wrist. Hers.

She raised an eyebrow at him, though he couldn't see the gesture. "I did what had to be done to ensure our survival. If things had gone the way you had planned, we would already be dead now, assimilated into the Frierd or else too weak to ever make it back to the warren once the Migration is over."

His eyes snapped open.

"Don't you dare speak to me that way," he hissed. "I am the Warlord. My word is law. I could have you killed for addressing me with such disregard. Even if you are my wife." He said the last word as if it were akin to saying that she was just another of his many possessions, like an additional goat for his herds.

Marvi threw back her head and laughed, ignoring the threat completely. "Let's not forget who put you there, Jenthro. Let's not forget whose schemes and plots have kept you from being overthrown by the next upcoming usurper time and time again. It was not you who defeated them. They were dead before they ever reached for their swords. Let us not forget who really ensures that the people get fed, trade gets secured, and our survival maintained. You may be the Warlord, but you do not lead the clan."

He sprang to his feet but did not approach her. His look was murderous, filled with hate. His hands clenched into fists at his sides. "I should never have consented to marry you. Treacherous snake. I am the Warlord. I *am* the clan."

"An empty title, Jenthro. It always has been, even when my dear late father held it, and he was a much better man than you. Power isn't something given to you. It is earned. Slowly, painstakingly, over the course of years. It is complete mental and emotional domination. If you have power you did not earn, it is because someone has earned it for you. And that, my dear, will always elude you."

He raised a fist as if to strike her and then spun on his heels and stalked off into the trees, his every step proclaiming his rage. Marvi watched him go, not bothering to hide her calculating expression. It was not the face she presented to the rest of the clan. This was the face of the spider pulling at strands of web, knitting lives together or pulling them apart. This was the face of the master weaver of the clan's life-web.

"In a way, I'm glad you chose him over me," a deep voice said from behind her.

A true smile appeared on Marvi's lips as Taren walked out of the trees, his bald pate glistening with sweat. She reached out and took his hand, squeezing it gently. He didn't return the smile, but his eyes twinkled as they always did when he watched her humiliate Jenthro. There were times when she did it just to see that gleam in his eyes.

"I think it is time to rid ourselves of him," Taren said as he turned to glance toward where Jenthro had disappeared. "He is becoming something of a nuisance. The blood of the Sidena who fell on our way here are on his hands. I think it's time we give them the justice they deserve."

Marvi's smile widened and she slid her fingers up his arm slowly, caressing.

He shook off her hand. "You're a married woman," he said, his voice hard.

"And you're a married man, full of spirit and vitality," Marvi replied, pointedly flipping his hand over to show the multitude of scars that crossed his wrist. The most recent one was still fresh, the scabs just beginning to peel away.

There had been a chance, long ago, where she could have been that first scar, and she secretly resented the four women the scars represented, especially the most recent. But both she and Taren had chosen different paths. She had chosen Jenthro instead and coerced him along the path that led him to where he was now. But she had never loved him. Taren had always had her heart, not because of his looks, for he had none, but because of his ambition. He loved power and did what he had to do in order to get it. In that, they were kindred spirits, and that ran deeper than a pretty face.

"That whelp was left for the genesauri," Taren said with a humorless snort. "She's in a far hotter place now."

Marvi nodded, acquiescing. Obediently she put her hands behind her back, waiting for Taren to repeat his earlier statement. She knew it would come. She'd know it for years, had paved the way for it little by little. She had Taren in the palm of her hand, the prize she'd always wanted. All he had to do was ask.

"Jenthro needs to step aside. His reign has ended."

"Agreed. But are you ready to step in and lead?" She already knew the answer—she had been instrumental in making sure that all obstacles in Taren's way, including her own sons, had been eliminated in one way or another.

Taren closed his eyes, breathed in a deep, earthy breath, and nodded.

* * *

When Jenthro had appeared in the meadow below him, it had taken all of Gavin's will power to not drop from the tree and attack the man. Elvira's grip on the other outcasts had started slackening the moment the man had brought out the three sickly goats as payment for their performance in the Sidena Warren. Gavin had always wrestled with his temper. But within only a few moments Marvi had appeared and then Taren. His grandmother would be proud that he had kept his cool. The clans were at each other's throats. That boded well for the outcasts currently scattered throughout the Oasis.

Gavin slid down the trunk of the tree, one of his hands wrapped around one of coconuts that grew at the top of the palm. His grandmother loved the milk hidden within, and Gavin enjoyed chewing the meat. It was a good source of continued moisture, though it wasn't much needed in the Oasis. There was water everywhere here.

He hit the ground with a soft thump. Brushing his hair out of his eyes, he slipped his tattered sandals onto his feet and tugged on a thin vest, glancing to where the three Sidena had retreated only once to make sure they were gone. His anger still stormed within him, but it was secondary now, cloaked in a blanket of pragmatism that bore his grandmother's admonishing tone.

"Do not let your emotions rule you," she would say. "Rule them. Emotions are a fuel for action, not the cause of them."

It had been her admonishing voice that had granted him the will to remain in the tree when Jenthro had appeared. She often told him of how the Rahuli clans were an arrogant folk, always looking down their noses at everyone around them. And when one is looking down one's nose, one never thinks to look up.

The smell of change was in the air. Only five of the seven clans had made it into the Oasis. The Heltorin and the Londik were still missing. The other clans spoke of it in hushed whispers, fear and disbelief keeping them from saying what Gavin had known to be true a month into the Migration. The genesauri had gotten them. And the rest of the clans were afraid. They had all lost people this time. The Sidena lost more than most, though no clan had escaped the devastation. And there were so few of the outcasts left, too. Only a handful of families remained, though that was not too unusual. Outcasts like Gavin didn't generally live long on the sands without the protection of a warren's walls around them. Exposure would kill them before almost anything else. His grandmother had done much to unite them into a semblance of a clan of their own by making them performers and pooling resources, but her hold, tenuous as it had been before, was slipping.

The ground sprang back under his feet as he jogged and pushed him onward. He loved the Oasis: loved the green, loved the life, loved the abundance of food and water. It was much better than sand. Sand was hot, enveloping, and invasive. It washed over everything and granted it the color and pallor of death.

Since he belonged to no clan, he had to skirt around the areas were their patrols passed, hugging the Oasis wall until he came to a shallow depression in the rock. He bent down and slipped into the cave.

His grandmother lay in the darkness, huddled in a thin blanket that rose and fell as she breathed. Her back was to him, but he could tell that she was still losing weight. His grandmother had always been small, but he could see the bones of her ribs even through the blanket. Her grey hair, once the brilliant orange of flame, was thinning and now bleached white by age. There was almost more skin showing on her scalp than hair now. The sight made him sick, shame and anger forming into a knot in the pit of his stomach. This early Migration, this hell, had brought his grandmother low.

He didn't want to wake her, but he knew that she needed to eat. If she didn't start putting on more weight, she would never survive when the rains forced them out of the Oasis. He gritted his teeth and placed a light touch on her arm.

She came awake instantly, turning over to gaze at him with bright, intense eyes.

Those eyes. Gavin had never known a moment when those eyes didn't seem as if they were peering into his soul, stripping away all the extraneous bits of superficial personality and laying bare his very being. Even now with her body succumbing to decay and age, her gaze pierced him and filled him with strength.

"Nana," he said, smiling, "I brought you some coconut."

He pulled one of the fruit from his bag and dug around in the sand until he found the sharp rock he'd hidden there. With the rock, he bored two small holes in the large fruit, one slightly smaller than the other. Her hands shook as she took the fruit Gavin offered her and greedily gulped down the milk.

He smiled at her, though his heart despaired. She was dying, and there was nothing he could do about it. Even the news he carried paled in the face of those black tidings. Pride sustained her now. Pride and stubbornness.

"Enough of that look," she rasped between mouthfuls of milk. "You could give storm clouds lessons on how to look ominous. Don't soil that pretty face of yours on my account."

Instead of cheering him up, the words only deepened his scowl.

"Tell me what news you've gathered then, little storm cloud."

Despite himself, Gavin felt the corners of his mouth twitch. He told her what he'd seen.

She watched him intently as he spoke, eyes cool and penetrating, showing more life and fire than they had in several fortnights. It was as if, for a moment, the age vanished from them and he saw once again the woman who had spent years teaching him the ways of the sands and how to survive without the aid of clan. The coconut spilled from her hand as his account came to an end.

Before Gavin could protest, she seized him by his vest and pulled him down toward her with a strength that she had not had in years. Her eyes glistened with intensity and—Gavin was terrified to see—worry and no small amount of fear.

"This is your chance," she said. Her voice was sharp and articulate, with none of the previous rasp. "Swear to me that you will complete your father's task."

"Nana," he said, trying to tug free of her grip, "you know I don't believe in the stories. It's because of them that we're outcasts. It's because of them that *you* had to raise me instead."

Her grip didn't slacken. "Swear it to me, Gavin. By the stones and sands of the desert, swear it to me. If you love me, you will do as I say."

"But—"

"Gavin," she said, "our people, the outcasts, they will not survive this change if they don't have someone to lead them. I'm dying, Gavin. I can't hold them together anymore. They need a strong arm to rely on. Your arm."

Gavin tried to pull away, but her arms held him. He wondered how her small frame could manage it. He was not a leader. She was, as his father had been. He didn't want this; he'd never wanted this.

"Don't talk like that," he said.

"Swear it!"

"I swear it, Nana," Gavin said, pulling at her wrists. "Now lay back down and rest. Drink your milk. Getting all worked up isn't good for you." He had hoped the news would give her the strength to move around again, come back to him, and not send her into another fit. She needed rest.

"By the sands and stones of the desert?"

"Yes, by the sands and stones of the desert I swear I will complete my father's task." He tried not to roll his eyes and added under his breath, "Or more likely die trying."

"Remember the stories, little storm cloud," she said, her voice dropping to a whisper. "Remember what I have taught you. Remember your oath. They will die without you."

She smiled weakly and closed her eyes, drifting off to sleep.

Gavin adjusted the blanket over her frail form before turning to harvest the fruit from the rest of the coconut. His grandmother snored softly beside him, a single glistening tear trembling on her weathered cheek.

That night she died.

CHAPTER 6

Despair

"The pressure is taking its toll. My bones ache, eyes droop. I feel that the clans are beginning to understand that there will be no escape from this. They begin to understand the enormity of my task. And I am coming to accept it, as well. I will continue, for there is no other cause left to me, but I know now that I may be proceeding in vain."

-From the Journals of Elyana

Lhaurel woke with stiff muscles screaming protest at the abuse. She stretched to ease some of the soreness and rolled over, unsettling the thin wool blanket she'd found in the room they'd given her.

"You know, you talk in your sleep."

Lhaurel jumped, head swiveling toward the voice. Kaiden stood just inside the doorway, leaning against the red sandstone wall, sword belted at his waist.

Lhaurel grabbed the blanket and pulled it up to her chin. He'd seen her in her smallclothes before, but this was different. This was her *room*. After the events of the previous day, she'd been given her own room to sleep in, which was far preferable to the eyrie floor.

"It's polite to knock."

Kaiden laughed. "I tried that, but you didn't hear me, obviously. Get dressed. Makin Qays wants Tieran and I to take you out today."

"Who?"

"You'll meet them soon enough." His smile said he was enjoying her discomfort.

Infuriating man.

"Wait for me outside, please," Lhaurel said, with a pointed look at the door.

Kaiden laughed again but did as she asked.

Lhaurel dressed quickly, wishing she'd had time to get her clothes cleaned. They still smelled of aevian and sweat, an extremely pungent combination. After fastening the last button, curiosity trumping her soreness, she opened the door and stepped out into sunlight.

The room was almost as large as the eyrie but open to the sky in the center with a far more utilitarian purpose. Dozens of smaller caverns opened up along the walls at floor level. Above each of these smaller caverns ran a ledge that spiraled upward to form rows and rows of interconnecting tiers that ran up to the large, irregularly-shaped hole in the ceiling. There must have been over a hundred rooms and a dozen other passages, the former marked by thick wooden doors or curtains. Between the openings were etchings on the walls, faded and worn, that had tugged at Lhaurel's memory when they'd brought her up here.

There was an overwhelming vastness to it that left Lhaurel in awe. She could have fit the entire Sidena clan three times over within them. It spoke of something ancient and powerful, something that predated the world that she currently walked.

"You ready, then?" Kaiden asked.

Lhaurel nodded and followed him around the ledge and down the ramp to the main floor. She only saw a few people busying themselves around the room. A pair of women was spinning yarn from a basket of raw wool very near the end of the ramp, whispering to each other and pointedly ignoring everything around them. She noted the lack of *shufari* curiously since she hadn't bothered to find herself a new one. A handful of men sparred in a large ring marked in the stone near the middle of the chamber, swords ringing faintly as they came together. Looking closer, Lhaurel realized that one of the combatants was, in fact, a woman. Not just any woman, either.

"Is that—?" she began, but Kaiden, following her gaze, interrupted her before she could finish.

"That's Khari, yes," Kaiden said. "One of the finest swordsmen we have in the Roterralar, and a mystic, too."

"Mystic?"

Kaiden chuckled and gestured for her to turn down a side passage leading away from the greatroom. "You'll find out soon enough, I'm sure."

Lhaurel bit off a response, annoyed with the vague answer, but let it go. She most likely would find out eventually. They were letting her be a part of the clan when they could have just as easily left her to die in the Oasis. She could give them a little more time, even if they *had* tried to trick her into escaping.

They turned down another passage, one that seemed vaguely familiar.

"Where are we going?"

"The eyrie."

Lhaurel smiled, picking up her pace as recognition dawned on her. At the end of the passage, she turned right, passing Kaiden and pushing the door open. The familiar smells and sights of the eyrie greeted her, and a chorus of aevian voices sounded recognition. There was a soft thump of wings, and the fledgling dropped onto the sand near her, chirping softly.

"How are you, boy?" Lhaurel asked, reaching up to gently stroke the aevian's beak. He chirped again and then scuttled away.

Aevians cried and chirped above and around them. A group of younger women were at work near them, butchering sailfin carcasses. Lhaurel wrinkled her nose against the smell of rust and mildew.

Kaiden walked up beside her, taking her arm in a firm grip and tugging her toward the eyrie's cavernous opening. Lhaurel pulled her arm free but continued to walk alongside him.

Lhaurel looked in the direction they were heading and noticed Tieran putting harnesses on a pair of aevians. She recognized one of them. Kaiden's aevian, Skree-lar, scratched at the rock with one foot, adjusting his wings around the harness and saddle Tieran had just put on his back. The other was probably Tieran's. It was larger than

Skree-lar and had a deep sandy-white coloring.

Tieran noticed their approach and gave a mock little bow. "Ah now, a pretty smile for a pretty face," Tieran said, noticing her slow smile.

Lhaurel let the smile slip slightly, becoming a mere shadow of a grin. "Where's mine?"

"Come on, little miss. I think we can find you something far softer to sit on." His grin widened as if he'd said something funny.

"You'll ride with me, Lhaurel," Kaiden said brusquely. He pulled a pair of harnesses from a bin off to one side. Tieran chuckled and gave Lhaurel a wink before going over to the bin and pulling out a harness for himself.

Kaiden handed Lhaurel one of the harnesses and showed her how to put it on. Lhaurel had seen several of the other warriors putting harnesses on in the weeks she'd been in the eyrie on her own, but she hadn't paid close enough attention to know where all the straps and buckles went. Kaiden had to reach out and correct her several times.

When the harness was finally attached to Kaiden's satisfaction, and with many side comments from Tieran, which Lhaurel mostly ignored, Kaiden gave a low whistle, and Skree-lar lowered himself to the ground. Kaiden vaulted up onto the creature's back and affixed two leads to the thick saddle there before turning back to Lhaurel and offering her a hand.

Tieran mounted his own aevian.

Lhaurel licked her lips. The last flight on Skree-lar's back had been exhilarating. It was an experience she desperately wanted to repeat. But it had also ended very badly. She wasn't sure she wholly trusted any of the Roterralar yet, and being up in the air would leave her little options.

"Are you coming or not?" Kaiden asked.

"Maybe she'd be more comfortable over here with me," Tieran said with a laugh. "Maybe you scared her last time."

Kaiden rolled his eyes.

Lhaurel hesitated a moment and then accepted Kaiden's hand, allowing him to pull her up behind him. He attached several of her leads to the saddle and then nodded to her. Lhaurel took a deep breath and wrapped an arm around his waist.

Flying was every bit as wonderful as it had been the first time. The takeoff was terrifying, but the sheer joy of flight quickly overcame the fear. Lhaurel whooped with delight as Skree-lar banked into a strong gust of wind and started to climb higher into the sky.

Tieran, a few spans above them, laughed.

"Where are we going?" Lhaurel shouted into the wind.

Skree-lar's wings hummed as they pushed them higher.

"You'll see," Kaiden shouted back.

Lhaurel groaned inwardly but allowed herself to relax into the joys of flight. Tieran took the lead, turning northward. Lhaurel studied the desert below her as they flew. Dunes of red sand moved across the desert below her, carried by the wind in an endless progression. Every now and then a bit of stoneway would appear to rise out of the sand like a silent testament of a forgotten time. Lhaurel glanced westward to where she could just make out the walls of the Oasis.

Saralhn.

The thought passed through her mind with a weight, dampening the joy of flight like a wet blanket over a fire.

Tieran whistled sharply from above them, and Skree-lar pulled his wings inward, turning into a steep dive. Lhaurel squealed, but the sound was ripped from her throat by the rushing wind. Her eyes watered, and she squeezed them tight. Her grip tightened around Kaiden's waist in anticipation of what she knew would be coming next. Her stomach heaved when Skree-lar pulled out of the dive and landed on a rocky surface, judging by the sound made by Skree-lar's talons.

Lhaurel opened her eyes. Recognition rolled over her immediately, her mind going numb. Kaiden unbuckled her harness from the saddle, but Lhaurel barely noticed. The cave-like entrance to the Sidena Warren lay before them. Memories of flashing teeth, pain, and death swam through her mind.

"What are we doing here?" she asked, slipping from Skree-lar's back before Kaiden had un-hooked himself.

Tieran dropped to the ground near her.

"We're here to see what the genesauri left behind."

Lhaurel swallowed and ran her tongue over dry lips.

Kaiden dropped to the ground next to her, sending sand and dust into the air. "Well, come on, then," he said, striding forward.

Lhaurel followed, letting Tieran come behind. There was evidence of the sailfins' passing all around them. Little piles and bursts of sand dotted the ground. Lhaurel was careful to avoid those. The passing of a sailfin left loose pockets a person could fall into if not careful. These were old and already mostly filled in, but she wasn't going to take any chances.

The rock around the cavern's mouth was scoured as if by long claws, though Lhaurel knew it was made by the passage of hundreds of sailfin spines. She shuddered at the thought of the writhing, swarming, monstrous bodies fighting for entrance into the warren.

They found the first skeleton a few spans into the passageway, metallic ribs glinting in the light filtering in from the cave's mouth. Only the bones remained, two and half spans from skull to tail. Even the spines were gone.

"They eat each other?"

Tieran grunted from behind her, and Kaiden paused momentarily, looking down at the massive skeleton.

"What do you think they eat when they can't get Rahuli?"

Lhaurel felt bile rise in the back of her throat. "But wouldn't they have killed themselves off by now, doing that?"

Tieran chuckled. The lack of humor unnerved her. "They only eat their own if they get injured. It's the blood. This one probably got cut on a rock or something, which started the frenzy. We'll find others, I'm sure."

"Besides," Kaiden called back from deeper in the caves, "they breed much too quickly for the ones they eat to make much of a difference. There's another one up here."

Several ribs were broken on this skeleton, as if something heavy had crashed into it. The broken ends were jagged and stained dark.

They moved on, finding three more skeletons before they even made it out of the main passage. Lhaurel steeled herself when they got to the offshoot. To the left were the hot springs, where she'd bathed before her wedding. A little further down and to the right, the passage opened up into the greatroom. The passage was dark, hiding the beads of nervous sweat on her forehead.

"Go that way, Tieran." Kaiden said, gesturing to the left. "We'll go this way to the greatroom. Meet us there when you're done."

Tieran nodded, though his expression was bleak. He smiled at Lhaurel as he passed, but it didn't reach his eyes. His shoulders were slumped, his posture limp.

Kaiden nodded to Lhaurel before turning down the passage on the right. Lhaurel bit her bottom lip and followed.

The greatroom was the picture of chaos and destruction. Lhaurel dropped to her knees only a few feet from where the passage opened up, ignorant of the darkened sand beneath her knees. New holes in the ceiling bathed the room in sunlight, illuminating the broken rock and metallic skeletons of dozens of dead sailfins strewn about the room. Broken baskets, furniture, and pieces of the ceiling lay amidst the dead, like cairns marking mass graves.

There were no human bodies left, not even skeletons. No, Lhaurel knew from how they'd left the hard skeletons of their own behind that there'd be nothing left of any human body. Only blood. Pools of it stained the sand. Splashes of it made the walls look wounded in a hundred different places. It smelled of death, rust, rot, and decay.

Lhaurel tried holding her breath, but she couldn't force herself to hold in the foul air for very long. Instead, she cupped a hand over her mouth and nose to try and filter the smell. It didn't help much.

"They were lucky here," Kaiden said softly. "I was able to warn them in time. Some of the others were hit harder."

"*This* is lucky?"

"Very. They could prepare. Some of them were already running when the sailfins hit. And this was a small pack, maybe only a hundred of them." Kaiden's voice was cold, detached, and factual. It made Lhaurel shudder.

"How many died?" Lhaurel asked.

"Sailfins? You can count the skeletons yourself."

"How many Sidena died?" she repeated.

Kaiden shook his head. "I don't know. A lot. Some of the others held off another pack while you ran and escaped afterward, if you recall. They said there were only a few hundred running toward the Oasis."

"A few hundred?" Lhaurel brought her other hand up to her mouth, though it wasn't for the smell.

Then Kaiden's words clicked in Lhaurel's mind. "Wait, the Roterralar *were* there. Why didn't you stop this? You could have protected them, couldn't you? They didn't have to die."

Kaiden sighed, and his expression darkened. "You'll have to speak with Makin Qays about that. The short answer is no, we couldn't have stopped it."

Lhaurel felt cold tears run down her cheeks. This was death on a level she'd never imagined. There was nothing that could stop this level of destruction.

Booted feet crunched on sand, and Lhaurel turned to see Tieran approaching. Kaiden turned toward him as well.

"There's nothing here worth saving," Kaiden said. "You find anything down there?"

"Just lots of blood," Tieran replied, "and this."

He reached into a pocket and pulled out a thin, white object. A wide-toothed comb made of bone. The comb Saralhn had given her, forgotten at the springs. Lhaurel reached for it, and Tieran handed it to her. She held it carefully, though with white-knuckled strength.

"Saralhn," she whispered, and she pulled the comb to her chest, rocking back and forth as she wept.

* * *

The door swung open. The scent of sweat and spice wafted in with the light.

Kaiden and Tieran had left her waiting in the small room when they'd gotten back from the Sidena Warren. Saralhn's comb rested in her waistband. She'd waited here, quiet and subdued, for what had seemed like an eternity. And—simultaneously—only an instant.

Lhaurel got to her feet, though the man who had opened the door remained standing on the eaves, framed by light and a strange red penumbra. She squinted against the sudden brightness.

The man's clothes were of a simple cut, practical rather than ornamental. His long grey-brown hair was held back from his face by an intricate silver chain and a long genesauri bone. A medium length beard adorned his chin. His skin was deeply tanned, browned by long years of toil in the blistering desert sun. He must have been in his fifth or sixth decade, which was extremely old by Sidena standards, almost as old as Old Cobb.

Lhaurel felt as if she were being weighed on invisible scales, though she did not know the bargain being struck or the measure of the counterweight.

"Are you coming in or going out?" she asked wearily. "It's hard to tell since, you see, you're currently halfway from doing either."

"Actually," the man said without taking his eyes from her face, "I am doing both. I am entering this room and leaving the passage behind. It is the nature of entering a place that you must, of necessity, leave the place you're already in."

Lhaurel gave him a wan smile.

"I believe that it is wise to start off a conversation with both parties being able to call each other by name," the man began. "I am called Makin Qays. You are called Lhaurel." He paused for a moment as if he expected her to say something but then continued on after only a heartbeat's passing. "I am the Warlord of the Roterralar—"

"How come I've never heard of the Roterralar clan before now? We all just think of you as the crazy people who wander into warrens from time to time." The question escaped her lips before she'd consciously decided on which of her hundred questions to ask.

"A worthy question. One I would have answered had you allowed me to continue with what I was saying. Please do not interrupt me again."

Lhaurel nodded.

He continued calmly, "I lead these people. What they do, they do by my command and with me at their head. Even the mystics follow me. We protect the clans from the genesauri. And sometimes even from each other."

Lhaurel sat up straight. "Protect us? How in the seven hells do you protect us from the genesauri? Where were you when the sailfin packs attacked my clan?"

Makin Qays put his arms on the table, interlocking his fingers. The short sleeves of his warrior's coat pulled back, exposing muscular forearms covered in an array of colorful banded tattoos. She counted seven different colors.

He leaned forward and placed his chin on top of his fingers. "We, the Roterralar, swear to protect and defend the Rahuli people. Defense, in part and in whole, from all enemies, from the enemy, and from all that threatens their existence. To this end, should our lives be required in this defense, then they are lain down. Hope is a solitary flame standing alone against a gale. What is the test of honor? To uphold the flame, or to snuff it out? This is our oath. We are always there, but never where you can see us."

Lhaurel frowned. *What?*

"Stop and think for a moment, Lhaurel. What would the clans do if they realized there were people who would be there to protect them? What would they demand of us then?"

"They'd demand that you do your jobs," she responded instantly, "protect them."

"All of them? Every time?" The look he gave her was sharp, penetrating.

"Yes! Every single one of them, every single time." Even as she said it, though, her thoughts returned to the memories of the Sidena Warren, broken and destroyed. How could anything stand against that? And that had been a small sailfin pack, according to Kaiden.

"Is that all they'd do? Demand that we protect them?"

Lhaurel paused, pushing aside her frustration, emotion, and memories to consider the question. No, they wouldn't just do that. "They'd probably fight you. They might even band together to take this place from you, or at least the aevians."

Makin inclined his head toward Lhaurel in acknowledgement. "The genesauri often attack in many places at once and in massive numbers. You've never seen a true sailfin pack. What makes it to the warrens is what remains after we get done with them. But we are not infallible. We barely have enough warriors to face one pack, let alone many. You saw what a small pack did to your warren. Imagine what a larger one is capable of. Imagine what *all* of them can do. And that's just the sailfins. The marsaisi are worse, the karundin hell incarnate."

"Why don't you get more warriors? There are over a hundred aevians. I've only ever seen a handful go out at one time."

Makin Qays smiled ruefully, shaking his head. The wrinkles on his face deepened, making him appear even older.

"It is not so simple as that. There are other factors involved. We have neither the resources nor the capacity to support more than the few hundred we have here. Less than a quarter are warriors, though they have all upheld the flame. Suffice it to say that we must remain hidden because we do not have the numbers to protect everyone, everywhere—including ourselves—from the rest of the Rahuli. We do what we can so that the race can survive. We get new warriors, but only a few at time by means where they will not be missed. Finding you was enough work on its own, an endeavor that took several years."

Lhaurel swallowed hard and clenched her fists to keep them from shaking. "You are all cowards," she whispered. She didn't really mean it, but it slipped out before she could stop herself.

Makin Qays rose to his feet slowly, keeping his gaze locked onto hers. His face didn't change expression, but his eyes smoldered with a deep blue flame. He raised one of his arms, brandishing the tattooed bands. There were over thirty banded rings on that arm alone.

"These rings represent each time someone dies because we couldn't protect them. We find each body we can and give them the honors that they deserve, no matter how grisly the remains. When you understand what it's like to have to choose which clan to protect and which to let flounder on its own, when you feel the guilt of each death as it is inked into your flesh as a reminder, when you kneel in the sand clutching a little girl's hand as her guts leak out of her stomach and her eyes slowly fade and there's nothing you can do but hold her, when you know what that's like, then you can call us cowards. Then you can presume to understand why it is that the clans do not know us."

He dropped his arm and turned around, pivoting on the heel of his boot. Without looking back he pulled open the door, exited, and shut the door behind him.

Lhaurel remained where she was. Slowly, her hand dropped onto the comb in her waistband for a long, lingering moment. Then her head fell into her waiting hands, and she cried. The tears were cold.

CHAPTER 7

The Strength of Steel

"We lost half the clans today in our struggle with the enemy. Briane cried over the loss of an uncle. What would it be like, I wonder, to have a family who cares about you? I didn't know how to comfort her, but she didn't seem to need much comfort after her tears were done. The cause, she said, was worthy of the sacrifice."

-From the Journals of Elyana

The first thing she noticed when she entered the room was harnesses. They hung from pegs on the walls, each line or lead neatly attached to separate pegs or hooks hammered into the rock so that none of the varying pieces of leather would get tangled. There were hundreds of them, stretching down both side walls, up and over the door, and even hanging from the ceiling. She was so enthralled by the sheer number of them that she barely noticed the man who had softly closed the door behind her. He stepped back into the shadows and watched her as she studied the room.

Lhaurel took a step forward into the long, narrow room to better view the furnace and metalwork that rested in the center, nearly dominating the middle section. A metal flume carried the smoke of the massive ceramic furnace up and out through the ceiling, the metal darkened with years of soot. The smell of leather and ash and the odd odor of heated oil hung heavy in the air.

The man cleared his throat behind her. She jumped.

The man was short, smaller than Lhaurel, with plain features and a wide nose. But what he lacked in height he made up for in sheer brawn. His arms alone were bigger around than both Lhaurel's legs together. A leather vest strained against a chest large enough to seem nearly grotesque. Corded muscles on his shoulders and arms showed through the skin like bands of iron. And his skin. It was flecked with small specks of a dull greyish cast, like freckles, but that glittered in the lamplight. It was almost as if long years working at the forge had infused flakes of metal to his skin.

"Welcome, Lhaurel," the man said, his voice raspy.

"Thank you . . . sir," she said.

He flourished one hand, gesturing for her to move back toward the center of the room, where the forge rested.

She obliged.

He shuffled along behind her, his step a rasping sound against the sand. The man walked with one leg trailing behind the other, almost dragging it along. It pulled against the loose sand, making the grating noise. He noticed her watching him and growled deep in his throat. She turned away hastily.

She stopped in the middle of the room but heard the man shuffle along behind and pass around her. Heat radiated from the open forge where coals glowed a deep, dark red around a layer of white.

Tieran had come to get her after Makin Qays had left. Khari had wanted him to bring her to see a man named Beryl. Despite herself, Lhaurel found herself liking the jovial Tieran more and more as they'd walked through the warren before he had deposited her here.

The man limped into her periphery, headed toward one of the various bins secreted beneath the long tables nestled against the wall. His limp gave him a decidedly hunched look, and Lhaurel almost took a small step back. "Why am I here?" she asked.

Beryl didn't respond. Instead, he righted and tossed something from inside the bin at her. A practice sword—straight blade, almost no guard. She caught it deftly as it twirled toward her. Lhaurel looked up at him quizzically, only to find him swinging a sword of his own down toward her head in a powerful overhead chop. She brought her blade up in a mad scramble to block. Wood cracked against wood. Pain shot up her arms from the force of the blow.

"What are you doing?" she demanded.

His answer came in a sudden flurry of blows. His eyes were hard, focused, as he spun his practice sword in a dizzying pattern of blows. The wooden sword seemed almost alive in his hands, spinning in and hitting her once, twice, three times in rapid succession before she could get her feet under her and slip into a middle guard position. With each blow that connected, her arms ached. The strength in his arms was incredible! She marveled that someone so crippled could move with such grace.

Suddenly, his onslaught slowed. He broke into a more measured, steady rhythm, spinning the sword in a sequence of moves that she recognized. She had memorized all the practice sequences that the Sidena warriors trained with and so slipped into the form designed to counter the smith's movements. Still, she was wary. Why was he attacking her?

The man shifted into a second sequence, and she responded in kind, slipping into its counter sequence and matching him blow for blow. The blood pounded in her ears, pushing adrenaline throughout her body, and her muscles loosened with the warmth of motion. The blacksmith was good, incredibly so, yet she almost smiled as she slipped into the forms. He shifted to a third sequence, and again she responded with the appropriate counter.

Their speed picked up, practice swords coming together with more force behind each blow. Lhaurel had never drilled so long before. Her muscles ached, her arm felt leaden with fatigue. But she felt a thrill of happiness running through her.

With a muffled grunt, the blacksmith executed a sudden twist on his blade, and Lhaurel's practice sword was ripped from her weakened grip and dropped to the sand.

Sweat dripped down Lhaurel's face. She breathed heavily, almost panting. The blacksmith didn't even look winded.

"What . . . " she gasped, "what was the point of coming at me like that?"

"Would you have fought an old cripple if he'd just asked you?"

She pondered the question for only a few moments before answering, "No."

"First thing you need to learn is to never trust what you see," the smith said, bending down with a groan and picking up Lhaurel's discarded sword. "Trust is more precious than water. You can't trust anyone, not even your own eyes. Trust only your weapons."

Lhaurel nodded, unable to articulate her words as she gulped down air.

"Do you know why you're here?" he asked. He shuffled over to one of the bins and dropped the wooden practice swords inside.

"Kaiden brought me."

"No, girl, I'm not talking about here with the Roterralar. I'm asking if you know why you're here with me right now?"

She shook her head. Hadn't she just asked *him* why she was here?

"Khari wants me to make you a sword," he said, voice becoming quiet and raspy again. "The fool woman thinks you've got enough promise to be one of the warriors. Well, maybe she's right. Rare to find a woman fresh from the clans that knows the basic forms. Knows them badly, but knows them."

"Badly?"

He ignored her. "Do you know what it takes to make a sword? Heat and pounding. Blood, sweat, and tears. Metal has to be thrown into the fire until it gets so hot that it can't bear another moment in the coals. And then it gets beaten down. Shaped. Harder metals take more beating and more heat. They get abused more, but they make by far the finer blades. And the proper fuel creates the proper heat. Everything has a cost, has a price to be paid. That is the second thing you should remember." He peered at her, eyes sharp and penetrating.

Lhaurel stared back at him blankly. *He's insane.*

The man rolled his eyes and shuffled around the furnace to the small opening that led deeper into the chamber. He muttered something under his breath, running one hand through his tufty, grey hair. His bad leg, the left one, dragged along in the sand, leaving a furrow in the ground.

"You coming, girl?" he asked.

She hesitated for a moment but then ran after him.

The heat intensified the closer that she got to the furnace, rising almost to an unbearable level when she tried to hurry through the narrow opening between it and a row of counters upon which various tools or unfinished works of metal or leather lay. She was already covered in sweat, but it poured anew from the intense heat. Lhaurel cursed softly as she hurried past the forge and into the room behind it.

Despite the heat blazing against her back, the contents of the space halted her in her tracks in stunned amazement. Long spears by the hundreds leaned against the sandstone walls. Racks upon racks of swords were neatly arranged in long rows, the weapons glistening and polished as if new. Dozens of bins rested against one of the walls, but even with the bins and racks, the room was arranged so that the center was completely bare of furnishing, leaving a large swath of clean, reddish sand. The back wall was also bare, devoid of any weaponry or ornamentation of any kind.

Lhaurel chewed on her bottom lip. It was incongruous to have one wall completely clear when every other available space was covered. Her eyes studied the reddish sandstone surface, trying to identify anything out of the ordinary. There, along the seam where the walls met each other and along the ceiling. There was a faint line that shone red like the eyelids did when gazing at the sun with closed eyes. A quick scan revealed cleverly hidden stone hinges along the left side. The whole wall was a door, one that opened out into the sands beyond.

The smith waited for her near one of the racks, his expression one of knowing humor. He leaned against his right side, easing the pressure on his bad leg, though it had not hampered him in the slightest when they had sparred. Lhaurel still felt a little winded from the encounter. It was either that or the sight of the weaponry making her hyperventilate.

She wanted to laugh. What the Sidena warriors would have given to be in this place now? The Warlord would be stunned. Taren—well, Taren would have taken everything he could get. Maybe to kill off another one of his wives. She smirked. Neither of them was here now. She was. She took a moment to bask in the irony and triumph of it.

She turned to the smith, her voice holding a touch of wonder. "Who are you?" she asked.

"They call me Beryl," he said with a little mock bow. "And you are Lhaurel." His tone warped the humor into sarcasm. "Now, do you want to come over here and pick a sword or do you want me to simply pick one for you?"

Lhaurel started, absently brushing wet hair back over her ears. "Didn't you just say that Khari wanted you to make me one?"

Beryl shook his head and snorted, throwing up his hands. "All you new recruits are the same," he said. "you think that making a sword is a simple matter, something that only takes a few hours. Well, you're wrong. I just told you all about it. It is an art, a craft that must be studied and practiced again and again until it becomes a part of you. The work becomes an outward expression of someone's heart and soul. That doesn't happen overnight. That doesn't happen in a fortnight. So again, do you want to come over here and pick a sword, or should I?"

Lhaurel hesitated, unsure of how to respond after his long-winded tirade. He hadn't answered the question that she'd asked. Or rather, Lhaurel was sure that he thought that he had, but not in a way that made any sense to her.

Beryl grimaced and threw his hands up in the air with a muttered, "Fine, then. I'll do it." He continued to mutter under his breath as he limped down the rows of sword racks.

Lhaurel chewed on her bottom lip and cocked her head to the side. She wasn't sure what she'd done to indicate that she didn't want to choose her own sword. She had merely been trying to figure out the man's answer.

"Here you are, then."

The blacksmith's voice right beside her ear sounded like the blast of a hunting horn. A hand flew to her chest as she turned, her heartbeat racing. Beryl held out a sheathed sword, hilt facing her. She reached out a hand that was shaking—either from the adrenaline that still raced through her blood or anticipation—wrapped it around the hilt, and pulled the sword free.

Straight and only sharp along one edge, the blade shone with a luster that defied the dull grey metal from which it was made. It came to a wicked point, and the hilt was wrapped in a thin wire to aid the grip. The cross guard was a single round piece of metal, unadorned and simple. It was beautiful.

"Take it and get out of here," Beryl said, proffering the sheath and a belt that had been worked in silver to appear like a *shufari*.

Lhaurel took the belt, trying hard to focus on the questions that she knew she should be asking. "Why are you giving this to me? I'm new here, and you can't trust me. I might as soon kill you as anything else."

Beryl gaped at her, the first real look of genuine emotion that Lhaurel had seen on his face. "Haven't you been paying attention? I'm making you a sword. Takes a long time, making a sword. Use this one until then. What did you think you were going to do when chosen to come here? Eat fruit and sip wine all day? And you're nowhere near good enough for anyone here to worry about."

"How in the seven hells am I supposed to know?"

"Not my problem," Beryl said, making a dismissive gesture with his hands. "Now take the sword and get out. I'm sure someone will find you and know what to do with you. Well, maybe not." He paused, his brow furrowing above his bushy eyebrows. "They've cracked your shell, girl, but you're not broken just yet, are you?"

"Broken?"

Beryl straightened suddenly, seeming to tower over her even though he was far shorter than she. He made dismissive gesture with one hand. "Leave me in peace."

Lhaurel opened her mouth to ask another question, but Beryl's expression tightened and he raised a massive hand, index finger extended to point toward the exit.

"Get out!"

Lhaurel left, but when she reached the door she came face to face with Kaiden.

"Could you move out of my way?" she said.

"Not even a 'please'? I brought you here to become part of something greater, be part of the protectors and not the protected. Here you can hold a sword in your hands and not be worried about being killed. Here you can learn to fight and kill genesauri. Here you can learn what equality means and the true price of freedom."

"Could you get out of my way, please?" Lhaurel said with a thin smile.

Kaiden snorted loudly and folded his arms. "You're as stubborn as an old goat, aren't you?"

Lhaurel opened her mouth to respond, her back stiff and her face twisted with anger and guilt, but a long brazen sound rolled through the passageway and echoed off the walls. Kaiden cursed and grabbed her by her barely healed left wrist, his grip strong enough to bring a squawk of protest to her lips.

"What are you doing?" she demanded, trying to pull free, though the sword in her hand got in the way.

Kaiden spun toward her, jaw forming a hard line and brow furrowing in concentration. There was such intensity in the gaze it made Lhaurel pause.

"There's a sandstorm coming, you idiot," he said. "We've got to find cover. Come on." His words slurred together in his rush. "Sands blow through these passages with enough force to rip the hide from your bones."

A few quick steps took him further down the passage, where he stopped and turned back, dancing on the balls of his feet. His eyes flashed with irritation, but he simply gestured for her to follow.

Lhaurel hesitated, though the mention of a sandstorm sent ripples of fear down the base of her neck. Someone appeared at the end of the hall, belabored breathing seeming to echo in the narrow confines. It was Tieran.

"Lhaurel. Kaiden," he gasped. "Get out of the halls. Get somewhere with a door."

The intensity cut through Lhaurel's distrust. The panic in his voice was real.

She dashed toward Kaiden as Tieran continued down the intersecting hall. The sword Beryl had given her weighed heavily in her left hand. When Kaiden reached out and grasped her by the wrist, Lhaurel didn't fight the grip, though her skin crawled at the feel of his rough hands. Images of leather, blood, and a flashing knife darted across her memory. Dread spread through her. Her vision swam and Kaiden swore, giving her arm an unusually hard tug that sent her stumbling.

Anger welled up within her. Before she realized what she was doing, she lashed out with the sheathed sword, catching Kaiden in the gut. He doubled over, clutching at his stomach, but Lhaurel followed up with a swift kick to the side of his legs, bringing him to the ground. Leaping to her feet, Lhaurel half drew her sword before she came to her senses in a wash of cold realization.

"I'm—I'm sorry," she stammered. "I—I didn't mean to. I—"

Kaiden waived her to silence. His eyes burned with a mixture of anger and pain. A dark stain spread across the lower half of his robes. Lhaurel couldn't tell if it was water or urine, but she wasn't about to ask.

The wind picked up, screeching down the passage like the sound of a sailfin pack. Lhaurel's robes fluttered in the wind, dancing up around her knees and revealing an indecent amount of leg. The smell of dust hung heavy in the air, filling her nose.

Kaiden cursed and struggled to his feet, the anger fading into a wary expression. He gestured for Lhaurel to follow him again, though it was a perfunctory motion, no heart in it. She followed him, not meeting his eye.

Kaiden threw open a nearby door and stepped inside. Lhaurel entered after him, and Kaiden shut the door.

Not even a single crack of sunlight drifted down through the sandstone. Torchlight cast a strange orange and grey pallor over the barrels and sacks that lined the walls of the small room. Kaiden grunted as he pushed around her, shoulders bumping with no small amount of force, and sat down on some of the sacks. A pair of rashelta scurried out from under the sacks and disappeared into the shadows, light glinting off the small spines that stuck up from their shells.

"What was that for?" Lhaurel said, rounding on him.

Kaiden dug around in the pocket of his robes and fished out a soggy piece of leather. It took Lhaurel a moment to recognize it as a small waterskin, one side split along the seam.

"That's two of these you've ruined now." He tossed the soggy leather at her.

"*I've* ruined?"

"Yes, you," he said, a biting edge creeping into his voice. "You're a wetta. Khari asked me to break you. I guess I succeeded. Fat lot of good that did me."

Lhaurel blinked. "I'm a what?"

Kaiden threw up his hands in exasperation, the flickering torchlight seeming to outline him in a thin reddish aura. Or at least Lhaurel thought it was exasperation. When she took a moment to comprehend what she was seeing, she realized Kaiden had tossed several small squares of metal into the air. She waited for them to fall to the ground, but they hung suspended in the air a few inches above Kaiden's head.

A wash of emotions crossed over Lhaurel's face. Fear, confusion, incredulity—all giving way to stunned disbelief as Kaiden flicked a finger and the metal squares threw themselves through the air with a whistle, piercing the shell of a scrabbling rashelta that had just wandered back into the torchlight. The shell gave way with a sickening crunch. The metal weaponry burst through the rashelta's belly and clinked against the rocks. Purple blood dripped into the sand.

Lhaurel backed slowly toward the door, her eyes wide.

Kaiden turned to her with a grin.

Her back hit wood. Her left hand scrabbled at the door's latch.

"You're a mystic," Kaiden said, his tone quiet yet fervent. "A magic user. One of three kinds. I am a magnetelorium. You are a wetta."

The stories were true. The tales tired mothers told their wayward children at night to keep them in bed, stories about the magic of the Roterralar and how they could kill you without ever raising a hand. They were all true. She'd never been one to believe the stories, especially not as she'd gotten older, but she had proof before her now. She'd thought Tieran had been joking when he'd called Khari a mystic but—

"What are you?"

Her hands twisted on the latch behind her back, but it wouldn't budge. She could hear the wind whistling behind her, could feel the sand beat against the outside of the frame. She knew the dangers of being exposed to such a blast. She'd seen flesh torn off a man caught outside the safety of the warren. Right now, though, looking at the twitching rashelta, she almost wished for the sands.

Blood dripped onto the ground.

Kaiden blinked and seemed to notice her fear for the first time. He sighed and rolled his eyes but got to his feet, holding his hands wide.

"Alright," he said, "let's start this over again. You can draw your sword if you wish, whatever will make you feel better."

Lhaurel felt a small flush of embarrassment. She'd dropped her sword as soon as the metal squares shot across the room. It lay discarded at her feet. She picked it up hastily and drew it, metal gleaming in the torchlight.

"What did you just do, demon," she asked, her voice harsh.

"Why is it always demons? The next time I visit the clans I'm going to have a word with all those mothers about the stories they tell their children. I'm tired of being called a demon by those I try to protect."

"What did you just do?" she repeated, bringing the point of her sword up to hover an inch from his face.

Kaiden focused on the blade. His expression was hard, tempered with the barest trace of contempt. "Metal. I manipulated the forces that pull metals together or push them apart. Anything made of metal I can control. For example—" He shifted and the sword wrenched from her fingers of its own volition, twisting in the air to turn back around and point toward her. It hovered in the air an inch from her left eye. "Useful, wouldn't you say?"

Lhaurel unclenched her fists with an effort. Who was he? Just when she'd started to understand one thing, something new had completely upended her world. "You are a wetta." The sword dropped into the sand, point first. "Which means that you don't manipulate metal. You manipulate water. You can find it, sense it. In the same way, you can sense and detect other mystics. Both useful in the desert climate."

"No, I can't." The denial came readily, the words leaping from her lips almost before conscious thought formed them.

"Pretending you can't feel the sandstorm's effects on your skin doesn't mean its not raging just behind the door," Kaiden said, the lines on his face sharpening. "I tell you that you are a wetta. Whether or not you accept that is irrelevant. It doesn't change the truth. We've watched you for years. The mystics who've come through your warren have been there to keep an eye on you. Since one of our wetta sensed you, we've just been waiting for the right moment to bring you into the fold. Tradition dictates it be close to your seventeenth year for women, though it can be earlier if something triggers a breaking before then."

The sword flipped up out of the ground and spun around so that the hilt was facing her at around arm height. The metal squares flickered in the torchlight, dripping purple flecks of blood as they returned to Kaiden's hands. He wiped them on the sides of his pants and deposited them in a pocket. He did it so casually. As if something so wondrously terrifying were commonplace and mundane. The sword bobbed in the air, gently prodding her arm. Lhaurel did her best to ignore it.

Fear tugged at her, giving her clarity of thought. She remembered Kaiden throwing her the sword when the sailfins had attacked the Sidena. He'd set her up—she was sure of it—set her up to be genesauri bait and—ultimately—bring her here.

Her hands reached behind her and struggled with the latch. It rattled loudly, and Kaiden arched an eyebrow at her, but she didn't stop. She didn't think she could even if she'd wanted to. Shrieks of anger assaulted the door behind her—the anger of wind denied passage at the end of a long journey.

"You're still in denial, aren't you?" Kaiden sighed and grabbed a fistful of his hair in frustration, "Lhaurel, we want you to join us. In fact, you've already sworn fealty to the Roterralar, so it's just a matter of acting the part."

"And what if I don't want to anymore?"

The lock clicked in the door behind her, the latch suddenly lifting in her hands.

"Then leave." His voice was cold, his eyes ice.

Would he really just let her leave? Lhaurel snatched her sword out of the air, opened the door, and hurled herself into the maelstrom.

Sand assailed her, cut into her skin, tore at her flesh. The force of it blinded her, filled her mouth and left her struggling to breathe. She stumbled onward blindly, one arm extended in front of her and the other futilely covering her mouth and nose. She stumbled into a wall, cutting open her hand. Sand filled the cut in moments, stopping the blood flow. With a muffled scream, she fell to her knees, which tore her robes and opened new wounds. Her mind screamed with the pain.

What was this place? Who were these people? All the rumors were true—demons taking human form. Mystics. Magic users. And she had let them use her.

She got to her feet unsteadily, fought the force of the wind threatening to push her over. She felt the skin peeling off her flesh, felt the sand tear it from her like thousands of hungry teeth. But she took one dogged step forward after another. She had to get away. Away from all of this. Away from the pain and the confusion and the blood. All the blood. What did Kaiden want with her?

She took another step forward. Another patch of skin joined the debris in the air.

How dare he accuse her of being one of them! She was no demon. She stumbled.

Maybe he was right.

The thought came small and dark, entering her mind like a thief in the night, leaving the footprints of a king. She coughed up sand, though more filled her mouth and nose than left. Why was she here? Why had the genesauri attacked early? Somehow the two questions merged in her overtaxed mind.

She took another step forward and tripped against a promontory of rock. She hit the ground hard, sucking in more dust and sand. This time she didn't get up.

What did it matter? She was dead now. Her life with the Sidena had been nothing short of the first of the levels of hell. This had to be the second. Death would be a pleasant relief to the pain. A freedom from thought, confusion, and . . . and . . . where was her sword?

It was gone. Oddly, she felt a twinge of sorrow at that. It had been a nice sword.

Sand choked her, cut off her air. She struggled to rise but didn't have the strength. She was dying, slowly suffocating with a mouth and nose stopped up with sand. The thought didn't seem to sadden her. Though her eyes were closed, her vision lightened, and she caught a glimpse of a far off meadow, the grasses green and verdant, calm and tranquil, like the Oasis would be about then. She smiled.

A face appeared in the light, resolving into a complete form, one whose arms were outstretched, holding up a large metal plate like a shield.

Kaiden?

She slipped into unconsciousness.

* * *

Blackness. Blackness and the faint sound of raspy breathing.

Consciousness was an elusive tendril of thought that refused to coalesce. Somewhere in the darkness, Lhaurel came aware of herself. The line between tangible and intangible was fuzzy. Thought, feeling and emotion become one. A feeling of safety and peace washed over her. She seemed complete—whole.

She was dead.

The thought should have bothered her, but it didn't.

"Lhaurel."

The voice came from a great distance. It was muffled and weak, as if it passed through the thick morning mists that sometimes assailed the Oasis.

"Lhaurel."

It came again, more insistent, forceful.

She opened her eyes.

Tieran looked down on her, face twisted in concern. Behind him, Khari peered over his shoulder.

Lhaurel blinked. What was she doing here?

Reality reasserted itself and her pains washed over her. She gasped, both from the pain and the sudden loss of perspective. The peace remained, though. The feeling of belonging, of being complete. Her mind felt fuzzy, as if it had not yet followed the rest of her consciousness back.

"Where am I?" she wheezed.

Tieran placed a waterskin to her lips. She gulped down water gratefully, feeling the brackish liquid clear the sand from her throat and ease into her stomach with welcome relief. A strange, tingling warmth ran across her stomach. Khari answered.

"You're in the healing chambers, deep within the warren."

A deep rushing noise reached her ears as if they had suddenly decided to start. It was a glorious sound, the gurgling, splashing sound of running water. It was the white foam of surf churned up by battling waves. The deep, blue-green tang of the sea and the sky. It was a transcendent symphony of hope, peace, and roiling emotion. *Sea?*

"Where's the water coming from?" she asked, though she could somehow sense its location. Tieran and Khari gave each other a significant look, and Khari almost smiled.

Then Lhaurel realized what she was doing. She had turned away from them when she had heard the noise. Neither of them was in her field of vision. How had she known that they'd looked at each other? How had she sensed it?

Dread washed over her like an icy wash of reality. What had Kaiden done to her? At the same moment, deep within her, something cried out in triumph at finally being set free.

"In the corner, there," Khari said. "It's a freshwater spring that feeds a lake deep beneath us. It's so far down we just use this spring for water."

Yes, Lhaurel thought, *there is a lake down there. I can sense it. It's enormous. Almost as big as the warren itself.* She cut off that line of thought. She didn't want to know how she knew that. And yet, at the same time, she hungered for the knowledge.

"What am I?" she whispered, closing her eyes.

"Tieran," Khari said softly, "leave us, please."

Lhaurel felt the man rise and walk to the door. She could sense him walking, almost feel his long stride, the crunch of the sand beneath his boots. She sensed the cold metal in his hands as he turned the knob, the shift of his weight as the door swung inward. He left, but long after the door had closed, Lhaurel still followed him in her mind, though the sense of him faded the further away he walked.

The bed shifted as Khari sat, pushing Lhaurel's bent legs aside to make room.

"Well, you can stop feeling sorry for yourself, girl. The man is gone and it's just me and you now."

Lhaurel didn't even open her eyes. She kept her face turned away, ignoring the other woman's presence. The bed shifted again, and Khari arose with a deep, exasperated sigh. The next thing Lhaurel knew, the bed was tilting, and she spilled onto the sandy floor in a tangled mess of bedding and limbs. Lhaurel struggled against the blankets that entangled her, but before she could free herself, Khari shoved her over, knocking her back to the ground.

"What in the seven hells are you doing?" Lhaurel demanded, her voice muffled by the bedding. She was tired of being pushed, dragged, and thrown around.

"If you're going to act like a child, then I will treat you like one."

Khari shoved her again and she toppled into the sand, rolling closer to the gurgling spring.

"You spent the last fortnight after answers, and now when you get them, you act as if the world is falling apart around you. You're told you have a chance to be part of something greater than yourself. To finally find that family, that inclusion you've been hungering for since birth. And you throw a tantrum like a spoiled child."

Lhaurel managed to free a hand and pulled a blanket off her head. "Some family," she said. "You locked me in a room with a demon, for sand's sake."

Khari laughed aloud, a single great guffaw of laughter that held more derision than humor. "A demon? Kaiden? Not likely. He's a mystic, and so are you. That's why we took such great pains to recruit you. The mystics are what keep the clans alive. Especially us wetta."

"I am *not* one of you."

"Oh, but you are," Khari continued over Lhaurel's protests, "and you secretly have always known that you were different. That you were better than those around you. You've never fit in, never followed the rules that others gave you. It is the nature of a wetta. Like the sea, you cannot be unwillingly tamed. You are one of us, and you have the chance now to fight for that which you crave. Freedom isn't given; it is conquered. You have to fight for it, for yourself and others. You have the chance to give life to the clans and protect them from the genesauri."

Lhaurel ran her fingers through her hair, listening to the intensity of Khari's words.

"Show them you understand that honor is more than just protecting and nurturing those that you agree with; it is also protecting and nurturing those with whom you disagree. That is what we're giving you the chance to become—a bastion of honor in a world where there is none. Let's face it. You're a woman. You have breasts and bear children. In the eyes of the Sidena, that is the only thing that you will ever be good for. Here we will teach you to fight, teach you to use the powers within you. You will be as equal as any man. You will never get that chance among the clans."

Lhaurel pulled the last of the bedding free and got to her feet, wary and ignoring the pain as her skin stretched and the raw flesh screamed in protest. The pain was much less than she had expected, but it was a passing thought, a diversion to her present situation. The discarded bedding made a jumbled pile on the overturned bed frame, behind which Khari stood.

Lhaurel didn't know what to think. Her emotions were a chaotic mixture of anger, skepticism and, buried deep beneath layers of scars and distrust, a small flickering flame of hope. She *wanted* to believe. She really truly wanted to think that she could become what Khari was saying. But past experiences weighed heavily in the back of her mind.

And the magic . . .

What was this power? What would it do to her? The image of the dead rashelta dripping purple blood onto the sand flitted through her mind's eye. Would she become the ruthless killer that she had seen in Kaiden during that moment?

It seemed that some of the rumors were true, or at least partially true. Could the others have some basis in fact as well?

Purple blood dripped onto the sand.

Another image crept into her mind, an image that she remembered only hazily, as if through a filmy mist. A man, standing above her and holding up a thin sheet of metal against the storm. A man protecting her. Kaiden. He could have left her. He hadn't needed to come out and save her. And yet he had. At least she thought he had. Why?

"Is Kaiden alright?" As soon as the words escaped her, she bit her bottom lip. She hadn't meant to ask that.

Khari raised an eyebrow at the question, perhaps curious at the line of reasoning that had brought Lhaurel to ask it.

"He is well. He and several others are out gathering information." Khari looked at her, eyes narrowed, appraising her.

Lhaurel realized for the first time how extremely pretty the woman was. Green eyes, short brown hair that hung just to her shoulders, and a slender build that belied her powerful frame. The grey that flecked her temples and the base of her hairline only added a grace and maturity to her beauty. She radiated strength and power more forcefully than Taren or Jenthro ever had.

In that moment Lhaurel realized she'd made her decision. The realization both thrilled and frightened her. Questions still hung unanswered in her mind, questions that demanded answers. She wasn't sure that she wanted them, though. She wanted what Khari had. Though she could barely admit it, even to herself, she longed for the promise of acceptance and freedom that Khari had dangled before her. And she was willing to walk this path to get it. She stood up straighter, the line of her jaw firmed. She looked up at Khari, who smiled at her.

"Welcome to the Roterralar."

CHAPTER 8

Clarity

"I have failed them. As they always thought I would. Our experiments have proven fruitless. There is some element missing—some means of combining the forces at work here that refuses to coalesce."

-From the Journals of Elyana

Makin Qays tapped on his chin as he listened to the report. A good leader finds solutions. When presented with a conflict, the good leader resolves it. When presented with a dark, difficult situation, a good leader makes it light by breaking it down into smaller parts and delegating each task. But what was a good leader to do when presented with a situation he didn't even understand?

"The genesauri appear to be moving northeast, toward the Oasis." Kaiden reclined in a chair at the other end of the table, his flight harness still attached over his dusty robes and his face stained reddish brown. He held a cup of wine in one hand, swishing it about absently.

Makin Qays sat opposite him, trying hard not to let his emotion show on his face. A half dozen other cast leaders sat around the table, murmuring amongst themselves and occasionally glancing at either him or Kaiden. A low buzz of conversation hung heavy in the air, and the smell of dust and drink intermingled left Makin Qays slightly nauseated.

SANDS

"Go over it again, Kaiden," Makin Qays said, leaning forward and cupping his chin with one hand, "from the beginning."

Kaiden stared down at his glass for a long moment, silent. Makin Qays cleared his throat and Kaiden glanced up, meeting the Warlord's gaze.

"What was that?"

"Again, from the beginning."

"Right. Well, the cast and I went north, following the line west to where we'd last sighted the Heltorin and Londik. Their tracks met up a few leagues south of the Oasis and then simply disappeared. We found nothing. We spent the night there, and then in the morning we flew north, following the signs of a large sailfin pack. It had been following a westerly course but then suddenly broke northward, straight for the Oasis. We split up then, half cast going east and half cast going north in large sweeping patterns. Every track we found traced back northward, almost as if something was forcing them to change direction. Over twenty sailfin packs are headed straight for the Oasis."

Twenty packs. Makin Qays wondered at the sheer number of the creatures. Even a small pack of sailfins generally numbered well into the threescore or fourscore range. Twenty packs was well over a thousand sailfins. Even with all forty aevian warriors they currently maintained, the Roterralar would never be able to stand against that many.

But why were the sailfins headed toward the Oasis? The massive stone wall had repelled dozens of previous packs over the decades. It had something to do with the magnetic rocks suspended in the sandstone, according to the mystics. Single packs happened across the area, but it was still an impenetrable defense as far as the clans were concerned. Thankfully the rains had stopped early this year and allowed the clans to take refuge in the Oasis despite the early Migration.

Not all of the clans, Makin Qays corrected in his head. Two were still missing.

They're dead. Makin Qays pushed the thought away, though it echoed on in the shadows. *They're all dead.*

"Do you have any idea what caused them to change course?" Rhellion asked.

Next to him, Kaiden shook his head. "No. We didn't see anything out there."

"Could someone be behind it?" Rhellion pressed, turning to Sarial. "A mystic gone rogue?"

The question sparked whispers throughout the room.

Sarial, however, snorted. "No one is that powerful. None of us can affect a single living genesauri, let alone twenty packs."

Makin Qays glanced down at the table. There *was* a mystic who might be powerful enough, but he never left the warren. And Makin Qays trusted him.

"How long?" one of the cast leaders asked.

Kaiden shrugged half-heartedly and leaned back further in his chair. "A fortnight, maybe a day or two longer," he said. "They're moving at a steady pace. Took us three whole days to catch sightings of them all."

"Numbers?"

"Well over a thousand strong, but we didn't get accurate counts. We had to avoid being spotted."

A note of emotion crept into Kaiden's voice at this, a hint of resentment and frustration. Makin Qays let it pass. He wasn't about to start the same old argument again, not when he needed to think with a clear head.

"Thank you, Kaiden," he said with a curt nod. "That is all we need for now. Senior warriors please stay. Everyone else is dismissed to their duties."

Several of the warriors, including Kaiden, stood up and shuffled out of the room. There was a measured reluctance to Kaiden's retreat, as if he longed to stay and participate in the council. Or perhaps it was simply the wine. The glass still in his hand had been filled more than once while going over the initial report.

Makin Qays met his gaze. For a moment, a transient flash of either anger or pain flickered in Kaiden's eyes. Then it was gone. He nodded slightly and exited the room, closing the door behind him.

Almost as soon as it closed, however, it opened again to admit

Khari. She moved with the lithe grace of a warrior and the air of one used to being in command. Before she had taken over care of the eyrie as the Matron, she had been one of the best warriors they had. Now she cared for the aevians and assisted new warriors in learning to ride the magnificent creatures. She was equally skilled in both these endeavors. Which was one reason that Makin Qays had grown to love her.

He turned away from the door and looked back at the assembled warriors. They were all cast leaders, except Sarial, and all but her and Tieran had enough years beneath their belts that wrinkles stretched across their faces. His senior council.

His eyes strayed to their exposed forearms, each one covered in tattoos. Kaiden wasn't the only one with difficulty severing ties. More than one of his senior warriors had tattoos that favored one color over the others.

He sighed. Divided loyalties were something he fought every day. He made a mental note to ask around about where loyalties lay. And he'd need to check in on the mystics. Maybe he'd get Khari to help him with that since she was one herself. He didn't need any more headaches.

A cleared throat brought his attention back to the matters at hand. He placed his hands flat on the table and gazed around the room once again, this time with purpose. Sarial sat at the far end of the table, a few chairs away from her twin, Tieran. Odd how they never sat together. Two of his other senior warriors, Gheinghal and Rhellion, sat opposite Khari. Tornan, a quiet cast leader with a sharp mind, filled the last chair.

"Well," he said, "what are we to do?"

"The clans will need to be warned." Gheinghal said.

"And we'll need to start harrying those sailfin packs," Tieran added, almost before Gheinghal finished his sentence. "Send out more patrols, full casts if needs be. Maybe we can cut down a couple of the packs or scare off some of the others."

Rhellion snorted. "Scare off a sailfin pack? You'd just as soon make the sun stop its journey across the sky."

"And what would you do, Rhellion? Let the packs hit the Oasis full force?"

"The wall has managed to repel the genesauri up until now. What makes this any different?"

Tieran ran a hand through his hair and grasped onto the long locks at the nape of his neck. "And what if this time they don't hold? What then?"

Rhellion gave him a look that quite plainly said that such would never happen.

Tieran opened his mouth to reply, his face reddening, but Sarial spoke before he managed to form words.

"Some action is required," she said, looking to both of them in turn. "There is no harm in sending out additional patrols to harry the packs headed toward the Oasis. And we have contacts among the clans. We can send messages to them or else send a mystic to push them in the right direction."

Rhellion scowled, and Sarial gave him a flat look.

"Just in case the wall doesn't repel them this time. That many packs may draw out the marsaisi early this Migration for all we know. We have no idea how the walls or stoneways would stand up to one of those."

Rhellion shrugged grudgingly and sat back in his chair. Tieran grinned impudently at him, which only deepened the scowl on the other man's face. Khari looked around the room at all of them, frowning. Tornan glanced at her and then simply shrugged.

"So, we're all in agreement that Sarial's plan holds the most merit?" Makin Qays said, breaking the silence. He had already decided along a similar path, but he had long ago learned that allowing his leaders to arrive at the conclusion for themselves proved the most successful. The nature of the Roterralar made them all too independent, too stubborn to be lead in a certain direction. They had to be prodded. It had taken long years of painful experiences for Makin Qays to finally learn that lesson.

Everyone nodded.

"Good," Makin Qays said. "We'll put it before the Gathering tonight. Until then, Gheinghal and Sarial, ready your casts for an additional patrol along the northern stoneways above the Oasis. You'll leave in the morning if the vote from the Gathering supports it."

They all nodded again except for Rhellion, who merely grunted.

Makin Qays closed his eyes and made a dismissive gesture, indicating that the meeting was over. Everyone arose and left without a word.

He would have to meet with them all individually later and discuss what was going on. They seemed to be more prone to talking one on one. Something was driving the genesauri toward the Oasis. Something had awoken them early. But what?

"Well," Khari's voice came from right beside him, "at least some good news can be found today. Lhaurel broke. Well, broke the rest of the way, that is. I guess Beryl and Kaiden were right about her."

He opened his eyes and looked into his wife's face. She wasn't smiling, but her eyes were bright.

"You've something to say," he said.

"I didn't hear the full report, but I got a partial summary on my way here. What I heard scares me. Something is driving the genesauri. Something is pushing them toward the Oasis. We need to figure out what's driving this. Find the reason."

"Now you sound like Kaiden," Makin Qays said with a sigh. "There's always a reason, isn't there? Rhellion seems to think it could be a rogue mystic." He gave her a significant look.

"Beryl is the only one powerful enough to do something that large. It's not him, but that doesn't mean Rhellion couldn't be right. One of the Rahuli could have broken during the initial Migration, someone young, powerful, and mad."

"It's possible. We'll need to do something, though. What would you have us do?"

"Sarial's plan has merit. Let's do what she suggested. Kill as many of them as we can and gather what information we can."

"We can't kill them all."

"I'm not saying we should spend our time hunting down all genesauri," Khari said, an edge creeping into her voice. "I'm not talking about exterminating them, though they would surely deserve it. We don't have the warriors to do that. I'm talking about sending patrols to follow the tracks back to where the packs originated. I'm talking about taking time to understand the whole picture. Strategy before tactics. Movement before battle." She recited the old admonition in a weary tone, as if the oft-repeated words had grown worn and tired.

"Perhaps," Makin Qays said, rubbing at his temples. "But for now we need to focus on the threat we know about. A fortnight is not a lot of time to stop twenty packs. I'm not as sure as Rhellion that the wall will hold them all at bay. Things are changing. We can't rely on any of our past experiences to hold true anymore. I'll take a cast out myself in the morning. I need to see this for myself."

Khari sighed and tossed her head, hair bouncing on her shoulders. "Well, at least we can agree on that." She smiled at him, and Makin Qays smiled back.

"I've decided to teach Lhaurel the sword," Khari said, turning to go. "It shouldn't interfere with my other duties."

* * *

Flames crackled and groaned, screaming as they ate the wood they were caressing. Even up on the second tier in the greatroom, the heat was enough to make sweat bead on Lhaurel's forehead. She sat with her feet hanging over the lip of stone to watch the people gathering below.

She was still sore, and even the smallest movement hurt, but most of the redness was gone from her skin, and the larger abrasions had completely healed over.

In the middle of the storm, it had felt like she was being torn to pieces, every last bit of skin torn from her body to leave only muscle and bone exposed to the elements. Yet her skin was whole and almost perfectly smooth. It didn't make sense. *Magic.*

The entire Roterralar clan was present, down to the last child and wee babe. She smiled as she looked down at one defiant infant suckling at its mother's breast. Every now and then, the mother winced as the hungry babe bit into flesh.

Lhaurel missed seeing children. It made her heart glad to see so many of them running around or huddled with their families. But it was a gladness tempered by regret and mild dusting of sorrow. There were so few of them. She had expected the Roterralar to have more people with how large their warren was. Altogether, including the children, Lhaurel only counted around a hundred people. Why were there so few of them?

Makin Qay's voice silenced the quiet hum that hung over the assembled throng. "My people. We bring dark tidings today. The Heltorin and Londik clans no longer exist."

Lhaurel brought a hand to her mouth. She winced in sudden pain and realized she'd bitten her lip so hard it bled. Her eyes fell upon Kaiden as she cursed. He was silent as well, head down and staring at his arms. In her mind, purple blood dripped into the sand.

"We all know that something woke them early this Migration. But now something else has happened. Something has turned the sailfin packs toward the Oasis."

"What is doing this?" someone from the crowd shouted.

"The wall will stop them!"

"Yes, the wall. They can't get past the wall."

Makin Qays held up his hands for silence. The shouts slowly died down, but the whispers remained. Husbands spoke to wives and clutched the hands of their children. Smaller children who didn't understand what was going on yawned and stretched out in the sand or else made faces at their elders. And the mothers hushed them all, turning their attentions back to the Warlord.

"Earlier today I met with the council, and we decided on a course of action. We cannot be sure the Oasis walls will hold off the genesauri this time. Things are changing, and we don't know why. We can't trust past experience to hold true. We don't know what's causing all this, but we intend to find out."

"So what do we do?" The voice was Kaiden's this time. Lhaurel felt a flush of irritation, even though she had the same question.

"We will send out half casts to harry the sailfin packs and try to track them back to their origin. Maybe we can find out what started all this and put a stop to it. Then we can simply ride out the rest of the Migration in relative peace. I will lead the first patrol. Gheinghal and Sarial will lead another group out as well. Those in favor?"

Most of the people raised their hands.

Lhaurel was stunned. The Warlord was letting the *clan* decide? She raised her hand as well, gritting her teeth against the pain of her bleeding lip.

"So be it, then. The casts will leave in the morning."

* * *

Lhaurel awoke adrift in a sea of blackness, awash with images that flickered and then faded, leaving her both relieved and saddened. Then she blinked, and the blackness faded. She became aware of the spring gurgling in one far corner of the room, felt it bubbling up from the depths below. Sensations of movement and people passed through her, as elusive as smoke.

Khari sat at the edge of her bed, a short, curved sword belted at her waist. Lhaurel sensed nothing from her. Nothing at all.

"Get up," the woman said, hand on her sword. "Grab your sword and come with me."

Lhaurel blinked and chewed on her bottom lip, hesitating. She'd gone to bed late after the Gathering, mind awash with questions and sensations brought about by strange powers and thoughts.

Khari arched an eyebrow. "Don't make me repeat myself, girl," she said.

So it's back to being mean again, is it?

Lhaurel finally shrugged and got to her feet, fishing around by the side of her bed until she located her sword. She was too tired to find the belt Beryl had given her, so she simply held it close to the hilt, wooden scabbard slick in her palms.

Khari didn't wait for her to change or even tie her hair back. Still holding her sword, Lhaurel hurried to follow as the woman left the room with a purposeful stride, leading her upward. The angle of the stone wasn't so steep that she would have noticed normally. In fact, thinking back, she'd had absolutely no sense of direction when walking through the caverns within the Roterralar Warren. Back in the Sidena, only long years of constant traipsing through the endless red sandstone passages had given her any sense of north, south, east, or west. Now she somehow knew that there were dozens of side passages and smaller rooms that branched off the main tunnel they were in, some with people or livestock in them and others without. Last night she'd been too confused with it all to put a name to the sensations, but this morning it was all much clearer. Sharper.

She shuddered and tried to shut it out. She failed.

Lhaurel hurried to keep up with Khari's fast pace. The woman didn't pause at any of the side passages but strode forward with dogged determination in each step, as if she regretted every one of them.

Several people worked in the passages they traversed, both men and women, some of whom she recognized from last night's Gathering. Drifts and piles of sand clung to the sandstone walls and clogged the walkways. It was a silent testament to the sandstorm that had passed. A memory of pain and fear. The image of a man crept into her mind. A man holding up a shield against the wind. A man protecting her. Overlaid with that image came one of a man calmly killing a rashelta. A man who had left her to die. She chewed on her bottom lip and pushed the thoughts away.

At some point, Lhaurel realized they were headed toward the greatroom. That was where she had first seen Khari in the dueling ring. There were people in the greatroom up ahead, five of them. Lhaurel sensed two working on the ground level and three others in various rooms on the other tiers. Lhaurel shook her head, trying to ignore it, but couldn't and ran headlong into a wall.

"If you can't even watch where you're going," Khari said without turning, "why am I wasting my time teaching you how to use a sword? You'll probably end up cutting off your own leg."

Lhaurel pushed herself off the wall with the hand that held her sword, the other nursing her bruised and damaged face. Blood dripped from a few small scrapes. The pain and embarrassment forced its way out of her mouth in the form of a barbed comment.

"You know, this bullying-the-new-girl routine is starting to get old. If you try smiling a little more it may work better for you."

Khari only chuckled.

In the greatroom, Lhaurel was unsurprised to see the same two women spinning yarn at a wheel along one side of the room. The fire ring had been removed and new sand tossed down where it had been stained black by the flames. One of the people in the rooms above had since left, leaving only the two still behind in their quarters. Khari walked to the far end of the room and drew her sword, turning and waiting for Lhaurel to catch up. A large circle had been drawn in the sand, within which rested two smaller concentric circles. Lhaurel approached, unsure whether she was supposed to draw her sword as well. As she got closer, she realized that the circles were actually made of stone, carved into the ground and then filled in with sand. She stopped at the edge of the larger circle.

Khari gestured for Lhaurel to remain where she was and then shirked her outer robes, which left her only in tight leggings and a thin vest. Lhaurel would have found it scandalous if she hadn't worn similar garb while practicing her sword work.

Khari dropped into a middle guard, muscles snapping into position with incredible speed and precision. She moved from the middle guard to a hanging guard while stepping backward. Almost immediately, she pivoted and spun back to the middle guard followed by a horizontal guard with such fluidity that it seemed but one long motion. She flowed through the forms, her feet tracing the circles of stone. At times she faced Lhaurel. Other times she faced away from her, sword flashing in dizzying arcs and spinning patterns that left blurs of silver-grey hanging in the air.

Lhaurel watched in awe as Khari moved through all of the basic forms and then transitioned into forms that Lhaurel had never seen before. The sword moved like a living thing, an extension of Khari's will rather than an inanimate weapon. It spun up over her head and then down at a stunning angle to flip into a reverse grip and complicated pattern of footwork that Lhaurel wasn't able to follow. It was more than sword work. It was artistry.

Suddenly it was done. Khari lowered her sword and turned to face Lhaurel, face glistening with sweat. Lhaurel felt a pang of loss as the moment, the majesty, faded.

"If you wish to enter this circle," Khari said, her voice barely above a whisper, "you must leave behind who you once were. That part of your life is over. If you enter this circle, you will be forevermore a Roterralar and no more of the seven clans. You must be committed, heart and soul, to a cause. Strategy before tactics. Movement before battle. Purpose."

Caught up in the moment, Lhaurel eagerly stepped into the circle.

An hour later Lhaurel had not once removed her sword from its sheath. It lay in the sand outside the outer circle. Lhaurel stood just inside the outer stone ring, feet spread to shoulder width and knees slightly bent. Khari stood just behind her, correcting her form with a few slaps of a thin rod.

"Knees bent," Khari snapped, "bent, I said. Your balance is off—I could knock you over with one hand."

To demonstrate, she did so. Lhaurel got to her feet again, blowing hair out of her face and brushing it back behind her ears. The scarlet locks dripped with sweat. She reset her stance and bent her knees as instructed.

Khari nodded appreciatively. "Good, now it's just doing that a few hundred more times before you have it ingrained into your muscle memory."

Lhaurel bit back a groan. Her legs ached, she smelled horrible, and the lesson had not gone anything like she had expected. After seeing Khari's stunning display, Lhaurel had expected to launch into forms, but the woman had instead set her back to basics. Stance and feet placement. Movement before battle, she said.

Lhaurel sighed.

"Oh, stop whining," Khari said with a sniff. "You'll live."

Lhaurel stifled another groan but couldn't resist rolling her eyes at Khari's back. The short woman was surly and blunt but effective. There was an economy and litheness to both her movements and her words that spoke of a sophistication hidden beneath the gruff exterior, something Lhaurel had noticed the first day she'd seen the woman, back when Kaiden had first delivered her here. Beauty hidden beneath layers of dirt and grime.

One of the women who had been spinning yarn brought Khari a waterskin. Lhaurel felt the water sloshing around inside the skin, felt each wavelike motion. She also sensed the woman walking away to rejoin her companion at the spinning wheel, even though she had turned so that her back was toward them. She shuddered.

Kevin L. Nielsen

Instinctively she turned to accept the skin from Khari. She sensed the water, not the woman, which Lhaurel found odd even though she couldn't explain why. The water was warm and brackish, tasting of leather and sweat, but it passed through her system like a small fire, spreading warmth throughout her limbs. Aching muscles eased and tension faded.

"Well, off with you then," Khari said, taking the skin from her and stoppering it without looking. "To the eyrie with you."

"The eyrie?"

A booted foot shot out and kicked her lightly on the rump, propelling Lhaurel forward. She squawked indignantly, but Khari's gruff voice drowned off her protests.

"What did I tell you about repeating myself? Off with you!"

Lhaurel would have argued, but it was pointless with Khari. Instead, Lhaurel picked up her sword and adjusted her clothes before breaking into a slow jog. The drink of water had given her a burst of restless energy that surged within her, granting her speed and strength. Though she had never traversed the paths to the eyrie from here, she could sense where the eyrie was located, could feel the aevians' presence within it, and somehow knew the way to get there. The pathways were clear, already devoid of sand.

She passed a few people in the halls, people garbed in the typical robes of the desert peoples, some with swords and some without. She couldn't remember seeing any of them before, but they didn't even pause to give her a second glance, not even the men. Some of the people wearing swords, some of the warriors, were women. More evidence that things well may be as different here as Khari, Makin Qays, and Kaiden claimed.

She couldn't decide if everything was what it seemed to be. There was too much fear for faith. She didn't even know if Kaiden was there to protect her or try to kill her. And behind all that was the threat of the genesauri. Something had caused them to change after centuries of constancy. No one knew what it meant.

The eyrie arose in front of her, majestic and vast. The aevians flew around the room, filling it with a cacophony of chirps, caws, flapping wings, and the sound of talons scraping against rock. A few women worked over sailfin carcasses near the door, carving up the meat for the aevians to eat. Several smaller aevians hopped in the sand near the pile of cut steaks, hungrily eying the bloody meat. One of the bolder ones darted forward, skittering on the sand. He seized one of the steaks in his pointed beak and leapt into the air, his wings throwing up dust as he flapped to a nearby ledge and began tearing bloody chunks free with a sickening, wet ripping noise. The others, emboldened by his actions, leapt forward and stole their own pieces.

The women kept on working.

"Lhaurel!" a well-known voice called. Tieran strode toward her, aevians scattering as his long strides ate away at the distance between them.

Lhaurel smiled and brushed a loose lock of auburn hair back behind her ears.

"Well, apparently you survived Khari." He said with a wide smile. "That takes a strange combination of stubbornness and a resistance to surly facial expression, but once you get used to that, she's alright. My wife likes her, so that's a point in her favor." He winked at her.

"Wife?" she said. "You're married?"

Tieran grinned and spread his hands wide. "What can I say? Love does strange things to people sometimes. Besides, I'm an outrageous scoundrel and notorious flirt. It helps to have a wife who is so supremely confident in herself that she doesn't wonder after a husband's failed attempts at humor. And every now and then it helps me remember my place when she sticks a sword in my face. So it works out on all counts." Tieran chuckled, a deep throaty sound, and gestured for her to follow him toward the opposite side of the eyrie.

She did, shaking her head and chuckling at the man behind his back. It was one of the first times that she had been able to laugh in a long, long time, and it was a welcome relief to the suspicions and frustrations that had become so commonplace. There was so little left in her life to be happy about. Tieran, somehow, still managed to find that glimmer of joy in almost all situations.

They reached the far wall where the storage bins were kept, and Tieran immediately pulled out a jumbled mess of leather and metal. He tossed the tangled mess to Lhaurel, whose confusion melted away when she recognized it as a harness. Her pulse quickened.

"Is this what I think it's for?" She asked, untangling leads so she could slip the contraption over her shoulder. She dropped her sword to the sand.

In response, Tieran grinned and then pursed his lips to produce a single, sharp whistle that rose in pitch. A piercing screech rent the air and a shadow passed in front of the sky. Lhaurel turned, sensing the aevian's dive. She knew who it would be even before the massive bird opened his wings and pulled out of his spectacular dive. She'd spent too much time with him to not recognize the presence of the fledgling. He landed on the edge of the cliff with surprising grace.

Steely talons dug into the sand. Light gleamed off coal black eyes. He clicked his hooked beak at Lhaurel expectantly, turning his body as if to allow her to inspect him. It had only been a few days, but even that short time had changed him. The few remnants of white, downy feathers had vanished. The black bands of adulthood worked up his legs and the underside of his wings, ending partway up his chest. A harness was fastened under each wing, across his chest, and extending around the legs.

"Hello, Fahkiri." She said softly. The name sprang from her lips unbidden, but it felt right.

He chirped, a quiet sound that was both intimate and personal. As if he were saying her name in return.

He lowered his head so they were almost eye to eye, a short distance, but enough to show he was deferring to her. Lhaurel reached out a trembling hand and stroked the warm feathers on the side of his jaw.

"Welcome to the Roterralar."

Part 3

Awakened

CHAPTER 9

Voices in the Dark

"The hope of our people rests in my hands—hands trained by the masters of the Orinai. Hands that could just as easily crush their hope as save it."

-From the Journals of Elyana

Marvi swallowed the mouthful of salted fish, savoring the strength of the flavor. She took another bite. The fish had been part of some negotiations Taren had played a part in with the Aeril clan. They were a strange lot, living in mobile tents in the northeast part of the Oasis, where a salty sea cut through the edges of the Forbiddence. The trade she'd worked out with the Frierd was working out well also, despite Jenthro's meddling. Taren had stepped in to assist with that as well.

Marvi took another bite of the fish, washing it down with a sip of wine. All in all, she was quite pleased with herself. Everything was going well, despite living in the dank, dark wetness of the Oasis. Everything, including Jenthro's death.

"This tastes like dirt." Jenthro shouted from the other side of the tent. He took his platter of fish and threw it across the room. "Give me lamb any day over this Oasis filth."

He had to stop then as a fit of coughing overcame him.

Marvi almost smiled. Almost. The cough was the only symptom of the poison she had procured. Thankfully coughs were something easily attributed to living in the Oasis. The wetness of it all was an easy and believable scapegoat.

"I'll have someone slaughter one for you," Marvi said. "We only have a few lambs left, but I'm sure we have one or two we can spare for you." She smiled at him pertly and turned back to her fish.

"Damn you, woman. I don't have time for your games today. The Warlords want to call another meeting about borders again. The Frierd are stealing every bit of space from us, and you sit there letting them, prattling on about the use of a well and goats."

"The clans do seem a bit restless this year, don't they?"

Jenthro raised an eyebrow. "Restless? They're at each other's throats." Another fit of coughs. "We've only been here a fortnight, and I'm already not sure how we're going to survive each other."

"The blood oaths will hold." Marvi said.

The fish really was amazing. Maybe she should negotiate for more.

Jenthro snorted. "The blood oaths are about as useful as the ones you swore to me on bonding day. They're both only as strong as the people who gave them."

Marvi pursed her lips and nodded. It was an astute observation for him. She studied him for a moment as he picked at the rug that covered the cursed grass blanketing the ground.

"What about the rumors?" she asked before turning back to her fish. It was almost gone, so she took small bites, barely enough to get the full flavor out of it.

"You mean the ones about the voices in the walls?" The scorn was evident by his tone. "Don't tell me you've started believing those, too? They're just tales told by the weak minded to try and increase the tension between the clans." He trailed off as if thoughtful, scratching at a spot on the back of his arm. "It's almost as if—as if someone were trying to get us all to violate the oaths. As if someone were trying to get us to fight one another here in the Oasis."

Marvi didn't look up, but she felt her pulse quicken slightly.

"Agh, I'll find my own lamb. Woman, you give me a headache sometimes." With that, Jenthro got to his feet, coughing only slightly, and pushed open the tent door and into the bright sunlight.

Marvi put down her fish and rubbed a hand across her forehead, feeling suddenly chill. There *was* something strange going on, but it had to be more obvious than she'd assumed if Jenthro was starting to see it, too. From the sound of things, the other Warlords were starting to question things as well. She'd have to reach out to her informants, spread some false rumors, and get the clans more interested in one another than they were of anything else.

A noise came from behind her. Marvi turned her head, pulling a small, poisoned dagger from a hidden sheath in her sleeve. It was only Taren.

"Oh, it's you," she said, stowing the dagger back in its sheath. "Would you care for some fish?"

Taren scowled. "That idiot was right about that, at least. The stuff is terrible."

Marvi shrugged, got to her feet, and served herself another helping from the larger platter off to one side. "It really is excellent fish. Are you sure you won't have some?"

Taren gave her a flat look.

"I just thought I'd ask." She took a seat on the ground across from Taren. "So what did you think about what he said? I assume you heard all of it?"

Taren nodded, unknowingly picking at the exact same spot on the rug that Jenthro had. "Tensions are high here, he's right about that, though I'm surprised he noticed. That one would miss a sandtiger eating his own feet."

Marvi smiled. The description was harsh, but accurate.

"His cough is getting worse." Taren continued. "We should increase the amount you're giving him."

Marvi took another bite of fish, chewing slowly. This one wasn't as good as the first one. There wasn't as much seasoning.

"What are you thinking?"

Marvi set aside her platter. "Maybe we shouldn't kill him just yet."

Taren's face immediately hardened, and he clenched one hand into a fist. The scars on his arms whitened with the pressure of his muscles against taut skin.

"And why is that?"

"With everything going on, it may not be the right time," she said. "If we kill him now, with tension between the clans so high, the clans may blame one another for the supposed assassination, even if we make it look like a simple sickness."

"And if they do?"

Marvi blinked. Of course he knew what they'd do. Why was he asking?

"They'll fall upon one another like sandtigers among sheep. The blood oaths would be broken. More death and destruction."

"It's a perfect opportunity," Taren said. "We can blame it on one of the other clans even. There aren't many of them left, actually. If we do this right, we could even end up the most powerful clan in the Sharani Desert instead of one of the weakest."

Marvi sniffed and raised an eyebrow. Was he really suggesting they go through with it? Taren got to his feet, stepping toward her.

"Think on it. If we do this right, we can rule the Rahuli people altogether. You and me." He looked down at her, his expression cool and appraising. Inviting. Marvi's pulse quickened.

"You're behind all this, aren't you?" she asked, staring back at him with a question in her gaze. "This tension, the rumors."

Taren raised an eyebrow and gave half a grin. "If only I was that capable. No, I'm not behind it, but I do plan on exploiting it now that it's here. Jenthro dies. Now's our chance."

Marvi looked into Taren's eyes, seeing the passion and intensity there. He was right. It was time to get rid of her husband.

* * *

Saralhn strode along the well-worn path, marveling at how fragile the grasses of the Oasis were. After only a fortnight, the Sidena had walked this same route to the market enough times that the soft, springy plant had died away, leaving behind a swath of brown dirt. Several other women walked with her, bantering back and forth as they walked. They carried baskets and smaller goods for trade.

Saralhn carried her own basket under one arm. She hoped it would be big enough. She'd had to start over after leaving the pack behind. Enril had beaten her badly for that. She still walked with a slight limp.

But she'd deserved it. Carrying the pack had been her responsibility, after all. It'd been destroyed when Lhaurel—

No, don't think about that. She shook her head in an attempt to banish away the memories.

"Alright there, Saralhn?" Jerria asked.

Saralhn gave the older woman a wan smile. "I'm fine. It's just all this water in the air. It fogs my mind sometimes."

Jerria nodded knowingly and pursed her lips. Around her, the other Sidena women made various signs of agreement.

"Ah, the Oasis is full of wonders, true, but sometimes I wish we could avoid this cursed place." Jerria said with a sniff. "It's just so . . . "

"Strange."

"Yeah, strange. All this green, and the water flowing everywhere. Give me good red sand and a warren over this any time." Another of the women agreed.

Saralhn let the women talk, falling into step. She wasn't sure what she thought about the oddities in the Oasis, but she wasn't sure she'd take the sand and rock any more than the grass and water. Neither one was really better than the other. They both simply existed. Both had a purpose and use where they were, or nature would have long since destroyed them.

Something in the conversation pulled her from her thoughts. "What was that?" she asked.

Maryn stopped talking mid-sentence, giving her a stern frown.

"My pardon," Saralhn said, "I didn't mean to forget my manners. What were you saying just now, mistress? My thoughts wandered off."

Maryn's frown deepened and she pointedly dropped a hand to a hip, drawing Saralhn's eye to the purple *shufari* about her waist. Saralhn still had a few more fortnights to go before she would even get to wear the brown.

Saralhn bit the inside of her cheek.

"Leave the child be, Maryn," Jerria, who also wore a purple *shufari*, said. "She was just saying her husband heard the voices last night while on patrol."

"The voices?"

"Yes, girl, the voices," Maryn interrupted, still frowning at her.

"My husband, Cobb, was on patrol duty last night. He was passing near the walls of the Oasis, near our border with the Frierd." Her frown grew into a scowl.

Some of the other women muttered under their breath. Something to do with water thieves.

"He heard the voices. Like whispers of dead men coming from the walls."

Jerria clasped a fist over her heart, a sign of warding protection against evil. "By the seven hells."

"It's the Frierd," Maryn said. "My Cobb says so, too. He thinks they're after more than just our water. It's a trick."

"Do you really think so, Maryn?" Jerria asked, looking anxious. "What if the voices really are the spirits of the dead, come to haunt us? The genesauri coming early this Migration, the death, old allies renewing strengths. What if this is a sign of the end?"

Maryn frowned at the woman, her brows coming together over her eyes.

"Shame on you for saying such things. Of course it's the Frierd. They've always hated us. This is retribution for our raid three moons ago. They're trying to scare us, but it won't work. We're Sidena, not Londik cowards."

"And if it is the Frierd?" It really wasn't Saralhn's place to get involved in a conversation between the two women, but she asked anyway.

Maryn glanced at her and then gave Jerria a pointed look. Jerria looked away, as if embarrassed.

"If it is the Frierd," Maryn said in a firm, confident voice, one bolstered by the look of absolute resolve on her face, "then they'll understand the true strength of the Sidena. And live to regret it."

* * *

The Oasis sat in a strange circle of grey and red stone, interspersed with pockets of a dull grey metal. The cliffs rose hundreds of feet into the air, reaching upward toward the sky and protecting the clans from the genesauri. They were a rough, craggy mass of stone and rock and metal with only two points of ingress, both of which were too narrow for even the smallest sailfin to pass through. Towering monoliths, they'd stood against sailfin and marsaisi for hundreds of years. His grandmother told him once that there'd been a time when the sailfin packs had come. Hundreds of them surged against the walls, but they were repelled.

She'd also told him the stories about the score of outcast brethren and sisters who had died trying to scale them. Gavin had lived through one of them. He hadn't understood what had driven his parents to try and do the impossible when he was a child. He didn't fully understand it now, though part of him still blamed the goading, taunting insults the Sidena warriors had lobbed at them. That wasn't entirely true, though. His father had talked about making the climb for years beforehand, talked of living up to the legacy of their ancestors. For Gavin's parents, the story of Eldriean wasn't just a story. It was a lesson handed down to them by their parents. It was fact, something they could hold on to as a chance at redemption from their lives as outcasts. He hadn't understood that then.

He climbed now, knowing he would likely meet the same fate as they. The walls had easy handholds for the first few spans, but they came farther and farther apart the higher he climbed. It was an impossible task, set to attain an imaginary goal. Yet Gavin climbed anyway.

His parents had died attempting this very task, something they had sworn him to do when he was just an infant, as his grandmother had sworn Gavin's father to do in *his* infancy. It was impossible, but he was going to do it anyway. He climbed for honor. He climbed to uphold an oath. And he climbed because there was nothing else for him to do. With his grandmother gone, the other outcasts had no more hope left. He'd seen it in their faces in the days that followed her death, while he'd visited each family in turn.

He reached up and seized a crag of sharp rock with a hand that was already slick with blood and weak from pain. Stiff fingers wrapped around the stone. It cut into flesh as he put his weight on it and pulled himself up another span, shifting his foothold to another crag. He paused and glanced down, taking a moment to rest as best he could while clinging to a cliff over a hundred spans above the ground. The tops of the trees looked like small tufts of grass from that height. He could no longer make out the details of the small cave where he had left his grandmother's body, sealing the mouth of the cave with rocks and mud. But he knew where it was. Neither time nor distance would dull that memory, or the poignancy of her final words.

Remember what it is that you have sworn to do.

He gritted his teeth as a gust of wind tugged at him, pulling at his clothes and tossing his damp, sweaty hair into his eyes. He would do what he had sworn to do, though he did not understand half the things his grandmother had told him. Legends, stories, hints of rumors and myth, she had recited them to him each night on the sands as if they were accounts of actual people. As if they were true. Stories of ancient heroes, kings and rulers, Warlords, and a history that was stunningly disparate from the reality around them. Tales of greenery. Legends of trees that grew with things called leaves instead of fronds. Myths of places without sand, where water fell from the sky year round. And cities. He hadn't ever figured out what they were supposed to be. They sounded like massive warrens filled with thousands of people, but that wasn't something he could really imagine. He doubted there were more than a few thousand people in all the clans together.

But somewhere in the stories and myths, she had instilled in him an understanding and a duty. She'd claimed they were descendants of the mighty Eldriean himself, the right of kingship their legacy. On the few times he had spoken to anyone else about the stories, they had claimed that both his grandmother and the stories were insane. But insane or not, he believed them.

He blinked, coming to that realization for the first time. He believed them.

His grandmother had raised him, given him everything he had. One look into her eyes as she spoke of the trees or the strange passings of weather and clouds in ancient times, and he knew that she wholeheartedly believed in what she taught him. And he had come to believe in it as well. To believe in the legends of a proud and noble people cast down from their lofty origins. A people that could be whole again, if guided by the right man. He'd never believed that man could be him. He didn't want it to be him. But his grandmother did. Her dying request was sacred, and he would see it through.

The wind died down, and Gavin resumed his climb. He ignored the pain, discarded the emotions that swelled within him at the memories of sleepless nights beneath the stars as a child, his terrors only calmed in his grandmother's arms and by the sound of her voice. He climbed to fulfill a promise. He climbed to escape the pain. He climbed because his grandmother pushed him onward, her encouraging words with him even after death.

Her legends spoke of a king that would unite the clans and drive out the genesauri, returning the desert to the land of lush greenery that it had once been. It was not a prophecy. She had been vehemently adamant about that. There was no such thing as fate or destiny. There were simply things proven and things disproved. Her legends spoke of a king who could unite the clans. She said that king could be him. He climbed to prove it true.

He reached out for another handhold, but it was just out of reach. Gavin adjusted his feet and tried again, stretching to his utmost to get his fingers around the lip of the tiny outcrop. His fingertips scrabbled at the rock.

Gavin's left foot slipped.

He swore as his right foot was pulled from its spot by the weight of his falling left foot. Rock cut into his left hand as his entire body weight fell onto it. Blood seeped out of his fingers and slickened the rock. He growled, scrabbling for purchase with his feet.

His fingers started to slip, the skin peeling back against the rock. Gavin screamed, summoning every ounce of his strength and will. His left foot found a hold, his right following a moment after. The relief on his left hand almost overcame the pain. Almost.

He clung to the wall, weight balanced on his feet to relieve his aching hand. He stayed there for several long moments, his breath coming in long, ragged gasps. Pain numbed his mind, dulling his thoughts. It was impossible. Gavin knew he was never going to make it to the top.

He kept climbing anyway.

CHAPTER 10

Flight

"I wish that my old mentor were here to help with this cause, but alas, he is gone from this world. I shall see him no more. The importance of my task weighs heavily on my shoulders. Should I fail, we shall join him, too."

-From the *Journals of Elyana*

Tieran reached up and checked the leads that connected Lhaurel's harness to the one girded about Fahkiri. Two thin leads hooked into the harness in front of her, and a long one extended from behind her. Lhaurel felt ridiculous, but Tieran assured her that she would need all three straps to stay seated on the aevian's back as he flew.

"Now, when you get more accustomed to the way he moves and his flight patterns," he said, giving the last lead a sharp tug to make sure that it was secure, "then you can remove most of the leads and leave just the one main safety tether in the back. For now, you need to get used to how he moves beneath you."

The man grinned and stepped back, giving her a wink as if letting her in on a joke.

Lhaurel smiled back awkwardly, not understanding, which only made Tieran laugh harder. Lhaurel shrugged and shifted her seat on Fahkiri's back.

A wide strip of leather served as a sort of saddle that stretched down the length of his broad back and protected his feathers from her movements on his back. A single handhold had been attached to the saddle where the aevian's head met its back. Lhaurel felt tall and a little unsettled, though a thrill ran through her as the aevian stepped up to the edge of the cliff face. She glanced down the thousand-foot drop, her vision swimming. She looked up again, twisting around as Tieran approached.

"Try and be careful," he said, "this is your first flight together as a warrior pair. You need to get used to each other. Let him fly; don't try to direct him. Let him take you where he will. When you're ready to come back, whistle sharply three times, and he'll return to the eyrie."

"Wait," Lhaurel said, eyes wide with sudden panic, "you're not coming with me?"

Tieran smiled, a twinkle in his eyes that was more impish mischief than jocularity. He stepped back and whistled once.

Lhaurel screamed as Fahkiri spread his wings in one massive burst of powerful muscles and launched himself over the edge, carrying Lhaurel with him. Fahkiri folded his sickle-shaped wings inward toward his back, becoming almost a perfect wedge the shape of a spearhead.

Wind rushed through her hair, sending it fanning out behind her like a flame. The ground approached at an astonishing rate, the sheer force of the wind stinging her eyes and making them water. Her pulse raced, and she screamed in fear or exultation or some combination of the two. They were going to crash into the ground. They were going to die. Gravity pushed her forward, and she felt the pressure increase on the straps of her harness as the safety lead in back held her in place. Her hands shot forward and wrapped around the pommel, holding it in a white-knuckled grip that threatened to crack bone. Her brain protested against the onslaught of pure terror and the absolute joy that battled for supremacy.

She sensed the motion before it happened. One moment they were plummeting toward certain death on the rocks and sand below, and then, suddenly, Fahkiri spread his wings with a violent, gut-wrenching shriek, only amplified by the sudden slowing and change of direction. He launched back upward into the sky with powerful wing strokes, climbing at great speed.

Lhaurel let out her breath in one explosive burst. Until that moment, she hadn't even realized that she'd been holding it.

They winged higher, turning in a long curving pattern that brought them around so that they were suddenly facing the massive expanse of cliffs that made up the Roterralar Warren. The plateau stretched high into the sky, higher than Lhaurel remembered, and continued onward to either side for thousands of spans. She wondered at that despite the thrill of emotions that was coursing through her. She'd only sensed a small portion of the warren, and it was nowhere near as large as the plateau itself. Why waste such a large space?

Fahkiri continued to turn, each beat of his wings taking them higher, though the pace had slowed.

She studied that plateau, noticing the cavernous opening to the eyrie as they turned and almost waved to Tieran, who still stood at the mouth. Something stopped her. He looked so small, so far away. They were easily a hundred spans above him now and at least twice that away. He probably couldn't even see her. This was her time, hers and Fahkiri's. Besides, her hands were still fastened so tightly around the pommel that she doubted that she could unclench them without serious effort.

They climbed higher.

A handful of other aevians screeched in greeting as they flew past, a pair of smaller aevians and a few of their larger counterparts out stretching their wings. Fahkiri whistled back, though it sounded almost dismissive, as if they were intruding upon his domain.

As they turned, Lhaurel looked out over the dunes and sand to the east. The dunes rolled outward like massive waves, though there were patches of oddly shaped dunes that disrupted the symmetry and pattern. No, Lhaurel corrected. Not disrupted, changed. The more she looked at it, the more she realized that even the apparent irregularities were part of the desert's strange beauty. Without them, the uniformity of it would have been bland and the majesty lost.

Lhaurel laughed in delight and leaned forward.

Fahkiri responded. He folded his wings and turned his beak toward the ground.

Lhaurel's screams were cut off as they suddenly plunged for the ground. They were thousands of spans above the plateau by then, but the aevian's body was perfectly shaped for such steep, sudden dives. They sped up. The wind dug into her eyes and tore at her hair, clothing, and skin. It forced the air out of her lungs, slammed her eyelids shut. Her mind was numb with sudden terror. Something warm trickled up her leg. She felt like she was falling off the back of him as they continued to fall faster and faster. She sensed the ground approaching at stunning, impossible speeds, felt the ground rise up to meet in its warm enveloping embrace.

Cutting through her terror, though, was the movement, the sudden turning, twisting, gut-wrenching motion as Fahkiri spun around and opened his wings. Air screamed through his feathers, and Lhaurel, unprepared, was slammed forward. Her head slammed into the pommel with bone-breaking force. Her nose shattered on impact, and she struck with enough energy that, for a moment, she blacked out. Only the tethers attached to the saddle and her harness kept her on Fahkiri's back.

Her vision swam as she slowly came back into consciousness. A ringing sound pounded in her ears and she was awash in sensations of simultaneous pain and numbness. Something salty dripped into her mouth and there was a spreading warmth along her legs. She coughed weakly and sprayed scarlet fluid over Fahkiri's back. *Blood?*

Hands gripped her shoulders. A blade flashed and she was being pulled free from the saddle. She blinked. Had they made it back to the eyrie? She didn't remember landing.

Someone said something, but it was garbled and muffled by the ringing in her ears.

Blinking rapidly, she fought the fog and stinging numbness that threatened to overcome her. Blood trickled down her face and into her mouth. Swallowing only brought the rusty taste of blood down the back of her throat. She was vaguely aware of Fahkiri screeching in agitation near her, feathers bristling outward at his neck and along his chest, but she couldn't seem to focus on anything else. The rest of the aevian himself was blurry mass of grey and black, outlined by an aura of painful brightness. She shut her eyes against the pain.

Someone touched her face.

It was as if someone had poured boiling water over her. Skin rippled and bubbled like the surface of a stew pot simmering on the fire. Lhaurel's breath caught in her lungs. Her blood seemed to froth and roil within her veins. Her eyes snapped open.

Khari stared down at her, eyes narrowed in concentration.

The pain vanished. Her vision focused. She swallowed and there was no taste of blood. She reached up a hesitant hand and touched her face. She felt only smooth skin and an unbroken, fully whole nose.

Fahkiri chirped his special chirp, obviously excited to see her moving and whole. Someone, probably Tieran, had removed Lhaurel's harness, but there was blood on her robes.

"You might want to practice the landing a little more," Tieran said. There was a grin on his face, but it seemed strained.

Khari rose, pushing herself up with her hands on her knees. She seemed tired, much more so than after her stunning display with the sword earlier.

"What did you do?" Lhaurel asked in a hushed tone.

Khari blinked rapidly a few times as she turned to regard her.

"One of the abilities of a wetta is healing, of others and oneself. Haven't you wondered how you survived before Kaiden found you?" she said, blinking.

Lhaurel struggled to rise and managed to pull herself into a sitting position.

Khari shifted slightly, moving as if she were going to sit down, and then suddenly collapsed.

Tieran was at her side in a moment. "She's out cold."

"Is she going to be alright?"

Tieran carried the matron of the Roterralar into one of the adjoining rooms. He placed her on the bed carefully, though he didn't appear to be overly concerned.

Lhaurel stood at the doorway to the small room, gnawing on her bottom lip. She had followed them after assuring herself that Fahkiri was safe. She didn't understand what had happened, but somehow Khari had healed her, and the act had left the woman close to death. Somehow she could sense the woman now when she hadn't been able to before. Lhaurel could feel a faint pulsing from the woman, as if her heart beat weakly. Khari's weakened state was her fault.

"She'll be fine," Tieran said, one hand on Khari's shoulder.

"Is there anything I can do to help?" Lhaurel felt sick. How had she ever distrusted the matron? This woman had just put herself at risk to heal her. Bile rose in Lhaurel's throat.

"All she needs now is a little rest and some water."

"I'll fetch her some," Lhaurel said immediately, not pausing for a response.

She turned and hurried back into the eyrie. She broke into a jog that sent aevians in all directions. Fahkiri screeched in indignation as she passed him by without pausing. The women cutting up sailfin carcasses looked up when Lhaurel approached them and skidded to a halt. The loose sand got kicked up over them and their meat.

"What in the seven hells!?" a woman shouted, but Lhaurel ignored her.

A waterskin lay on the ground between the women, set aside for later use in washing or drinking. Lhaurel snatched it up without asking for permission and then dashed back across the eyrie floor. Shouts of anger and protest followed her. The aevians were smart enough to get out of her way ahead of time, even Fahkiri.

"Here," Lhaurel said breathlessly, bursting into the small room with sudden fervor and handing the skin to Tieran.

He took it, though the corner of his mouth twitched slightly. "Thank you." He stifled a cough with the back of his hand.

"Is it enough?" she asked, shifting her weight from one foot to the other and then back again. "I can go get more."

Tieran unstopped the skin and held the tip to Khari's lips. A small trickle of water escaped the nozzle and dripped down her lips and the side of her cheek. Her lips parted in response to the cool liquid, and Tieran poured a little into her mouth. Khari's chest rose and fell, and she took in a deep breath. Her eyes flickered open.

"This is more than enough," Tieran said with a smile.

Khari sat up and reached for the waterskin, gulping it down gratefully.

Lhaurel felt lightheaded with relief. She felt Khari's strength returning, swelling within the woman with each gulp of water. Slowly, Lhaurel sank to her knees in the sand. Khari noticed her.

"Where's your sword?"

Lhaurel blinked and suddenly started laughing, a deep, powerful, heartfelt laugh that worked its way up from the pit of her stomach. After the emotional highs and lows, Khari's question seemed so ludicrous.

Khari arched an eyebrow at her while she stoppered the waterskin and passed it back to Tieran, who was also grinning like a fool.

"Explain yourselves," Khari demanded.

Tieran spread his hands in an expression of innocence, though his grin belied the gesture. The grin turned into a great, booming bark of laughter.

Lhaurel looked at him for a moment, and then comprehension dawned. "I, um—" She looked at Tieran and couldn't suppress a laugh. "Well, I thought something was wrong and Tieran—"

Lhaurel didn't even have to finish. Khari groaned and shot the man an exasperated look as he chuckled. Lhaurel's laughter died away when Khari turned back to face her, Tieran's words and Khari's expression cutting through the ethereal humor.

"Thank you for your concern, Lhaurel," Khari said with a tight smile, "but I was never in any danger. I was already in the eyrie when Tieran whistled and called your aevian back. He has some unfortunate timing sometimes, and I witnessed your little accident. Healing leaves me weakened for a time, but it passes quickly enough, especially if I am given a drink of water. We can heal ourselves that way, too, through consumption of the water, which fuels our power. Forgive Tieran his jokes."

Lhaurel sniffed, unsure of how to respond. Tieran had let her panic, let her think something was deathly wrong with the matron of the Roterralar. She must have seemed the fool. Instead of feeling angry, she simply shook her head and smiled. She was too tired to be angry, and it was just like Tieran to pull something like this.

"I had it coming, I think. He did tell me you'd be fine. That's what I get for not trusting him in the first place."

Tieran grinned impudently and winked at her.

She smiled back. There was something endearing about the man. He treated her the same way he treated everyone else: like an equal.

Khari looked from her to him and back again and then let out a small sigh. "Leave us, Tieran."

He gave her a quizzical look.

"Please," she added.

He shrugged and got to his feet, leaving the waterskin laying on the sand next to where he had been sitting. He smiled to Lhaurel, gave Khari an exaggerated wink, and then left, closing the door behind him. The room was cast into semidarkness, the only light the orange glow of torchlight sprinkled with a wan light filtering down through the craggy sandstone.

Lhaurel shifted in the sand and toyed with a stray lock of her hair that had fallen into her eyes.

Khari regarded her coolly, the same stolid appraisal she had given Lhaurel earlier when she had invited her to enter the training circle. Lhaurel's skin crawled, and she shivered under the scrutiny.

"I know what you're feeling right now, Lhaurel," Khari said softly. "Fear, anger, confusion, pain. So many things are happening all at once. Your whole understanding of life has been upended. You're at the bottom of a lightning sand pit and there is no up. You've heard about the Roterralar vagabonds your whole life. Heard about the evil magic they do. Heard how they sacrifice small children. And yet here you are, experiencing the wonder of flight and a place where women are afforded a station equal to men, contrasted with the stunning supposed cruelty of keeping you locked up and imprisoned in the darkness of servitude. You catch glimpses of the light only to be shoved further into the confusing black.

"I've been there. I joined the Roterralar when I was close to your age, and the matron at the time broke me just as I was forced to break you. Well, as Kaiden and I were forced to break you. The nature of our abilities requires a shattering of barriers that would otherwise block their use. I—" The woman hesitated, the first time Lhaurel had ever seen her do so. She sensed a loosening of barriers that let Lhaurel catch a glimpse of the woman behind the matron. "I'm sorry for the way you were treated, Lhaurel. For the way *I* treated you. It was necessary.

Please don't hold it against Kaiden. He was only acting under my direction. I noticed how he seemed to get under your skin the first time you used your powers."

Lhaurel pursed her lips but didn't disagree.

"I will train you in the ways of the wetta and with the sword if you want to learn. You have but to ask, and I will respond to any question that it is in my power to answer."

Lhaurel sniffed and released a breath that she had not realized she had been holding in. It escaped her in a sigh that blew dust through the air. She brushed a lock of hair back into place as she contemplated what to say. She had gotten so used to simply being told what to do that she found it hard to find one single question to ask. Dozens flitted through her mind, but she finally settled one.

"So what do I have to do to get out of this place?"

Of all the questions that she could have asked, Khari's reaction told her that it was the one that had been the least expected. The woman recovered quickly, though.

"At this point, if you leave, you're dead."

"Why?"

"Because you know too much about us now. We function because we are not known outside these walls. No one who leaves knowing what you do could be allowed to live." Khari's tone was slow, guarded.

"What is so bad about the clans knowing about all this?" Lhaurel asked, gesturing vaguely around the room to encompass the entire warren. "Why is the only thing I've ever heard rumor and stories about Roterralar? You don't even wear red robes here."

Khari's eyes narrowed, and she sat up straighter, knuckling her back. "Have you ever seen a parent raise a child and do absolutely everything for them? Protect them from every little danger so that they never learn how to do anything for themselves?"

Lhaurel grimaced, recalling a few such children among the Sidena. A young man from one of the families she had spent time with as a child had had a completely overprotective mother. She even went so far as to lay out his clothes for him and help him lace his boots. There had been a time when his mother had not been around to lace up his boots for him. He had turned to Lhaurel, who had been salting some dried meat for the morning meal, and demanded that she do it for him. She'd been astounded to realize that, at fifteen years old, he still did not know how to lace up his own boots.

She'd refused. The beating that came later was one of the worst she had ever received.

"The clans are very much like children, Lhaurel," Khari said, scratching the back of her head. "And the genesauri are the dangers that they must learn to face. We protect them as best we can, but if they knew that we were out there, fighting the genesauri, riding the backs of the aevians with the mystics' magic alive within us, they'd expect us to save them every time. They would never learn how to function on their own. And, more importantly, they would destroy us even as we protected them."

Lhaurel paused a moment to consider what Khari was saying. It seemed so cruel, so heartless.

"What do you mean, 'it would destroy us?'"

"How many Roterralar have you seen within the warren?"

"Less than a score."

"Well, you've seen about a fifth of the entire population," Khari said. "And only two score of them are warriors. Even fewer are mystics. We don't have enough people to defend everyone everywhere. If we revealed ourselves to the clans, all of them would demand that we protect them from every genesauri attack. There aren't enough of us to be effective in any more than two groups. But what if three clans were attacked at once? What if there were four attacked at once? We'd be forced to try and protect them all, and we'd be too few in number to do any good. We would fall faster than we could help anyone out. We would be dead before the Migration ended."

"Which is why you recruited me and made me figure things out on my own," Lhaurel reasoned. "Because I was already dead and because you needed more people."

"More or less."

"It seems to me that you could do both. You could reveal yourselves to the clans, and then all of you could fight the genesauri together. There are more than enough aevians, and all the clans together could make a strong front."

Khari smiled and gave a soft laugh. "You've hit on one of the major debates among us. What is the test of honor, to uphold the flame or snuff it out? Do we remain hidden and fight the battles that we can with the resources that we have? A delaying action at best? Or do we reveal ourselves and rally the clans into one people to stand against the genesauri and, eventually, wipe them off the face of this land?"

Lhaurel nodded her agreement, shifting into a kneeling position. "Yes, why don't you simply do that?"

"The clans are not so easily mixed," Khari said with a tired shrug. "Even among us. If you watch, you'll see that those of us from rival clans originally have a hard time not following the same prejudices, even though we've all renounced our ties to the old clans and sworn our lives to the Roterralar. A change of name does not really change what many feel is in our blood."

Lhaurel's shoulders slumped, and she looked down at her hands, one thumb idly tracing out a thin scar on the back of her other hand. "And if you revealed yourselves and the clans were still divided, suddenly all you'd have would be a bunch of children trying to use the adult's tools."

Khari nodded. "An astute observation. And then there is a question of the magic."

Lhaurel looked up.

"I believe that it is time we confronted that particular subject."

CHAPTER 11

Choices

"The joy of success and conquest makes the quill in my fingertips shake and tremble. The child, Briane, held the key. That beautiful, wonderful, blessed child. Her ideas. Her efforts. Her heart. They made this possible. The cause was worthy of our sacrifice."

-From the Journals of Elyana

Gavin continued to climb even though the pain in his arms was beyond the point of continued bearing. His hands were cut and bloodied, though still useable. His booted feet were still somewhat protected, but the goat hide leather was split in a dozen places and coming apart at the seams His shirt had been torn into strips to cover his hands when he'd found a small ledge to rest on partway up the cliff.

And still he climbed upward. Hunger gnawed at his stomach and exhaustion clouded his mind, but in the midst of the fog, a voice recounted ancient words, words that he had come to believe somewhere between the ground and where now climbed on the wall. His grandmother's words.

It was the final words of a long tale, his grandmother's favorite. It detailed the might and power of the greatest Warlord in legend and history. The one who had defeated the enemy. Questions had assailed him for many years after this story. Gavin remembered one night, camping out on the sands during the Dormancy, the light of the fire casting odd shadow against the dunes, asking his grandmother what had gone wrong. If Eldriean had defeated the enemy, then why were the genesauri still there? Had they come back? She'd smiled at him, a warm, special smile that so infrequently brightened her wrinkled face, and said, "Enemies come in all shapes and sizes, Gavin. Some from without and some from within. We must confront them both." Though he hadn't understood, he still remembered her words.

Enemies from without and from within. Had Eldriean had more enemies than just the genesauri? Had someone betrayed him? What answers lay atop the cliffs? These questions drove him, guided him onward as his grandmother's voice swelled once more within his mind. Someone had to find out the truth. Someone had to complete what had been started so long ago. The clans had to be united and the genesauri driven from the sands.

The sun set and rose again before Gavin made it to the top of the cliffs. Rest had come in the form of a small crevice discovered just as the sun had set. A pair of rashelta had been hiding there. Their shells had proven to be poor pillows. They had scuttled away when he'd forced himself into the space, finally relieving his aching muscles and broken skin.

He ate some food he'd carried with him. His body was too tired to eat much of it, but sleep had not come easily. Nightmares haunted him.

In the morning, he drank some brackish, dirty water he found pooling in the crevice and forced down the last of his food. He wished he'd brought more. As long as he was wishing, he might as well have wished for wings. But he resumed his climb anyway.

When his arm finally crested the top of the cliff and the ground felt flat beneath his broken, bloody skin, he was so wearied and tired that he didn't even realize it until he'd pulled half of his body up over the edge. He gasped his relief, his breath ragged and weak, and pulled himself all the way over the edge, scraping his chest without registering the pain. He lay there for what seemed like an eternity, staring into the sky and letting the sun bake the blood onto his skin. At some point, he slipped into blackness.

* * *

"Wait!" Lhaurel said, leaning back, "What about the genesauri? Do we know why they're awake early this year? What are we doing to stop them?"

"We?"

Lhaurel bit her lip, realizing that she had included herself as a member of the Roterralar. Well, she was now. At least, she thought she was.

"Yes, we."

Khari smiled. "We are conducting raids, killing those we can. We have patrols out trying to figure out the change in pattern and direction. We have not been idle."

"And?"

"And what?"

"What do we know?" Lhaurel's voice had a bite of impatience to it.

Khari raised an eyebrow at the tone but replied anyway. "What we know is that we don't know much. Now we must move on to your wetta training."

Lhaurel ground her teeth in frustration. It was obvious that Khari knew more than she was saying. So much for truly being a part of the Roterralar. What were the clans doing in the Oasis? Had the last two clans made it there safely? Makin Qays had said that they had been lost. Where were they? She opened her mouth, but Khari held up a hand.

"Enough, Lhaurel," she said. "Don't press me more right now. I know I told you that I would speak freely, but on this one area I am forbidden. Let us proceed with your lesson. Don't make me repeat myself again." The stern edge crept back into her voice, hardening along with her features.

Lhaurel huffed, but swallowed the question she had been about to ask. She wasn't giving up, but Khari's expression made it clear that she would get no further satisfaction if she pursued that line of questions. Lhaurel would simply have to figure out some other way of getting the information she needed.

"You are a wetta," Khari began. She slipped to the ground

and knelt in the sand in front of Lhaurel. All signs of her previous weakness had vanished completely. "The clans say that we mystics consort with demons and have magical powers that can change the world around us. Well, it is true. At least in so much as having gifts that can manipulate the world around us. Our demons are no more or less real than those of any others within the seven clans, though no less powerful or personal as the denizens of the seven hells. Those who can use these gifts are called mystics."

"Wetta." Lhaurel rolled the foreign word over on her tongue. The power didn't seem as frightening now.

"Don't interrupt me. A wetta is a specific type of mystic. Your gifts lie in the understanding and manipulation of water. Though the other two types of mystic have gifts that are more situated for military prowess, ours is by far the most important. For without water in the desert there can be no life."

Lhaurel silently agreed.

"Though they do not know it," Khari continued, "they could not survive without our wettas. It was wettas that found the warrens and their hidden springs and wells. Wettas that found this place, with its rich underground reservoir. And it was wettas that discovered the ocean on the other side of the sands far to the north of here."

Khari suddenly paused as if she had said too much. It was that, more than anything, which made Lhaurel suddenly realize what had been said.

"Wait," Lhaurel said. "The Sidena only moved to their new warren two years ago when their last spring dried up. Are you saying that—"

Khari cut her off. "Forget that I said that. We must focus on the lesson."

"But . . ."

"No," Khari said. "Suffice it to say that the wetta are more important than what the other mystics sometimes make us out to be. That's probably why there are so few of us. Regardless, you are a wetta. You've already shown your power twice before that we know about, both involving a broken waterskin and a rather annoying magnetelorium."

Lhaurel scowled, and Khari, upon noticing the expression, smiled.

"Yes, Kaiden can have that effect on people."

Lhaurel nodded grudgingly and tossed her head, her red locks cascading around her face.

"That's what we call a 'breaking.' When someone born with the ability to use the mystics' powers gets so mad or scared or elated that the barriers which hold the magic back are broken, those powers burst free in random, wild ways. In your case, the magic seized upon the closest water source, which was inside Kaiden's waterskin."

Lhaurel remembered the feeling of dread and nausea too well to refute what Khari was saying. She hadn't believed it when Kaiden had confronted her during the sandstorm, had refused to acknowledge the evidence that was, even at that moment, coursing through her veins. But she couldn't deny it any longer. She could feel the powers within her, just as she could feel the water reservoir deep beneath her and the presence of Khari and the other four score people that wandered through the massive labyrinthine warren.

"Our first lesson will be similar to our lesson with the sword. Practicing the basics. And the most basic place to begin with these gifts is becoming familiar enough with them to access them without having to be in an extreme emotional state."

Lhaurel sighed. She wasn't sure that she was going to enjoy having Khari as her trainer for both the sword and this.

Khari crossed her legs beneath her and then arranged her arms so that her forearms rested across her knees. She formed circles with her thumbs and forefingers and let her hands touch over her crossed feet. She nodded for Lhaurel to do the same.

Lhaurel shifted, copying the position.

"Close your eyes. Breathe in through your nose and out through your mouth. In and out. In and out. Good. Now, picture in your mind a puddle of water. Its surface is calm. Unbroken. Perfect. A drop of water falls onto the surface. It merges with the water, forming ripples. Travel with the ripples. Find the moment that they fade into the water's surface once more. That is the place where the power dwells."

Lhaurel gasped from the sudden shock as dread spread through her, clutched at her heart, and froze in her veins. No, not dread. She recognized it now. It was a cool, icy power that coursed through her blood, that pumped through her being with every beat of her frantic heart. She felt it there, burning, hungry, eager to explode from her in one enormous burst of fantastic might. And at the same time, she felt a calm hinting of endless patience and a careful storage of strength.

She opened her eyes.

The power vanished.

Khari stared at her with an expression of bewilderment on her face. "Well, that was . . . interesting," Khari said. She held a broken waterskin in her hand, the very waterskin that Lhaurel had taken from the worker women earlier.

Lhaurel breathed out, feeling suddenly drained. "How so?"

Khari held up the broken skin. "I was expecting something else. Most wetta, on their first true sojourn into their powers, pull the water from a skin and dissipate it to mist or else simply hold it in the air. When you reached out to the water, it simply exploded outward, as if it could no longer remain where it was."

"Meaning?"

"Meaning there's no control," Khari said bluntly. "There's only an ability to touch the water, but not to hold onto it."

Lhaurel sniffed again and pulled her knees up, wrapping her arms around them. She felt suddenly cold.

"Don't despair," Khari said, surprisingly tender. "You're new. Control comes to everyone with time."

Khari got to her feet and then helped Lhaurel up.

She felt weaker than she had expected, as if she had just done an exorbitant amount of work rather than explode a waterskin. And her powers seemed to have been dulled. Her sense of the warren was diminished, much less expansive than it had been before. She could only sense herself and Khari, whose presence had grown steadily stronger throughout the ordeal. Lhaurel could sense nothing within the eyrie. She found this discrepancy troubling.

A hesitant knock sounded at the door. Khari opened it, casting sunlight into the room.

Tieran stood highlighted in the doorway. He peered inside the room with a grin plastered on his face. "Lessons a little frustrating?" He winked at Lhaurel as if to say that Khari often got mad.

"Whatever do you mean, Tieran?" Khari asked. Her flat tone made his smile falter slightly, but he hitched it back up in an instant.

"Well, a moment ago all the water gourds shook so bad that we feared they would topple over. The aevians all flitted about as if they thought another sandstorm was coming. Kaiden and some of the others wanted to storm in here and find out what happened, but I just laughed and told them that you'd probably gotten mad at your ward. That was you just now, wasn't it?"

Khari's expression was all the answer he needed.

She turned to Lhaurel with a troubled expression on her face. "We really must focus on teaching you control. You will need to meditate each night. I will show you what to do."

Tieran interrupted her then. "That will need to wait. The reason that Kaiden and the others were in the eyrie just now is that they were looking for you and I. They have called a meeting of the senior warriors, and since Sarial is off on a patrol, Kaiden is to fill in for her. Makin Qays thought you'd want to be there, too."

"And we're already late," a cool voice said, bringing a sudden chill to the back of Lhaurel's neck. "We should be going."

Kaiden stepped up behind Tieran, looming over the shorter man. He wore a black leather vest and loose leggings. His eyes darted to the broken waterskin in Khari's hand and then to Lhaurel. He grinned at her, though the humor didn't reach his eyes. "Well, at least it's not my waterskin this time," he said. "Come along now, Khari, Tieran." Lhaurel wasn't invited. "We don't want to be late to this meeting. I think we've gotten word from contacts in the Oasis. There's news to report." He was taunting her.

"And what exactly should I be doing while you're all off chatting about the clans in the Oasis?" Lhaurel asked, trying to keep the biting edge out of her voice.

Kaiden shrugged. "You could go have words with your aevian. He seemed somewhat agitated when I walked over this way, and there was blood on his saddle. Yours?"

Lhaurel ignored the quip.

"Stay here in the eyrie," Khari said, shooting a glare at Kaiden. "Unsaddle Fahkiri and clean up your saddle. Then practice your stance until I come back."

Lhaurel rolled her eyes at the trio's retreating backs as they left. Kaiden glanced over his shoulder at her once and winked. She longed to chuck a rock at the back of his head. The man irritated her to the very core. And, at the same time, she felt guilty for being irritated.

She bit her lip and sighed. There was so much new information to process. Just when she got comfortable with one thing, something else was added. And what had Tieran meant about all the water gourds shaking? She was sure that she had been the cause—Khari had made that plain—but how had she done it? It had all happened too fast. And that meeting—what was it about? Who were these contacts in the Oasis? She longed to be able to hear what was going on. There were far too many secrets among the Roterralar.

She shook her head and walked into the eyrie, shooing the stubborn birds out of the way. Though even the smallest of their number was larger than she, the aevians parted before her. She paused for a moment at the water gourds, studying them for a moment before taking a swig of the cool, refreshing liquid. Nothing seemed any different about them than before. As she walked, she felt her powers returning to her as larger portions of the warren returned to her awareness. She could sense the aevians around her, sense the people moving around in the warren. The worker women that had been cutting steaks earlier had left, leaving her alone in the eyrie. She sensed Fahkiri to the northwest and turned in that direction.

She had only taken a single step when she suddenly froze mid-stride. She'd *sensed* Fahkiri? She'd never been able to tell one person's presence from another's before. But she was sure that it was Fahkiri that she felt. Her pace sped up. Yes, there he was, sharpening his beak on a rock, saddle stained along the pommel with her blood. She *could* pick out individuals.

Fahkiri noticed her and paused in the act of dipping his head back toward the rock. He straightened and eyed her beadily, clacking his beak and ruffling his feathers.

"What's wrong, Fahkiri?" She stepped toward him.

He clacked his beak and shuffled around so that his back was toward her.

She sighed and moved up to pull the saddle off his back. He stayed still long enough for her undo the two buckles that held the entire contraption on his back, but as soon as it came free, he scuttled away and launched himself into the air.

"What did I do?" she shouted after him.

The sound of someone clearing a throat made her turn. She had been focused on Fahkiri and hadn't noticed a young woman approach. Now, Lhaurel felt her presence as well as saw her.

"Can I help you?" Lhaurel asked, somewhat peevishly. She was annoyed with Kaiden and Fahkiri and more than a little confused by her unreliable skill with magic. The young woman, unfortunately, got the brunt of her frustrations.

The girl smiled at her, though it was a brief grin that only danced at the edges of her lips before fading. "He's just upset because you ignored him earlier when you stole my waterskin." She nodded in the direction Fahkiri had gone.

"I—well, um—Khari needed the—I can't return it. It sort of exploded." Lhaurel began.

"Oh, I'm not upset," the girl said with another quick grin. "It was an old waterskin anyway. I was just explaining. I know a good deal about the aevians. Sometimes people find my knowledge useful."

"I haven't seen you around before."

"Well, while you were in here the Matron kept all the riders busy with other things. Let me tell you, probably one of the worst days of my life. Slaving away atop the plateau for Kaiden and Skree-lar, ugh. That was unpleasant."

"What?" Lhaurel asked.

"Kaiden," the girl explained, rolling her eyes and lowering her voice conspiratorially. "He refuses to sleep in the greatroom with the rest of us. He sleeps atop the plateau. Something about how we could house the entire population of the clans within our warren but are simply choosing not to. He doesn't think we should be separated so much from them. So he chooses to sleep up top. He's gained quite a following. They have their own little camp up there and everything."

"So he's grumpy with everyone, then," Lhaurel said with a smile, "not just me."

"Not everyone, but almost everyone. He's nice to Sarial, but he probably has to be. She leads the mystics as a whole." The girl's grin matched Lhaurel's and then fell slightly, "Kaiden does have more cause to be irritable than some, I guess."

Lhaurel looked at her questioningly. The girl glanced around and then answered.

"Before he was a Roterralar, Kaiden was part of the Londik. Everyone thinks his clan is dead. Not all the Roterralar truly give up their old lives. I mean, some of us still have family among the clans. Or *had*, I should say."

Lhaurel didn't know what to say. Maybe there was more to the man. Maybe there was more to the Roterralar than what she'd thought. They remained aloof from the clans, hidden from sight and knowledge, while they still had family, friends, and connections among them. Lhaurel hadn't had that connection with her own clan. Well, maybe with Saralhn, but that was gone now. They must truly believe what they practiced in order to leave so many behind.

Lhaurel let the silence stretch almost to the point of being awkward before changing the subject.

"I always wondered why I never saw Skree-lar in the eyrie. But you were saying about Fahkiri?"

The girl smiled. "Like I said, your aevian is upset because you ignored him earlier. Just like any male, bring him some food, and he'll forgive you. I'd cut you up a nice sailfin steak, but they already picked clean the carcasses we have on hand. There's not another raid scheduled until tomorrow, so you'll just have to wait until then."

Lhaurel smiled at the girl's rambling, lilting tone. "I'll have to try that," Lhaurel said.

The girl smiled and gave Lhaurel a small bow, turning to leave.

"Wait," Lhaurel said. "The meeting that everyone was going to. Where is it being held?"

"Up in the council room, but it is only for the senior warriors." She noticed Lhaurel's confused look and added, "Those who have been around long enough to become cast leaders."

"Thank you," Lhaurel said vaguely.

The girl left.

Lhaurel waited a moment and then followed her. Dealing with Fahkiri's hurt feelings would have to wait until tomorrow anyway. She wanted to find out what was going on, and if past experience was any indication, they weren't about to simply tell her. She'd have to find the information for herself, which meant eavesdropping on the meeting. She couldn't tell when she'd decided to try and sneak in—probably when Kaiden had taunted her—but her mind was set.

CHAPTER 12
Division

"The news of this success will rekindle their hope. There is still much work to be done. Much work indeed. Size augmentation is the primary concern. Then multiplication.

"The work would move faster if Briane were here. She vanished on the eve of our our great success and has not yet returned."

-From the Journals of Elyana

"Someone should go and warn them."

Rhellion banged a fist down on the table, the sound reverberating in the small room. "Enough, Kaiden. You are here to fill in for Sarial, not rehash old decisions already made well before you were born."

Kaiden sat as far forward on his chair as he could without falling off. "Some of us are not so coldhearted as you," Kaiden said softly. "Some of us think that the old ways are not what you older gentlemen believe. The stories and legends speak of a time when all the desert people were one, not divided as we are now. On the eve of this crisis, it may warrant another discussion." He finished his words with a pointed look at Makin Qays, though the Warlord returned his look with impassivity.

"This is *hardly* a crisis," Rhellion retorted, picking up his glass of wine and sipping it carefully.

Makin Qays sniffed at the indulgence but didn't say anything. It was little wonder that the younger warriors, like Kaiden, were fond of the drink when their elders acted in much the same manner.

"The wall around the Oasis will hold the genesauri back, as it always has," Makin Qays said. "The marsaisi are much too large to fit through the narrow openings, and the sailfins are repelled by the strange magnetism the walls put off. You should know that better than most, magnetelorium."

Kaiden grimaced and opened his mouth to reply, but Khari placed a hand on his arm and he swallowed what he was going to say. He pushed back in his seat and slumped down, lowering his head and crossing his arms beneath his chest.

"What we need now is to gather more information," Khari said. "Strategy before tactics. The patrols are not back yet, and this news doesn't change anything. It only lets us know that the clans are at each other's throats. This isn't the first time. What we need is more information."

Kaiden shifted slightly in his chair, but said nothing.

"Agreed," Makin Qays said. "We will need to wait for the patrols to return before we can decide on any further action. If there are no further questions, I think this meeting is over."

* * *

Lhaurel darted around the corner just as the council room door creaked open. It had been surprisingly easy to sneak up to the council room. In fact, there hadn't been any need to do any sneaking at all. There hadn't even been any guards. These people were much more trusting than they should have been.

She dashed down the first side passage that broke off from the main hall she followed. Waiting there in shadow, she reached out to feel the presences of the senior warriors leaving the room. It was so easy now. She did it almost without thought.

They were all there, the senior warriors, moving down the larger passage back toward the long, wide passageway that Lhaurel had begun to start thinking of as the main artery through the Roterralar Warren.

Someone grabbed her arm, strong fingers wrapping around her

wrist and squeezing in tight.

"I knew you wouldn't be able to resist." Kaiden yanked on her arm and spun her around to face him, half drawing her sword.

"Let go of me!" Lhaurel demanded.

He released her with a smug expression, a look that appeared at home on his normally plain features. No . . . looking into his eyes at the moment, she decided that his features were far from plain. They certainly had nothing supremely distinctive about them, but it was more the expressions that so often frequented them that made the man forgettable. He was too unyielding, too stolid. But when he let true emotion show, like the smugness he now wore, then his features came alive. His face took on a depth that was memorable, if not truly handsome. And the memory of his standing over her with a shield during the sandstorm. That had been a moment of beauty.

"You set me up," Lhaurel said, massaging her wrist.

Kaiden shrugged. "Not all of us go as complacently as the Roterralar might think sometimes. I remember the fire in you when you were chained there on the rocks and left to die. I had to hold the chains down so you wouldn't break out of them on your own." He grinned.

Lhaurel grinned back. "You put me there."

"No, you put yourself there," he corrected, "I simply hastened your inevitable end and then saved you from it."

"You make it sound so noble. From where I was sitting, it was rather churlish."

Kaiden shrugged again.

The nonchalance left Lhaurel feeling suddenly irritated again. "Well, since you knew I'd be listening, why didn't you stop me? Why did you confront me alone instead of in front of everyone?"

And why didn't I sense you coming? She was loath to ask the question out loud. She wasn't about to let Kaiden know her inability to sense his approach irritated her if she didn't have to. He didn't need to know anything else he could use against her.

"Maybe I wanted you to hear."

"If you did, you would tell me what news you received, since I missed that first part."

Kaiden spread his hands wide and smiled. It really was a pretty smile when it was genuine.

"But of course. It seems that your husband has aspirations of power."

"He is *not* my husband."

"True, I believe your supposed death absolved you of that rather burdensome arrangement. Your Sidena Warlord has taken ill, and it's pretty clear who is behind it. Taren and the Warlord's wife are currently planning his demise so Taren can take over."

Lhaurel was silent for a moment. That Marvi would conspire against her own husband came as no surprise. Anyone who had ever lived among the Sidena and had more than half their wits knew that Warlord Jenthro had little in the way of leadership skills. The clan only survived by Marvi's efforts. The woman was devious and manipulative, which was the only reason that she had survived so long. Any other woman would have been stoned to death or strung up on the rocks for such impertinence. And most likely at Marvi's order. She was the harshest enforcer of the gender roles, though she violated them daily.

"What about the water oaths?" Lhaurel asked. "They forbid the normal succession duels. How are they going to pull it off?"

"So you're not surprised?"

"Marvi plot against her own husband? Taren wanting to be in charge? Are you surprised when the sun comes up in the morning? That's just the way they are. You didn't answer about the water oaths."

"That's right. I didn't. Probably because the information didn't say."

Lhaurel grimaced, but set that aside for the moment. "So what else was there? Why were you saying that someone needs to warn them? Warn them about what? What did you mean about the legends and stories talking about when we were all one people?"

"Do you ever stop asking questions?"

Lhaurel frowned. "Do you ever not answer a question with another question?"

"Well, the genesauri seem to all be headed directly toward the Oasis. None of those old fools thinks the clans should be worried.

Nothing I say can get any of them to see the danger. I *have* to figure out how to get them to take this threat seriously." He spoke with iron resolve. Lhaurel's half-formed response died before reaching her lips. She sensed someone approach. Someone familiar. She focused, trying to distinguish whom it was. Recognition hit her the moment before Khari rounded the corner. The short woman regarded them both with an expression that was either knowing or angry. Or both.

"Lhaurel," Khari said, ignoring Kaiden completely, "I have need of you tonight. Come with me, please. We have little time to ready ourselves."

Lhaurel looked from Kaiden to Khari and then back again, chewing her bottom lip. Kaiden rolled his eyes and walked away without a single word of parting, undermining any hesitancy Lhaurel had been feeling.

"What do you need?" Lhaurel asked, distracted.

Khari began talking, but Lhaurel only half listened. Her mind was elsewhere, following Kaiden's retreat even without being able to feel his presence.

Khari led Lhaurel back to her room to grab a red robe for each of them. Lhaurel felt odd wearing them, though they fit surprising well. Then Khari handed her a leatherwork belt inlaid with steel rings to replace the more ornate one Beryl had given her, and Lhaurel gladly belted her sword onto it.

"So what exactly do you need me to do?" Lhaurel asked for perhaps the dozenth time as she and Khari walked down the passageway toward the eyrie, red robes encircling them.

Khari groaned and rounded on her. "As I said before, I need to gather some information tonight. My informants don't know enough about us to even realize what questions to ask. I need someone who is familiar with the Sidena's current politics to help me find out where to prod and who to approach."

"But won't they recognize me?" Lhaurel asked.

"They think you're dead. They won't be looking for your face beneath a Roterralar hood. We survive through mystery and intrigue. The more mysterious you seem, the more likely it is that they will pay more attention to you. And the closer attention they pay to you as a Roterralar, the less likely they are to actually see *you*."

"Alright." *That didn't make sense at all.*

* * *

Gavin blinked and sucked in a long, ragged breath. Time returned with the sound of his beating heart.

Thump.

He tried to sit up, but his muscles refused to respond. He groaned, a weak, wet sound.

Thump.

He lay there for what seemed like an eternity, though by the count of his heartbeats it was far less than that. The sun beat down, warming the rocks upon which he lay and burning his exposed, bloody flesh. He had no idea how long he'd lain there, but it was long enough that a few carrion eaters, including a few rashelta, poked around near him without the slightest hesitancy.

He strained and struggled to rise, finally succeeding in rolling onto his stomach and then back onto his knees so that he could slip into a sitting position. His vision swam and a shock ran down his arm. The carrion-eaters scattered.

Slowly, his vision came into focus, coalescing on the red-grey rocks that formed the cliffs that encircled the Oasis. Heat radiated upward from the cliffs, giving the whole area a look of a mirage. The rock extended in a massive circle around the entire perimeter, stretching for miles along the circumference of the almost perfect circle. Though mostly flat, there were sections that had become broken and jagged where pieces of the cliff had broken. These ragged towers dotted the otherwise unbroken circle in several places, but the only true gap in the wall rested above the narrow canyon-like entrance to the Oasis, a few hundred spans to the south of Gavin.

Gavin groaned, low and pitiful, and brought his hands up to inspect the damage. They were a ragged, broken mess, some completely devoid of anything resembling flesh. He could still use them—they all bent and none of them were broken—but movement brought pain.

Why?

The question burned through the shock and the pain. What had driven him to such self-destructive actions?

Remember what it is that you have sworn to do.

It had been said that the end of the great and final battle against the enemy had been fought here, upon the cliffs. Literally on top of the plateau-like ring that protected them from the genesauri during the Migration. The stories claimed that what had happened atop the cliffs had brought them both salvation and destruction.

His grandmother had told him that his parents had died trying to discover the truth behind these stories. His father had tried to scale the cliffs more than once but had never completed the climb. The burden of discovery and proof now fell to Gavin. Somewhere atop these cliffs was the proof that he and his family had searched for for generations. Somewhere there were the answers that he sought.

Muscles screamed in protest as he struggled to get to his feet. Strength failed him and he stumbled and fell. He screamed, and his screaming gave him strength. A gust of wind whipped up around him, scattering dust and driving sand into his wounds. Teeth clamped together against the searing pain, Gavin rose to his feet, defying his weakened muscles and remaining standing on sheer will alone.

His grandmother's oaths pushed him onward . . .

. . . and something else. Something deep and primal within his very blood . . .

He took a step forward and then another, broken boots falling from his bloodied feet. He concentrated on the steps, counting each one as he walked, though never getting past two.

One, two. One, two. He walked.

After what seemed like an eternity, he tripped and sprawled out onto the rocks. He groaned and pushed himself to his knees, spitting out blood. He glanced back the way he had come, his path clearly marked by his jagged, bloody footsteps. His path was wayward, but he noticed, with a sudden discordant surge of pride, it retained its forward progression.

A small beetle scuttled across the rock near him. Without thinking, Gavin reached out and grabbed it between two stiff fingers. The pain was excruciating, but he didn't let go. He popped the insect into his mouth, ignoring the scuttling, flailing legs that kicked at his tongue. Chewing was painful, but he bit down on the hard shell, feeling a satisfying crunch as the bitter juices washed over his tongue. He'd never tasted anything quite so satisfying. He tried to stand up, but strength failed him. He needed rest and time to heal.

The sun rose and fell three times before Gavin had the strength to move with the speed and alacrity he was used to. There were plenty of beetles and small crab-like creatures to sustain him, though the diet was bland. Water came in shallow pools near the Oasis side of the walls. His hands had healed, so the pain was only a dull ache. The sun rose over the Forbiddence, barely visible from his current vantage, warming the rock.

He popped a beetle into his mouth and chewed.

He swallowed and pushed himself up to his feet, stifling a groan. His grandmother's voice drifted across his memory, recounting the stories of his youth. It gave him strength. The wind whipped at his brown hair streaked with red, tossing it around his face where it wasn't plastered to his scalp by dried blood and dirt. The wind smelled of dust and heat and blood.

He took a step forward and then stopped. On the other side of the Oasis walls, something glinted in the early morning light. An outcropping of rock jutted out from the otherwise flat surface of the plateau. Something glinted at its apex. How had he not noticed it before?

It took him the better part of the morning to circumnavigate the top of the Oasis wall, eyes constantly straining to try and make out what was reflecting the light. When he was close enough to see what it was, the sight made him halt. A sword was thrust into the rocks, part of the blade and the hilt remaining exposed to the elements. And there was something at its base. He resumed his walk, though more quickly than he'd gone before.

The dull white thing took shape as he neared. A skeleton, ancient and broken. It lay against the red sandstone, limbs sprawled out as if it had fallen from a great height. The blade was thrust through the broken ribs exactly where the heart would have been.

Gavin studied it, fascinated. The proportions were off. The person would have stood over seven feet tall and, judging from the thickness of the bones, been a massive behemoth of a man. And the skull was odd. The head was more narrow and pinched at the front than he had expected and the teeth—they had been filed to points, like the fangs of a genesauri.

"This can't be Eldriean," Gavin said aloud, wonderingly. He stepped closer, his movements coming more fluidly than they had been before. He reached out and laid a bloodstained hand on the sword's hilt. The sword toppled free with a crunch of rock. Gavin struggled to catch it before it fell, his fingers protesting the abuse. He grabbed the sword hilt as the ground beneath his feet gave way, and he fell into darkness with a terrified scream.

He hit hard. He heard something break, though he couldn't tell if it was one of his bones or his entire body. He coughed, spitting up blood and phlegm as dust poured down around him and chunks of broken rock hit the floor.

Somehow he'd maintained his grip on the sword. It seemed lighter than he had expected.

When the dust settled and the rocks stopped falling from the crumbling mess of sandstone above, Gavin used the sword like a cane to support himself. He struggled to his feet. Nothing felt broken, but beneath the pain from the wounds he had already sustained, it was altogether possible that he had broken any number of bones and simply couldn't feel it. Regardless, nothing was damaged enough to keep him from walking, though his movements were slower again.

"This is for you, Nana," he said, to give himself strength. "There *was* something up here. You were right . . . you were right." His voice echoed strangely in the chamber.

He looked up, noting the distance he had fallen, only a few spans. The sword must have extended down into this hollow chamber beneath the skeleton, slowly weakening it until Gavin's light touch on the hilt caused the whole section to collapse. Thankfully, the cliff itself hadn't fallen.

He stepped forward and something crunched under his foot. Bones, he realized, looking down. The behemoth's bones. That was what he had heard breaking. Ancient, brittle, and bleached by ages in the sun, the bones were now little more than dust and jagged white flecks mixed in with the red and grey sandstone.

He pressed his hands against the sides of the wall, searching for purchase, but found nothing. It was too smooth, too polished. Like glass.

It *was* glass. It lined the inner walls in a thin sheet. It was a startling discovery, one that made him re-assess the nature of this cave. This wasn't a natural structure. It had been made by human hands.

That meant that there had to be an exit somewhere. He felt his pulse quicken. There was more here to be discovered. As he shuffled forward, coughing as dust entered his lungs, he wished that his grandmother and parents could have been here to discover this with him. They were still with him in memory, but he longed for their physical presence by his side.

Eventually, he found the expected exit, hidden in shadow at the far end of the chamber. He paused a moment to gain his strength, leaning against the greatsword, and then stepped into the darkness.

* * *

Beryl closed his eyes and reached out with his senses, selecting a large block of metal and pulling it toward him. The cold, grey lump of hardened steel rose out of the bin as if in defiance of gravity's laws, floating through the air toward where Beryl waited. His eyes remained closed. He didn't bother stoking the flames of the forge. He really didn't need to, though at times the physical turmoil of forge work was a boon to his troubled, crowded mind. His work lay scattered across the desert, like the grains of the sand itself, but this weapon would be different. This weapon he made because he wanted to, not because he was bidden.

This girl, this Lhaurel—she was different. Khari and Makin Qays had visited him earlier, both congratulating themselves on another successful breaking. One of the voices told him they were wrong. It was the voice of someone he had once been, someone from long ago.

"'They think the girl is broken.' He whispered in response to that voice. "The sandstorm, Kaiden, the trauma, it only widened the cracks. She's not broken yet. No, it takes a more complex breaking to open up complex magic."

He remembered his own breaking like a distant echo. Even after all the other memories had faded, that one was as fresh and poignant as if it had occurred just yesterday.

"How long must I be the weapons maker?" he asked.

He raised his hands before him, flecks of metal in his skin reflecting the light, and gestured at the block hovering in the air before him. It *shifted*. The metal began to elongate and flatten, manipulated by the will of one who was as old as the metal he worked and twice as hard.

"The curse." He spat, willing the metal to thin more. "Why must they keep fighting? Isn't there enough death? Why must I keep giving them more weaponry? Why don't they ask where the weapons come from—where the fuel comes for the fires?"

He knew the answers.

"They were the dregs of society to begin with. And the slaves. They are the lesser children of a greater father." He shuddered, memories playing through his mind like flashes of lightning in a storm.

The metal he was working shimmered and warped for a moment, but a simple gesture smoothed out the transmuted edge and the work continued.

How long would his torment continue? He'd been the first thrown into this desert, this eternal hell. He was the first of the lesser lords. The first magnetelorium. Did any of these remember their ancient heritage? No. Of course they didn't. It was lost to them, lost in memory and legend. The outcasts, those crossbreed mutants now so interbred that the original purpose of the imprisonment was lost to them, they still told some of the stories. Twisted and warped versions of them, but at least that was something. But these Roterralar, those here to protect the others, they didn't understand a hundredth part of what they thought they knew. Not even when they sat upon the very spot where it all began. Not even then. Thanks to Elyana and the genesauri.

"Oh Elyana," he said, voice soft and eyes still closed.

The hilt formed on the sword, and the cross guard flattened and formed to separate the hilt from the blade.

"You will never know what you caused. When you created your *salvation*, did you understand what you were doing to this people? Did you know what effects it would have?"

Her cause had been just, and it had performed its intended purpose, though Beryl wondered if it was perhaps just a delaying of the inevitable. The enemy had been driven back, but a new one took its place. How was this any better? And when the current enemy was removed, how long before the old one returned? The Sharani were a doomed people, imprisoned in their desert without any idea of what went on beyond the Forbiddence that enclosed the sands. In truth, Beryl no longer remembered, either. Those memories were foggy things, lost to the annuls of time and history. Yet he had been here before the desert, been here before the crimson scourge had made a sport of this all.

Things were changing. Beryl could feel it. It had started with the genesauri shifting their hibernation pattern. But that was only a beginning. This was only a part of a larger whole. Things had been set in motion that were simply better left undone. The world was about to change. The girl, Lhaurel, she reminded him of times past.

Beryl closed his hands, blade finished, and the weapon dropped from the air to bury itself in the sand, point first. Another blade completed. Another sword made to kill Rahuli. He was about the task appointed him, the same task for which his life had been spared.

He laughed suddenly, a strange, short bark. It was the laughter of a broken man, a man whose existence and sanity danced on the edge of a knife. The laughter of a man doomed to eternal creation and eternal damnation. He was a bringer of death, a supplier of the implements of destruction.

A quick swipe crumpled the sword into a useless lump of metal once more, flinging it back into the bin.

The laughter that followed did little to hide the wet streak of a tear slipping down his cheek.

Then the metal lump rose and began forming itself into a sword again. He'd lost track of how many times he'd fashioned this sword. Maybe a dozen or so this morning. Twice as many yesterday.

He laughed and then shrugged, pushing aside the despair and

emotion welling within him. For now, he would allow himself to be simply Beryl, the smith. For now, he could forget the pain and the madness. Beryl opened his eyes and pulled on the bellows, stoking the fire. This time he would do it the mundane way. Maybe he could ignore the voices then. Maybe this time he could ignore the small part of him that was screaming.

CHAPTER 13
Shifting Sands

"My work is taking a toll on me. Sleep greets me with the echoes of children screaming. When awake, the dreams linger, the echoes giving me an anxiety which slows the progress we so desperately need. But Briane was right. The cause is worthy of the sacrifice. I must fight on."
-From the Journals of Elyana

It had taken much more than a simple bribe to get Fahkiri to come down from his roost. By the time Lhaurel climbed up to him and not only apologized but also begged for him to come down, Khari was ready to simply leave her behind. But the aevian had eventually relented and allowed Lhaurel to saddle him and clip her own harness into place on his back. They had managed to launch from the eyrie's cavernous opening an hour before sunset and wing their way southward.

Lhaurel loved the thrill of flight, but her racing heart was filled with a small measure of trepidation. Her harness was completely secured, but she rode more stiffly in the saddle now, clutched more tightly onto the pommel. She didn't want to repeat the terrifying plummet that had happened earlier.

Khari's aevian had been none other than Gwyanth, Fahkiri's mother, though there didn't seem to be any familiar love between the two anymore. Gwyanth was as cold and distant towards Fahkiri as her rider was to Lhaurel.

Khari pushed them hard through the blazing sun, though as high up as they were in the air, the heat was bearable, even in their long robes.

Lhaurel scanned the red sands below them. The evidence of sailfins passing was everywhere. Small piles and depressions dotted the sands, like pockmarks on an old man's face. The wind was slowly filling them in, but even the relentless wind needed time to erase so many. Lhaurel shuddered at the memory of the Sidena Warren, destroyed by only a small sailfin pack.

She shifted her gaze as Fahkiri climbed a little higher on a gust of wind. Kaiden was right about where the monsters were headed. The pits and piles of sand pointed in the same direction they flew, straight toward the heart of the Sharani desert, the Oasis. Eventually the evidence stopped, showing where the sailfins had stopped to rest or whatever it was they did when they weren't on the move.

Lhaurel scanned the ground, hoping to spot a fin or two poking up out of the sand or evidence of a marsaisi—she'd never seen one, only heard the tales—and almost missed the large depression in the sand. A long, wide pit cut through the dunes, stretching for over a hundred spans in width and over twice that in length. A genesauri nest? She made a mental note to ask Khari when they landed.

Before too long, the high stone walls of the Oasis appeared on the horizon, and Khari signaled that they were to land with a sharp whistled pattern that she had taught Lhaurel in the Roterralar eyrie. Lhaurel held on tightly as they descended, though she felt Fahkiri shift before he dipped into his dive and was ready for the gut-wrenching fall and sudden stop. She still rocked forward at the sudden change of direction, but not far enough to snap the safety lead or slam her face into the pommel, which was already stained with her blood.

Lhaurel unclipped the harness and dropped to the sands, her feet sinking a few inches into the loose, red-grey terrain. They were still a hundred spans away from the Oasis. She'd forgotten how much she hated walking in the loose sands of the desert. The warren floors were all coated in a thin layer of sand, true, but beneath it was solid rock. In the dune fields and outside of the stoneways, the sand had nothing beneath it except for more sand, where each step forward also included several inches of sliding backwards and down.

"What was that massive depression back there?" Lhaurel asked, checking her sword.

Khari slid down off of Gwyanth's back with more grace than Lhaurel could have ever mustered, though the woman's face was dark and brooding. She landed and bent at the knees to absorb the blow, her red robes billowing up around her for a moment and exposing form-fitting tan leggings beneath. Khari checked her sword and divested herself of the leather riding harness before responding. "That is trouble." She pulled out a waterskin and took a small mouthful. "The depression is made when a kalundin, the third type of genesauri, breaks the surface of the sands."

Lhaurel's eyes widened. "A kalundin?"

Khari glanced back over the sands where they had come. She rubbed the palms of her hands against the sides of her robes, shoulders hunched. "There's only the one. That point where the two paths crossed—we see them from time to time during Migrations. From what we can tell, the kalundin eats the sailfins."

"The whole pack?"

"In one go."

Lhaurel swallowed, her mouth dry. Something that large could devour an entire clan. Something that large could destroy the Oasis on a whim. Maybe the Roterralar were right to remain hidden.

"What's it look like?"

Khari shrugged and turned back to face Lhaurel, expression more firm. "No one knows. We've never been able to see it, just the evidence of its passing."

Lhaurel swallowed vainly again and then took out her waterskin and took a small sip. "So what now?"

"Now we head into the Oasis, where I'll meet with my contacts. I'll tell Makin Qays about the karundin when we return. We'll be gone from here first thing in the morning." Khari tossed her harness up Gwyanth's back and attached some of the leads to keep it in place. As she did so, the sleeve of her robes pulled back, exposing the tattoos on her wrists and forearms. Lhaurel puzzled over them as she copied Khari's actions, removing her harness and stowing it on Fahkiri's back.

Lhaurel wondered whom the woman had lost.

The short woman took a few steps back in the sand, cursing softly as she stumbled on the loose footing. Lhaurel walked up next to her and the woman let out a shrill dismissive whistle. Their two aevians launched into the air, winging their way toward the setting sun.

"I'll call them when we're ready to leave in the morning," Khari said, and she turned to walk toward the Oasis. Lhaurel hurried after her, half tempted to take out her sword to use as a walking staff to aide her in climbing the slippery sides of the dunes. The thought was discarded as quickly as it entered her mind. The sword, even a loaned one, was worth far more than any discomfort she experienced walking through sand.

Khari seemed to have almost no trouble at all moving through the sands. Her steps were light and springy, barely leaving an impression on the sand. By comparison, Lhaurel moved with the grace of a sailfin.

"Why are we doing this, Khari?" Lhaurel called.

"We protect the clans as best we can. That's our job. We assail the genesauri, protect them during the Migration, etc."

"So I've been told." Lhaurel said.

"Well, that's only part of it. We also watch out to make sure that the clans survive themselves *and* the desert. There wouldn't be much use for us if the only things we could do for the clans were during the Migration. We try and help steer them politically and, when necessary, we help them find places to live and ways to adapt to this ever-changing environment. In a way, we are their guardians and protectors."

"Yes, as if the Roterralar are the parents of all the clans," Lhaurel interjected.

"In some things, perhaps, but in many ways we are more like the child than the parent. The Roterralar are formed from the other seven clans. They are a part of us and we are a part of them. You, for example, were once part of the Sidena." Khari paused for a moment and hiked up one of her sleeves. The banded tattoos stood out on her skin, though all were older, faded. "Just as many small streams joining together forms a river, so too do the seven clans join together in us."

"What does that have to do with the tattoos?"

"Even those of us who were born a Roterralar have relatives or ancestors who were once a part of the seven clans. They are our fallen family. When we swear fealty to the Roterralar, we renounce our ties to the clan that gave us birth and we cement our ties to all the clans. Each color represents a particular clan, the width of the band the number lost. When we go out to protect and defend, we remember those who we were unable to save. Each member of the party has at least one new band to add. We track back and count the number of the dead each time. None of them are forgotten if we can help it.

"Makin told me what you said to him. How you called us all cowards. Perhaps we are, but not for the reasons that you called us such. If we are cowards it is because we do not have the strength to let them survive as nature and fate see fit. Perhaps we are cowards because we seek to postpone that which is inevitable."

Lhaurel rankled at the words, slogging through the sand to grab Khari by the shoulder and spin her around. "Nothing is inevitable if you fight it. Yes, the clans fear the genesauri Migration, and there are those who die. But our people die defending them, allowing them the freedom to live as best they can."

Khari smiled, ignoring Lhaurel's grip on her shoulder. "That, Lhaurel, is called duty. Often the price of freedom is someone else doing their duty. These bands," she said, holding up her arms and shaking the sleeves down to show the tattoos, "remind us why we get up every morning to do our duty and protect this people. Even if those who find out about us think us cowards." She softened the last remark with a wink and then firmly removed Lhaurel's grip from her shoulder and resumed her walk.

Lhaurel stood still a moment, lost in thought, before hurrying after Khari. There was still much about the Roterralar that Lhaurel didn't fully understand or agree with, but she was beginning to realize that much of what they did was steeped in rich traditionalism and duty. They were a people fighting to protect as best they could with the resources that they had available. She wasn't sure if she agreed with or even understood why they kept themselves aloof from those they were protecting, but they were doing what they did for a reason. They weren't overtly unkind; they were simply performing their duty in the best way they knew how. And that, above all else, was something that Lhaurel could understand.

The walls of the Oasis grew larger as they neared. Lhaurel had been inside the protective embrace of those enormous walls, but something was different this time. She could sense something coming from the walls. Almost a presence, like she could feel off the Roterralar except with Kaiden and Khari on occasion, but somehow *different*.

As they neared the cliffs, the sense intensified. There was something ominous to it, something not quite right. It made the hair along her arms stand on end and sent shivers through her bottom lip. She bit it to keep the quivering from showing.

They approached the narrow canyon that led into the hidden lushness of the Oasis. Lhaurel cringed away from the sickly sweetness that exuded from the walls.

Khari turned to her. "Pull your hood up," she whispered. "And stay quiet. No matter what."

When Lhaurel had done so, the matron of the Roterralar entered the narrow opening without any trace of hesitation in her step.

Lhaurel followed much more slowly. It wasn't just the feeling of wrongness that came from off the walls. The pathway they walked was narrow, barely wide enough for them to walk through without their shoulders touching the rough sandstone. Lhaurel remembered years where some of the cattle, large, well-fed beeves that had grown fat in the relative safety of the warrens, had been unable to fit through some of the narrow passageways and had to be slaughtered and carried through in pieces.

It was a hard enough passage in full daylight, with the sudden twists and turns. It was twice as difficult a task in the semidarkness. There was something else, too, besides the cloying claustrophobia of the narrow canyon. Lhaurel, suddenly free to do many of the things she had wanted so desperately to accomplish in her youth, was walking back into the arms of her original tormentors. People who had literally sentenced her to death.

Ahead of her, Khari cursed. "Damn rashelta."

Lhaurel paused when another voice, a deep male one, spoke up in response to the outburst. She hadn't sensed his presence beneath the overwhelming sense of foreboding that surrounded her.

"Halt! Identify yourself!"

Flint sparked in the darkness, and a torch crackled to life. The flickering orange flame threw the speaker, an older man bearing a large spear and with a sword girded at his waist, into sudden relief. He stood directly in their path, blocking their way. He squinted at them, unable to make out much until his eyes adjusted to the sudden brightness. His furrowed brow stuck out over his eyes like fronds on a coconut tree.

"Oh, you," he said when his eyes had adjusted fully. "What do you want? We ain't had any wandering types here in the Oasis in seven years. What is going on now? Bringing more ill tidings, are you? Come on now, speak up."

"We come seeking shelter. That is all." Khari said. "We will be gone in the morning."

"A woman?" the old man said, voice incredulous, "Well, I'll be a sun-crazed fool. I never seen a woman Roterralar afore. Shelter, you say? Well, I reckon that won't be too hard to find around here. So long as you don't go stealing anything during the night."

"You can't let Roterralar into the Oasis." Another voice cut in from behind the old man. "We've bad enough luck as it is without bringing in the bad fortune they will give us."

The first man turned, shouting back at the other guard behind him. "They're women. What harm will it do? I'm letting them in, so get outta the way back there."

"Thank you, sir," Khari said with a slight bow when the older man turned back to gesture them forward.

"Name's Honric, and I'll not leave a woman out for the genesauri, Roterralar or not. Just promise me that you won't do anything—well, anything unnatural tonight. Alright?" The tone of his voice was almost pleading, something that Lhaurel had not expected to hear from any man.

It felt odd to be standing there, in Roterralar robes, being the object of suspicion and discomfort. And yet she knew now it was justified. The Roterralar were a strange people with many secrets. But not the kind these men believed.

"On our honor, Honric," Khari said.

They followed him down the narrow passage, his torch casting odd shadows.

"You must forgive Shelton," Honric said, his voice echoing slightly against the rocks. "He's superstitious, and with everything going on, he's got every right to be. We're all a might nervous."

"What's happening? Besides the genesauri, of course. That was the worst of all luck this year, I'd say." Lhaurel smiled beneath her hood, though it was wan.

"Well, I have it on good authority that there's a new Warlord among the Sidena, see. The old one up and died all of a sudden. I never met the man, seeing as I'm Olarin myself, but I've got a friend of a friend who knows some of the Sidena women, see. And they told me that the old one, he wasn't old exactly, you know, just saying that he was the old one 'cause there's a new one now—anyway, they told me that this old one went to bed last night and didn't wake up again this morning. He was all stiff as a water-logged cactus, if you'll pardon the expression, and with lips as blue as the water from the springs here. And his wife, the Matron, she found him like that when she woke up the next morning. Wailed for hours, so I hear. How do you figure that if not for bad luck? Just up and died in his sleep. No one knows what to make of them blue lips, neither. Leastwise no one is saying anything."

Lhaurel was taken aback at the torrent of words. The more passionate that Honric got, the faster the words came out and sort of slurred together. All that Lhaurel had understood out of it was that the old Warlord, Jenthro, was dead and a new one had taken his place. Did that mean that Taren was the new Warlord?

"That is bad luck," Khari agreed. "And they replaced him already?"

"Aye, that they did." Honric said with a nod. "They held a big vote, so I hear. Seeing as the water oaths forbid the shedding of blood in the Oasis, I guess a vote is as good a way as any to decide who's going to lead a person. Some fellow called Taren is the new Warlord."

Taren was the Warlord now. Lhaurel suppressed a small shudder.

"Will you shut up already, Honric?" Shelton's voice echoed from ahead of them. "You don't need to tell them all this. For the love of water, man, they're Roterralar! They'd as soon use what you just told them against us like as not. You're a foolish old man."

"That I may be," Honric shouted back, "but I can still best the likes of you and yours any day. So quit your whining and move along before I shove my spear up your skinny arse."

Lhaurel stifled a weak laugh.

Honric turned to glance back over his shoulder at Khari, an apologetic look on his wrinkled face. "Pardon me for the language," he said. "That fellow is a bit of a fool. I didn't want him to sit watch with me, but you know, orders is orders. What was I supposed to do except let him tag along?"

"You are a good and obedient soldier, Honric," Khari said, patting the man on the shoulder. "I'm sure that fortune will place water and shade in your path throughout your life."

"He's just a little jumpy, see. These younger warriors don't know how to ride out the tension. They want to react to everything. Always got an answer, they do. Take the two missing clans, for example. Me, I figure they's just late, or else managed to hole up inside their warrens. It's been done before, see. They're high enough up, some of them, that they could do it. But clans are nervous. Most of these here are young. They think that the genesauri got them all, the whole clan." Honric shrugged. "Well, maybe they did, but that doesn't affect us here. Life goes on in the Oasis. There's no use fretting over it if there's nothing to be done about it."

Two missing clans? Both Makin Qays and Tieran had mentioned that there were two clans that hadn't yet made it to the Oasis, but she had forgotten about it. She had just assumed that they had made it eventually. It had been almost three fortnights since Kaiden had arrived in the Sidena Warren and upended the life of the clan. Surely something must be known about them.

"So you've not heard anything from them? Not even by pigeon?" Khari asked. Her voice seemed off-hand, only mild curiosity mingled with politeness driving her to keep the conversation going. But Lhaurel noticed the tension of her shoulders, the slight tilt of her head. The woman had expected something different, hoped for better news.

"Not a word. Leastways, nothing that anyone has told me. My

clan isn't too close with either of the two missing clans, see. Maybe some of the others would know better than me. Ah," he said, gesturing broadly, "here we are."

The narrow canyon walkway ended abruptly, as narrow at the terminus as it was where it began. Some of the omnipresent oppression from the cliffs faded. It was too dark to see much outside of the small pool of light provided by Honric's torch, but Lhaurel sensed vast amounts of water and thousands of people arrayed in camps in the space ahead of her. It smelled of life and the sharp musty smell of wetness and dirt.

"We thank you for your kindness, Honric," Khari said, placing a hand on his arm. "We will go our way now and let you get back to your watch."

Honric grinned. "It was nothing. Come on, you."

Shelton stood at the edge of the torchlight, hidden in shadow. He grumbled something unintelligible but followed Honric back into the canyon. Lhaurel sensed him go and then hesitate once he was far enough into the passage to not be seen. Honric moved on, taking the torchlight with him.

"Where to, Lhaurel?" Khari asked. "We need to get to the Sidena camp."

Lhaurel didn't answer immediately. She could sense the sullen man creeping slowly closer. She bent down and felt the ground until her hand found a small rock. In one smooth motion, Lhaurel stood and hurled the rock back into the narrow canyon. She smiled when a yelp suddenly sounded from the darkness.

Khari spun toward the sound, sword half out of her sheath.

"Don't worry," Lhaurel said. "He's leaving."

"How can you tell?" Khari asked.

Lhaurel hesitated. "I can sense him leaving."

"You can sense him? So he's a mystic? Odd, I don't sense him at all."

Lhaurel almost chuckled. "I don't think so. Mystics feel different," she said, realizing the difference for the first time, "like the difference between salt and fresh water."

"You're telling me you can sense *everyone*?" Khari's voice was incredulous. She sheathed her sword, the sound a slick hiss of metal on leather.

"Yes. You said that one of the abilities of a wetta is locating people."

"Not people, mystics. Normal wetta can only sense mystics. They can't sense everyone. How long have you been able to do this?"

"Since the day after the sandstorm," she said, "but it's not constant. Sometimes I can sense everyone and sometimes I can't." Lhaurel shrugged and glanced back down the canyon one last time.

Khari muttered something that Lhaurel didn't catch but then spoke up more loudly. "So, which way to the Sidena camp?"

Lhaurel pointed to the northeast and then realized that the gesture was meaningless in the darkness, so she simply started walking in that direction. Khari followed.

Though it was dark, their eyes quickly adjusted to the little light offered by the stars and the edge of the moon that poked up over the top of the Oasis cliffs. Lhaurel led the way, careful to skirt the guards of the two clans whose territory they had to pass through in order to reach the section that was controlled by the Sidena. Though Khari didn't say anything, Lhaurel could tell that she was troubled. The information the talkative old Honric had given them was certainly cause for concern. Taren was Warlord. Two clans were still missing.

Lhaurel swallowed and refused to let herself be cowed. The ground sprang up beneath her feet. She breathed in the sweet pungencies of earth and plants. She'd always loved the Oasis, and compared to life within the Roterralar Warren, it was even more beautiful now. Lhaurel stopped next to a narrow stream that bisected a section of meadow abutting the Oasis walls. Though she couldn't see it well, it was enough to recognize the boundary of the Sidena territory. She could make out the tiny pinpricks of light to the east that marked their camp.

"The camp is over there," she whispered.

The area was surprisingly devoid of guards. Lhaurel couldn't sense anyone closer than the edge of the camp in the distance. Something registered this fact as discordant in the back of her mind.

"Good. Well, then, who should I approach?" Khari asked, stretching and suppressing a stiff yawn.

Lhaurel thought a moment and then came up with the only name she could honestly recall. "You can try Ami. She had a daughter about my age who was the only one in the clan that I was somewhat close to. She'll probably talk, given enough encouragement."

"As good a place to start as any. You stay here—and stay out of sight. Hide if anyone comes. At the very least, don't do anything stupid like try to run away on me. I spent long hours talking Makin into letting you come with me. Please don't make me regret this."

"He didn't want me to come?"

Khari didn't answer. Instead she turned and walked off toward the distant lights.

CHAPTER 14
Trembling

"How does an ant rise to the challenge of defending its colony from the threat of invasion? How does it defend itself from the booted heel that crushes it?

"A multiplicity of numbers. Soldiers. Unity

"But what if the ant became suddenly a larger thing? Able to fight against the boot and win as an individual? What then? Would the colony's ability to swarm then make it so that all booted heels would cease to crush their kin? I think so. And if we harness this strength?"

-From the Journals of Elyana

The stars shone in the sky far above, twinkling like fires on a distant sea of black. Lhaurel lay on her back in the thick green grass, gazing up at them. There were so many of them. The Oasis afforded an unobstructed view of the sky, which allowed her to bask in the glory of the various night scenes and constellations. Her favorite, a group of three stars that some called the "witch's *shufari*," shone like a beacon in the western sky. The moon was only half formed, resting just above the rim of the wall.

Lhaurel breathed out a long sigh of contentment. After the confinement of the Roterralar Warren, the open air was a welcome relief and afforded her a sense of freedom. Freedom from the Roterralar; freedom from this new life that had been thrust upon her; freedom from strife and stress and pain. This was the sort of night she lived for.

She stifled a yawn.

Khari had been gone a long time. Lhaurel could sense her, vaguely, intermingled with a number of people within the Sidena camp. As with Fahkiri, Lhaurel found that she could pick out Khari's presence from the others with only a little more focus.

Khari could spend all night speaking with the Sidena for all that Lhaurel cared. She tilted her head back and closed her eyes, sighing in contentment. Water dripped somewhere, lulling her toward sleep and forcing her thoughts more deeply adrift.

Someone approached where she was laying. She sensed them before she saw them. One of them was far larger than the other, and the other one was being pulled along behind them. The smaller figure stumbled and fell. The larger one bent down and made a sharp motion with one hand. Even from where Lhaurel stood, she heard the sharp crack of flesh striking flesh. Then shouts came.

"Get up, woman," the larger one, a man, shouted. "Get on your feet before I have to drag you myself."

Another sharp crack sounded, and the smaller figure was tossed to one side as she tried to rise.

"You're a lazy, worthless creature," the man shouted. "I don't know how I ever let Taren talk me into marrying you. With as many times as I have bedded you, a decent woman would have let my seed take root and given me a son. And now I know why. Consorting with Roterralar. You've cursed yourself and my seed. Worthless."

The woman crawled on all fours, head sagged toward the ground and sobbing in short, pained bursts.

"I should rid myself of you now," the man said. He pulled his leg back to kick the woman at his feet.

In that moment, Lhaurel lived in memory. Once again she stood before the women of the Sidena, feeling their eyes upon her and demanding that they stand up for her. She looked into their phantom eyes, and this time, she didn't see a lack of emotion. Instead she saw her own questions reflected in their eyes. Where was she when they were being abused? Where was she when they were forced into marriages that they had not wanted? She had been as silent and shaken as they.

The foot never fell.

Lhaurel didn't know how she suddenly made it to where the man was. Perhaps she had already started running while he had been busy yelling. Perhaps he took a lot longer to ready himself to kick out than a normal person did. Regardless, Lhaurel found herself in between the man and the sobbing woman. Her sword glittered in the moonlight, the tip bouncing with the slight trembling of her fingers. Her power coursed through her, summoned by her anger. It burned in her blood, clutched at her heart, and froze in her veins. The wind whipped her robes up around her, enshrouding her in a halo of red cloth.

"If you touch her," Lhaurel said, her voice thick with anger, "I will kill you."

The man gulped, looking down at the blade dancing just beneath his chin. Then his face hardened. "How dare you draw your sword against me," he said in a snarl. "Do you know who I am? We'll never let another of your kind into the Oasis."

The earth seemed to tremble beneath her. The blood pounding in her veins turned icy. The hand holding the sword steadied. She could feel the blood swirling through her body, could feel it swirling through *his* body. For years she had been what this woman was now, chastened by the Warlord for acting in a way different than a proper young woman should, punished by Marvi, abused and tormented and tortured for years. But she was no longer powerless. Now she had the sword and the power. The blade inched closer, drawing a thin line of blood that dripped down the man's neck like a scarlet bead of sweat.

"I think," a voice said softly, "that you should leave, warrior."

Khari stepped out of the shadows into a pocket of moonlight, her sword in hand.

The man grumbled something but raised his hands and took a step back.

Lhaurel reached out a quick hand and snagged a part of his shirt. He tried to pull away, but Lhaurel's grip was strong, stronger than even she expected. She stepped up to him, pulling him down so that she could whisper in his ear. Her sword was pressed against his side.

"If you touch her again, I will know. I will find you. And I will kill you."

She shoved him away, sending him staggering back with an expression of terror on his face. He scrambled to his feet and dashed into the night, his presence fading.

Lhaurel turned back to Khari, her blood still pounding, but Khari wasn't where she'd been. She was on the ground, holding the woman as she sobbed.

"Stop that, Lhaurel," Khari said. "You're scaring her."

"Stop what?" Lhaurel asked, stepping forward to kneel in the grass.

"Making the ground tremble. I think you scared Saralhn as much as you scared her unfortunate husband."

Lhaurel nearly dropped her sword in shock. Her racing blood stilled and color drained from her face. *Saralhn?* They'd told her Saralhn was dead. Kaiden—Kaiden had broken her with that news.

It had been a trick.

Lhaurel reached out a weak hand and placed it on the trembling woman's shoulder.

"Saralhn," she said, "it's me, Lhaurel."

The woman looked up. Her face glistened with tears and blood, yet her eyes reflected the moonlight. They focused on Lhaurel and, for a moment, appeared confused. Then recognition dawned and returned to confusion.

"You're dead." Saralhn stammered. "They left you on the rocks. Khari said you were still alive, but I didn't believe her." Her voice was weak and she coughed wetly.

Lhaurel wrapped her arms around her and pulled her close. Saralhn shifted for a moment, as if she were about to pull away, but then she collapsed into Lhaurel's arms. Lhaurel felt close to the woman, closer than they ever had been before.

"I lived," Lhaurel said, stroking Saralhn's hair.

"I'm sorry that I didn't arrive any sooner," Khari said. "I saw him drag you away, but I couldn't leave then without arousing suspicion."

Saralhn gave a barely perceptible nod. Her eyes were locked on Lhaurel's face.

Lhaurel, for her part, registered the strange comment a moment delayed. "What was that?"

"I saw Saralhn's husband drag her away while I was speaking with some of the other women. He'd seen me talking to her and his look was murderous. I knew she was in trouble, but I couldn't get away."

"Well, at least someone was here to protect her," Lhaurel said harshly.

"He was drunk and angry," Saralhn coughed. "His uncle had just died and the senior warriors had voted Taren in as Warlord over him. I—I was just the tool he used to let out his rage."

"He would have killed you!"

"I don't think so." Saralhn's arguments sounded hollow and empty. She hung her head again and fresh tears dripped down her cheeks.

Khari gave Lhaurel a hard look and shuffled closer to the sobbing woman. "Saralhn, you must do as I have asked. You must be our eyes and ears here within the Sidena. We can't protect you unless we know what is going on. Lhaurel scared your husband bad enough tonight that I doubt he will ever touch you again for fear of calling down the witch that makes the earth rumble and who has the strength of ten men. We will protect you."

"How can you protect me when you're not even here? You're Roterralar—no one trusts Roterralar. The saying 'as wayward as a Roterralar' came from somewhere. Lhaurel, how could you be one of them?"

Lhaurel sniffed and tried to ignore the sting of the words, the mistrust and confusion in Saralhn's words. Saralhn had always been far more superstitious than Lhaurel had been herself.

"It's alright, Saralhn. They—we—are not what the stories make us out to be. We're normal people, just like you."

Khari reached out and wrapped a hand around Saralhn's shoulder. The woman winced in pain, but Khari did not let go. "I have messenger birds hidden throughout the Oasis. I will tell you where they are. Send us one bird every three days. If we don't hear from you by the third day after your last bird, we will come."

Lhaurel looked over at Khari, gratitude evident in her expression, though the darkness obscured it. Saralhn coughed but was silent for a long moment, contemplating.

"Alright," Saralhn said at last, "but not for you." She turned to look at Lhaurel, her eyes tear-filled. "If Lhaurel agrees to come if I need help, then I will be your eyes and ears."

Khari nodded and released her grip on the woman's shoulder. "Thank you, Saralhn."

Khari got to her feet and gave Lhaurel a significant look. Even in the darkness, Lhaurel could feel the seriousness of the expression.

"Can't we take her with us?" Lhaurel asked, suddenly feeling protective and more than a little frustrated at the sudden turn of events. "Just until she's healed?"

"No, Lhaurel." Khari shook her head. "She can't come with us. She needs to stay here and keep an eye on this place for us. She'll heal with time, maybe even faster with some help."

Lhaurel missed the significance of the remark for a moment, clouded in disbelief and anger, but then it dawned on her. Could she do it? Khari had healed her twice now. Once after shattering her nose on Fahkiri's pommel and, she suspected, once after her terrifying encounter with the sandstorm. But she'd never shown Lhaurel how to do it.

"I—I can't." Lhaurel stammered, shrinking in on herself. "I—"

"It's alright, Lhaurel," Saralhn gave her a wan smile that twisted into a grimace as she struggled to her feet. "This isn't the first time he's beaten me, and it wasn't the worst, either. I'll be ok. I will still find water and shade before my time is through."

Lhaurel realized that she couldn't have healed Saralhn anyway.

The clan would be suspicious if a beaten woman came back looking like she hadn't been touched. The realization brought her relief that soured with guilt.

Saralhn limped over to Lhaurel and put her arms around her. Lhaurel basked in the sudden warmth, the joy of friendship and acceptance. She hugged Saralhn back, clutched at her hair and breathed in the salty, tangy mix of her scent.

And then the moment was gone. Saralhn released her and turned to Khari, hand extended before her in a gesture of respect and gratitude. Despite the bruises on her face and the funny way she leaned to one side to take the weight off of her damaged ribs, the woman radiated strength like a beacon of hope. When had Saralhn suddenly gotten so strong-willed?

Khari smiled and returned the gesture.

Saralhn nodded once, smiled at Lhaurel, and then shuffled off into the darkness, limping slightly but straight-backed and proud. Noble.

"She's got almost as much fire in her as you do," Khari said once the woman was lost from sight.

Lhaurel looked over at the other woman, following Saralhn's retreat in her mind. "She's not the same girl I left behind. She didn't have that kind of strength before. The Saralhn I knew would never have agreed to go back and face that man again. She would never have had the courage."

"Maybe you didn't know her as well as you thought. Strength like that isn't something that just appears overnight. The seed of it is born within you. It doesn't just come from outward defiance. Sometimes strength comes from learning when to bend and silently follow."

"Won't she get into trouble? Her husband's going to know we spoke with her."

Khari snorted and gave a short laugh. "Do you really think a Sidena warrior is going to admit he was bested by *women*?"

Lhaurel smiled and shook her head. *No, he most certainly would not.*

Lhaurel turned away, gazing back toward the Sidena camp. Perhaps she'd never given Saralhn the credit she deserved. It was something to consider.

"What did you learn?" she asked.

"Not as much as I would have hoped." Khari's voice was suddenly sour. "Taren should never have been made the Warlord. Jenthro's sons are far more prominent in the clan, even if Taren has the most experience. There's something going on there besides simply murdering the old Warlord."

"Murder?"

"The blue lips. It's a sign of the cawlhasi flower's unique poison. The flower is extremely hard to find and even harder to distill down into a poison. Very few people have that sort of knowledge or the ability to get it. In fact, it only grows on the cliffs of the Frierd Warren. But come on, let's walk as we talk. It will be dawn soon."

Lhaurel hurried after Khari, her mind chasing down the

implications of what Khari had just said. "So you're saying that Taren is somehow involved with the Frierd?"

"Maybe," Khari said over her shoulder, "but I don't think so. This is something different. Power duels are constant. Warlords change often. But Taren is different. He seems too cold, too calculating. And too hungry. I don't think that he's going to be satisfied with where he is for very long, though I'll be a sand-blasted fool if I can figure out what else he's up to."

Lhaurel shuddered as memories of Taren's eyes on their wedding day swam through her mind. Cold, calculating, and hungry were perfect descriptions.

"Marvi is helping him." Lhaurel said.

"Yes, I know," Khari replied absently.

They approached the narrow canyon that would lead them out of the Oasis. Much of the majesty of the area had faded, pushed out of Lhaurel's mind by the night's events, but the oppressive wrongness of the walls returned in full force as they neared the dark opening. She sensed a deep and profound darkness radiating from the stone, as if her presence tore at the very fabric of its reality. Lhaurel shuddered.

"Well, if it isn't the two Roterralar women." The voice was cold, harsh. Lhaurel recognized it with a grimace. The presence from the walls obscured her senses, including her magic, but she did sense someone near, or maybe . . .

A torch flared up, revealing the scowling face of Shelton. This time, though, he was not alone. Two other men stood with him, large muscular men with corded muscles that bulged under their tight jerkins and faces set in what appeared to be permanent frowns, arms folded across their chests. Cudgels of a light brown wood hung at their belts and they didn't carry a spear. Not swords, cudgels. These were not guards.

"Where's Honric?" Khari asked. She halted at the edge of the torchlight, falling into a seemingly nonchalant stance, though Lhaurel recognized the sudden tension in her posture.

The man chuckled. "He decided to take a little nap. He's old, you know, and I don't think we should wake him up. Do you?"

The other two men with him sniffed as if they found their

companion tedious, but they said nothing.

Khari frowned and stroked her chin. "No, we wouldn't want to wake him."

Lhaurel pushed out, extending her consciousness to try and find Honric. The strange sensation from the walls resisted, like a film of oil over water, but somehow she shoved through it, stumbling across Honric's presence somewhere within the canyon. She was surprised that she could so easily pick him out, but then the surprise gave way to disgust and fear.

Honric's presence was weak and fleeting. She could sense it struggling against something that was slowly enveloping it in blackness. The blackness seemed to draw her in, pulling her deeper and deeper. Breath came in quick gasps. The darkness closed in, strangling her.

Honric's presence faded away.

Lhaurel coughed and dropped to her knees, sucking in air in massive gulps and clutching at her chest. It burned as if on fire, and her head felt fuzzy, almost like it had when she'd slammed into Fahkiri's pommel. Her back arched, and she screamed, a low, desperate, pain-stricken scream.

The men stared at her as if she'd suddenly gone insane. Even Khari took a hesitant step back, face twisted in an expression of surprise.

Lhaurel struggled to stand, gasping for air, and tense muscles screamed in protest and fought to bend, to tighten. Her mind worked furiously, struggling to comprehend what it had just experienced. Honric had just died. She had *felt* him die. She had died with him.

"You killed him," Lhaurel said. Her voice sounded hollow, emotionless. She took a step forward.

"What are you talking about?" Shelton said.

The wind kicked up dust around her and made the torchlight flicker.

Coughing raggedly, she stood upright, the memory of Saralhn's dignified expression giving her strength.

"You killed him," Lhaurel repeated, drawing her sword. The wind whipped her robes up around her, obscuring her vision in a haze of red.

One of the larger men ripped the cudgel free from his belt, raising it threateningly before him. His companion drew his cudgel as well and advanced. Shelton remained where he was.

Lhaurel breathed in, filling her lungs with air and reaching out with her mind. She felt the men approach. Sensed them on such an intimate level that she felt their movements before they made them. Her eyes closed.

The first man swung in hard, crossing downward toward her left shoulder a beat ahead of his companion's blow toward her right. Reversing her grip, Lhaurel brought her sword up, slipping in and under the cudgel's swing and digging into the flesh of the man's armpit. The sword continued upward as Lhaurel took a quick step backward and she pivoted around to parry the other man's blow. Wood struck metal and stuck fast. A twist of the blade tore the cudgel from the man's grip. It went spinning into the sand, torn free from the sword blade.

Lhaurel didn't stop. She flipped the sword behind her, spinning, and thrust it with all her strength. The blade took the man on her right through the belly. He gasped as hot, red blood poured from his gut. He stumbled backward, sliding off Lhaurel's sword.

Lhaurel's eyes snapped open. The wind died. She felt the man's pain. She felt his presence begin to fade, and his lifeblood poured into the sand. She felt him dying. Bile rose up in her throat and suddenly she was vomiting uncontrollably. Vomit mingled with blood in the sands.

The other man, the one she'd cut under the arm, stumbled away into the darkness, shouting incoherently. Shelton took one look at Lhaurel and the dying man and followed.

Khari hurried over to Lhaurel's side. "What in the seven hells?" she yelled.

Lhaurel coughed and wiped her mouth with the back of her hand. Behind Khari, the man's presence faded and was gone.

"We've got to get out of here," Khari said, tugging at her arm. "Help me find Honric so that we can figure out some excuse for all this."

"Honric's dead."

"How do you know?" Khari demanded.

Lhaurel coughed and spat bile, staring at the sword in her hand as if she'd never seen it before. Why had she wasted so much of her life longing to possess one? It was an instrument of destruction. A tool of death. She slipped it into its sheath even though it was still covered in gore.

"I felt him die. They killed him. Beat him over the head with one of those cudgels." She said it simply, but her voice still trembled.

"What in the seven hells are you?" Khari asked. Her hand on Lhaurel's shoulder shook.

"Sick," Lhaurel said. "I'm sick."

Khari stood, composing herself and returning to her normal scowling visage. She grabbed Lhaurel's shoulder and pulled her to her feet, giving her a shove toward the exit.

Lhaurel didn't need much more encouragement. She wanted to be far away from this place. Far from the blackness of death. But Khari's words haunted her. What was she?

As she stumbled through the narrow canyon, the sticky wetness on her hands reminded her. She was a bringer of death.

Khari was the first to stumble across Honric's body. She cursed as she tripped but caught herself against the wall. Small fingers of light stretched red and purple rays across the deep blackness of the sky, which made the specter of Honric's body all the more grisly. Lhaurel took one look and heaved again, but there was nothing left to come up. Even Khari's face paled as she bent down over the man's stiff form. One side of his face was a broken mass of bruise and blood, caved inward beneath the force of the blow that had killed him. One of his arms was bent back over itself.

"He fought back," Khari said, wiping her mouth with the back of her hand. "He faced them down. How did you know, Lhaurel?"

Lhaurel heaved again, spitting bile and phlegm. Coughing, she righted herself and looked down at Honric's still form. Part of her guilt dropped away.

"I told you," she said, "I felt him die. I felt his pain. Why, Khari? Why would they kill him?"

Khari scowled and looked back the direction they had come. Her gaze was contorted in an expression of murderous anger, and her hands rested on the hilt of her sword.

"Because they wanted us, and they knew that Honric would stand in their way."

"What would they want with us?"

"What does any man want with a woman?" Khari nearly shouted, whirling around to stare at Lhaurel with narrowed eyes. "Rape us, kill us, take our swords. Who would miss a couple of mystic women? Who would come to defend us?"

Lhaurel swallowed hard. She gazed down at Honric, wishing that she could have done something more for the man. At least she had been able to avenge him partially. Somehow, the thought didn't comfort her.

"What do we do now?" she asked.

"We leave. Enough rumors about our meeting will be left behind that we may not be able to come back. Then again, they may be so frightened of us that we'll never have problems like this again." Khari glanced over her shoulder once more, as if convincing herself not to go back.

They buried Honric in a shallow grave just outside the canyon. There was no marker. The sands would have covered anything they left behind anyway.

The sun had broken over the horizon, though part of it still remained hidden behind the Oasis walls.

Lhaurel felt somehow less after he was buried. She had only known the man for a short time, but he had died defending them. He may not have known it at the time, but he had. As she mounted Fahkiri, she couldn't help but wonder if Honric would still have been alive if she hadn't thrown that rock.

CHAPTER 15

Quenching

"Briane still has not returned. I searched, but there was no indication of why she'd left or where she'd gone. I cannot begin to comprehend why she would have left on the eve of our great victory. The clans were delighted that we had been successful, and Briane's disappearance was given cursory investigation. I fear something may have happened to her."

-From the Journals of Elyana

Lhaurel could feel Fahkiri shifting beneath her, preparing for his descent, and she adjusted her weight and position accordingly. His presence was weak, though, even astride him. Not weak like Honric had been, but weak because her ability to sense it had diminished. She couldn't even feel Khari or Gwyanth from a few spans away.

Fahkiri turned into the dive, aiming toward the shadowy opening in the cliff face that led into the eyrie. Atop the plateau, Lhaurel could just make out a rough grouping of tents nestled near an outcropping of rock toward the center of the plateau. Kaiden's area.

Fahkiri pulled out of the dive with a deafening screech. Prepared, Lhaurel shifted with the sudden change in momentum, pushed back against the incredible forces pulling her downward, and sat up straight when the aevian landed with a proud, triumphant chirp.

Gwyanth landed nearby, and a group of younger aevians skittered out of the way, squawking indignantly.

The only person in the eyrie was Kaiden. He sat to one side of the water urns, back up against the wall. He was wearing a black long-sleeved shirt and a brown vest, both trimmed with a silver metal. His leggings were also black. The one splash of color on his was a white sash, almost a *shufari*, that he wore at his waist. He grinned at her when he noticed that she was looking.

Lhaurel groaned quietly as she unclipped herself from Fahkiri's back and slid to the ground, pulling off her harness almost as soon as her feet hit the sandy floor. She was in no mood to deal with the intractable man.

"I need to go speak with Makin and the others," Khari said, tossing Lhaurel her own harness. "Go get some rest. You could use it."

Lhaurel shrugged.

"Oh, and Lhaurel?"

Lhaurel turned.

"You may want to wash up. You've still got blood everywhere."

Lhaurel looked down as Khari hurried from the room. Brownish black stains covered her hands and parts of her arms. She smelled of blood and sweat and aevian mustiness. An overwhelming desire to be clean came over her, and she hurried over to the water urns, leaving the harnesses in a pile on the ground. She poured ladles of water over her hands and scrubbed at the blood until nothing remained. But she kept washing, let the cool water drip down her arms and over her flesh, washing away the blood and the sweat and the guilt. Or at least masking it. The smell remained, though, forever burned into her nostrils. She put the dipper to her lips and swallowed, feeling vigor and strength return.

"Looks like your first return to the motherland was interesting," Kaiden said from beside her. She hadn't noticed him get up and walk over.

"What do you want, Kaiden?"

"A little moody today, are you? It was a simple observation." He spoke with a hurt voice. She knew it was fake from the smile that tugged at the corner of his lips.

The smile reminded her of Honric, and her emotions flared. "Go away. Leave me in peace." She turned to walk away.

"But I want to know what's happening in the Oasis," he said, holding out a hand to block her path. "And I'm sure there's a good reason why you showed up just now covered in someone else's blood."

"Go ask Khari."

"I'm asking you."

Lhaurel blew out a long breath and ran a hand through her tangled auburn hair. "And if I tell you will you go away and leave me alone?"

Kaiden smiled. "Possibly."

"Fine. Taren is the Warlord of the Sidena now. He poisoned the old one with something from the cawlhasi flower, Khari said, which is somehow significant."

"Because it's only found near the Frierd Warren," Kaiden interrupted.

"Yes, something like that. Now shut up and let me finish. Jenthro is dead, Taren is Warlord, I scared a bunch of people, and Khari has a new contact to send her messages. End of story. Now go away." She made a shooing gesture with her hands.

Kaiden frowned, brows furrowed, and scratched at his chin. "And where did the blood come in?"

"You know, I'm tired, and I want to get some sleep. Just go talk to Khari, ok?" She didn't want to relive what she had done. She couldn't see Honric's face one more time without bursting into tears. The guilt was too strong, the wounds too fresh.

"Come with me," Kaiden said, holding out a rough hand. "I want to show you something."

Lhaurel groaned loudly and shook her head. "Are you not listening? Leave. Me. Alone."

"Just come with me already," Kaiden said. "I'll just keep asking until you come, so you might as well give up."

"Fine, but only to get you to shut up."

Kaiden grinned and took her hand.

* * *

SANDS

The forge lay dormant when Khari opened the door to the blacksmiths' workroom and stepped inside. The room was still sweltering hot, though the coals had been banked and covered in ash and sand to keep them warm for later use. A pair of lanterns on one of the counters were the only source of light.

Early risers within the warren were just now going about their labors for the day. Beryl, though, preferred the solitude of the night. The thick stone walls and heavy wooden door prevented the sound of his work from penetrating too deeply into the passages, so his odd work schedule rarely presented difficulties to anyone else.

"How can I help the Matron today?" Beryl's voice said from right beside her.

Khari would have jumped, but long years of training kept her still and poised.

She hadn't noticed the smith standing there when she'd entered, but that wasn't unusual. Beryl was so quiet and unassuming in demeanor on the outside that he was often overlooked. And that often proved to be to their great undoing. For beneath the misshapen exterior lay a mind and a passion unparalleled within any of the clans.

Khari had known the man since childhood. She had thought him old then, though he hadn't seemed to age in the intervening decades. It was one of the benefits of being a mystic, though none of the others had ever reached quite the same age that Beryl had obtained.

"It's about Lhaurel," she said, turning to face him.

The short man leaned against his crippled leg, resting against the wall. He lay obscured in shadows and the long leads from the dozens of harnesses that hung from the wall and ceiling around him.

Something gleamed at his side. As he shuffled forward, the glittering object resolved into a sword, unsheathed, yet complete and polished. Metal clinked together as the harness leads struck each other as a result of Beryl's passing.

He looked up at her with a hint of smugness. "Have you finally come to believe what I said earlier?" The rasp in his voice was even more pronounced, deep, and grating.

Khari nodded, studying the sword in his hand. Beryl's work was normally masterful, but the sword he carried went beyond mere mastery. It was a thing of beauty designed to kill. Perfectly straight, the weapon's single edge shone with razor sharpness and the metal whorled in layers of differing shades of gray that made it appear like a raging storm had been trapped within the metal. The brass guard was far wider than normal and was rectangular in nature except that it had been bent. Eight triangular sections had been cut out of the guard, though small and mostly ornamental in nature rather than strategically placed for ease in disarming an opponent. The handle itself was simple, long enough to be used either with one hand or with two. A brass endcap shone on the pommel. It was simple yet elegant, and the contrast made it beautiful.

"That is a masterful sword, Beryl."

The smith grunted. "What do you want, Khari?"

"I wanted your opinion on something. Concerning Lhaurel."

"Why now?" he asked, "You and Makin Qays were convinced that she was broken and that you knew everything you needed to know."

"I know, but in the Oasis today she displayed powers that no other wetta has. She can do things, feel things, which defy reason and explanation. Is this some new form of magic? We know so little about it, and what little we do know, we've had to learn ourselves." It wasn't an apology, but it was the closest thing that Beryl was going to get.

"What sorts of things?"

"She can sense people, not just mystics, but all people. A man was killed by some degenerate fools for defending us, and she felt him die. And her first attempts at controlling the magic were odd. Instead of manipulating the water, she made it explode."

Beryl's brow furrowed, and the hand not holding the sword reached up to scratch at his chin. The forge flared, bathing the room in reddish light. Khari glanced at it. She'd though it dormant.

"And what about the other wetta skills?" he asked. "Healing, and discovering water sources?"

Khari shook her head. "I don't know. She hasn't been exposed to anything like that, but you should have seen her in the Oasis when she felt that man die. I swear I could see the anger radiating from her when she attacked the men responsible. I've never seen such stunning sword work. It was both beautiful and terrifying."

"Not much to go on."

Khari raised her hands and sighed. "It's all we have."

"Well, she has been through a lot recently. It's like working metal. When metal is hot, it becomes malleable and can be shaped. But it is also unstable and will begin to show you its flaws. If the heat is too intense, or not strong enough, when you go to quench the piece it will show its true strength. If there are flaws, it will either become brittle or remain too soft and malleable. The perfect combination is somewhere in between. But you can never really tell which it will be until you quench the metal."

"A lovely analogy, but what do you suggest I quench Lhaurel in?"

"I suggest you let her cool down. Keep stresses out of her life. Let her find something relaxing and peaceful. Don't overwork her. Like the metal, both she and her magic will cool, and then you should be able to see what sort of flaws come to the surface, if any."

Khari nodded. Beryl always had astute advice.

"Oh, and when you see her, ask her to come see me. This is hers," he said, holding up the sword.

"I will." She turned to leave but hesitated.

Beryl arched a bushy white eyebrow at her as she turned.

"Do think someone is controlling the genesauri?"

The forge flared again, and Beryl frowned. The light from the forge illuminated half of Beryl's face, leaving the other half bathed in shadows.

"No one is that powerful," he said. "Not even me."

Khari pursed her lips into almost a frown and turned to leave, but before she got through the door Beryl spoke again.

"Oh, and Matron—she isn't broken yet."

* * *

Kaiden strode through the darkened passages with long, lithe strides, holding aloft the torch he had taken from a wall bracket. The sand lay thick in these tunnels. The cleaners either hadn't gotten down this far after the sandstorm, or they simply didn't clean down here. Kaiden strode purposefully onward. He obviously knew the path well and fully expected Lhaurel to follow him. Lhaurel didn't know why, but she did.

She walked along behind him, cursing the sand, but otherwise her thoughts and mind were pleasantly blank. She followed not because she had any interest in where Kaiden was taking her, but because the walking calmed her mind and granted her a measure of peace. Intermingled with the emotions that ran high concerning Honric's death were other, less powerful, yet equally troubling thoughts and feelings about Kaiden.

The man was somewhat of an enigma. There was something endearing about him, yes, but at times he simply seemed an arrogant little toerag bordering on cruelty. So cold at some points, and then so warm and inviting at others. The memory of the first time she had seen him, among the Sidena, made her smile through her tiredness. He'd been so cool, arrogant, and sarcastic among the Sidena. Yet he had treated her with respect even in the face of such barbarity as was going on around them. And then there was the way he had treated her during the sandstorm. Slaying the rashelta to demonstrate his powers and standing over her in the storm, facing the winds to protect her. He was a contradiction wrapped in the guise of a man.

Yet she followed him anyway. Where was the sense in that?

At the moment, she simply did not care. She just walked and allowed her mind to go blank, unable to do much more than focus on putting one foot in front of the other. Her mouth and throat were dry, but she didn't have any water on her. And she was not about to ask Kaiden for his. Her numb sense of things left her with no way of knowing where they were within the warren.

Eventually, though, her curiosity got the better of her.

"Where are we going?"

"Not far."

"That's not a very helpful answer."

"It wasn't meant to be. It wouldn't be much of a surprise if I told you about it, now would it? Just trust me."

"I'd really rather not."

Kaiden laughed. "It's a momentary trust, fleeting at best. You can go back to not trusting me afterward."

"How much further?"

"Not far," he said again. If she'd had a rock somewhere, Lhaurel would have tossed it at him.

The passageway grew dank and cold as they walked farther. Moisture dripped from the walls and ran in little streams down the crevasses of reddish-grey rock. Lhaurel felt oddly comforted. When she trailed her hand through the water on the walls, she felt strength surge through her, and her senses seemed to come alive. She felt Kaiden walking a few paces in front of her, sensed his presence. She felt the water running down the walls. The massive underground water source that she had felt earlier rested just on the other side of the wall. It was so large, so incredibly vast. It swirled with currents and eddies, budded with life. The place felt right. Safe.

They rounded a corner.

"Here we are." Kaiden said, raising the torch high.

Torchlight glittered off the surface of a vast underground lake. It stretched out several hundred spans, reflecting the light off its shimmering surface. The sound of dripping water echoed against the walls, a harmonious symphony that sang to Lhaurel's heart. A narrow pathway of stone led through the lake toward the far wall like the stoneways through the sand toward the Oasis.

Kaiden let her soak in the grandeur of that much water all in one place for a moment and then motioned with the torch that they were going to follow the path. The flickering light cast odd shadows across the water's surface and on the cave walls around it.

Kaiden led the way. Lhaurel followed, breathless.

As they neared the far wall, the light revealed what Kaiden had obviously brought her there to see. An enormous mural covered the face of the entire back wall. The paint or dye was faded in some places, worn with the age and covered in layers of mildew and dust, but it depicted a world and a life different from any that Lhaurel had ever known. Strange drawings of plants that looked like bushes but with only one massive brown stalk and far too much green on them. Animals that were clearly the workings of some child's imagination. Bodies of water that were bigger than anything that would have survived long in the desert climate above.

And central to it all were depictions of a people. People who worked and farmed and hunted together, all standing or working with their eyes turned upward toward one figure wearing a thin crown and bearing a strange-looking sword. Along the edges, an odd reddish brown cloud and streaks of white lightning were drawn in a ring, enveloping the mural as if it cut it off from everything else. There were other drawings etched into the stone that looked older still, but they were faded and worn, the message lost.

Beneath the mural, along the bottom two spans of the wall, hundred upon hundreds of little rectangular repositories had been cut into the stone, each one lined up in dozens of rows and columns. Little symbols were carved into the stone around each opening, but Lhaurel had no understanding of their meaning. As she stepped closer, her mouth hanging partly open in awe, Lhaurel noticed that within some of the repositories there was something placed, something that shone and reflected the light.

"What is this?" she asked, reaching out a hesitant hand.

Behind her, Kaiden moved the torch so that she could see what it was she was touching. A glass tube with a metal cap. There was a rolled up length of parchment inside, but it was too dark to make out any markings. "Depends on who you ask," Kaiden said, stepping up beside her. "Some say this is simply a pretty picture, drawn by people who had been driven mad by the genesauri. Some say it is a remnant of a time long past that will never be again." His voice was quiet, respectful—almost reverent.

"And what do you think?"

Kaiden turned to look at her, and his gaze was serious. His brows furrowed above his eyes and then suddenly relaxed. Looking away, he gazed up at the mural on the wall.

"It's a depiction of what used to be. And what can be again," he said. "It doesn't matter if it really happened or not. It's an ideal. A unified people working together, guided by a wise and powerful leader. A time without the genesauri. It's what freedom looks like, Lhaurel."

Lhaurel stared at the man, stunned. Who was he to talk so longingly and majestically of freedom? In order to long for freedom, one must first have tasted the bitter gall of imprisonment. But his words rang with the beauty and power that only came through truth.

She looked up at the mural again and caught a small glimpse of what Kaiden was explaining. She chewed on her bottom lip, suddenly trying to reconcile her image of Kaiden with the surprisingly poetic soul he had just revealed.

"And what are these?" she asked, holding up the glass container.

Kaiden smiled and winked at her as if she had asked something clever. Lhaurel found herself blushing, which somehow made her angry with herself.

"Well, my guess is that they are a record of our past and how this," he said, gesturing to the mural, "somehow became the hell we live in now."

"Your guess?"

Kaiden shrugged. "Well, everyone knows this lake is down here, but few come down this far. It's somewhere I go when I need to find peace. It's too sacred, too perfect, for me to feel comfortable showing it to just anyone. Actually, anyone but you. I haven't even shown Sarial."

For some reason, that made Lhaurel smile. "So why did you show me?"

"Because you understand what it is like to fight for freedom. Not just freedom for yourself but freedom for those you care about. I've seen it in you. Once they identified you as a possible mystic a few years ago, we watched you. We saw the way you rankled under the pressures of being a woman. I personally saw your little acts of rebellion and how you tried to show the other women that they didn't just have to capitulate. Oh, nothing too dangerous. Like teaching yourself the sword, for example. Freedom is in your blood."

Lhaurel flushed at hearing how she had been watched for several years. The last month of constant scrutiny had been bad enough, but years?

"And, for a moment today, you looked like something had taken away that thirst for freedom. When I feel like that, I come here. It reminds me why I fight each day. Why I struggle to provide freedom to all."

"I—" she began and then hesitated. Did she trust him? Maybe she was starting to, but it was still a small thing, a seed just barely taking root.

It only took her a few minutes to relate what had happened in the Oasis, culminating in the death of one of the brigands at her hands.

He listened, impassive, as the torch sputtered in the dank, musty air. His expression changed to one of outrage when her story reached the part about the three men.

"You were too merciful." His harsh voice echoed in the cavernous confines. "I wouldn't have left any of them alive."

Lhaurel almost recoiled from the sheer force of his animosity. She had expected Kaiden to question her actions, interrogate her on how she had felt Honric die, or even lecture her on diplomacy.

"But I killed a man. He wasn't a genesauri or a sandtiger. He was a man." Kaiden's expression softened somewhat, if steel could be said to soften.

"Sometimes killing is the only way to protect others. This won't be the last time someone dies on your blade. Sometimes there is simply no other way to protect either your own or someone else's freedom. You killed to protect. There isn't any better reason for death than that."

Lhaurel bit her bottom lip. "But how do I know that I really was protecting? I just got so angry that my body forced me to act. It was as if I was watching myself do it from behind a stranger's eyes. Did they really need to die?"

Kaiden reached out his hand and gripped her shoulder. His grip was iron. "People don't change that much, Lhaurel. If they were going to attack you because you were Roterralar women, then they had already made their choices that lead to those actions a long time ago. Once men get it in their heads that there is one way of doing things, then that's the only way for them. There is no going back. What you did helped save future lives." His voice was passionate, sharp, and strong. Yet there was a mixture of bitterness to it, as if the conversation had somehow opened up old wounds not yet healed.

Lhaurel sniffed, and Kaiden released her shoulder, dropping his hand to his side.

"Come on," Kaiden said, "I'll take you back up to the greatroom. You look like you could use some sleep."

Lhaurel nodded but then hesitantly reached out and grabbed his arm. He stopped and turned to face her.

"Thank you for this, Kaiden," she said with a grandiose gesture that took in the entire room. One side of her mouth twitched upward in a small smile.

Kaiden winked at her and shrugged. "It was nothing."

* * *

Lhaurel entered the smithy with measured hesitation. Before she and Kaiden had made it back to the greatroom, a young woman had met them with a message for Lhaurel. Beryl needed to see her. Again. Lhaurel had almost forgotten that the man had been working on her own sword and that the one at her belt was only a temporary companion. Lhaurel felt relieved that she would not have to keep the weapon that had shed another human being's blood.

Yet her trepidation now came for another reason. After bidding goodbye to Kaiden and the young messenger, Lhaurel had checked the blade that Beryl had loaned her only to find it stuck fast with blood. Despite her best efforts, which, admittedly, were somewhat hampered by her revulsion at the sight of the reddish brown stains, the blade was still coated with it.

The ever-present harnesses hung from the ceiling, though after her experience with the broken strap, she now understood why there were so many of them. The forge was dormant, but some heat still radiated from it, and a pair of lanterns on one of the counters provided a little illumination. Beryl was nowhere to be seen. Lhaurel peered over each of the counters and even looked into the dark shadows in the corners of the room.

She sighed. It made sense that the smith would be in the other room, the armory, but she had hoped to not have to go in there. The sheer vastness of the room left her in awe, and she was not sure how she'd feel about being surrounded by such an array of weapons.

She found the smith standing just on the other side of the forge as if he had been waiting for her. A beautiful sword rested in his grip. He offered it to her without a word. Lhaurel took it, wrapping her fingers around the slightly too-long handle, and then handed him the sword that he had loaned her. The new sword somehow felt right in her hands, much more so than the other one ever had.

"Thank you," she said, threading the weapon's sheath onto her belt.

Beryl ignored her, instead drawing the blade she had given him and inspecting the bloodstains on it. He grunted and slammed the sword back into its sheath.

"Khari told me about what happened," he said in his gruff voice. "Well done, young one. Those your age shouldn't have to be put in those situations. You should be with people your own age instead of being forced into life's hard lessons."

Lhaurel swallowed and half smiled. It seemed an appropriate response.

Beryl tossed the loaned sword toward a pile of weapons that lay in a corner. A cloud of reddish-grey seemed to form around Beryl as the sword continued to sail over the pile of discarded weapons and float, suspended in midair, into a bin of scrap metal. The weapon landed with a clatter and the cloud around Beryl faded.

"You're a magnetelorium!" Lhaurel said, realizing that the misty clouds she sometimes saw around people marked when someone was using their magic.

Beryl nodded. "That I am. There are a few of us here."

"Like Kaiden."

"Yes, like him." Beryl said then hesitated, his brow furrowing in an expression of concentration. "He's about your age, isn't he? Maybe you should spend some time with him and enjoy your youth. Leave the hard life lessons for later."

Lhaurel smiled and turned to leave. Beryl didn't stop her.

CHAPTER 16
Eddies and Falls

"What is the nature of dreams? Are they real or purely illusory? If they are real, what is the nature of this realm of dreams? If illusory, why do they have such a powerful effect upon the dreamer? I think the enemy has somehow found Briane, and they have pried from her the nature of our plight. They have found a way into my dreams. I see blood and steam and fire. The enemy taunts me with visions of things that simply could not be . . . no, they could never be true. Images of blood and fire and pain. And a girl child screaming."

-From the Journals of Elyana

Lhaurel ducked Khari's high vertical thrust and then rolled out of the way of her follow-through. Lhaurel's feet shuffled backward and to the left, following her opponent's blade and bringing her own sword up under Khari's guard. The older woman tried to dodge but not quickly enough. The leather-clad blade smacked hard against her side, most likely leaving an angry red welt even beneath the leather and the layers of cloth. But there was no time for Lhaurel to gloat.

Khari grunted away the stinging pain and spun back in, forcing Lhaurel back into a defensive stance that backed her up to the edge of the training circle.

Around the edges of the circle, more than a dozen spectators watched the duel with more than idle attention. Several younger women, mere children in all actuality, watched in open admiration as they danced around one another. Older women and men watched with less open emotion, though it was still apparent that most of them were impressed. Tieran stood to one side, grinning foolishly as Khari scored a hit on Lhaurel's leg. On the other side of the circle, Kaiden winced and shouted words of encouragement to Lhaurel. Hearing him, she gritted her teeth and launched back onto the offensive with renewed vigor.

In the week since she had come back from the Oasis, Lhaurel had spent almost every waking hour either training with Khari, flying with Fahkiri, or else, surprisingly, with Kaiden. The magnetelorium, despite his surliness and arrogance in many situations, was fast becoming her dearest and closest confidant. The night after he had shown her the mural and the underground lake, he had shown her the camp he'd formed atop the plateau. "Topside," he called it. She'd marveled at the stars and the sense of camaraderie and acceptance she'd felt among the people gathered there. Several of the people she had met there had come to watch her fight. She'd found her own tent and slept there that night and every night since. In all truth, she hadn't ever spent a single night in her room within the warren itself.

Khari darted in with a spinning reverse-gripped cut. Lhaurel's training had progressed rapidly, far more rapidly than Khari had expected, but despite that Lhaurel barely managed to get her blade up in time to deflect the blow. Their blades locked, the hilt of Khari's sword only inches away from Lhaurel's blade.

Lhaurel's eyes locked onto Khari's, and suddenly Lhaurel saw a small glimmer of triumph in them. Before she could react, Khari punched forward with her hilt and struck Lhaurel a resounding blow on the temple with the sword's pommel. Lhaurel cried out in pain and sudden dizziness, blinking back tears and seeing stars. The flat of Khari's blade came to rest on Lhaurel's neck.

Lhaurel gasped, the smell of leather and sweat filling her nose and distracting her from the throbbing in her temples. "I yield. You win."

Around them, the crowd clapped and a few even cheered. Tieran's booming laugh carried over the din as Khari gave Lhaurel a tight-lipped smile and then removed the blade from her neck.

"Expect the unexpected, Lhaurel. Strategy before tactics. Maneuver before battle. Every action you take with the blade should either foil something your opponent is doing or else give you an advantage. The masters do both at the same time. Remember that."

"And don't forget when you're beating one of the best after owning your own blade for less than a week that Khari plays dirty," Kaiden interjected, his voice dripping with a mixture of sarcasm and mirth.

Khari shot him a withering look, but Lhaurel sent him a wan smile. Tieran laughed as most of the crowd dispersed to be about their other duties, some shouting consoling words to Lhaurel or congratulating Khari as they left.

Wincing, Lhaurel probed her temple with one finger. There would be a bruise later if there wasn't one already. Her face on that side already felt puffy, and it hurt to blink. If she was lucky, Khari would offer to heal it later, but she doubted it. Her teacher felt that the marks were good reminders of what happened when your skill was not up to a level deemed acceptable. And Lhaurel suspected there was another reason behind it. One that dealt with her other training.

Lhaurel herself had not been able to master the healing art or do much else that Khari said was normal for a wetta. Kaiden said that it was typical for new mystics to struggle with their powers, but Lhaurel didn't think they were talking about her particular challenges. More likely Khari was still curious about why Lhaurel could do things that other wetta couldn't and why she was apparently incapable of doing things that *were* normal wetta skills. And the most frustrating part about it all was that Lhaurel herself had no answers to give.

She scowled and stalked over to where she'd stowed her things and bent to retrieve them.

Kaiden approached as she belted on her sword and settled it on her hip. "It was a good match," he said. "Until she hit you, that is."

Lhaurel scowled at him, but he ignored her.

"Anyway, I'll have to catch up with you later. Sarial and the others got back while you and Khari were busy bashing metal sticks together, so I'm off to see what they found."

All brooding vanished from her countenance in an instant. "I'll come with you," Lhaurel said.

Kaiden shook his head. "I'm afraid you're not invited. They sent a runner for me earlier, but I decided to stay to watch the end of the match. Makin Qays will curse me to the seven hells for it, but I figured I'd get to see you roughed up a bit, and I couldn't really miss that. Besides, Makin won't start without Khari anyway."

Lhaurel punched him on the arm as hard as she could. Considering that her arms were tired from her recent duel, it didn't amount to much of a hit.

Kaiden winced dramatically and left with a half-hearted wave. As he passed Tieran, he tapped the man on the shoulder. Tieran nodded and followed him from the room.

Khari had already left.

Lhaurel sighed, put down her things, and picked up her sword. She might as well practice some more.

* * *

Lhaurel slumped into the sand sometime later, completely exhausted. A lock of her bushy auburn hair rested between her teeth, but she didn't really notice.

"Are you alright?"

Lhaurel glanced to her right. Sarial stood there over the corpse of a sailfin, which was already half butchered. One of the recent raids had brought back so many corpses that they were working on them throughout the warren. Two neatly butchered carcasses lay barren on the sand next to her.

"I'm fine," Lhaurel said, realizing the meeting must be over. How long had she been sitting there practicing?

"Good, I'd hate for you to have hurt yourself somehow. You know, I used to be afraid of these things," Sarial said, kicking one of the sailfin corpses. "Massive teeth, the keening noise they make when they travel through the air, the packs."

Lhaurel nodded.

"But then Khari had me do some butchering, and I'm not so scared of them anymore. I'm actually somewhat fascinated with them."

"Fascinated? With these monsters?"

The older woman nodded, her expression growing grim. While Sarial was only a decade or so older than Lhaurel, her expression made her seem far older. "Well, yes. Haven't you ever wondered how they can fly? Or why their flight is so jumpy and sporadic? I mean, creatures like these simply shouldn't exist."

"What do you mean?" Lhaurel asked to get her to continue. She had wondered about those things. Everyone had.

Sarial grinned and pushed her hair back out of her eyes. "Look here." She pointed at the milky white sinew and metal-encrusted bone on the half-butchered corpse. "See these sinews? They hold a power that shocks, like lightning, but on a much smaller scale. When wrapped around metal, this power gives the metal a magnetic charge."

Lhaurel's face must have betrayed her confusion.

"Like what Kaiden can do. It makes it so that the metal can push off against other metals. So when the sailfin, or any of the genesauri, for that matter, starts crackling along those black spots, that means the shock is charging the metal. Kaiden says there's a whole plateau of metal beneath the sands against which the genesauri push their bodies, making them fly, but only for as long as the charge holds."

"That's—that's interesting." Lhaurel said. She hadn't meant it to sound so doubting, but Sarial immediately stiffened.

"I can prove it."

Lhaurel backed up as Sarial stretched out one hand and wrapped it around one of the metal encrusted bones. A nimbus of white and red seemed to glow around the woman, and suddenly her hand crackled with brilliant white energy.

The corpse lifted off the ground.

Lhaurel gasped, raising a hand to her lips. The nimbus around Sarial faded, and the corpse crashed back to the sand. The woman sighed and sank to her knees, breathing deeply.

"You're a—" Lhaurel asked, searching for the right term.

"A relampago, yes." The tone of the woman's voice made it clear that Lhaurel should have known this.

"So you . . . "

"I can create the same energy the genesauri can." Sarial's tone was blunt. "What do you and Kaiden talk about when you're together? Or is talking not something you two do?"

Lhaurel blushed but felt her temper flare at the same time. Sarial couldn't be *jealous, could she*?

She held up a hand before Lhaurel could respond. "I shouldn't have gotten upset like that," Sarial said softly. "I did a little too much charging that corpse. It takes a surprising amount of energy to get one of those to lift up."

Lhaurel frowned and waited for more of an explanation.

"I am Sarial. I lead the mystics. Tieran is my brother."

Lhaurel nodded but didn't ease her frown. She knew who the woman was, even though they'd never been introduced. Did this woman really think she had a chance with Kaiden?

"I'm sorry I didn't believe you."

"I'm used to not being believed. People tend to find my ideas a little strange."

"Well, I believe you now. They really are a—um—fascinating." Lhaurel grimaced as she said it.

"It's hard to admit, isn't it? But that's not even the most fascinating part. Since Kaiden and Khari have neglected their duties with you, I'll have to teach you some of this myself."

"What is the most fascinating part?"

Some of Sarial's fatigue seemed to have vanished. She smoothed some of the sand near her and began to draw, speaking as her finger traced out a design.

"The Roterralar—well, really the Rahuli—have three distinct abilities. The wetta." She drew a teardrop shape. "The relampago." She drew two jagged lines that crossed behind the teardrop. "And the magnetelorium." She drew three parallel lines behind the teardrop as well, centered on the fat part of the drawing. "Three elements working together for the good of the people. All three of these elements— metal, water, and energy—are present in the genesauri, too. There's a symmetry to it."

Lhaurel studied the drawing. It seemed oddly familiar, though she couldn't place where she'd seen it before.

"What does it mean?" she asked.

Sarial shrugged. "I really don't know. I just know there's a connection."

Silence stretched between them for a long moment. Lhaurel picked up a waterskin and played with the stopper. It sloshed around inside the leather. She could feel it churning, pulsing. Mirroring her thoughts.

"So you're a wetta, then?" Sarial asked, though it was obvious she already knew.

Lhaurel nodded.

"Good, we can always use another healer."

"You're a—relampago, was it?"

"Yup. I can manipulate energy to an extent. Outside of battle it's not much use to anyone. I mean, we can make glass, but outside of pretty ornaments, what good is glass?"

"How does energy make glass?"

Sarial laughed, though it wasn't a pleasant sound. "Glass is just heated sand. When you run energy through sand it heats up and melts into glass. The genesauri, do it too. Genesauri nests aren't really nests at all. When they crackle with energy, it melts the sand and forms a thin glass tube. Then sand gets blown into it but stays loose instead of getting all packed together." She got to her feet, legs a little wobbly. "Well, I need to get back to my work."

Lhaurel nodded, getting to her feet as well. "Thanks, Sarial."

"For what?"

"For reminding me to never be afraid of what others think of you." She smiled wryly.

Sarial gave her an odd smile, obviously not sure how to respond, and then left.

Inside herself, Lhaurel laughed.

* * *

The tent flap rustled as Taren stepped inside, his cold eyes taking in the small dark room and alighting on Marvi's still form along one side of the room. She watched as his silhouette drew near and reached out a hand to wake her.

"I am awake, Taren," she said.

He grunted, unsurprised at having found her awake.

She half sat up, curiosity overcoming her tiredness. Since becoming Warlord, Taren had not spent much time within the camp. As was customary, he'd spent a large amount of his time with the other Warlords, boasting of past conquests and forming new alliances or renewing old rivalries. In Marvi's opinion, it was inevitable that men would take any excuse they could find to swill down some wine and brag about highly embellished deeds of yesteryear. But she had expected other things from Taren. Especially after all she had done to aide him in his quest. She had, after all, killed her husband for the man. And helped him bypass her own sons for leadership of the clan.

"Get up, woman. The clans are all gathering at the well." His voice was gruff, and Marvi detected more than a trace of irritation. Or arrogance. It was hard for her to tell with Taren sometimes.

"What's going on?" she asked as she rose and pulled on clothes that lay near the bed.

Taren ignored her and pushed out the door into the night outside.

She had heard movement outside her tent earlier but had simply written it off as one of the patrols sweeping through camp a bit too vigilantly for their own good. She had meant to have words with Taren about that later but never got the opportunity. Now, as she pulled the tent flap door out of the way and stepped out into the cool night air, she realized that the sound had been the noise of the camp emptying. She joined the throng of people hurrying from their tents, all headed in the same direction. Warriors were scattered amongst the throng, carrying swords or spears, but they were sparse. More common were women wearing the yellow *shufari* or mothers with children clutching sleepily at their mother's skirts. She nearly knocked Saralhn over as she hurried to catch up to Taren.

"What's going on?" Marvi asked, grabbing Taren on the shoulder.

He spun around and backhanded her across the face, knocking her to the ground.

She fell hard, clutching at her bruised face, eyes wide with shock more than fear or pain. No one even stopped to see if she was alright or to help her to her feet.

SANDS

Taren stood over her, one hand resting on the hilt of his sword and the other pointing down at her. "Never touch me again, woman," he said, voice soft. "You are no longer the Warlord's wife. You do not wear the blue."

Cold anger flashed through her, but she quelled the bitter retort on her lips.

She no longer wore the blue *shufari*, it was true. Instead she now wore the white of a widow, the same as so many others. But Jenthro had not defined her before. Authority was earned. She had put Taren in the position he was in now. She could just as easily take it back away from him or allow it to be taken from him. Her expression hardened, and in her mind, she began planning her first moves.

"As you wish, Warlord," she said, her eyes hard as ice. Whatever passion she had felt before was gone.

Taren grinned wickedly and turned back around, disappearing into the crowd.

Marvi made to get to her feet and felt a pair of hands grab her right arm from behind to help hoist her up. Marvi looked over her shoulder. Saralhn stood there, supporting her weight. In the light of a passing torch, Marvi could make out a large purple bruise on the young woman's cheek.

She pulled her arm free and dusted off her clothes. "Go," Marvi said curtly.

Saralhn nodded, melding with the passing throng.

Taren stood atop the speaking stone at the exact center of the Oasis. He looked out at the assembled masses that were huddled together in familial and clan groups. Marvi noted that the Frierd were short on numbers, but the Sidena were fewer still. The journey to the Oasis had cost them dearly.

What was Taren doing leading the meeting?

He reared himself up and began to speak. "Brethren." His voice boomed out through the darkness. "I have called this gathering to share with you glad tidings before fell news. There is hope once more for our people."

Somewhere in the crowd, someone yawned loudly, and another voice called out, "If it's not about special fruit that can make you fly, it's not good enough to get us out of bed."

Taren's face remained outwardly calm, but Marvi, who was studying him closely, saw the tightening of his jaw, the set of his shoulder.

He grinned through tight lips and continued onward. "This is the defining moment of our civilization."

His soft voice quieted the crowd as easily as if it had been a thunderclap.

"And with as much magic in it as your special fruit." Taren drew a small knife and began to idly trim his nails while he talked, not looking down at his hands while he worked. "I ask you, brethren, how is it that we take down a sailfin? How do we defend ourselves against genesauri when we are not walking the stoneways or here within the Oasis? I answer for you. We band together. Two or three warriors pool their talents and skill to fell the foul beasts, each one defending and protecting the other. The strong survive and the weak are left to die."

There was a murmuring note of agreement from the crowd. Many of the warriors were nodding. The women mostly had their heads down, tending to tired children, though even those that had no children seemed intent on the intricacies of the sand at their feet.

Marvi, for her part, pressed careful attention to every word. What was Taren about? He was getting powerful if no one had stopped him yet. Too powerful, maybe, for her to take down.

"Unity," Taren continued. "It is a lifeline against futility and loneliness. It is a flame of hope against the darkest night. I will never be able to describe the joy of being faced by death and having one of your brethren spit in the devil's eye and bring you back to life again. We are brothers-in-arms against danger. Protectors of each other."

The yawner from earlier repeated his prior show of boredom. It was a large man with a thick black beard and long hair tied back behind his ears. He was muscular and tall, if a little on the uglier side. The moonlight highlighted the silver scars that scoured a line down the middle of his nose, giving him an ethereal cast.

Taren pointed at him with the dagger he'd been using to trim his nails. The people around the man shied away as Taren spoke.

"You there, warrior, speak your mind."

The man grunted and shrugged, shifting his weight from one foot to another. It was obvious that he didn't like the attention he was getting, nor did he want to speak, but pride forced him to respond.

"What do you want, man?" he asked, his voice a deep rich drawl. "I know yeh don't want nothing to do with unity. Yer just making a show of all this since yer a new Warlord. Cut out the crap and get to the point."

Marvi let out a small silent whistle of grudging admiration and incredulity. The man had no small amount of courage. Maybe he wasn't half bad to look at. The scars gave him character.

Some of the women who had had their heads down glanced up for a moment, looking to see who had spoken.

Atop the speaking stone, Taren regarded the man coolly and then turned slowly where he stood, raising his hands high, one hand still clutching his dagger. "What do we do when there is a sandtiger amongst the flocks?" He fell silent, waiting for the crowd to respond.

"Chase it away," several voices shouted.

Taren smiled and shook his head with a small chuckle. "A temporary solution at best. What do you do?"

"Move the sheep away," one of the women called.

Again Taren shook his head and smiled. The hand holding the dagger flourished slightly so that the weapon flipped over and left him holding the blade by the point.

"Worse answer yet. You band together, and you eliminate the threat. If you do not, the sandtiger gets it in its head that this is an easy source of food.

"This is a simple way to survive. You subjugate yourself to it since it will keep coming back until the problem is gone. Not only that, you track it back to its nest and eliminate its mate, its cubs, all of them. You wipe out the threat once and for all."

He was facing away from the man who had spoken, but Marvi saw Taren's body tense a moment before he spun at the torso and his arm pumped, letting the dagger fly. It was a masterful throw, one only a handful of warriors within the Oasis could make, but the dagger spun through the air end over end, glittering in the torch gleam and moonlight, before finding its mark in the man's eye.

He slumped to the ground with a silent, futile groan.

The assembled clans immediately cried out in anger, shock, and surprise. Marvi tensed and clutched at her throat. What had Taren just done? The water oaths that governed the actions of all the clans within the Oasis forbade the shedding of another's blood. They protected the clans from each other and from themselves. For three months each year, there was peace within the Oasis. Not in living memory had that been violated. It was one of the things that actually kept the clans together. Violations of the water oaths were punished by the clans as a whole, not by any one Warlord, but by all of them together. She expected one of the other Warlords to shout out in protest, but none of them spoke up. In fact, she didn't see any of the other Warlords in the crowd. Other voices cried out in the din, asking the same questions.

"The water oaths!"

"Murderer!"

"What have you done?!"

Saralhn pushed through the crowd, going to the man's side and rolling him over. She checked his pulse as shouts assailed Taren. After a moment, she moved her hand away from his throat, dripping with blood, and shook her head.

Taren raised his hands for silence, and the shouting slowly died away. He radiated a sense of confidence that Marvi found disconcerting. He didn't seem even remotely concerned that he had violated every oath that the desert people held sacred. In fact, he seemed coldly delighted.

Marvi felt a strange itch creep down her arms, and she hugged them to her chest.

"The genesauri are coming," he said. "All of them. They are coming here. If we do not stand united, we will be destroyed. We will be their easy source of food. Just like the sandtigers, we have to hunt them down and destroy them."

"Are you mad?" Someone shouted, bravely voicing what everyone else was thinking.

Taren arched an eyebrow, his wrinkled face growing even more wrinkled at the gesture.

"This man was an enemy of the unity. I am upholding the water oaths. I am preventing the shedding of innocent blood. Those who do not stand with me only further their own destruction. The genesauri are coming, and we will destroy them. And I will lead you in that great battle."

Silence reigned. But it was more than simple silence. Among the women, the silence was the silence of despair and resignation. The silence that fills a room after the death of a loved one. The loss of hope and peace in the face of devastating truth. Among many of the warriors and men that made up the lesser half of the group, the silence was of disbelief and anger, the silence of a man who simply did not know what to say or how to say it. Yet among the children the loudest silence lived. Among them was the silence of fear. Fear because they simply did not understand but felt the emotions radiate from their parents and those around them.

Marvi looked out into this silence and found herself a participant in all three.

After a long moment someone finally spoke. "The Warlords will not agree to this."

Taren smiled and then whistled shrilly. Marvi felt a twinge in her left knee as horror welled up within her and clawed its way toward her mouth. At the edges of the crowd, shapes began to take form. Shapes of men with weapons drawn, glinting in the torchlight. The approaching men formed a ring around the crowd, weapons pointed inward. Marvi recognized the middle warrior as Alarian, Warlord of the Frierd. Three of the men stepped forward in front of the others and raised round objects into the sky. Each man held the head of one of the other Warlords.

Taren smiled and looked down at the man who had spoken. "I really don't think they'll object."

Marvi raised a hand to her mouth, horrified. How had she let this man take charge of her clan? Looking back, she could clearly see how he'd manipulated her, pulling on her strings like some outcast puppet. He'd planned this from the beginning, hoping to take over not just the Sidena, but all the clans. He'd eliminated all the competition.

She stopped as realization hit her. She looked up at him. His gaze fell on her, and he smiled. She realized, as pain blossomed in her back and a dagger worked its way toward her heart from behind, that she'd supported the wrong man. * * *

Lhaurel paused halfway through the form she had been practicing, one foot raised about a foot above the ground. She held her balance perfectly, unconsciously, as she recognized Kaiden's approach.

He was out in the hall still, but she had mastered isolating her ability down to a certain area or even to a particular person. Khari had helped her discover how to do it even though she didn't fully understand how Lhaurel could feel everyone's presence.

Shifting out of her stance, Lhaurel lowered her sword to her waist and sheathed it before Kaiden burst into the room, sending an aevian that was preening near the door skittering away with a screech of indignation.

His face was a storm of emotion. Lhaurel noted with concern that anger and frustration were the foremost, though it was intermingled with a smattering of resignation and, oddly, eagerness. He noticed her, and his expression slipped smoothly into one of surprise.

"What are you doing here, Lhaurel? Weren't you in the greatroom?"

"I needed some fresher air." She smiled and then noticed on the edges of her senses that others were approaching the eyrie, too. Tieran and his twin were among them. "What's going on?"

"Sarial thinks she found what's driving the genesauri," he said carefully. "Makin Qays has ordered two whole flights to investigate and destroy the place if possible. That should stop them from being driven toward the Oasis."

There was uncertainty in his voice, an edge of indecision.

"What is it?" Lhaurel asked.

"Sarial wasn't very specific. But something big."

Lhaurel rolled her eyes but let his sarcasm pass. He seemed distracted.

"Well, be safe. And watch out for Sarial." She knew that if she were allowed to tag along, he would have mentioned it already. Yet a part of her wanted to go with him. She was only half surprised to realize that only part of it was curiosity about what was driving the genesauri. The larger part was a desire to be with Kaiden.

"Why? Because she thinks you're stealing me away from her?" He smiled and winked at her.

SANDS

Lhaurel felt warmth spread across her chest and color bloomed on her cheeks. So he *knew* Sarial had feelings for him, too. It had taken Sarial's little show earlier for Lhaurel to realize her own feelings for Kaiden were growing into something beyond friendship. She found that odd, considering how much she'd distrusted him. A small part of her still did, but the seed was slowly starting to grow.

He stepped forward suddenly and kissed her on the cheek.

"Stay safe," he said. Then he was off, hurrying to call Skree-lar as the other members of the flights entered the eyrie.

Lhaurel watched him go, one hand on her cheek where the feel of his lips still burned.

Part 4

Mystic

CHAPTER 17
A Lake of Tears

"Briane. Dear, sweet Briane. I know the voice of the girl child screaming. What have they done to you? I cannot believe these dreams. They are illusions brought about by the enemy. I cannot believe them. I simply cannot.

"I know the voice the of the girl child screaming. Am I the cause of those screams?"

-From the Journals of Elyana

Pain is the thief's mask in the dead of night. It creeps up in the quiet moments when there is nothing else around and steals away hope and love and pride. It is the silent messenger that comes to announce that the best efforts are futile. But it is also a lie.

Gavin trudged doggedly through the long, dark passages. The greatsword was still a cane in his hands, an extra limb to grant his aching body support. The pain in his chest had turned to a fiery inferno long since. He had thought before that maybe some of his ribs were broken. Now he was sure that at least two of them were. If he only had some numbweed or nettleberry sap to chew to dull the pain. But as long as he was wishing for what he didn't have, he could use a torch, some water, and something to eat, preferably a juicy haunch of lamb. His mouth watered at the thought, and his stomach grumbled in protest.

Rest stops came every time he passed through ragged patches of light that streamed down through jagged openings in the ceiling. As he rested, he studied the breaks and the rubble strewn beneath them. Invariably, the edges of the breaks were worn smooth with age, pounded by the wind and sand until they had been rounded down. None of them were fresh and none of them were in a position where they offered him any chance of escape.

After an indeterminate time, his arms became leaden and his legs too weary to move, yet he forced himself to simply put one foot in front of the other. Left and then right. Left and then right. He repeated the words in his mind, using them like a beacon to guide him forward. It was a testament to his pure and all-consuming exhaustion that he walked right by a lit torch crackling in a sconce set into the wall without even noticing it. He kept on walking, putting one foot in front of the other and almost dragging the greatsword along behind him. The hilt was locked in his swollen grip, as if the weapon had somehow become a part of him.

A cool breeze caressed his cheek, touching him with the strength of a falling feather and then passing on again. He blinked and stumbled in his step. The breeze came again. It washed over him with the strength of a sandstorm wave, though it was over and done within the space between two breaths. It was as if someone had infused new energy within him. His eyelids fluttered and his gaze snapped back into focus. Pain faded to the background. In a sudden burst of understanding, Gavin realized he was standing in a lit hallway.

Torches meant people. The wooden brands had very short lives and burned up their fuel relatively quickly. They would only last for a few hours at the most. That meant that very recently, someone had been through this very passage to light the two torches.

He straightened and adjusted his grip on the greatsword. What were people doing inside the walls of the Oasis?

Aches and pains set aside for the moment, Gavin crept forward, gaze intent for signs of movement within the tunnels. The breeze picked up again, cool and refreshing on his bruised and sweaty face. Vestiges of exhaustion still clung on stubbornly, so it took him a moment to realize that the breeze, along with being cool, carried moisture with it. Water. His stride lengthened, and he moved with a more confident step. Need made him bold, as it does to all men. Even the lowliest churl, addicted to the euphoric effects of the nettleberry pods, became bold when his addictive need drove him to obtain more of his addictive substance. Or so his grandmother had said.

The passageway curved to the right and sloped downward, leading down into the wall. Gavin followed it and passed several other torches set into the wall. The walls here showed the signs of recent and frequent use. Blackened walls behind and above the torches where soot had not yet been scrubbed away. A clear path in the sand and dust on the passageway floor where feet had trodden recently. From the breadth, depth, and number of tracks, Gavin guessed that anywhere from six to eight men had passed through there as recently as an hour ago. His grip on the greatsword's hilt tightened.

What was going on? Maybe he'd hit his head harder than he thought, or else he was so badly wounded that he was beginning to hallucinate, like a man driven to heat exhaustion by prolonged exposure to the sun.

Several side passages branched off from the main artery, but Gavin ignored them and continued to follow the main passageway downward and to the right. His aches were beginning to return with a vengeance, and he hadn't run across anyone else in the passage despite the signs of their passing. He had to stay vigilant. He had a strange feeling that whatever was going on here wasn't natural. There was a sense of the ethereal to it.

The passage ended in a cavern large enough to hold all the clans together and have room to spare, a room whose entirety was completely covered in water except for a narrow strip of grey-brown stone down the center that lead toward the opposite wall. Torchlight glittered off the surface of the vast lake. It stretched out several hundred spans, reflecting the light off its shimmering surface. A symphony of dripping water echoed off the walls.

Without conscious thought on his part, Gavin stumbled forward, lost in the alien beauty of such vast amounts of water collected in one place. A cool mist dusted his face as he walked, his step suddenly surer at the touch. He neared the far wall and realized his own insignificance in the face of such grandeur.

Light cast odd shadows against the base of the wall. The narrow walkway widened, creating a narrow patio along the wall. Hundreds of small cubbyholes were carved into the rock. Most of them had strange glass bottles in them that shone dully in the torchlight. The dust hung thick upon them, a grey-brown patina of age dusted with neglect. Switching the greatsword to his left hand, Gavin reached out to pull one of the glass cylinders free.

Before his fingers closed over the bottle, a murmur of echoing voices reached his ears. His heart raced. Years of his grandmother's constant nagging asserted themselves within his mind. *Those who remain calm while others are in panic are those who can create change. They are those who can rule.*

Clutching the bottle and the greatsword to him, Gavin hurried into the shadows where two walls met, resting at the edge of the stone in a crouch. The shadows played along the wall and atop the water's surface around him. That, coupled with the dust and grime that still covered him from his earlier fall, served as a ready shield against prying eyes.

Presently, a handful of figures came into view from the mouth of the cavern, voices raised in heated debate. The voices echoed over one another, distorting the words and dulling them as if they had been shouted during the middle of a sandstorm. But as the figures drew closer, the meaningless words resolved into a fierce argument between two men.

"Yes, they had to die." The speaker's voice was light. "When one of the goats in the herd becomes diseased, a wise shepherd kills it before it can infect the others. Only an ignorant man would let the sickness spread. Yes, the remaining goats will now look at their master in fear, but perhaps that is for the best. Fear is a great motivator of obedience."

"But we're not talking about sick goats." The other man's voice was hard and cold. Angry.

"Ah, but we are. These were but the first deaths. There will be more. There *must* be more. The herd is infected, and the sick ones have to die. You agreed to this. It is all a part of the plan. We must stand united, or we will all die."

The two men came close, stopping at one of the cubbyholes and taking out a glass canister. The second man kept silent as the pair turned around and headed back out the way they had come.

Gavin let out his breath in a low hiss. What in the seven hells was going on?

* * *

At first Lhaurel didn't understand what she was seeing. A small bird fluttered through the cavernous eyrie mouth and alighted on the ground near her. Smaller birds avoided the eyrie as if it were a den of snakes. The aevians would devour anything foolish enough to stray into their territory. It wasn't until she saw the narrow strip of parchment attached to the bird's leg that she realized why the bird was there and why none of the aevians had so much as given it a passing glance.

She turned to one of the worker women busy cleaning the genesauri carcasses. "Go get Khari."

She reached out a hand and the bird obediently hopped up onto her finger. She carefully untied the note, and the bird leapt from her hand and flew away, back toward wherever it was that Khari kept her messenger birds. Lhaurel was just about to unravel the small scroll when she sensed Khari approaching.

Since the casts had left, everyone in the warren had been on edge. The tension had led to more than one spat with Khari during training, which generally meant that what little training there was occurred in the first few minutes of the lesson before either of them could get into the stride of an emotional outburst.

Khari pushed open one of the doors with more force than was necessary. From the set of her shoulders and the expression on her face, it was clear that she and Makin Qays had been arguing again. Lhaurel had never heard them expressly fight, but she suspected that their arguments revolved around how to respond to the growing threat to the Rahuli.

Lhaurel handed Khari the note. The woman snatched it out of her hands without a word of thanks.

"It's addressed to you," Khari said after a moment.

Lhaurel held out a hand for it, but Khari unraveled it herself and read the brief text. Her brow furrowed, and then suddenly she swore.

"Damn him to the seven hells," she said, nearly tearing the note in two. "Damn him."

"What?" Lhaurel asked.

Khari turned to her and distractedly handed her the miniature scroll. It read, *Lhaurel. Taren has taken over rule of the clans. Other Warlords are dead.* It was not signed.

"But how—" Lhaurel started, but Khari cut her off.

"We've got to tell Makin," she said, spinning on her heel and almost running back the way she had come. "Gather those you can to the council room."

Lhaurel waited a moment, and then she ignored the order and ran after her. She caught up just as Khari was passing the news to Makin Qays.

"Sidena has taken over the Oasis." The force of her words made Makin Qays turn to regard her with furrowed brow. "All the other Warlords are dead. Taren leads them."

Lhaurel wondered how detailed the reports were that Khari gave him that she could refer to Taren by name.

Makin Qays's furrowed brow contracted even further. He reached a hand up and scratched at his scraggly beard. It was the first time that Lhaurel had seen him look so disheveled.

"If it's true, this isn't good. What does he want besides the power?" Makin Qays leaned forward. "We need to confirm this report, though I will make preparations here either way. Send someone to the Oasis to double check."

"I don't think that's a good idea," Khari interjected. "We've never been well received even when protected by the water oaths. If they really have killed the other Warlords and this Taren has taken charge as some self-proclaimed king, then the water oaths are worthless. Anyone who goes would be risking their lives, especially after the last time."

"We risk our lives every time we go out there," Makin Qays said.

Lhaurel found that she was chewing her bottom lip and stopped herself. Khari looked like she was about to speak further, but Lhaurel interrupted up before she could.

"Warlord," Lhaurel said in a somewhat hesitant voice. "I agree with the matron. It would not be wise to send someone in right now. Especially not a woman."

Makin turned to regard her as he leaned back in his chair and cupped one hand under his chin. He raised an eyebrow at her. "What makes you say that?"

Khari looked over at her, too, awaiting her response.

"I don't know much about politics and leadership," she said. "But I do know this man, Taren. I was married to him for a short time. He loves control and spends a great deal of time showing people his power over them." She raised her arm to show him the fresh scar on her wrist where the marriage dagger had sealed the bond. "I was his fifth wife."

Makin Qays blinked. "Then we should proceed as if this message is correct for now and make plans accordingly. What is Taren's plan? Why is he doing this? I will meet with the cast leaders and Sarial when they return from their mission. The genesauri are the more present threat right now, but perhaps the two are not unrelated." He nodded to Lhaurel as if thanking her for her opinion.

"I'll see what I can do about getting more information to see what this Taren plans as well," Khari said.

Makin Qays nodded, both in agreement and in dismissal. Lhaurel inclined her head toward the man slightly and turned to leave.

Just then, a deep, resonating sound reverberated through the room, a rolling, thunderous note. Lhaurel instantly reached out her senses, pushing them to their furthest limitations. The warren sprang to life in her mind, each individual within it passing through Lhaurel's consciousness with a light touch before she found what she was looking for.

"Kaiden and the others are back," she said, fixing on his presence. "They—" She hesitated. There was something wrong about the way he felt. He felt somehow lessened, weaker, like—like Honric did before he died. Without pausing to give an explanation outside of the color draining from her face, Lhaurel turned and dashed down the passageway toward the eyrie.

SANDS

Her breath came in long, labored gasps, but she pushed herself onward, bursting into the eyrie only a few minutes after leaving the council room. To Lhaurel, it had felt like an eternity. A throng of people and aevians bustled about at the opposite side of the room, a cacophonous wave of indistinguishable sound rolling from them. She caught pieces of conversation and whispers between them among wails of grief and despair.

Lhaurel didn't slow her run as she raced toward the group. Pushing through the birds and people there, not caring if she offended anyone, Lhaurel forced her way to the center of the group. Kaiden and another cast leader were there, stretched out in the sand and being attended to by a swarm of women.

"Tieran, the others?" she wondered aloud.

At the sound of her voice, Kaiden looked up. There were cuts and scrapes all over his face, and his clothes were torn and bloody. Lhaurel hoped the blood wasn't his.

He met her eyes with tears in his own. He shook his head. "The kalundin hit us."

* * *

Later that day, after Kaiden and those who'd survived had had their wounds bound and had given their reports to Makin Qays and the others, Lhaurel found herself wandering down toward the underground lake. The news of the deaths had spread through the warren like the sands from a storm. Lhaurel herself felt numb. Nearly a score of people were dead. Most of them were people that Lhaurel knew at least by sight. And Tieran. Dear, sweet, lovable Tieran. She still half expected him to appear from behind a corner and wink at her roguishly, explaining that it was all part of some elaborate scheme.

But she knew he wouldn't. The look in Kaiden's eyes when he'd shook his head had told her everything she needed to know. She hadn't seen Tieran's wife since, but she had searched for her with her powers. The woman was locked in her rooms, and Lhaurel was not about to disturb her. Instead, she searched out the one person that she did want to comfort. The story of what had happened had spread with the rumors as well—the story of the desperate battle that had ended the lives of so many. Too many. The party had come upon the location that the first patrols had found, a patch of sand that shone like glass and was ringed by dozens of thin metal poles that stuck up into the air. When they had landed, they hadn't discovered anything of interest other than a confirmation of what they had already assumed. Something had turned the sand to glass.

They had been just about to leave when disaster had struck. Genesauri had burst up out of the sands around them, but not sailfins. Worse. Marsaisi. Lhaurel shuddered. She'd never seen one of the colossal beasts, but stories said that they were almost thirty spans long and could swallow a dozen men with room to spare within their gullets. They were also nearly impossible to kill.

And then the kalundin had appeared. No one would speak of it, but the despair and terror were like a wildfire, burning away hope.

Lhaurel stepped into the misty air of the lake chamber and felt an overwhelming sense of calm and peace wash over her. Torchlight glinted from the far wall, flickering in a silent war against the shadows. Lhaurel walked along the path toward where Kaiden rested, his back against the wall. His head didn't turn as she approached, but his eyes followed her. Lifeless eyes, sunken and hollow. She took a seat next to him and hugged her legs to her.

"Hi," she said. Kaiden didn't look at her, but when he spoke, his voice was cold.

"You don't see it, do you? You're just like Makin Qays and the rest." The contempt in Kaiden's voice was palpable. "Look at this place. There are enough rooms to support thousands of people here. We have running water, walls high enough to keep the genesauri at bay, and the aevians to take us wherever we wish to go. And yet we keep it to ourselves. We hoard what we have instead of sharing it. We let others die because we are too possessive of our power to take them in. And we justify our role as deity by remembering those we've lost with bands on our arms."

He sighed in disgust and turned away from her, waving a dismissive, bandaged hand. A thin red mist seemed to envelope him, and some small bits of metal on the floor rose up and started spinning in intricate patterns in front of him. Lhaurel shifted closer and placed a hand on his sleeve, pulling it upward to reveal the strange banded tattoos that ran up his arm where bandages did not cover them.

"Tell me."

His head shifted as if he were going to look at her, but then he stopped, tugging at his sleeve until it slipped from her grip and slid down over his arm to cover the tattoos.

"Not all of us are as lucky as you, Lhaurel," he said softly. "Not all of us were saved when our families were taken by the genesauri. My clan didn't know that I'd fallen. They didn't stop when my father fell or when my sister suddenly vanished in a shower of sand and gnashing teeth. They didn't know. They had to run."

Lhaurel waited expectantly, similar memories washing through her mind. She had thought that he would start talking about the battle now, about how he had managed to escape. But this was something else. Something much more personal.

"I fell back to help my father. He'd stumbled on a rock and rolled down the side of a dune not far from where the Stoneways were. I leapt down after him, but before I had even made it down the side of the dune, before my father could even draw his sword, a sailfin shot up out of the sand and tore off his head."

Lhaurel gasped and put a hand to her mouth.

"I still remember the hot, salty smell of his blood. I still see the genesauri's fangs tear into his flesh. And that is when I broke. As my clan ran off down the stoneways, I felt the power swell within me. Felt it burn. My father's sword came alive, killing the sailfin before it could return to the sands. I watched it die.

"And then Makin Qays showed up. Plunged out of the sky on the back of his aevian. They had waited until my clan was out of sight. They had waited. A few moments earlier they could have saved him. They could have saved him. I should have saved them." His voice caught.

"Them?" Lhaurel asked, placing a hand on his shoulder. He shrugged it away, still not looking at her.

"When they brought me here, I fought them. I fought them every single minute of every day. I hated them all. Hated that they could just sit there and let my father die. Hated that they could just sit here and make these grand claims that they've given up allegiance to their clans, but they still find ways of protecting those they care most about. They only saved me because one of their wetta sensed me break. They usually wait until they're older, like you, but I broke young.

"I hated the Roterralar. I vowed that one day I would make each one of them pay the price for the blood on their hands. They would pay for their selfishness." A sound broke through his words, a ragged, broken sob that only intensified with the echo. "Now I'm one of them. I let them die. I should have saved Sarial. I should have saved Tieran. I should have been able to save them all."

His sobs grew hard and Lhaurel wrapped her arms around him, letting his tears drip onto her arms and roll into the lake.

CHAPTER 18
Crumbling

"Sleep eludes me. The dreams haunt me in that realm of eternal blackness and illusion. Dreams that I cannot escape. The work holds me now. Only the work. The creatures doubled in size in the first week. They seem to have slowed now. I had hopes that perhaps they would double again, but it appears that they will not reach that size. But there are others that I could try. Now that we have had success, we can try again with others."

-From the Journals of Elyana

Makin Qays drummed his fingers against the thick wood of the table. The staccato sound echoed only lightly against the walls, but even if it had sounded like a drum, he would not have heard it.

The world was quickly devolving into chaos around him. The stability he had worked so hard for during the last several decades was gone in the space of only a few fortnights. Half the Roterralar were dead, and the genesauri were descending upon the Oasis. For some reason, a part of him doubted that the walls would hold them at bay.

He swallowed and cursed his foul mood. Then he swallowed again and cursed his cursing. He had every right to be in a foul mood. The leader of the mystics was dead, Tieran was dead, and the responsibility of all the lives in the desert were suddenly resting upon his shoulders in a very real sense for the first time since he had gotten his first patch of grey hairs. He had always been the Warlord of the Roterralar, but the clans had needed little in the way of protection of late. Simple raids, diversionary measures, and the occasional assistance in finding a new warren where the water supply would more readily be found.

And now this.

He grunted and began to pace. His choices were limited. He could let the genesauri roam rampant and unchecked, or he could kill what he could before they reached the Oasis. The nagging, cautious part of him argued that the clans in the Oasis, united or not, would need the smaller numbers. He simply could not rely on the walls to keep them at bay. Maybe they could get the sailfin packs to turn back if they harried them enough. They'd only tried a few smaller raids. Maybe it was time to try something larger.

He grimaced and called one of the younger aevian riders to him. He gave the order.

* * *

Lhaurel fought down a wave of emotion as she tightened the girth strap on Fahkiri's saddle and then checked the straps on her own harness. Four full casts were there, almost a score of aevian riders and a handful of mystics. Kaiden worked near her, his hands methodical but quick on the straps. He noticed her looking at him and smiled. She smiled back. He was recovering well.

She had not expected him to come on this raid, but he appeared along with the rest of those who had survived the disaster of the day before. There were still bandages on his arms, though he had removed the ones from his hands. She had held him long into the night while he let his emotions run. The intimacy had been overwhelming. Part of her had longed for him to reach up and kiss her, or hold her in return, his strong arms wrapping around her body and holding her tight. She blushed slightly as she remembered the dreams that had come that night after she had drifted off to sleep. They had involved far more than kissing.

Kaiden moved closer to her and whispered, "Stay close to me. Just do what I do, and you'll be fine." What was he doing comforting *her*?

He was the one who should have been nervous. And yet her hand shook as she leapt up into the saddle and set about attaching the support leads.

Kaiden put a hand on her leg and opened his mouth to say something, but Fahkiri hissed at him. He shrugged, walked over to Skree-lar, and climbed into the saddle.

Lhaurel continued to feel the warmth of his touch on her leg long after he let go.

Near the mouth of the cavern, Khari leapt atop Gwyanth's back and shouted for quiet. Tieran's wife sat astride a small aevian behind her, her face dark and brooding. Lhaurel felt a pang of sadness that she'd never learned the woman's name.

Makin Qays appeared through one of the side caverns, outfitted in fine robes of deep blue and with a sword belted at his waist. A large axe poked over one shoulder.

The few remaining whispers broke off.

"This is not a normal raid," Makin Qays shouted, his voice carrying a weight and solemnity Lhaurel had not heard before. "We're not there to just kill a few and run. We're not fighting to delay. We are fighting to destroy."

The stillness and silence that fell over the assembled warriors was deafening.

"Scores of our brethren have fallen. Let us repay them in kind!" Makin Qays whistled sharply and a massive aevian dropped from its roost high along the wall and landed in the sand in front of him. The majestic creature stood well above any of the other aevians, white plumage spotted with black and gold. Makin leapt up onto the creature's back, not bothering to clip in, and the aevian lunged into the air.

"Follow me," Kaiden shouted to Lhaurel over the din of flapping wings and shouts from the riders. "Bank left once you're away and follow me down."

"Down where?" Lhaurel tried to shout back, but her voice was lost in the rush of wind as Fahkiri launched into the air.

Lhaurel was buffeted by swirling wind from the aevians ahead of her. Her hair flapped and tugged at the base of her scalp as Fahkiri banked and followed the other aevians, turning in a great arc that took them back toward the face of the red sandstone cliff that hid the Roterralar Warren. She wished that she had tied it back or at least tucked it into her clothes. For a moment, she considered doing it as they flew, but just then Fahkiri banked again to avoid a group of aevians and their riders winging back up from beneath them. Light glinted off the sharp steel of the long spears they now clutched.

Skree-lar winged around to get in front of them. Kaiden gestured sharply to the left and Lhaurel glanced in the direction he was pointing. There was an opening in the sandstone wall, almost as large as the entrance to the eyrie, through which the aevians were entering and exiting again almost as quickly as they had landed. Beryl's smithy.

Fahkiri landed a moment behind Skree-lar. As soon as they had, a pair of the long spears flew toward them through the air of their own accord. Kaiden snatched his out of the air and tucked it under one arm, the long haft extending a few spans upward and behind him. It was so long, in fact, that it would have dragged along the ground if he had been holding it anywhere close to the middle of the haft.

"Hold the lance like this," Kaiden said. "Watch me when the fighting begins. Fly high. The smaller aevians are the bait. We are the real fighters."

Lhaurel grabbed the lance from the air and mimicked Kaiden's movements, holding it beneath one arm. Someone shouted at them to get out of the way, and with a sharp whistle from their riders, Fahkiri and Skree-lar wheeled about and launched themselves into the air as several other aevians landed in the forge. Lhaurel felt a thrill as they flew back along with the group. Part of the group climbed higher while a much larger portion dove toward the ground and remained a few spans above the dune tops. The young aevians, small and quick. They and their riders flew in intricate patterns over the sand.

Lhaurel fell into the joy of the flight. Wind tugged at the long lance in her hand. The haft was of pure, solid metal, though it was far lighter than she would have expected. The length was unwieldy and that added a sense of weight without having any real effect. The blade itself, almost a span above her head, was almost two feet in length and had a thick crosspiece at its base. She wondered what that was for.

SANDS

They flew for what seemed like an hour. The walls of the Oasis appeared on the horizon, growing larger as they flew. There came a sudden shout from below and suddenly a high-pitched screeching filled the air. The scream of a sailfin.

Lhaurel looked down over Fahkiri's wing.

Long, lithe bodies burst from the sands by the score, wind making the flesh on their long yellow fins vibrate and produce the irritating keening. And flying among them, swords, lances, and talons flashing, were the young aevians. They darted in between the masses of sinuous sailfin bodies, almost as agile as the genesauri themselves. Talons flashed, ripping gaping holes in genesauri flesh. Lances drove in behind the heads, piercing through the other side and getting stopped by the crosspiece. The riders left the lances embedded in the corpses, letting them fall back into the sand and getting in the way of the sailfins that continued to burst upward. Those who had already dropped their lances drew swords and lashed out, cutting sailfins out of the air, some falling back to the earth in more than one piece.

High above, Lhaurel reached out with her senses. She felt the blood coursing through the Roterralar veins. Felt the thrill of adrenaline and fear that drove them onward. The aevians felt of pride and anger, lashing out against these perversions of nature with all of their might and strength. There was an abiding hatred there, a sense of generations of enduring, pervasive animosity that manifested itself in their unabated desire to kill these creatures that plagued the sands.

Makin Qays lead a group down. Lances pierced sailfin flesh, pinning corpses to the ground to be devoured by their companions. Makin Qays rolled out of his saddle, landing in the sand and throwing up dust. Above him, Lhaurel watched with a panic-stricken grip on her lance as Makin Qays pulled his axe free and dashed across the sand, dodging the sinkholes left by earlier sailfins. The man was crazy. He was going to die.

He dashed toward the nearest group of sailfins, a roiling mass of spines and flesh tearing into one of their fallen companions. His axe spun in a dizzying arc. Blood spurted and sailfin bodies joined those pierced by the lances. Makin Qays seemed to disappear among the contorting forms, and then he appeared on the other side, axe dripping blood. His aevian dropped to the sand a moment later and Makin Qays leapt into the saddle, a cry of victory springing from his lips. The Roterralar rallied around him.

Stunning pain ripped through Lhaurel's body, pain so intense that it made her muscles seize and she almost lost her grip on the lance. Only the safety tethers on her harness kept her in the saddle. Below her, a young woman on her aevian screamed in the jaws of a sailfin. Then the scream cut off. Her aevian sent a ragged screech into the air and dove into the pack of sailfins that swarmed over the fallen Roterralar like ants on a drop of honey. Talons flashed, blood flowed, and shrieks rent the air from both genesauri and aevian alike. And then all was silent.

Lhaurel gasped and tore herself away from the scene, pulling her senses back, bruised and bloodied. Before she had pulled back, she had sensed the genesauri below the sands. Sensed all of them. They extended outward for hundreds of spans. Thousands of them. Only one small group fought them here. One small group of many. Fear and despair clutched at her heart and stilled her pounding blood. Below her, more shrieks and screams made a jarring symphony of death and pain. Lhaurel refused to look down, but some part of her couldn't resist the pull. She looked just as the larger aevians and their riders dove in a glorious wave of steel.

They shot through the air with speed unmatched by any other creature upon the sands. Lances held out before them, Makin Qays and Khari at their head, a wave of aevians crashed into the sailfins below with devastating accuracy. Blades pierced sailfin bodies and drove them into the ground. The lances remained buried in the sand as the aevians pulled out of the dives in a swirl of wind, sand, and feathers, swords hissing out of sheaths. War cries filled the air as wave after wave of the larger aevians plunged toward the earth and killed genesauri by the dozen. Makin Qays raised his bloody axe in the air, signaling another attack. Until that moment, Lhaurel had never understood why he garnered the respect he received from the Roterralar. Now she saw. He was a warrior at heart, not a leader of a peaceful people. This was a man who fought battles with his own hands, who rallied people to him when hope seemed lost.

SANDS

Kaiden and Skree-lar appeared in the chaos and press of bodies. From so high up, Lhaurel couldn't make out many details, but she could see that he didn't have a sword, and his lance was no longer in his hand. For a moment she felt a hint of panic as a sailfin burst out of the sand and surged through the air straight toward him. Without even pausing to think about it, Lhaurel whistled sharply and urged Fahkiri into a dive. He screeched a war cry and plunged toward the earth, aimed at Kaiden. The wind bit at her eyes, but Lhaurel refused to close them. They remained locked on Kaiden and the approaching jaws of the sailfin. She willed Fahkiri to go faster, urged him downward. She readied the lance.

The sudden impact nearly tore her arm from its socket. The lance pierced genesauri flesh as easily as if it had been passing through butter, but then it struck something solid and was wrenched free from her grasp. She let it fall and readied herself against the sudden lurching, gut-wrenching change of direction that she knew was coming.

A single clarion note cut through it all, a solitary thought that gave her both peace and stability against the chaos and noise and death that filled her eyes and ears and nose around her. Kaiden was safe. She had saved him.

And then she and Fahkiri slammed into the ground. Her head struck something hard and the leather leads in her harness snapped. Momentum carried her off Fahkiri's back. Sand filled her mouth and ground into her flesh, tearing the skin. As quickly as she could, Lhaurel scrambled to her feet, spitting. Dazed confusion clouded her mind for a moment, but then her gaze fell upon her brave aevian. Dark blood pumped from the hole through his chest.

No. Lhaurel dropped to her knees, ignoring the blood that flowed from a dozen wounds. *Not Fahkiri. Please, no.*

The sailfin's corpse lay a few feet away, lance through its middle, purple spines along its back lay broken and covered in blood, the same deep, red blood that stained Fahkiri's feathers and painted the sands. Lhaurel ignored the sounds of fighting around her, ignored the geysers of sand that heralded the arrival of even more genesauri.

Fahkiri cried weakly. His legs twitched spasmodically as the sailfin venom worked its way through his veins. Black eyes met Lhaurel's.

There was sadness there.

No, she was not about to give up on him so easily. Hands went over the wound, a meager bandage against the flow. Blood pumped up between her fingers, hot and strong. She could feel it. She could *feel* it.

She gasped and reached out to the other part of herself, the mystical part of her that rushed through her blood. The powers answered. The sense of the blood was much stronger than when she had felt the water. She could feel each pump of Fahkiri's heart with a sudden clarity that wrapped around her and gave her strength. A thin film of red mist enveloped her. With every bit of strength she could muster, she willed the blood to stop flowing, willed it back into the aevian's body. A reservoir of untapped power had suddenly opened up to her. Khari's training provided her the path to channel it downward between her fingers.

The pool of red around her knees shrank. Blood flowed back up into Fahkiri's body, forced back through the wound. Flesh knit together beneath her fingers, the blood within it obeying her command. She was master of the substance. She ruled it, and it bent to her will. The bloody mist around her dissipated as the wound sealed itself back up and Fahkiri rolled awkwardly to his feet, his screeches sounding as awed and confused as Lhaurel felt.

Lhaurel fell back onto her buttocks, realizing that she was shaking. Her hands trembled and shook, but they were clean of blood. Every last drop of it had been forced back through Fahkiri's wound.

The aevian stretched his wings experimentally, afraid that he wouldn't be able to. When he didn't feel any pain he stretched his wings to their fullest, reared back his head, and screamed into the sky. Behind him, a sailfin dropped to the ground and sent a shower of sand into the air. Chunks of the sand hit the ground near Lhaurel and dusted her with a fine gritty spray.

She blinked and raised a shaky hand to brush the sand from her face. As she did so, the ground beneath her trembled. Something massive burst out of the sand next to her, sending her tumbling down the side of a dune. Fahkiri screeched in anger, rage, and pain as a genesauri as big around as a dozen sailfins together shot up out of the sand and then arched back downward, swallowing Fahkiri whole and plunging back into the depths of the sand.

Something inside Lhaurel broke. She felt it shatter as she watched the marsaisi's long, stocky body and spotted tail slip back beneath the sand.

She had just saved him. Fahkiri had been dying and she had healed him. She had just saved him.

Her mind felt numb, and yet at the same time, a torrent of swelling power grew within her, and her senses blasted outward like a raging storm. The wind kicked up and shot outward from her as her power grew, the sands radiating outward in a circle and following the path of the whipping wind. The sand rolled outward in waves like ripples upon the surface of water.

Lhaurel felt the genesauri in the sands beneath her feet. She felt the marsaisi turning in the sand, pushing upward against the force beneath the sands that let it pass into the air. She felt it, felt the blood pulsing within it. Felt it and reached out to it.

A red mist formed around her. Power blossomed in her chest, a bittersweet burgeoning of pure strength that made the earlier reservoir seem like a candle beneath the sun. The red cloud grew as she continued to pull on the blood. The marsaisi burst up from the sand, twisting and writhing in a great and terrible pain.

Lhaurel stared at it without pity, ignoring its flailing body and the waves of sand that flew in the air and were blasted away from her by the screaming wind. She reached out to the blood within it. Reached out to and drained it from the creature's body. And as she did, the power within her grew, grew to a strength that she simply could not contain. The wind screamed around her, whipping up dust. A scream of pure agony and terror and ecstasy ripped from her throat. The red cloud of blood and sand grew and thickened until she was hidden within it, a pool of red that bubbled and hissed as if it were steaming.

The marsaisi seemed to shrink, the skin wrinkling and desiccating until all that remained was skin plastered against bone and a thick, plated skull. It flopped onto the sand and remained there, lifeless. A dozen sailfins burst from the sand, screeching toward her.

Kaiden landed in front of her, shards of metal flying from both his hands in a steely cloud. The metal shards whipped through the air, forming a protective ring around him and Lhaurel. Anything that got close was torn apart by the swirling metal, spraying the air with blood and bits of ragged flesh.

Lhaurel remained in the pool of blood, laughing in the sheer power of it. It raged within her like a tempest contained within a bottle. Her blood boiled and then turned icy in turns, racing through her veins in time to the throbbing, roiling masses of the blood that surrounded her in the air. A horn sounded, calling for a retreat. She sensed them leaving, sensed the hundreds of dead and dying genesauri here. And then she knew no more.

CHAPTER 19

Choosing Death

"The clans have given me another to assist me. I do not know her name. I fear to ask it. Will the enemy use her against me, too? Perhaps I will send her away before it happens. She shouldn't be here."
-From the Journals of Elyana

Gavin sat with the greatsword across his lap, reading one of the scrolls in the torchlight. The scrolls were in the ancient script of his people, the Orinai, the language that his grandmother had spent so long teaching him. As a child, he had thought it wonderful to have a secret language that only he and his grandmother knew. As he'd grown older, he had wondered at its use. But now, reading the scroll, he thanked his grandmother for her constant, persistent teachings.

Hope is a solitary flame standing alone against a gale. Will alone cannot keep it alight—it requires fuel. Our hope rests close to me now, a feeble force against the coming storm. But it is all we have. There are some among the elders who would not have me try.

But the people have spoken. They accepted my plan. Me. The one that they call crone. Witch. Outcast. Now their lives rest in my hands.

What is the test of honor? To uphold the flame, or to snuff it out?

The decision has fallen to me.

The enemy has come.

The rest of the page was faded, but Gavin shuddered as he carefully rolled up the scroll and placed it back within the glass. As he did, he pondered the question in the message. What was the test of honor? His grandmother's dying wish was that he uphold the flame.

The writings here spoke of things that didn't exist in the Sharani Desert. Green plants and "flowers" and animals that would never survive the harshness of the desert adorned every page as if they were commonplace. They reminded him of the stories his grandmother had told him, tales of Eldriean and the time before the enemy came.

A noise sounded down the hall, echoing strangely against the surface of the lake. Gavin stilled, listening as it grew steadily louder and louder until the distinctive sound of it became plain. Footsteps. Someone was coming. He stowed the scroll into a pocket and rose into a crouch, greatsword held at the ready. Stepping back into the shadows, he waited in silence.

Voices drifted down to where he hid, different than the first and much less refined.

"You'll get the work done, or you'll be the first ones we feed to the genesauri." A commanding voice, the contempt not even masked in the slightest.

"I don't answer to you, m'lord. I'll do as I'm told by me and mine." The second voice was firm, yet there was a careful edge to it, as if he were not sure how the man he spoke to would respond.

A sickly hiss echoed through the room, the sound of bare steel sliding against leather.

Gavin almost smiled as the first speaker spoke again, his voice now flat. "You can answer to me, or you can answer to my dagger here. The choice is yours."

The rest of the exchange was lost as the voices faded away and the speakers moved on. Gavin relaxed slightly but decided that it was time to move. He wished that he could have taken more of the scrolls with him, but the one he had would have to suffice. He needed to see more of this place, travel through the halls and see what was going on. He had a growing suspicion that this place had once housed an ancient and forgotten people, the Orinai, or some of their first descendants. His grandmother would have loved to have seen this place. He felt compelled, now, to walk it for her. And a part of him burned with curiosity to discover exactly who it was that now called this place home.

He moved forward cautiously, crossing the narrow walkway in the middle of the vast lake as quickly as he dared without creating too much noise. His wounds slowed him. He paused at the entrance to the lake room, but upon hearing nothing he moved on. He only made it a few steps before he came face-to-face with an unfamiliar, aged face.

The man's eyes widened slightly in surprise, and then they narrowed, and he reached for his sword.

Gavin hesitated for only a moment less. With a sudden burst of strength, he shoved the man aside before he could draw his sword and dashed down the passage behind him. He turned down the first turn he came to.

Behind him, the man shouted for aide, screaming of intruders. Gavin recognized the voice through his panicked flight. It was the dagger-wielder he had overheard before.

Gavin burst into another room, large and spacious in its expanse. It was a dead end. In desperation, he searched for another way out, but there was nothing.

Behind him he heard his pursuer enter the room and slow to a measured walk. A cautious man, one who knew the folly of leaping into a situation blind.

Gavin cursed. He turned and came face-to-face with the older man again.

The man smiled, revealing gaps in his otherwise straight teeth.

"What's a little whelp like you doing down here?" the man asked.

The only response Gavin offered was to raise his sword.

The old man's eyes narrowed again. He recognized the surety of Gavin's movements.

Gavin almost smiled back at him but forced his expression to remain blank and calm. His grandmother's teachings sounded in his mind, reminding him to remain in the moment where the ripples on a pond faded and stillness began. That was the moment of balance.

The older man shifted into an aggressive stance and waded in without any further preamble. Gavin spun his blade up to block the blow, his arms tingling from the power behind it, and then shoved the blade way. They exchanged a series of quick blows, each one trying to get a gauge on the other. The other man's smile slowly returned, and Gavin felt a cool chill prickle at the base of his skull.

The man's blade slipped through his guard and scored a minor cut along his leg. Gavin cursed at the searing pain that raced down his leg and felt the warm, stickiness drip down its length. He slapped the blade aside before it could dart upward and do any more serious damage, but he realized in that moment that he was seriously outclassed. He knew the forms, knew them as well as anyone could without actual combat, but the man before him had weathered a thousand battles against man and beast alike. This man was the embodiment of practical application.

No! He would not die here at this strange man's hand. He had survived without a warren or a clan to protect him since he had been a small child.

Gavin steeled himself and attacked, the greatsword in his hand spinning in rapid, arcing cuts that worked his opponent's blade up and kept the man rocking back on his heels. Gavin stepped forward and forced the man back a step. Wind sounded in Gavin's ears, and he felt *something* surging through him and up his arms.

Gavin's blade spun in, seeming to glow with a crackling white light, and scored a small hit on the old man's arm. It was small and barely drew blood, but the old man spat a curse and screamed in pain, stumbling back.

Gavin had survived the deaths of his parents and grandmother, had done the impossible, had conquered the Oasis walls. Energy crackled along his blade. He let it go.

He blocked a series of rapid thrusts and then deflected the older man's blade slightly to the right, letting go of the hilt with his left hand and bringing his elbow up to smash into the other man's nose. It shattered.

He had scaled the walls of the Oasis and discovered the place where legends claimed that the enemy had been driven back. He was not going to die here.

With a shout, Gavin took two quick steps forward and brought his sword spinning down in a great overhead chop, the glow from the sword illuminating the crags in the old man's face, now running with blood. The old man smiled suddenly and drew his dagger in a lighting-quick motion. He caught Gavin's blade between his dagger and sword, which he'd crossed before his face. Before Gavin could reset, before he could even react, the old man pulled the dagger out from underneath the sword and slammed it into Gavin's gut.

* * *

Makin Qays sat with his chin in his hands, elbows resting on top of the thick wooden table in the council room. Blood still stained his robes from the morning's battle. Only Khari was in the room with him, cheeks stained with the tears of grief. There was no one else to fill the empty chairs. This was not a council meeting. This was a meeting where a man and his wife discussed their inevitable deaths.

"Is there any sign of them?"

Khari moved around behind him and placed her arms around his neck, leaning in close. She massaged his shoulders, though her own face was strained and the grey in her hair appeared more white than grey.

"The last anyone saw of the two was when Kaiden picked her up and got her onto Skree-lar's back. Everyone else was so busy with the regroup they didn't see if they actually made it into the air."

"So they're lost now, too, then?"

"It may be that our time has ended, dear one," she said, her voice quiet and resigned. "I do not know why the genesauri have come. But much blood has been spilt because of them. We must have killed over a hundred of the beasts, and yet they continued onward as if fleeing the flames of the seven hells. I—" She hesitated, and her hands stilled on his shoulders. "I don't know what else to do but continue on with honor."

"You saw them on the way back here, my wife," Makin said, taking her hand in his own. Both were spotted with blood. "There are thousands of them. They'll fall on the Oasis like a sandtiger on a lamb. They'll be slaughtered. I can't order the Roterralar to die along with them."

Khari removed her arms from around his neck and rounded to sit on the table in front of him. She took his head in her hands and looked deeply into his eyes.

"When you became Warlord of the Roterralar, you swore an oath to protect the seven clans. You vowed to uphold the flame. You swore that you would protect them until the last breath of life left your body and the last drop of blood dripped from your veins. We must uphold that oath, or all the deaths are meaningless. Sarial died in vain. Tieran died in vain. All of them."

"You'd have us die, then? Throw away our lives for people that don't even know we exist?"

"If we are to die," she replied, her eyes hardening, "then we die together. We die with them, defending the Oasis from the genesauri that would wipe them out."

"We'd reveal ourselves." It was not a question.

"We have no choice. The Roterralar barely survived with the numbers that we had before the deaths. Now we number only a few score. We either rejoin our parent clans, or we will cease to exist altogether. Our choice has been made for us. The time for decisions is over. The time for action is upon us."

Makin Qays slowly lowered his hands onto the table, curling his long, worn fingers inward to form tight fists. He raised his head to look at Khari and his eyes blazed with a sudden fire.

"So be it."

A few minutes later he stood in the greatroom, the remnants of the Roterralar arrayed below him. Makin Qays looked down at them, studying each face in turn. Wives and mothers clutched children or held their husband's hands. Yet there was no fear in their faces, only resolve. He smiled.

"The time has come for us to uphold our oaths," he said, not even needing to raise his voice to be heard by everyone in the room. "I leave for the Oasis as soon as I am done here. The Rahuli will know we are here after today. The Roterralar will cease to exist, one way or another. Anyone who will come with me to uphold the flame is welcome, but know that we go to die."

He turned and headed for the eyrie. Everyone old enough to hold a lance came with him.

* * *

Beryl looked up from his work when Khari entered. Sweat beaded on his brow and dripped down with a sharp hiss onto the hot metal he was working. He could have finished the task using his other abilities a dozen times over in the amount of time it had taken him just to get to this initial heating, but his mind needed the work. He had to keep the *voices* at bay.

"We're emptying the warren, Beryl." Khari said, approaching him despite the heat. "Everyone that can hold a lance or ride an aevian is needed."

Beryl grunted, turning back to his work. He knew what she wanted, but she was going to have to ask. It wouldn't change his answer. He couldn't go back out there. He didn't want to see what had become of his home. He didn't want to see what Elyana had done so many years ago.

"Beryl, we need you." Khari stepped closer, near enough for the sparks from the metal when his hammer struck it to come dangerously close to hitting her. "You're our strongest magnetelorium. You've been around for as long as any of us can remember."

Beryl shook his head. The voices in his head clamored for a chance to speak. Yes, he could fight again. He had the strength, had the power. It swelled within him, strengthening the voices—heightening the madness.

"No!"

"But you must!"

Beryl set down his hammer. The forge furnace flared near them, washing them in a wave of heat. Beryl clenched his teeth, dampening his temper and struggling to keep the voices as bay.

"One crippled old man won't make any difference," he said softly.

Khari stepped up to him and put a hand on his arm, gripping it firmly.

"I've never understood you, Beryl. Neither did my father. Why will you not leave the warren? Your abilities are strong enough to kill even a marsaisi, I'm sure. You were the one who showed Kaiden how to manipulate metal. You're the most powerful mystic alive."

Beryl growled, a low, deep sound of earth trembling beneath their feet. A marsaisi? He could tear one of those apart with his bare hands. He didn't even need his powers for that. Only the karundin would give him pause. But that wasn't because of what the Rahuli slaves thought, one of the voices whispered. What would stop Beryl, the smith, would be the memory of what the creature had once been. The memory of its creation. Khari took a step back as Beryl leveled his gaze on her.

"I will not go. This is your fight. I fought mine long ago and lost. I'm still fighting it every day. Go, fight your fight. The lances will be ready."

In the back of Beryl's mind, a small voice begged him to go. It yearned to fight. It screamed at him.

"I will not go!"

Khari backed away, clearly shaken. Beryl growled again and picked up his hammer. The metal had cooled enough that shaping it with the hammer would be useless. He struck it anyway, the sound masking the door shutting behind Khari's retreating form.

He laughed suddenly, a strange, short bark of a laugh that held neither humor nor any hint of levity. It was the laughter of a broken man, a man whose existence and sanity danced on the edge of a knife. The laughter of a man doomed to eternal creation and eternal damnation. He was a bringer of death, a supplier of the implements of destruction.

Inside his mind, one of the voices screamed.

CHAPTER 20

Allegiance

"We have had success again! These are already much larger than the first, much more robust and of far greater stature. I released a number of the first into the sands despite the clans' objections—the enemy will soon encounter this new threat. Let them taste fear. Let my creations haunt them as they haunt me. Let them take revenge for Briane. The enemy is vast—but then, so are my creations."

-From the Journals of Elyana

Lhaurel knew she was alive because she felt the pain. Not just the physical pain from the dozens of minor wounds that covered her body from head to foot, but also the pain of failure and loss.

Darkness surrounded her on all sides, wrapped her in its loving embrace and swaddled her in the soothing arms of confused forgetfulness. The last thing she remembered was Fahkiri's death. Everything else was shrouded in a red, misty haze, like a fog painted with blood.

The blackness and the pain mingled into a swirling vortex of black and red, twisted in her vision, and did nothing to lessen the confusion or deaden the pain. If anything, both intensified.

Lhaurel's ears started working in slow bursts of sound and silence, each sounding more loudly than the last. The silence was loud. The following sound was quiet. Yet mingled in with the quiet whispers of ghost voices and calumnious shouts was a soft, rustling laughter. A laugh that grew from the silence of not-so-distant memories and resolved into the painful intensity of the present.

Her eyes opened from blackness into nightmare. A gap-toothed smile filled her vision, and hot breath that smelled of rot filled her nose.

"Taren."

"Hello, my dear," he said, stepping back slightly so that she could see more of him in the dim light. "It's been a while."

Lhaurel blinked and closed her eyes, willing this to be a dream, a nightmare. How had Taren gotten here? Where was she? There was blood on his face that looked like it had been hastily cleaned.

"I would think by now you're wondering where you are," Taren said slowly, stepping back again so the most of him was lost in shadows. Whatever dim light it was that filled the chamber barely had the strength to illuminate the small section of it where Lhaurel lay and didn't reach much further. "You'll just have to keep on wondering, my dear wife."

The words brought a rise out of Lhaurel. From somewhere deep within her, a small burst of strength and spirit flared.

"I am *not* your wife," she spat.

From the shadows came the sound of steel clearing leather, a sound that caused Lhaurel's flesh to crawl and a small shiver to run down her spine. She swallowed a momentary flutter of panic and steeled her expression. If she was to die here, she would not do so clouded in fear, huddled and weak. She would not back down before Taren.

Light flashed off steel as a thin blade spun through the distance separating them and buried itself in the sand a few inches from Lhaurel's face.

She spat sand. Her eyes focused on the quivering blade before her. Did he miss? Recognition answered the question for her. It was the sealing dagger.

"Your blood in my veins says differently."

In response, Lhaurel spat at him, though the spittle fell far short. It was futile, a waste of pure water, but it made Lhaurel feel less helpless.

Taren laughed, cold and hard, and sunk down to his knees. "Ah,

Lhaurel. You are such a fool. You could have been part of something great. You really could have. Even before Jenthro approached me to petition for our union, I had my eyes on you. Stubborn. Strong. Willful. The perfect match for a future king. Once you had been properly broken, of course. Even then the plan was in place. Marvi helped me with that, though she didn't know what she was doing. The correct pieces were moved to prepare for this final day. I wanted your power for my own. But your blood wasn't good enough."

Lhaurel was trying her best to ignore him completely. There was blood on the dagger, fresh blood that shone red in the flickering light. Despite her best efforts, Taren's voice rang through her closed ears.

"My blood?"

Taren grimaced, pointedly scratching his arm where the sealing dagger had left its mark five different times. "The magic you mystics have has something to do with your blood. We thought mixing blood during a sealing would work, but yours was too weak. He said that's why they wait to take women until they're older, for the mixing of blood."

He stepped forward and retrieved the dagger, his expression hard.

"If the choice had been mine, this would be your end, too, along with the mystics and Roterralar, but alas, the choice is not mine." His voice remained flat and emotionless.

It took Lhaurel a moment to realize that something was off about what he had said. Her brain wasn't working like it should. It was as if her thoughts were trying to run through loose sand.

"The mystics?" she asked. What did Taren know of the mystics?

Again Taren answered with a laugh, though this one seemed to carry a genuine, if minuscule, amount of humor to it. "Come, now, Lhaurel. Don't play dumb. We both know that you're anything but dumb. Yes, the mystics and the Roterralar, supposed protectors of the seven clans. Rulers of the sands and keepers of the magic that keeps us safe. Those that do not join us today will die here upon the sands."

Lhaurel's head pounded with each beat of her heart, which only heightened her confusion. Taren was suggesting that he would kill the Roterralar? He may control the seven clans now—or five, now that two were missing—but even with all of the several thousand people,

Khari could wipe out most of them herself. Kaiden could kill them all before they ever even came close enough to lob a spear at him.

She tried to lick her lips, but her mouth was dry and all she managed was to crack the scabs and dried blood that lined them. She tried to rally the strength to sit up, but she couldn't find the will. Her muscles refused to respond. Even her thoughts seemed sluggish.

Taren leaned forward, his eyes suddenly gleaming and his voice filled with eagerness. "And when the Roterralar have fallen or been pulled back into the fold," he said, "then I will be king, standing at the head of the clans when we face the enemy at the gate. And at my side will be one who can stop them."

"You're mad."

"Not mad," a familiar voice said from the shadows. "Just fervent."

Kaiden stepped out of the darkness. Lhaurel looked up at him, eyes wide and mind clouded with confusion and a sudden, overwhelming sense of relief. He was here to save her. Blinking, she waited for him to draw a sword, or manipulate metal and attack Taren, but he simply stood there, watching her. Watching how she would react to seeing him there.

Taren glanced over at him and nodded once. Curt and low enough that the deference was plain.

Realization dawned with the cold fingers of dread clutching at her heart.

"Leave us, Taren," Kaiden said.

Taren's face contorted for a moment, eyes narrowing, but he stood without a word and walked into the shadows.

A creak of iron hinges sounded in the shadows and then the soft thunk of a wooden door slipping into the embrace of its frame. Then silence.

"I am sorry about Fahkiri," Kaiden said at last.

Lhaurel nearly laughed at the sheer, mad impossibility of it. "That's what you have to say? You're sorry about Fahkiri? You're in this with Taren. You're behind the genesauri too, aren't you? It's you. It's always been you."

Kaiden nodded.

"How? I heard them in the council meeting. They said no one was powerful enough to control the genesauri."

Kaiden smirked. "They think too narrowly. They always have, Lhaurel. I don't have to control them when I can simply change the direction of their flight."

"What?" Lhaurel strained against her bonds, but they wouldn't budge. Why couldn't she feel her powers?

"Sarial explained it to you. The genesauri fly using a form of magnetism. The Oasis walls are filled with magnetic metals that have pushed against the genesauri for as long as anyone can remember. Since the Oasis was created, actually. I simply changed it so the genesauri were drawn toward it instead."

"Why, Kaiden? Why? Do you know how many people you've killed?"

In reply Kaiden raised his arms to show his tattoos, flicking the sleeves so that each of them were exposed. "I know how many I haven't been able to save," he said, "and I know how many the Roterralar let die in their own ignorance and fear."

"And you think if they hadn't hidden they could have saved more? You're as mad as Taren."

Kaiden shook his head and crouched down beside her, pulling out a waterskin and holding it up for her to drink. She almost refused, but the sensation of water so close was simply too much to ignore. She swallowed gratefully and felt strength surge through her.

"Is it mad to want to protect everyone? Is it mad for a shepherd to kill a diseased goat before it can infect the others? And if he can used that diseased carcass to also kill the predators that hunt the other goats, how much better is it? Would that shepherd be considered mad or visionary?"

"We are not goats."

"Some are sheep and some are shepherds," Kaiden said. "And some who are shepherds are really sheep. And some sheep are really shepherds who have simply forgotten who they are."

For a moment, Kaiden's words resonated in the depths of her mind and stirred her soul, tugging at emotions and anger that had grown dormant in the time she had spent with the Roterralar. And then an image danced through her mind. A rashelta dying, purple blood dripping into the sand. Broken crockery across the floor. An image in red.

"You can burn in the fires of the seven hells, Kaiden." Lhaurel closed her eyes. She steeled herself for the blow she knew would come. She waited. The crunch of sand beneath booted feet reached her ears as Kaiden slowly walked away. She opened her eyes as he passed out of the light and was lost in shadows.

He shot a parting retort over his shoulder toward her over the creak of hinges protesting their use.

"Ask yourself which you want to be, Lhaurel. A sheep or a shepherd. Our understanding of this world is about to change. The enemy is coming."

The door closed.

* * *

Saralhn swallowed hard and felt a tremble in her calves as they threatened to give out beneath her. Sweat broke out on her forehead, and a sudden dryness afflicted her mouth. But she didn't move.

"I said, stand aside," the warrior said between gritted teeth.

Behind Saralhn, the young woman she was protecting whimpered and hugged her face in both hands, trying desperately to cover the bruise that was slowly blossoming across her cheek. Fruits lay scattered across the sand, toppled from the basket next to the young woman. A crowd gathered around them, some curious, others afraid. Only Saralhn stood between the soldier and the young woman.

"What did she do?" Saralhn asked, raising her chin to look the man in the eye.

He scowled, a scar on one side of his face twisting and making one of his eyes squint. "None of your business, woman," he said, brandishing his spear.

Saralhn felt a small flicker of fear but didn't let it show. She wondered why no one else in the crowd even glanced at her or the young woman behind her. For a moment, she thought them cowards. But then she stopped herself. A fortnight ago she had been just like them. That Saralhn seemed like a memory. She understood now why

SANDS

Lhaurel had always seemed so frustrated with her when she wouldn't help with any of the schemes and chores that would have labeled her a rebel.

Things were different now, though. Her message had gotten no response. For all Saralhn knew, Lhaurel was dead. There wasn't anyone else here to defend those who needed defending.

"I am making it my business."

"Get out of my way." Holding the spear like a quarterstaff, the soldier moved to push Saralhn out of the way with it.

Saralhn grabbed the wooden haft and pulled forward, using a trick she had seen one of the soldiers use during one of the early scuffles in the power struggle. Having expected resistance, the soldier overbalanced as Saralhn's pull yanked him forward. Instinctively, she twisted her grip and wrenched the spear from the soldier's grip. He overbalanced and landed face first in the dirt.

"Run," Saralhn said to the young woman behind her. She didn't need telling twice. The girl grabbed her fallen basket, not bothering to grab any of the fruit, and scurried off into the stunned and silent watchers.

Turning back to the soldier, who was cursing and getting to his feet, Saralhn tossed the spear aside, scattering stunned observers in all directions. Her palms were sweaty and her hands trembled, but her stance remained firm and resolute. The soldier righted himself and spun on her, spitting curses, hands balled into fists.

She raised her chin.

The blow struck her with enough force to knock her to the ground. Her ears rang and her head pounded with blood that rushed to color her cheeks. Blinking against the sudden brightness of the sun, Saralhn put her hands beneath herself and pushed off. She was halfway up when a booted foot caught her in the side and sent her rolling across the sand. She gasped from the pain and sucked in air in great gulps.

"I'll teach you to stick your nose where it doesn't belong," the soldier said, sending another kick into her side which threw her even further across the sand. "I'll teach you how to respect a man."

He kicked her again.

Saralhn blinked rapidly, a vain effort to banish the splotches of blackness that were crossing her vision. She looked up into the faces of the silent crowd around her. She noticed an old woman, face wrinkled and hair as grey as the errant wisp of cloud high above the desert, look down at her with pursed lips. She frowned down at Saralhn as if she were angry at her for even attempting to stand up to a man. It was a face of ingrained tradition and resignation. A defeated face.

Saralhn blinked to clear away the fog. There was something deep within the woman's eyes. Hope. Shame. Guilt. Pride. So disparate from the expression on the woman's face.

She glanced over to the next person. A man, yet a young man, clutching the hand of a woman who wore a yellow *shufari*. His expression mirrored hers. Expressions of grim acceptance of a way of life that had always been that way. Condemnation of what she had done and mild indignation. Yet their eyes showed the truth of it. They took pride in what she had done. But they would not help her.

She looked from face to face, marking each expression, looking deeply into all the eyes. They were all the same. Each face bore a mask. Each pair of eyes spoke the truth. Mostly women, but among them were a few younger men. Saralhn felt a mild note of surprise at this, which cut through the pain. She blinked again. Where was the next kick?

Her ears suddenly started working, and she heard a familiar voice filled with iron resolve crack like a whip.

"I said that was enough!"

Saralhn turned and grit her teeth against the pain.

Maryn stood between her and the soldier, short stature suddenly seeming larger. The ends of her purple *shufari* fluttered in the vagrant breeze.

The soldier scowled at her, scar crinkling his eye again. His hands remained in fists, but there was a hesitancy about his movements, as if he were unsure how to handle the older, stern-faced woman.

"Why should I listen to you?" he spat.

"Because, you dolt, I said so. My husband could kill you without breaking a sweat. If you touch her again, you'll have to move me aside to do it. If you touch me, my husband will kill you. Slowly."

The soldier seemed to lose some of his bluster. The scowl never left his face, but his fists slowly unclenched. Saralhn coughed and got to her feet, choking off a scream of pain as her ribs creaked and grated against one another. No one offered to help her.

"Fine." The soldier bent down and picked up his spear. "I've wasted enough time on the little wench anyway. Just watch yourself, woman. Next time I'll just stick my spear in you and be done with it."

Saralhn didn't know if he was talking to her or to Maryn, but the older woman responded anyway. "I'd say you're out of practice with your spear work. It may be a little dull, too. I'd be careful where you try and stick it if a little wisp of a girl can take it from you like that."

This brought a murmur of noise from the assembled watchers, and the soldier's face flushed. His knuckles grew white on the haft of his spear, but he simply scowled and walked away, shoving through the crowd with more force than was necessary.

Saralhn sighed and sank down into the sand, clutching her ribs. The crowd dispersed, a low hum of noise accompanying them as they left. The sound was a comfort after the deafening silence.

"Did you even know that girl?" Maryn asked. Her voice sounded weary.

Saralhn looked up at her, blinking, and shook her head. The motion made waves of dizziness wash over her like the cool waters of the salt spring back in the Sidena Warren. The thought made her smile as memories surfaced. Lhaurel would be proud of her.

* * *

Inside the walls of the Oasis, Lhaurel walked slowly behind Kaiden, sore muscles protesting the relentless pace. It was dark in the passages, and the sandy floors were slippery. Lhaurel struggled to keep her balance, her arms pinned awkwardly in front of her by metal shackles. She stumbled, but before she lost her balance, she felt a tug on the shackles and she righted. Even in the darkness, the reddish-grey mist surrounded Kaiden each time he pulled her back up.

"Come now, Lhaurel. Quit playing games," Kaiden said without looking back. "We both know you have better balance than this. I've seen you in the training circle, remember?"

She ignored him, though inwardly she cursed the long days spent letting him watch her spar with Khari or simply practice the forms. She'd been a fool to ever start trusting him. Hadn't he shown his true colors often enough? He had betrayed her to the Sidena, had been the cause of all the pain and suffering she'd experienced among the Roterralar. He'd shown how he would kill mercilessly simply to prove a point. How had she ever trusted him?

She knew it was more than that, but in the face of everything that had come to light, she was too ashamed to dwell on the truth.

Kaiden led her to a dead-end chamber, large and spacious in its expanse, filled with wide pillars carved in dull grey stone. Except, as Lhaurel leaned against one, she realized that it wasn't stone at all, but pure, solid metal. She noticed, absently, that drying blood pooled in one corner of the room, long smeared streaks leading away toward the entrance. This had to be the place where Kaiden brought those he wanted to kill. A torture chamber of sorts.

Kaiden walked to the center of the room and stood with his arms outstretched, his eyes closed and his head tilted back. His back was to the chamber's entrance. Behind him, a figure Lhaurel recognized entered the room. Sarial.

"You too, huh? I should have known," Lhaurel said, despairing.

Sarial grinned down at her with barely masked contempt. "I don't know why you're still alive, girl," she said. "We took care of the other fools who wouldn't join us."

"Your own brother? You killed Tieran?" Lhaurel said.

Sarial extended a hand, and white energy crackled along its length. She approached Lhaurel, arm outstretched. "Don't ever say his name again. I told you to stay away from Kaiden. You didn't listen. Now you can watch as we bring down the walls and let the genesauri in. You can watch while we destroy the Roterralar and I rule at his side."

Sarial turned away from Lhaurel, walking to one of the pillars and placing both hands on it.

"It's time," Kaiden said. "Freedom awaits."

Reddish-grey mist surrounded him. An instant later, Sarial was enveloped in a cloud of reddish-white, and crackling energy burst from her fingers to wrap around the metal pillars. Kaiden's face hardened in concentration, and Sarial started groaning. The energy swirled up the pillar, coming in stronger and stronger waves.

The ground began to shake. Lhaurel curled into a ball as stones were knocked loose from the ceiling, falling to the ground near her.

Kaiden screamed, falling to his knees.

The walls shook and trembled and then, with a sound like thunder multiplied a dozen times over, fell away, tumbling outward in a shower of dust and rock and sand.

Part 5

Broken

CHAPTER 21

Unity's Lies

"My new assistant is missing. Again on the eve of success. The enemy must have spies among the mystics. Maybe she was one of them. I never thought she was trustworthy. I can no longer trust any of them. The enemy is set upon stopping my work—they are afraid of me, as well they should be. My new creations are growing—already triple the size of their older brethren. Tomorrow I will embark on the last of my quests—the final weapon against the enemy. They will pay for what they have done to me. They will suffer for what they have done to Briane. Briane. Even awake now I can hear it. The sound of a girl child screaming."

-From the Journals of Elyana

"You're saying Taren is in league with the Roterralar and that they are planning to kill us all?" Saralhn asked. The skepticism in her voice was thick and apparent.

Maryn flicked her head to the side and sniffed. "No, I'm saying that Cobb followed Taren into the walls. They're hollow, and they're planning to lure the Roterralar here and kill them all. It's a trap. And it involves us and the genesauri. People are going to die."

"What can we do about it?"

"They're holding someone captive up there. Cobb heard them talking. He's going back up to see what he can do. I'll go gather the other women, but you need to rally the people here. Get them to believe."

Saralhn snorted, but a look from Maryn silenced her and made her swallow the words she was about to say. She was serious.

"I'm going in to free the woman. Maybe she can make some sense of all this. You are going to ready the clans. And if you see the Roterralar anywhere, warn them."

Saralhn blinked in confusion. "Me? But I can't . . ."

"The woman I just saw had the support of everyone watching. Word of what you did will spread. Strange things are happening. Tradition and law are crumbling to dust and being blown away on the wind. They need someone to look up to."

"I can't lead," Saralhn protested.

Maryn reached out and grabbed a handful of Saralhn's robes and pulled her forward so that they were only a few inches apart. Saralhn was so startled that she didn't even struggle.

"I'll tell you a secret, Saralhn," Maryn said. "The clans are not ruled by men. The men are figureheads. Their wives are the ones who make sure there is food to be eaten and clothes to be warmed. We women know what it is like to follow. And only by following can we understand the motivation it takes to lead someone. Now stand up."

Saralhn tripped as Maryn released her and stumbled backward. Pain lanced through her side, and she bent wrong trying to catch herself. Her ribs creaked together. She sucked in a breath and opened her mouth—

The earth shook.

It trembled and rumbled and jerked up and down in a rapid shaking movement that knocked both women to the ground. They bounced and jostled with the rumbling earth. A massive cracking sound rent the air, followed by another, and then an enormous cascading avalanche of falling stone and sand billowed out from one of the Oasis walls right near the main entryway. Between bounces, Saralhn twisted enough to see the cascade tumble outward in a billowing cloud of dust.

A gaping hole over a hundred spans wide lay in in its place. Above the tumultuous noise of falling rock and stone, though, another noise could be heard, one that turned Saralhn's blood to ice. It was the high-pitched keening of tight flesh against the wind. A cacophonous, intertwining symphony of hundreds upon hundreds of sailfins.

* * *

K hari was the first to spot the billowing cloud of dust rising over the Oasis. Her breathing quickened, and sweat broke out on her forehead. Something was terribly wrong. They would not survive this encounter with the genesauri. She knew it with cold certainty. But perhaps some of the clans would survive. At least then the death would be meaningful.

Old age would not be what brought her to the funeral pyre. The thought brought a small smile to her lips.

She whistled sharply, two notes close together, one pitched higher than the other and gestured ahead of her. The message was relayed until all forty warriors could see the rising plume. Above her, at the head of his flight, Makin Qays whistled a sharp command. Fly straight. Kill genesauri. Duty. Goodbye.

Adjusting the grip on her lance, Khari grit her teeth and urged Gwyanth to fly faster.

* * *

L haurel coughed and spat. The dust filled her nose and wedged into the small spaces between her teeth. No matter how much she spat out, she couldn't get the salty taste to go away, nor could she escape the stinging in her eyes or the ringing in her ears. Sound returned in bits and pieces, broken rumblings and the silent echoes of what could have once been a conversation but was now simply fragmented words and vague periphery noises.

Someone touched her arm. "Come with me," Kaiden shouted in her ear, though it sounded like a whisper.

He pulled her to her feet, though she sensed he was unsteady. Lhaurel stumbled after him, unable to do much more than simply follow. Somehow, amidst the twists and turns they followed and the encompassing field of dust and gloom, Lhaurel sensed they were moving upward. Light broke through the gloom as they reached an opening.

Kaiden paused there for a long moment, hands on his knees. Lhaurel thought about trying to make a run for it, but her hands were still bound, and she couldn't muster the strength. Kaiden pushed her up the ladder after a moment, and Lhaurel hurriedly clambered up, gulping in the clear air. Kaiden moved up behind her and scrambled onto the rocky plateau. He pressed a waterskin into her hands. She drank gratefully as Taren appeared from down below and walked up to the edge.

Her fatigue and the ringing passed from her in a rush. In its wake, feeling and sensations returned. Death reigned below. She passed through the deaths in tandem with those below. She stumbled forward in a sudden wave of dizziness, her eyes drawn downward to the chaos and death below.

No! Lhaurel dropped to her knees, hands clasped over her mouth in complete and utter horror.

The genesauri poured through the breach in the Oasis walls, descending upon men, women, and children without discrimination. Sailfins dove through the sand in long graceful arcs, dragging souls down to hell with them. Marsaisi skimmed the surface of the sands, flesh nigh impervious to the swords, arrows, and spears launched at their massive bulk. And where the massive genesauri passed, death was left in their wake. And building in the sand came a massive, enormous berm, rolling forward like a giant wave. The karundin. Lhaurel screamed a scream of pure, unadulterated terror.

The Roterralar swooped down through the sky, defending what they could, but the sheer numbers of genesauri were more than they could handle. They didn't stand a chance. They fell almost as quickly as the other Rahuli. The sounds of death and despair reached them even atop the cliffs.

Kaiden stood atop a broken pinnacle near her, hands clasped behind his back, expression wan, though his gaze was intense. *Unite or die.* The words echoed in Lhaurel's mind from the council meeting she had spied on. Words that Kaiden had shouted in angry defiance. *We must unite or die.* Then it had sounded like an omen. Now it sounded like what it really was. A threat.

Kaiden's skin seemed to glitter in the sunlight. It took Lhaurel a long moment to realize that bits of metal showed through his skin like they did on Beryl. The smith had been right. There was a cost for using magic.

A rock skittered across the stone. She reached out, sensing Taren approach even before he spoke.

"All those we would save are away, sir." Taren came into view, his sword stained red with dripping blood. "We met some resistance in the caves down below, but I took care of it."

Blood. Blood everywhere. Dripping into the sands from Taren's sword. Dripping into the sands from the bodies down below. Sands stained red with blood. Blood coursing through Kaiden and Taren's veins. One a sign of death, the other of life. A bloodred sunset, and a crimson sunrise.

The wind whipped up around her, tossing her robes and hair around her thin frame. Taren steadied himself against the gust, though Kaiden ignored it, turning back to the battle below.

Lhaurel felt her heartbeat, sensed the flow of her blood, in and out. Down below people screamed. They died. Spilled blood into the sands. Her heart beat.

Taren grinned and stepped up next to Kaiden at the edge of the plateau. Aevians died. A group of women ceased to exist as a marsaisi fell among them, jaws flashing. Lhaurel felt it. By the seven hells she felt them all! The genesauri, the clans, the people, the aevians, Kaiden, Taren—she could feel all of them. Felt the lifeblood pumping through their veins, felt it being stolen away as they died. She knew it, experienced it with them. She felt their pain. The wind howled.

Her muscles seized up, her back arched, and from her depth a primal, primitive scream ripped from her trembling lips.

* * *

Saralhn scrambled to her feet amidst the chaos, pains forgotten beneath layers of terror and pure horror at the death and slaughter around her. The spear she had tripped over skittered across the sand and then came to a rest. Maryn had disappeared, and she absently wondered what had become of her. A woman covered in blood and missing a hand ran in front of her, the dust making her appear wraithlike

A sailfin burst out of the sand. Teeth gleamed.

Terror melted in the face of instinct. Saralhn dove aside and tucked into a roll, coming up with her hands wrapped around the haft of the spear. The sailfin twisted in midair and came at her with a sound that was halfway between a growl and a hiss. Saralhn clutched the spear in sweaty palms and licked her lips. Blood pounded in her ears. Time seemed to slow.

Glistening teeth bristled in front of her. The smell that issued from the creature's gaping maw was that of death, decay, and rot. Saralhn felt sick. Then the beast was upon her. It slammed into her and took her to the ground. The spear was wrenched from her fingers, and she screamed as a billowing cloud of dust rose into the air around her. Heavy, coiled muscles writhed and twitched above her.

Is this what death feels like? She had thought there would be more pain involved. Not this surreal sense of detachment. People described death as a cold embrace, but this was far from that. This was hot and dusty and . . .

Still.

It took her a moment to realize the writhing coils above her had stopped moving. The pressure on her chest was simply that of massive weight threatening to flatten her, not the crushing embrace of sailfin jaws. Flailing, she kicked herself free and scrambled to her feet.

A foot of broken wood stuck out of back of the sailfin's body, piercing the fin and slick with its blood. Its eyes were clouded over in death. Saralhn felt wetness on her cheeks and realized that she was crying, tears of helplessness and fear and a euphoric sense of relief. She didn't remember killing the beast, but it was dead all the same. It must have rammed itself onto her spear. She had aided its suicide.

Saralhn laughed at the thought, a crazed broken laugh that held little humor in it. But it cut off as quickly as it had begun, and the reality returned to her in the form of another sailfin bursting up and spraying her with earth. A shriek rent the air. For a moment Saralhn thought it was the sound of another sailfin coming from behind her, but then a large bird appeared out of the sky, rider on its back and long spear held out in front of it. The spear pinned the sailfin to the ground as the bird's rider released the spear, and the bird pulled out of the stunning, majestic dive. The rider saluted her with a raised fist as the bird winged back into the sky.

Saralhn blinked. She knew that face. It was the Roterralar woman, Khari. Lhaurel's friend.

Saralhn rushed forward and wrenched Khari's spear free from the dead genesauri, mind racing. Lhaurel was somewhere among them. She hefted the spear. It was light despite its cumbersome length. She had an idea.

* * *

Kaiden didn't even look over his shoulder at the sound of Lhaurel's scream. His gaze was focused downward on the battle below. Aevians fought and battled genesauri. People screamed and died. Yet the Roterralar fought hard to form a wall of death between the broiling mass of sailfins and the people of the clans. Few escaped the line, but those that did wreaked havoc amongst the unprepared people.

"You're just going to let them die?" Lhaurel said, crawling up to the edge of the plateau and watching in revulsion as people died, as a part of her died with them.

Kaiden didn't turn his head. "Those who deserve to live are not here. Those worth saving have been saved. If any survive this fight, then they will have earned their place among the sands. I will give them a world free of genesauri, but they must earn it. They must have the requisite strength to survive the descent of the enemy."

"But you told me we need more numbers," she said, mustering everything she could to try and make her voice sound persuasive. "How can you unite them if they are all dead? How can you hope to stave off the genesauri without enough warriors?"

At this, Kaiden did look over, a wry grin on his face. "You know so little. I called the genesauri here. I can drive them away. They are nothing but the crucible within which the dross is consumed. I unite those worthy of being united. After today, there will be no Roterralar and no clans. There will simply be the tribe."

Kaiden turned away from her and glanced at Taren, who stood a few feet away, watching the battle below. "Take Lhaurel below," Kaiden ordered, whistling shrilly to summon Skree-lar. "Lock her up for now. I have work that needs doing."

Taren scowled but saluted.

Lhaurel cried.

CHAPTER 22

A Breath of Stale Air

"Am I the cause of those screams?"

-From the Journals of Elyana

Khari spun in a shimmering dance of death, sword a metallic blur that dripped scarlet. Somewhere she had lost her Gwyanth. It had been a quick death, thankfully, but now she was forced to continue fighting on foot. That was fine by her. She fought better with her sword than with her lance anyway. In the back of her mind she knew that without her aevian she would not have any chance of leaving this place alive. That, too, was fine by her.

A sailfin burst upward from the sand on the far side of the broken Oasis walls, a powerful leap to take it over the broken red sandstone and into the Oasis itself. Khari pulled her blade free from the creature she had just killed and, following the momentum of her feet, clove the genesauri perfectly in two. The two pieces dropped from the air and plummeted onto the rocks, renewing the stain.

It was no wonder that the sands were red. Red from countless centuries of death and destruction. Years of countless painting with the blood of its defenders. The blood of its people.

The berm on the horizon continued to draw nearer, though slowly. She knew what it was, though fear had long since died within her. Khari would be here on the rocks to greet it. She was a master of the blade. She was death.

The karundin was said to be the mother of the others. Perhaps that was it. Khari had never been blessed with children. Those she helped lead among the Roterralar had been the closest she'd ever come to experiencing what it was like to be a mother. She would be here to wreak vengeance for her surrogate children.

She paused for a brief moment to take a drink from a waterskin, one of many at her waist. The liquid rushed through her like a raging fire, urging her to act, renewing her strength and her power. Her lips formed a thin line. Her eyes narrowed. A marsaisi breached the top of the sand, bony headplate a dull, metallic grey.

Thick bone covered most of its head and a small section of its back. But right between the neck and the headplate was a tiny crack. Khari leapt from atop the rocks, blade extended downward in front of her, point aimed at the narrow crack. Blood dripped from a dozen wounds, but the sword found its mark. Her sword was wrenched from her grasp, but she found a discarded spear that she collected, letting it dance in her hands.

The heat of the contest washed over her, burning away pain and fatigue, but also smelting time. It passed in large dollops, a double handful at a time, or else seemed to slow to the speed of a tortoise arising in the predawn haze.

A dozen sailfins surged upward over the rocks in an effort to cross over into the Oasis. But at the very crest of the broken mound Khari danced, spear spinning up, over, and around her. It was neither her favored weapon, nor the one with which she was most skilled, but at that moment it sung a perfect harmony to her dance of death. Only three of the dozen sailfins made it back down into the sand on the other side.

The red-grey stones ran slick with blood, but the gritty sandstone gave Khari the purchase she needed. On the other side of the hill, the berm of moving sand continued to push forward, driving packs of sailfins and marsaisi toward the Oasis. Khari didn't mind it. She was one with the spear. She was one with the pulse of her own beating heart. She was death.

The berm exploded outward as a horrendous, toothy head burst out of the sands.

Death trembled.

* * *

The sound of sobs echoing in a small, dark chamber had an eerie cast about it. At times, Lhaurel thought the returning echo of her own cries sounded like the murmuring gurgle of a distant spring, sending water up to the surface from a hidden reservoir far below. Other times is sounded like a dam bursting, a cacophonous din of sound caused by too much water trying to escape from too small an opening. And sometimes it simply sounded like the pitiful sounds of a broken will.

It was the last that finally broke through her mental barriers. The pain of experiencing so many deaths all at once had left her without feeling, left her clinging to her own life with as much strength as she could muster. That left little room for much else but tears. A simple manifestation of a wide range of emotions or none. And yet, hearing her own sobs coming back to her, she realized the time for tears was gone. The clans were dying. Kaiden was wiping them out one by one. The genesauri were his weapons.

Someone had to do something. In here she could no longer feel them. The oppression of the Oasis walls kept out the sensation of death and destruction.

She felt weak and tired. The manacles on her hands clinked, and she scrubbed under her nose and wiped away the moisture that had pooled there. As she did so, her eyes fell upon her fellow prisoner. She could only make out his outline in the darkness, but she could sense the gaping wound in his stomach. Blood dripped into the sands beneath him.

She grit her teeth and struggled to her knees. It took effort, but she managed to drag herself over to him. She was helpless to save the people dying outside, but this one she would save. This one would not die if she could protect him.

Pulling him onto his back, Lhaurel felt his hot breath on her face. The smell of blood filled her nose. He was close to dying, hovering on the verge of the darkness. Placing her hands over the wound in his stomach, she reached out to her powers. It answered her call easily. Red mist formed around her, a cloak of blood. This man's blood and hers mingled in the air as fuel for her power. Energy surged through her. Grasping at it, Lhaurel willed the flesh back together. She pushed the blood back through the open wound and back through his veins. She could feel his heart begin to beat faster and faster as the torn flesh knit itself together between her fingers.

The man gasped, and his eyes snapped open, the whites showing clearly even in the darkness. An icy chill swept through Lhaurel's body, and without even thinking about it, she pulled at the red mist in the air around her. The mist dissipated, returning to her body. The chill vanished, replaced by a wondrous feeling of euphoria. A quick tug on the chain that held the manacles together sent the links scattering across the sand. Where had she gotten such strength?

The man sat up, feeling at his stomach with hesitant hands.

"Who are you? I should be dead."

"I healed you." Lhaurel stood and felt along the edges of the room until she found the door. Testing it, she found it locked.

"I am called Gavin," he continued. "One of the outcasts. My water is yours. May you ever find water and shade."

Lhaurel blinked. So formal.

"Lhaurel," she said.

"Lhaurel. Okay, Lhaurel. Would you mind telling me what is going on? The last thing I remember was fighting an old man."

"Taren?" she asked, ignoring his question.

"Is that his name?" The man, Gavin, sounded oddly light-hearted for having almost died.

Lhaurel placed an ear up against the door but heard nothing coming from the other side. Her muscles still trembled with strength and she clung to the vestiges of power that still surged through her. She could sense Gavin, behind her, and felt strength and power radiate from him, as well. He was a relampago; she could feel the power within him. Did he know? The thought was a comforting one for some reason, like the warmth of the sun on a cool spring morning.

"I overheard his plans down below. He said he was going to be king. But how could he . . . " He trailed off, standing. "I take it he succeeded, then."

Lhaurel paused and turned to look at him.

A noise sounded in the passageway behind the door, the sound of metal striking against rock.

"Get back," Lhaurel hissed.

Gavin lay back down in the sand and curled up how he had been before.

Lhaurel secreted herself behind the door, strength still surging in her arms. If people came in, she would deal with them. She had to get out and find Kaiden. Put an end to this.

A key scraped in the lock. The door swung inward, and light flooded into the room. The smell of pitch and the way it flickered revealed it was a torch. As soon as the door opened, Lhaurel's senses shot out into the passageway. The person in the door was Sarial.

With a muffled shout, Lhaurel slammed her shoulder into the door. The heavy wooden door slammed into the woman and knocked her to the ground. Lhaurel spun around the door, but before she could get to Sarial, Gavin was there, slamming a double-fisted blow to the side of Sarial's head as she struggled to rise. She slumped to the ground, motionless.

"Come on, then," Gavin said, grabbing the sputtering torch. "Let's get out of here."

Lhaurel hesitated, looking down at Sarial's form, the only movement the slow rise and fall of her chest as she breathed. It would be so easy to simply pull the dagger hanging from her waist and end it there. Spill her blood onto the sands. It would be easy. She'd done it to her own brother. She didn't deserve to live.

Lhaurel reached for the dagger and pulled it free.

"Good idea," Gavin said, reaching down and pulling free the sword belted at Sarial's waist. "We'll need these." He switched the torch to his left hand so that he could hold the sword in his right.

Still Lhaurel hesitated.

Gavin gave her a curious look. She recognized him then. He was the outcast who had told the story of Eldriean so long ago.

She sucked in a breath and shook her head. Enough blood had

been spilled.

"Help me move her in here," she said, stowing the dagger in her belt. "We'll take the key and lock the door. That should buy us more time if anyone comes looking for us."

"Good idea."

They were done quickly.

Lhaurel turned the key in the lock and then stowed it in a pocket. "Let's go."

"You're not going anywhere," a cold voice said.

Taren and a woman Lhaurel did not know blocked their way. Taren held Gavin's greatsword in one hand.

Gavin stepped between them, putting himself in front of Lhaurel.

Taren laughed. "Isn't that sweet. He's going to protect you, Lhaurel. Poor fool. This time, I'll make sure he's dead when I leave him behind."

A red mist formed around the woman, and crackling energy formed on her fingertips.

Lhaurel reacted without thinking, letting instinct reach out to her. Just as the woman raised her fingers to attack, Lhaurel pulled the bloody mist around the woman to her, dispersing it into the sand. The energy on the woman's fingers died.

"What—how?" the woman stammered, a look of stunned disbelief on her face.

Taren tried a much more pragmatic approach. With a lazy salute, he charged forward, sword raised before him. Gavin was ready for him. Their swords met once again, and Gavin pushed forward.

Lhaurel ignored them for a moment, drew her dagger, and advanced on the woman. Red mist formed around the woman again and energy crackled. Lhaurel dismissed it again. The power was in the blood—that was what formed into clouds of mist around the mystics, carrying the individual powers with it. She realized consciously now what she had known almost from the moment she'd first acknowledged her powers. Without the blood, there was no magic. And Lhaurel was master of blood. She wasn't a wetta at all. She was a blood mage.

"Enough," Lhaurel said, skirting around where Gavin and Taren fought. "Your magic is useless. I will continue to dispel it."

The woman grit her teeth in frustration and drew her sword with a shriek. "Fine, I'll just kill you the old fashioned way. You're nothing but a slattern, a mangy whore. I don't know why Kaiden prefers you to Sarial. But with you dead, no one will stand in her way." She dropped into a middle guard and waited.

"She can have him," Lhaurel said.

The woman took a step forward and then suddenly stiffened. Her mouth opened wide, as if she were about to scream, but no words came out, only a thin, bloody bubble of spit. For a moment, Lhaurel was confused, but then she saw the bloody tip of a blade sticking out of the woman's chest between her breasts and sensed the presence of someone else standing behind her. The woman slumped forward to her knees, fingers clenching and unclenching and scrabbling at the sand. Behind her, an old man stood clutching a bloody short sword in steady hands. His face was twisted in disgust.

"Cobb?" Lhaurel's voice was thick with incredulity.

The older man looked up at her, eyes going wide for a moment. Then they slipped past her to the battle that was taking place behind her. His expression hardened. With a shout, Cobb hurled the short sword in his hand with all his strength. For a moment, Lhaurel thought that the man meant to kill her, but the sword tumbled passed her, wide by a considerable margin. He'd been aiming for Taren.

It missed Taren by less than an inch, struck the wall in a shower of sparks, and then dropped to the sandy floor. Both men leapt back, turning to see who had thrown the blade. Taren spotted Cobb and cursed. He tossed his sword at Gavin, who dodged out of the way. Taren seized that moment to scurry away, slipping around Gavin while he was distracted and vanishing into the shadows.

Lhaurel turned her stunned gaze toward Cobb, dagger still half raised before her. His face bore a grim note of satisfaction, though his eyes were full of pained tears. Blood poured from one of his legs.

"What are you doing here?" Lhaurel asked him as Gavin cautiously approached.

Cobb glanced over at her without turning his head and then turned back to the body on the ground.

"Last I checked," he said, voice filled with pain, "you were dead."

Gavin made a small noise, halfway between a snort and a laugh, but Lhaurel silenced him with a look.

"I'm alive, but we won't be if we don't get out of here soon. Something terrible is happening in the Oasis!"

Cobb grunted and leaned back against the wall. He looked at Gavin. "You there, retrieve my sword. I'll need it. Lhaurel, take this tunnel down until it turns to the left. Take the passage there to the left, and it will take you down to an opening on the Oasis floor. The two missing clans are running around in here like ants over honey. Best not to be seen."

"Aren't you coming with us?" Gavin asked.

"Not with this leg, boy. I've done what I can. Now bring me my sword and get out of here."

Gavin didn't move until Cobb shot him a withering glare. When he finally did yield, it was grudgingly. "Here," Gavin said, handing Cobb the sword. "May you always find water and shade when the shadows come to take you."

Cobb grunted.

"Let's go," Lhaurel said. A sense of urgency gripped her and drove her onward. She took the sword from him and held it in one hand.

* * *

Makin Qays shouted a defiant challenge as the monstrous beast rose up out of the sands before the Oasis walls. Fangs larger than a man was tall jutted up from the karundin's lower jaw. With blunted nose, ebony eyes, and deep, dark, greyish-green skin, the creature surged upward, its head a hundred spans across and just as long. From atop his aevian, Makin Qays felt no fear, though his mind was numb from the sheer size of the beast.

It continued to rise up out of the sand, spiked head bending downward as it rose. Its long, armored, serpentine body continued surging upward, coiling around and around at the foot of the Oasis walls. A small fin rose along its back as it bent its head downward, back toward the sand as if to enter the Oasis itself.

Makin Qays was sure if it had wanted to, it could have leapt the

Oasis walls before part of it had collapsed. Makin Qays raised his axe in one hand and his sword in the other and screamed in death's face. He supposed he looked like a small insect buzzing at a man about to squash it to those below him.

Something glinted in the air above the creature. Makin Qays glanced up, expecting to see reinforcements. Instead, Kaiden dropped through the air, sword held in one hand. Skree-lar shrieked and flew away. Kaiden landed on the karundin's back, digging his sword into the creature to steady his landing. The karundin shrieked, a massive, bellowing sound that nearly deafened Makin Qays. Kaiden looked up at him, his expression an open challenge.

* * *

Saralhn wiped blood from her brow and spat to the side. The spittle was red. Stumbling, she ran forward, spear held out before her in raw fingers. Screams and the smell of death filled the air around her. The salty tang of blood mixed with the bitter scent of urine. She tried to ignore the bodies, but her numbed mind saw everything. She had to find Khari and provide a warning. She had to—

A sailfin burst from the sand in front of her, teeth bared. Without conscious thought her spear came up and sliced the creature from jaw to jaw.

Where was the woman? She burst into a jog, and then something slammed into her. Pain lanced up her foot as it was seized in iron jaws and she was dragged into the sand. She screamed, but it was a single note of fear amidst a symphony of terror. Sand closed in over her head. She struggled to break the surface, to gasp one last breath of fresh air.

CHAPTER 23
Surrogates

*"The witch, Elyana, is dead, killed by her last great 'creation.'
Her monsters, the genesauri, proliferate the desert sands, killing with
abandon. They have driven the enemy away. How were we so blind,
so afraid, that we fought the enemy at the gate and ignored the threat
within the keep? We should have known when Briane went missing. We
should have known when the first of those cursed beasts reared up out of
the sand and massacred our clans. Now there are too many.*

*"We will keep this record as a testament to Briane and Arrelone
and place it among our other records in the hidden grottos. They were
killed by the witch's hand to feed our hope for salvation. These records
will remind us that desperation and fear are not justification for being
in league with devils.*

*"The enemy has left us, but it seems Elyana has done their work for
them. We have killed ourselves."*

*-From the Journals of Elyana, notations added by Eldriean,
Warlord of the Rhiofriar*

Lhaurel burst out onto the Oasis floor into the midst of chaos and
death. She nearly collapsed from the sheer scope of *feeling* that washed
over her from the hundreds of fear-stricken people that were around
her. A double handful died, and she died with them, nearly blacking
out from the sheer pain and terror of the surrogate death. She felt it
and was a part of it. Only Gavin, coming up behind her and noticing
the sudden weakening of the knees, kept her from toppling over
entirely in the face of the emotional barrage.

He caught her around the waist and held her up. "Are you alright?"

Lhaurel didn't have the strength to answer. It required all her remaining strength to cut off the part of her mind that sensed the presence of others and return just to her own emotions. Yet even then, the momentary experience left her drained and emotionally raw.

"Water," she said softly.

Gavin searched around, coming up with a half empty skin that had been left nearby.

Strength returned to her. She stood up straight, shrugging out of Gavin's hold. He took a step back and looked out over the scene of chaos and death unfolding before him.

"Look at them," he said, his voice taking on a tone of deep sadness underlined with indignation. "Fighting in pockets. Why don't they gather? Form a defensive line?"

Lhaurel looked out at the people. The few warriors that had managed to retrieve weapons were indeed fighting in small groups, warriors arrayed in tight circular or square formations around the women and children. Dozens of these groups stood in the center of the Oasis, yet none of them were close enough to assist the others. They stood apart, often hidden beneath waves of sailfins or the massive body of a marsaisi. A handful of aevians and their riders dove through the air, picking off the odd sailfin or else harrying a marsaisi until it returned to the sands, but their numbers were few, far fewer than Lhaurel had hoped, despite her surprise at even seeing them.

"Clans," she said. "They're fighting in clans. That's the only way they know how."

Gavin growled, deep and low in his throat. He raised his greatsword. Wind kicked up a cloud of dust around them and a faint red mist formed around the man. He surged forward in long graceful strides.

Lhaurel watched in open astonishment as he scaled a large mound of boulders, slicing a sailfin in half almost without turning to look at it. At the top, he raised the sword high into the air and shouted out, a loud pure note that rose above the din of the battle.

"Brothers!" he shouted. "Sisters! There is strength in unity! To me warriors of the clans! To me women and children. Let us drive these creatures from our home. Fight with me!" His voice rang out and echoed off the walls.

SANDS

Two different sailfins surged upward out of the sand, writhing through the air. Gavin's sword spun in a twisting series of moves that flashed and glittered in the sunlight. Two dead sailfins fell to the rocks below, headless bodies on one side and bodiless heads on the other.

"Fight with me! Don't give in to fear! As long as there is breath left in this body I will defend you. Look to the fallen. Look at the slain. Brothers. Sisters. Children. Parents. Fight now for them! Fight with me!"

Slowly at first, as if they were afraid to believe, but then more quickly, the small pockets of people gravitated toward Gavin and then suddenly surged forward in a great wave that swarmed over the rocks like ants over a hill. Women and children were pushed to the center, but even the women looked suddenly grim-faced, and many of them bore small knives or the broken hafts of spears. Their faces were not of women lacking in strength. They were the faces of women willing to lay down their lives in defense of their children. These were the faces of women who were willing to die defending freedom. They knew their duty and accepted it with honor and strength.

Lhaurel felt herself swept up along in the tide, only her dagger clutched in one hand. Someone else darted by her, though, pausing only long enough to shove her out of the way.

"Nice speech, outcast," Taren said, scowling. "It will make my job easier now they're all together. I appreciate it." He made a gesture with his sword as if shooing away a fly.

Gavin raised his sword and dropped into a ready stance. A space opened around them, Rahuli fighters defending their lives from all sides.

"Let's get to it, then," Gavin said. And they charged.

* * *

Lhaurel pulled her dagger free from the sailfin corpse with a wet hiss. Blood dripped from it into the sand. Part of her mind screamed and trembled as it felt people dying around her, participating in their deaths. Blood pounded in her ears, almost deafening her in its intensity. She tried to push it out of her mind, but she couldn't. With each death the pull of her power grew somehow stronger. She felt the genesauri surging through the sands beneath them, felt the strange power by which they flew surging upward from far beneath them. She knew and understood the people around her intimately. She felt their fear and their pain and was fueled by it.

Yet somehow, she managed to still put some of her focus into the present moment. A woman near her shouted as another sailfin burst out of the sand. Two other women fell upon it with long knives and a spear, cutting it out of the air before it could latch onto someone and drag them into the sand.

Lhaurel took a moment to breathe. Her eyes unconsciously sought the fight on the rocks above them.

Gavin and Taren battled back and forth, their swords a blur of metal. Gavin countered each of Taren's strokes, but Taren was a veteran of hundreds of duels. Gavin's unorthodox technique was more fluid, depending upon speed and agility rather than strength, which countered Taren's more aggressive strength. Still, it was not going well for Gavin. He bled from several small wounds, and Taren's attacks were relentless. Lhaurel knew that it would not be long before Gavin slipped up and Taren ran him through. Again.

Almost as if in response to Lhaurel's thought, Gavin tripped on a loose stone and stumbled backward. Taren smiled, and his eyes flashed in triumph.

A cloud of red and white mist erupted around Gavin just as crackling energy surged down Gavin's arms. The energy leapt from Gavin's fingers with a sizzling hiss. It hit Taren just as he moved to bring his sword down. The bolt of energy blasted completely through Taren's chest.

A noise sounded through the Oasis, a powerful, nightmarish bellow that shook the earth.

* * *

The creature that arose out of the sand in front of Khari was a thing of nightmare. A hundred times larger than the biggest marsaisi, it seemed to blacken out the sky in front of it. Thick skull plate and spikes adorned its head, and massive, metallic fins jutted out from each segmented section of its long body. It appeared almost like a cross between a millipede and a rashelta, but with each section armored separately and teeth that shone grey and lifeless.

Standing before it, looking up at teeth larger and taller than she was herself, Khari knew the moment of her death. She stared at it and then looked down at the spear in her hand. It shone slick with the blood of scores of genesauri. A smile stretched across her bloodied face. She was death. And death cannot die. She leapt from the rocks.

* * *

Makin Qays leapt from his saddle, ignoring the fact that he was falling toward the back of the karundin. He landed on the creature's armored back and, as he'd seen Kaiden do, slammed the spike of his axe into the creature's armor to steady himself.

Kaiden smiled. "Hello, Makin. I'm not dead. Sorry to disappoint."

Makin Qays sucked in a breath. He'd hoped, for a moment, that Kaiden was here to help, had come to do the impossible and help him destroy this hellish monster. But he'd known, deep down inside, as soon as he'd seen Kaiden's defiant face staring up at him.

Makin Qays raised his sword. "You're somehow behind all this, aren't you?"

Kaiden smiled and made a small gesture with his free hand. Makin Qays's sword flew out of his hand. Beneath them, genesauri erupted from the sand or else dove back into it, filling the air with dust and sand. People screamed distantly.

"This is all because of you, my dear Warlord." Kaiden took a step forward as he spoke, a bit of metal appearing from a pocket of his robes and spinning in a slow circle around him. "These deaths are on your hands."

"You're insane." Makin Qays pulled his axe free, balancing as best he could as the kalundin continued to pull its massive bulk out of the ground.

He took a step forward, readying his axe, but Kaiden made another contemptuous flick of one hand and the axe flew out of Makin Qays's grip.

"You denied them the protection of your presence among them. You hid yourselves. Your cowardice made it so that dozens died needlessly. The tattoos on your arms name you what you really are: traitors to the vows you uphold. Hypocrites."

Makin Qays grimaced and balled his fists. "This is your fault, Kaiden. You set this up. People are dying here, defending themselves and others. What possible purpose does this have? You are the hypocrite. We are here, upholding the flame. You are here to snuff it out."

Kaiden stopped and looked at him, eyes hard, yet seemingly distant. "Why am I here?" He pointed his blade at Makin Qays. "To fulfill a vow."

The blade shot from his hand like an arrow. Makin Qays barely felt the pain of it entering his chest. He dropped to his knees and then slid to the side. He hung there for a moment, eyes and thoughts clouding over, and then slipped over the edge.

"For my father," Kaiden said, and he whistled for Skree-lar.

* * *

Lhaurel uncovered her ears, eyes straining through the dust and chaos of the Oasis floor, but couldn't see anything. Desperately, she reached out with her powers, dread clutching at her heart.

Something massive loomed just outside the Oasis, a giant evil with but a single great purpose: To eat anything living. She sensed Makin Qays fall, his life giving out before he hit the sand. She felt Kaiden leap onto Skree-lar's back and race toward where she was now.

Lhaurel dropped to her knees, clutching at her temples. Behind her, Gavin shouted out orders, rallying the fighters around him. Kaiden and Skree-lar winged closer. Lhaurel felt Kaiden leap from his saddle, plunging through the air toward her as if he could sense her, too.

Time slowed. Something inside Lhaurel screamed out. Something deep and primal that she had felt only twice before clawed to the surface and unleashed a torrent of seething energy and rage. She reached out, pulling blood from the sands and from the dead around her. A red mist enveloped her and shrouded her with power. And with it surged new strength.

That primal instinct tugged at Kaiden then, pulled at the lifeblood within him just as he neared the ground. Kaiden hit the ground in a cloud of dust. Red and grey mist formed around him like it did when he was using his powers, blood mixed with the metals in the sands, but it flowed away from him instead of toward him, flowed outward and to Lhaurel, joining with the cloud of bloody mist that surrounded her. The power within Lhaurel doubled, and she screamed from the sheer, painful ecstasy of it.

Kaiden also screamed, but his was one of pain and horror. His eyes widened, and his face seemed to age. Skin wrinkled and turned pale. The flesh sagged, and muscles lost their strength. His sword slipped from his fingers.

Pain lanced through her frame, shooting through her like a thousand volts of electricity. It pounded through her body. By reflex, she seized at her powers, pulled at the source of healing and strength with everything that she had.

A woman near her that was an instant from death died a moment early as Lhaurel pulled the blood from her dying body.

An older warrior, grey at his temples and with an old silver scar down one arm, gasped as he felt himself growing weak. He'd been wounded and knew that his time was short, but he hadn't lost too much blood yet. He sank to his knees. Maybe he'd lost more blood than he'd thought. He blinked once and then died.

Lhaurel screamed again and flopped on the sand as she realized what she was doing. Yet she could not stop the forces running through her. Power raged, churning through her body, changing her, channeling the blood of the dead and dying through her. She felt each person. Felt each genesauri. The powers within her raged like the storming sea. It screamed at her as wind whipped the sands and the sky overhead seemed to darken as clouds rolled in from afar.

She gasped as she sensed something massive near the mouth of the Oasis. Something massive and ancient and powerful. The energy flowing through her reacted as well. It surged and pulsed as if in recognition of an ancient foe.

The clans were broken and dying. Even if they survived this moment, they would not survive another Migration.

The genesauri were all here. Every one of them within the desert, from here to the Forbiddence that encircled the massive desert the clans called home. Every one of them. They had to die here, all of them, or the clans would eventually die. The effort would likely kill her.

The storm raged on within her body, but now she directed the flow. She didn't pull at the blood anymore; she pushed it, forced it to expand. Sailfins burst apart, splattering gore. Pockets of sand grew wet as the creatures beneath the surface burst as well. Marsaisi seemed to bleed from all the places where their armor met. And the blood flowed through the sands toward Lhaurel. She called it to her.

The red mist around her swirled and began to spin, becoming a vortex of blood and wind. It screamed and howled. Genesauri died, and she died with them. Her fingernails became a deep, dark crimson. Her hair, already a rusty red, darkened as if it, too, had absorbed the blood. And her skin grew even paler than before, a shade away from white.

The storm hit her. And with a last fading scream, Lhaurel tasted blood on her lips.

* * *

As Khari fell, she felt something swell and surge from behind her. A chorus of screams hit her ears. Yet she didn't falter. Her spear spun, point held before her. Her only hope was to land somewhere close to the open maw and ram it up into the brain.

The creature trembled and coiled in around itself.

Khari hit the rocks and stared up at it, awestruck. A red band seemed to be pouring out of its mouth, like a massive piece of wool yarn died red. But it wasn't yarn. She recognized it for what it was. Blood.

Something was pulling the blood out of this monster. Something was draining it.

Lhaurel. She knew it with an absolute certainty.

Khari watched, stunned, horrified, and grateful all at once, as the creature fell from the sky, bits of its armor crumbling from it as it fell, and then seemed to deflate. Somehow, Lhaurel had killed it. And it had probably cost her her life.

From within the Oasis came the sound of a ragged cheering. Soft at first, but then growing louder and louder, the shout rose until it echoed off the walls of the Oasis and reverberated out over the sands where Khari stood. Cries of victory, joy, and sheer, emotional relief.

Khari looked down at her hands and studied the blood there. She looked to the side and saw the bodies of the fallen warriors around her. Women and children's bodies were interspersed with those of the men.

They had upheld the flame and won. Had it been worth the cost?

* * *

Gavin looked down at the man they called Kaiden. Near them, some women clustered around Lhaurel's fallen form, conversing in hushed tones. They said she was still alive. Gavin leaned against his greatsword and watched Kaiden's body slide down onto the rocks. Kaiden looked suddenly old, as if he had somehow aged thirty years in a moment.

"You fools," Kaiden rasped, blood leaking form the corner of his mouth, "the enemy is coming. You cannot stand against them without me."

Gavin looked out over the sands, surveying the clansmen who still lived. All of them clustered together around the rock upon which they stood. They raised weapons in the air. Men, women and children. The genesauri lay dead around the Oasis, bodies dripping blood into the sand. As one, the survivors took up a chant, voices mingling into one cacophonous sound.

"Freedom!"

"We've already won," Gavin said.

Kaiden blinked a few times and struggled to say something, but all that came out was a gurgling noise that could have been taken as a laugh.

Gavin turned away from him. He basked in the sound of voices united. Men and women hugged one another or else clasped small children to them, tears streaming down their faces despite the lack of pure, precious water. People from different clans, even outcasts, laughed and cried and shouted their victory to the sky. Arm in arm. Hand in hand. He wished his grandmother could have been there to see it.

He raised his greatsword high into the air.

"Peace!"

Epilogue

Khari paused for a moment at the back of the procession, squinting up into the sky. Were those *clouds*? The strange, billowing balls of fluff floated through the air like grey sheep that had learned to fly. In the distance, she heard a distant sound of thunder. The rains were coming early, too. After the Migration, after everything they'd just been through, they had to deal with more change?

Khari turned back to the convoy and resumed walking, quickening her step so she could catch up to the two litters being born across the sands and trying to hide a scowl. Lhaurel lay on one of the litters, straining and thrashing against the loose bonds that held her in place and kept her from injuring herself. Khari put a hand to the woman's wrist, checking the weak pulse. Looking at her, Khari couldn't suppress a small shudder. She didn't fully understand what had gone on, but it was clear now that Lhaurel was not a wetta at all, but something else entirely. Something far more powerful and sinister.

"Is she going to make it?"

The voice was young, yet strong and genuinely concerned. Khari looked up into Gavin's eyes, walking along on the other side of the second litter. Khari knew nothing about the young man other than what had been told to her following the battle, but the clans, those who were not Roterralar, were treating him as if he were king. He'd killed Taren and, to the Rahuli, that was worthy of their honor and respect.

"I don't know," Khari said, honestly. She'd tried to heal Lhaurel, but whatever was going on inside the woman was not something over which her powers held sway.

"She—she looks different."

Khari didn't answer right away. It was obvious, looking at Lhaurel's blood red hair and nails and the absolute paleness, almost translucence, of her skin.

"Power comes with a cost. It always comes with a cost. If she comes through this, I'm not sure she'll ever be the same. With what she did, the mental strain alone could have completely crushed her mind. I really don't know."

Khari trailed off, looking over to the other litter. Kaiden rested there. Wrinkles covered his face and hands now, and his hair had bleached white as if aged. Immediately, Khari felt a flare of sharp, hot anger. He'd betrayed them all. He'd killed Makin, killed Tieran. He was nothing short of a murderer. If Khari had had her way, Kaiden would never have gotten up off the rocks. But Gavin and several of the surviving clan leaders had defended him, if only for the sake of gathering information. Gavin walked near him, Khari was sure, partly to ensure she didn't try anything. Regardless, Khari wasn't even going to attempt to heal him.

"Are you sure your warren will hold us all?" Gavin asked. He'd already asked the question before, so he had to be trying to draw her attention away from the man.

"Yes. As I said, we'll be safe there, though we'll face some logistics problems soon. We don't have the stores to support this many people."

"We'll face that challenge when we come to it. But if what you say is true and your warren has protected you from the Migrations for all these years, why haven't you shown yourselves before?"

Khari sighed. She'd wondered when that subject would come up.

"I don't have to explain my or my people's actions to anyone. Let's just worry about getting there."

Gavin nodded and looked out over the procession. She was a little surprised he didn't push it any further.

The surviving Rahuli trudged through the sand, the Oasis already a small blip on the horizon behind them. There were so few of them left, perhaps only a few hundred. The remains of the two clans who had hidden within the Oasis walls walked at the center of the procession, surrounded by warriors from the other clans, those who could still hold a sword. No one but the children had escaped unscathed. These ran around the procession, subdued but delighting in the sudden release from the confines of the Oasis. That the two traitorous clans had not simply been abandoned was another of Gavin's doings. They needed unity, he claimed. Khari wasn't so sure.

"Khari."

Khari jumped, looking down.

Lhaurel stared up at her, eyes open wide.

Khari rushed to her side, marveling that the woman could be awake. When she got close, though, Khari realized Lhaurel's eyes were unfocused, gazing off into some unseen distance. There was no recognition in those eyes.

"Death," Lhaurel whispered. "Death and blood—death and blood—dead—dead everywhere. Can't escape . . . "

Lhaurel's voice trailed off, and she began thrashing against the bonds again, her mouth still moving in a silent chant.

Thunder rumbled in the distance behind them. A single tear dripped from the corner of Khari's eye, but she blinked away the rest before they could fall. Crying was a waste of precious water.

* * *

Within the confines of the Roterralar Warren, Beryl huddled in a dark corner of the weapons room, wind screaming against the thick leather door through which the aevians entered. His bad leg lay sprawled out in the sand, the other pulled up tight against his chest, held there by his thick, muscular arms.

"Bloodlines," he muttered, slowly rocking back and forth. "The bloodlines have converged. She is one of them."

The rocking stilled, and his hands relaxed, his expression hardening and his lips curling into a slow smile. He'd felt her break, felt the powerful wave of massive strength and energy. She had killed them all. Such *power*.

"One of us," he said in a strong voice.

His grip tightened again, and the rocking resumed. His voice fell to almost a whisper.

"The Orinai must be told."

He sent the signal.

About the Author

Kevin Nielsen's journey into writing began in the 6th grade when an oft-frustrated librarian told him there simply wasn't enough money in the budget to buy any more books. She politely suggested he write his own. He's been writing ever since (and invading libraries and bookstores everywhere).

Kevin currently resides in Utah with his amazing wife and two wonderful children. He's still writing and continuing a lifelong quest to become a dragon rider.

Connect with Kevin:
Blog: http://kevinlnielsen.com/
Twitter: www.twitter.com/kevinlnielsen

Discover More Remarkable Books
from Future House Publishing

Never miss a book release.
Sign up for the Future House Publishing email list.

www.futurehousepublishing.com

www.facebook.com/FutureHousePublishing

http://twitter.com/FutureHousePub